MEDUSA'S COIL
AND OTHERS

MEDUSA'S COIL
AND OTHERS

THE ANNOTATED REVISIONS AND
COLLABORATIONS OF
H. P. LOVECRAFT
VOLUME II

Edited, with an Introduction and Notes

By

S. T. Joshi

2012

Introduction

The revisions and collaborations of Lovecraft's final seven or eight years differed markedly from those of the earlier decade or so of his career. Although his third and last ghostwritten tale for Zealia Bishop, "Medusa's Coil" (1930), is pretty much in line with his earlier stories for her and for Adolphe de Castro, and although his five tales ghostwritten for Hazel Heald are among the strongest of his revisions, Lovecraft gradually began working with younger colleagues who regarded themselves as his disciples and even his fans, with the result that these works, the product of their original authors' extreme apprenticeship, are on the whole aesthetically inferior to his earlier revisions, although they speak volumes for Lovecraft's skill and generosity in nurturing young talent.

"Medusa's Coil," by all odds, must rank as one of the most disappointing of Lovecraft's more substantial ghostwritten tales; for it depends precisely on an interplay and conflict of character that even his most devoted supporter would rank as one of his lesser literary skills. Let it pass that the tale is also racist, in that the culminating horror is the revelation that the enigmatic Frenchwoman Marceline Bedard is a negress; Lovecraft's notes to the story suggest that this element may have in fact been the contribution of his revision client. Those notes are of interest in themselves not only in revealing the care that Lovecraft took to plot out a ghostwritten tale—very much along the lines of one of his own tales—but in showing how dutifully he applied his basic principle of writing *two* synopses, one giving the events of the story in order of occurrence, the other in the order of narration; the substantial divergence between these two sequences often points to the structural complexity of a tale.

The accidental manner in which Lovecraft stumbled into many of his revisions or collaborations is revealed by his assistance to the professional pulpsmith Henry S. Whitehead in "The Trap," a story long known by virtue of its inclusion in Whitehead's first Arkham House volume, *Jumbee and Other Uncanny Tales* (1944), but which was not known to be a Lovecraft collaboration until I discovered a letter to that effect. The story appeared in *Strange Tales* under Whitehead's own name—a point on which Lovecraft no doubt insisted, since he regarded his assistance as purely a friendly gesture to a fellow writer, even though he seems to have written the latter three-fourths of the story. There is a certain irony in that Lovecraft's own tales were systematically rejected when submitted to Harry Bates's magazine, so that "The Trap" remains his sole "contribution" to this short-lived but well-paying pulp magazine.

Another story by Whitehead, "Bothon," may or may not have had input from Lovecraft. He speaks of it in several letters, referring to it under its original title, "The Bruise." The most revealing passage is as follows:

I'm now helping Whitehead prepare a new ending and background for a story Bates has rejected. The original told of a young man who bumped his head and thereafter heard sounds as of a mighty cataclysm, although the city around him was quiescent. It was supposed to be due to a result of the bruise—which made the fellow's head a natural radio and enabled him to hear the Japanese earthquake—which was occurring at the time. Bates rightly thought this tame, so I am having the cataclysm and its causes somewhat different. I am having the bruise excite cells of hereditary memory causing the man to hear the destruction and sinking of fabulous Mu 20,000 years ago![1]

This letter was written in April 1932. Whitehead died in November, leading Lovecraft to wonder if the tale "was ever put in final publishable shape."[2] Apparently, it was not—at least, not by Whitehead. However, the story, now titled "Bothon," did appear posthumously—almost simultaneously in *Amazing Stories* (August 1946) and in Whitehead's second Arkham House collection, *West India Lights* (1946). This long delay in the publication of the tale raises suspicions. A. Langley Searles, discussing this story and another posthumously published tale, "Scar Tissue," notes that both "fall below Whitehead's usual level of quality. There is evidence to show that 'Bothon' . . . is not wholly Whitehead's work."[3] In private discussions with me, Searles was more forthright: he thought it a distinct possibility that August Derleth, finding notes that Lovecraft wrote for the revision of "The Bruise" (or perhaps even reading the above letter), wrote the story on his own and passed it off as Whitehead's. Derleth took pride in passing off his story "The Churchyard Yew" as a work by J. S. Le Fanu, and he also extensively rewrote a tale by William Hope Hodgson for one of his Arkham House volumes of the 1960s. Whatever the case, "Bothon," as published, does not appear to bear any Lovecraftian prose, but may still be regarded as a kind of "shadow revision."

Of the Hazel Heald revisions much can be said. This woman from Somerville, Massachusetts, who appears (if the testimony of Muriel E. Eddy is to be believed) to have had a faint romantic attraction to Lovecraft, was the ideal revision client as far as Lovecraft was concerned: she evidently generated the simplest of plot-synopses or plot-germs and let Lovecraft write them according to his own wishes. As a result, the five stories published under her name (and she published nothing else) are tantamount to original fiction by Lovecraft. At the least, they gave him practice in fiction-writing at a period when—because of the nearly simultaneous rejection, in the summer of 1931, of *At the Mountains of Madness* by *Weird Tales* and of a proposed story collection by G. P. Putnam's Sons—his own creative instincts were at a low ebb. As with the Zealia Bishop revisions, these stories, however substantial, are probably ones that Lovecraft would not have written on his own, but they are otherwise thoroughly Lovecraftian in style, flavor, and mood. They were probably all written in 1932 or 1933, even though the last of them was not published until 1937. It is very likely that one of them, "The Horror in the Museum," is a parody—a parody of Lovecraft's own evolving pseudomythology, to which such other writers as August Derleth, Clark Ashton Smith, Robert E. Howard, and Donald Wandrei had made their initial additions. Heald was, accordingly, regarded as another "disciple" of Lovecraft's, adding what many readers believed were her own new "gods"—Rhan-Tegoth and Ghatanothoa—to the Cthulhu Mythos. Of these stories, "Out of the Aeons" is probably the best on purely aesthetic grounds. "The Horror in the Burying-Ground" has faint suggestions of parody (or, at the very least, of in-joking), being a kind of half-comic play on Lovecraft's tales of primitive backwoods denizens in New England, in the manner of "The Dunwich Horror" (1928).

By this time, Lovecraft had attracted a cadre of young enthusiasts who looked up to him as a revered figure in weird fiction. Robert Bloch (1917–1994) was one of these, and his correspondence with Lovecraft reveals that the older man helped the teenager with all manner of stories, some of which do not survive. Whether Lovecraft contributed any actual prose to any of Bloch's early tales—even the one published as "Satan's Servants" in *Something about Cats and Other Pieces* (1949)—is, however, open to doubt.

One youngster whom he did help more concretely was R. H. Barlow (1918–1951), who first came into correspondence with Lovecraft in 1931, when he was only thirteen. By 1933 Barlow was beginning to write horror—or, more properly, fantasy—fiction, and in recent years some very early specimens have been unearthed. These tales—including "The Slaying of the Monster" and "The Hoard of the Wizard-Beast"—were not published at the time, and they are in every sense apprentice work. And yet, what is remarkable is the rapidity with which Barlow developed as a fiction writer. Already by 1935, when he and Lovecraft wrote "'Till A' the Seas,'" he was producing creditable work; and the very next year, when he was scarcely eighteen years old, he wrote two splendid specimens largely on his own, "A Dim-Remembered Story" (which has no Lovecraft input) and "The Night Ocean," to which—as the recently discovered typescript attests—Lovecraft contributed no more than 10% of the prose. In this sense, the latter scarcely qualifies as a "Lovecraft revision." Lovecraft waxed rhapsodic when he read "A Dim-Remembered Story":

Thanks for the honour of the dedication of "A Dim-Remembered Story"! Have only just read the latter—since sealing this note. Holy Yuggoth, but it's a masterpiece! *Magnificent* stuff—will bear comparison to the best of C[lark] A[shton] S[mith]! Splendid rhythm, poetic imagery, emotional modulations, & atmospheric power. Tsathoggua! But *literature* is certainly your forte, say what you will![4]

That last comment refers to Barlow's wide-ranging interests of the period, which included music, publishing, and pictorial art. Barlow did not in fact continue to pursue literature; but his later celebrity as a Mexican anthropologist speaks well of his innate ablities.

We can, of course, not leave Barlow without noting the two whimsies, "The Battle That Ended the Century" (1934) and "Collapsing Cosmoses" (1935), written when Lovecraft was visiting his young protégé in Florida in the summer of 1934 and 1935, respectively. The former in particular is a highly amusing send-up of the entire weird fiction gang, while the latter mercilessly parodies the "space opera" brand of science fiction. That tale—a fragment of scarcely more than 300 words—was written alternately by Lovecraft and Barlow as a kind of live round-robin tale; and the latter ended up writing considerably more than the former, also writing some of the better jokes.

Another young colleague, Duane W. Rimel (1915–1996), was the recipient of Lovecraft's help in two (or perhaps three) tales. The earliest, "The Sorcery of Aphlar," probably has so little Lovecraft input that it cannot truly qualify as a Lovecraft revision, so it has been placed in an appendix to this volume. The other two, "The Tree on the Hill" (1934) and "The Disinterment" (1935), are more substantial. The former is still a bit crude and immature, but it revealed such progress on the part of its author that Lovecraft made the effort to write at least (and probably at most) the entire third section of the tale as a hands-on tutorial on fiction writing. But even Lovecraft was not prepared for the radical advance in quality shown by Rimel's "The Disinterment," which is as faithful an echo of Lovecraft's early manner (especially "The Outsider") as can be found in the work of any of his colleagues. It does not appear, however, that Rimel was able to duplicate his mimicry of Lovecraft in any subsequent tales.

If "Collapsing Cosmoses" was an informal round-robin tale, "The Challenge from Beyond" was a much more carefully planned one—although the plan did not proceed quite as scheduled. This was the brainchild of Julius Schwartz, who wished to run the story (along with a round-robin science fiction tale of the same title) in the third anniversary issue of *Fantasy Magazine,* and who managed to sign up some impressive writers—notably A. Merritt, Robert E. Howard, and Lovecraft himself—for the "weird" version; but Merritt's high-handed balking at providing the actual impetus of the plot almost scuttled the project, and it was left to Lovecraft to salvage the tale by actually making it go somewhere. The fact that he cribbed from his own unpublished tale "The Shadow out of Time" need hardly concern us: as an unpaid lark, the story was not one in which Lovecraft could invest much aesthetic effort; and yet, the fact that he generated a fairly elaborate set of notes, complete with drawings of the worm-creatures he placed on stage, suggests that he devoted considerably more effort than he need have done.

One of Lovecraft's last revisions, "The Diary of Alonzo Typer" (1935), is at once sad and touching: sad because the original story that Lovecraft received from his hapless colleague William Lumley (reprinted here in the appendix) was so confused and illiterate that it is remarkable how anyone could have made anything of it; and touching because, although Lovecraft's version is not without confusion and incoherence of its own, it speaks as poignantly of his generosity in time and effort as any single act could. To compound the situation, the manner in which Lovecraft worked on the story required additional (unremunerative) work on his part, as he wrote to Barlow:

> Speaking of story MSS.—my sympathy for old Bill Lumley has caused me to break my new anti-collaboration rule & fix up a tale of his . . . so that he can get the satisfaction of seeing it printed somewhere . . . by Hill-Billy [William L. Crawford] or somebody. I had meant to ask somebody else—perhaps yourself— to share the philanthropic enterprise to the extent of typing the 23-page finished product; but when I looked at the MS. I realised to my horror that no eye but my own could ever decipher it! The MS. you've just deciphered [i.e., "The Shadow out of Time"] was child's play in comparison. So all I could do was to groan & tackle the thing—which I did at the cost of a night's sleep & a prostrating headache. But now, gawddam it, it's done! In view of my task, the title of this immortal work has a peculiarly ironic significance— "The Diary of Alonzo *Typer*!!!!!"[5]

For Lovecraft, whose horror of typing had by this point reached phobic proportions, the act of typing the story appears to have been far more arduous than that of writing it.

That remark about his "anti-collaboration rule" refers to E. Hoffmann Price's frequent requests to collaborate on another story, whether it be a sequel to "Through the Gates of the Silver Key" (not included here because of its wide availability in other editions) or a new tale. Lovecraft put Price off repeatedly, chiefly because he recognised that Price, a prototypical pulpsmith, had a fundamentally different attitude toward the craft of fiction than Lovecraft, so that any resulting collaborative work would inevitably be unsatisfying to both parties—as, in fact, "Through the Gates of the Silver Key" itself was. A few months after making that statement, however, Lovecraft did violate his rule to the extent of helping the young Kenneth Sterling (1920–1995) with a tale that was not entirely suited to his temperament, the science fiction narrative "In the Walls of Eryx" (1936), which was the last of Lovecraft's avowed collaborations. We would love to have the version (estimated by its author at 6000 to 8000 words) that Sterling initially wrote, but it apparently does not survive; what does survive is a 12,000-word draft that, although entirely written by Lovecraft, no doubt incorporates as much of Sterling's prose as he could feasibly manage. If the result is an anomaly in Lovecraft's corpus—it is a kind of science fictional *conte cruel*—it nonetheless displays his ability to widen his fictional palette well beyond the bounds of his customary genre of supernatural horror.

Lovecraft was always ready to lend a helping hand—both to those who, like Lumley, had no chance of becoming talented professional writers, and to those who were indeed on the way to making careers of writing. His laborious instructions to Henry Kuttner in the revision of "The Salem Horror" (1936) have now been revealed by the publication of his letters to Kuttner. He does not appear to have assisted C. L. Moore on any actual tales, but his extensive discussions with her on the need to preserve aesthetic sincerity even in the face of the financial need to cater to crude pulp standards were no doubt of invaluable assistance to her, and their results show in the work she did in subsequent decades. It sometimes seems as if Lovecraft could scarcely let a manuscript pass over his eyes without tinkering with it, even if he were not specifically requested to do so; and if some earlier colleagues, such as Wilfred Blanch Talman, took umbrage at the unasked assistance, his younger fans and disciples were no doubt grateful to receive such concrete aid in the mechanics of story writing.

In sum, there can be no denying that Lovecraft's revisions and collaborations are on the whole inferior to his original fiction; a few of them, notably "The Mound" and "Out of the Aeons," stand out as verging close to his original work in quality, while others, such as "The Disinterment" and "The Night Ocean," are exceptional because their original authors contributed the lion's share of their merits. On the whole, the revisions form an interesting pendant to Lovecraft's own work: we know of no other writer who engaged—or, at least, engaged to such an extent—in this specific activity, and the result is an array of works that, while highly mixed in abstract quality, remain intrinsically entertaining and also shed distinctive light on Lovecraft's creative processes.

—S. T. Joshi

Medusa's Coil

With Zealia Bishop

I

The drive toward Cape Girardeau had been through unfamiliar country; and as the late afternoon light grew golden and half-dreamlike I realised that I must have directions if I expected to reach the town before night. I did not care to be wandering about these bleak southern Missouri lowlands after dark, for roads were poor and the November cold rather formidable in an open roadster. Black clouds, too, were massing on the horizon; so I looked about among the long, grey and blue shadows that streaked the flat, brownish fields, hoping to glimpse some house where I might get the needed information.

It was a lonely and deserted country, but at last I spied a roof among a clump of trees near the small river on my right; perhaps a full half-mile from the road, and probably reachable by some path or drive which I would presently

come upon. In the absence of any nearer dwelling, I resolved to try my luck there; and was glad when the bushes
by the roadside revealed the ruin of a carved stone gateway,
covered with dry, dead vines and choked with undergrowth
which explained why I had not been able to trace the path
across the fields in my first distant view. I saw that I could
not drive the car in, so I parked it very carefully near the
gate—where a thick evergreen would shield it in case of
rain—and got out for the long walk to the house.

Traversing that brush-grown path in the gathering
twilight I was conscious of a distinct sense of foreboding,
probably induced by the air of sinister decay hovering about
the gate and the former driveway. From the carvings on the
old stone pillars I inferred that this place was once an estate
of manorial dignity; and I could clearly see that the driveway had originally boasted guardian lines of linden trees,
some of which had died, while others had lost their special
identity among the wild scrub growths of the region.

As I ploughed onward, cockleburrs and stickers clung
to my clothes, and I began to wonder whether the place
could be inhabited after all. Was I tramping on a vain er-
rand? For a moment I was tempted to go back and try some
farm farther along the road, when a view of the house ahead
aroused my curiosity and stimulated my venturesome spirit.

There was something provocatively fascinating in the
tree-girt, decrepit pile before me, for it spoke of the graces
and spaciousness of a bygone era and a far more southerly
environment. It was a typical wooden plantation house of
the classic, early nineteenth-century pattern, with two and
a half stories and a great Ionic portico whose pillars reached
up as far as the attic and supported a triangular pediment.
Its state of decay was extreme and obvious; one of the vast
columns having rotted and fallen to the ground, while the

upper piazza or balcony had sagged dangerously low. Other buildings, I judged, had formerly stood near it.

As I mounted the broad stone steps to the low porch and the carved and fanlighted doorway I felt distinctly nervous, and started to light a cigarette—desisting when I saw how dry and inflammable everything about me was. Though now convinced that the house was deserted, I nevertheless hesitated to violate its dignity without knocking; so tugged at the rusty iron knocker until I could get it to move, and finally set up a cautious rapping which seemed to make the whole place shake and rattle. There was no response, yet once more I plied the cumbrous, creaking device—as much to dispel the sense of unholy silence and solitude as to arouse any possible occupant of the ruin.

Somewhere near the river I heard the mournful note of a dove, and it seemed as if the coursing water itself were faintly audible. Half in a dream, I seized and rattled the ancient latch, and finally gave the great six-panelled door a frank trying. It was unlocked, as I could see in a moment; and though it stuck and grated on its hinges I began to push it open, stepping through it into a vast shadowy hall as I did so.

But the moment I took this step I regretted it. It was not that a legion of spectres confronted me in that dim and dusty hall with the ghostly Empire furniture; but that I knew all at once that the place was not deserted at all. There was a creaking on the great curved staircase, and the sound of faltering footsteps slowly descending. Then I saw a tall, bent figure silhouetted for an instant against the great Palladian window[1] on the landing.

My first start of terror was soon over, and as the figure descended the final flight I was ready to greet the householder whose privacy I had invaded. In the semi-darkness I could see him reach in his pocket for a match. There came a flare as he lighted a small kerosene lamp which stood on a rickety console table near the foot of the stairs. In the feeble glow was revealed the stooping figure of a very tall, emaciated old man; disordered as to dress and unshaved as to face, yet for all that with the bearing and expression of a gentleman.

I did not wait for him to speak, but at once began to explain my presence.

"You'll pardon my coming in like this, but when my knocking didn't raise anybody I concluded that no one lived here. What I wanted originally was to know the right road to Cape Girardeau—the shortest road, that is. I wanted to get there before dark, but now, of course—"

As I paused, the man spoke; in exactly the cultivated tone I had expected, and with a mellow accent as unmistakably Southern as the house he inhabited.

"Rather, you must pardon me for not answering your knock more promptly. I live in a very retired way, and am not usually expecting visitors. At first I thought you were a mere curiosity-seeker. Then when you knocked again I started to answer, but I am not well and have to move very slowly. Spinal neuritis—very troublesome case.

"But as for your getting to town before dark—it's plain you can't do that. The road you are on—for I suppose you came from the gate—isn't the best or shortest way. What you must do is to take your first left after you leave the gate—that is, the first real road to your left. There are three or four cart paths you can ignore, but you can't mistake the real road because of the extra large willow tree on the right just opposite it. Then when you've turned, keep on past two roads and turn to the right along the third. After that—"

Perplexed by these elaborate directions—confusing things indeed to a total stranger—I could not help interrupting.

"Please wait a moment! How can I follow all these clues in pitch darkness, without ever having been near here before, and with only an indifferent pair of headlights to tell me what is and what isn't a road? Besides, I think it's going to storm pretty soon, and my car is an open one. It looks as if I were in a bad fix if I want to get to Cape Girardeau tonight. The fact is, I don't think I'd better try to make it. I don't like to impose burdens, or anything like that—but in view of the circumstances, do you suppose you could put me up for the night? I won't be any trouble—no meals or anything. Just let me have a corner to sleep in till daylight, and I'm all right. I can leave the car in the road where it is—a bit of wet weather won't hurt it if worst comes to worst."

As I made my sudden request I could see the old man's face lose its former expression of quiet resignation and take on an odd, surprised look.

"Sleep—*here?*"

He seemed so astonished at my request that I repeated it.

"Yes, why not? I assure you I won't be any trouble. What else *can* I do? I'm a stranger hereabouts, these roads are a labyrinth in the dark, and I'll wager it'll be raining torrents outside of an hour—"

This time it was my host's turn to interrupt, and as he did so I could feel a peculiar quality in his deep, musical voice.

"A stranger—of course you must be, else you wouldn't think of sleeping here; wouldn't think of coming here at all. People don't come here nowadays."

21

He paused, and my desire to stay was increased a thou-sandfold by the sense of mystery his laconic words seemed to evoke. There was surely something alluringly queer about this place, and the pervasive musty smell seemed to cloak a thousand secrets. Again I noticed the extreme decrepitude of everything about me; manifest even in the feeble rays of the single small lamp. I felt woefully chilly, and saw with regret that no heating seemed to be provided; yet so great was my curiosity that I still wished most ardently to stay and learn something of the recluse and his dismal abode.

"Let that be as it may," I replied. "I can't help about other people. But I surely would like to have a spot to stop till daylight. Still—if people don't relish this place, mayn't it be because it's getting so run-down? Of course I suppose it would take a fortune to keep such an estate up, but if the burden's too great why don't you look for smaller quarters? Why try to stick it out here in this way—with all the hard-ships and discomforts?"

The man did not seem offended, but answered me very gravely.

"Surely you may stay if you really wish to—*you* can come to no harm that I know of. But others claim there are certain peculiarly undesirable influences here. As for me—I stay here because I have to. There is something I feel it a duty to guard—something that holds me. I wish I had the money and health and ambition to take decent care of the house and grounds."

With my curiosity still more heightened, I prepared to take my host at his word; and followed him slowly up-stairs when he motioned me to do so. It was very dark now, and a faint pattering outside told me that the threatened rain had come. I would have been glad of any shelter, but this was doubly welcome because of the hints of mystery about the place and its master. For an incurable lover of the grotesque, no more fitting haven could have been provided.

II

There was a second-floor corner room in less unkempt shape than the rest of the house, and into this my host led me; setting down his small lamp and lighting a somewhat larger one. From the cleanliness and contents of the room, and from the books ranged along the walls, I could see that I had not guessed amiss in thinking the man a gentleman of taste and breeding. He was a hermit and eccentric, no doubt, but he still had standards and intellectual interests. As he waved me to a seat I began a conversation on general topics, and was pleased to find him not at all taciturn. If anything, he seemed glad of someone to talk to, and did not even attempt to swerve the discourse from personal topics.

He was, I learned, one Antoine de Russy, of an ancient, powerful, and cultivated line of Louisiana planters. More than a century ago his grandfather, a younger son, had migrated to southern Missouri and founded a new estate in the lavish ancestral manner; building this pillared mansion and surrounding it with all the accessories of a great plantation. There had been, at one time, as many as 200 negroes in the cabins which stood on the flat ground in the rear— ground that the river had now invaded—and to hear them singing and laughing and playing the banjo at night was to know the fullest charm of a civilisation and social order now sadly extinct. In front of the house, where the great guardian oaks and willows stood, there had been a lawn like a broad green carpet, always watered and trimmed and with flagstoned, flower-bordered walks curving through it. "Riverside"—for such the place was called—had been a lovely and idyllic homestead in its day; and my host could recall it when many traces of its best period still lingered.

It was raining hard now, with dense sheets of water beating against the insecure roof, walls, and windows, and sending in drops through a thousand chinks and crevices. Moisture trickled down to the floor from unsuspected places, and the mounting wind rattled the rotting, loose-hinged shutters outside. But I minded none of this, nor even thought of my roadster outside beneath the trees, for I saw that a story was coming. Incited to reminiscence, my host made a move to shew me to sleeping-quarters; but kept on recalling the older, better days. Soon, I saw, I would receive an inkling of why he lived alone in that ancient place, and why his neighbours thought it full of undesirable influences. His voice was very musical as he spoke on, and his tale soon took a turn which left me no chance to grow drowsy.

"Yes—Riverside was built in 1816, and my father was born here in 1828. He'd be over a century old now if he were alive, but he died young—so young I can just barely remember him. In '64 that was—he was killed in the war, Seventh Louisiana Infantry C.S.A.,[2] for he went back to the old home to enlist. My grandfather was too old to fight, yet he lived on to be ninety-five, and helped my mother bring me up.[3] A good bringing-up, too—I'll give them credit. We always had strong traditions—high notions of honour—and my grandfather saw to it that I grew up the way de Russys have grown up, generation after generation, ever since the Crusades. We weren't quite wiped out financially, but managed to get on very comfortably after the war. I went to a good school in Louisiana, and later to Princeton. Later on I was able to get the plantation on a fairly profitable basis—though you see what it's come to now.

24

"My mother died when I was twenty, and my grand-father two years later. It was rather lonely after that; and in '85 I married a distant cousin in New Orleans. Things might have been different if she'd lived, but she died when my son Denis was born. Then I had only Denis. I didn't try marriage again, but gave all my time to the boy. He was like me—like all the de Russys—darkish and tall and thin, and with the devil of a temper. I gave him the same training my grandfather had given me, but he didn't need much training when it came to points of honour. It was in him, I reckon. Never saw such high spirit—all I could do to keep him from running away to the Spanish War[4] when he was eleven! Romantic young devil, too—full of high notions—you'd call 'em Victorian, now—no trouble at all to make him let the nigger wenches alone. I sent him to the same school I'd gone to, and to Princeton, too. He was Class of 1909.

"In the end he decided to be a doctor, and went a year to the Harvard Medical School. Then he hit on the idea of keeping to the old French tradition of the family, and argued me into sending him across to the Sorbonne. I did—and proudly enough, though I knew how lonely I'd be with him so far off. Would to God I hadn't! I thought he was the safest kind of a boy to be in Paris. He had a room in the Rue St. Jacques—that's near the University in the 'Latin Quarter'—but according to his letters and his friends he didn't cut up with the gayer dogs at all. The people he knew were mostly young fellows from home—serious students and artists who thought more of their work than of striking attitudes and painting the town red.

"But of course there were lots of fellows who were on a sort of dividing line between serious studies and the devil. The aesthetes—the decadents, you know. Experimenters in life and sensation—the Baudelaire kind of a chap. Naturally Denis ran up against a good many of these, and saw a good deal of their life. They had all sorts of crazy circles and cults—imitation devil-worship, fake Black Masses, and the like.[5] Doubt if it did them much harm on the whole—probably most of 'em forgot all about it in a year or two. One of the deepest in this queer stuff was a fellow Denis had known at school—for that matter, whose father I'd known myself. Frank Marsh, of New Orleans. Disciple of Lafcadio Hearn[6] and Gauguin and Van Gogh—regular epitome of the yellow 'nineties. Poor devil—he had the makings of a great artist, at that.

"Marsh was the oldest friend Denis had in Paris, so as a matter of course they saw a good deal of each other—to talk over old times at St. Clair Academy,[7] and all that. The boy wrote me a good deal about him, and I didn't see any especial harm when he spoke of the group of mystics Marsh ran with. It seems there was some cult of prehistoric Egyptian and Carthaginian magic having a rage among the Bohemian element on the left bank—some nonsensical thing that pretended to reach back to forgotten sources of hidden truth in lost African civilisations—the great Zimbabwe, the dead Atlantean cities in the Hoggar region of the Sahara[8]—and that had a lot of gibberish connected with snakes and human hair. At least, I called it gibberish, then. Denis used to quote Marsh as saying odd things about the veiled facts behind the legend of Medusa's snaky locks—and behind the later Ptolemaic myth of Berenice, who offered up her hair to save her husband-brother, and had it set in the sky as the constellation Coma Berenices.[9]

"I don't think this business made much impression on Denis until the night of the queer ritual at Marsh's rooms when he met the priestess. Most of the devotees of this cult were young fellows, but the head of it was a young woman who called herself 'Tanit-Isis'[10]—letting it be known that her real name—her name in this latest incarnation, as she put it—was Marceline Bedard. She claimed to be the left-handed daughter of Marquis de Chameaux, and seemed to have been both a petty artist and an artist's model before adopting this more lucrative magical game. Someone said she had lived for a time in the West Indies—Martinique, I think—but she was very reticent about herself. Part of her pose was a great show of austerity and holiness, but I don't think the more experienced students took that very seriously.

"Denis, though, was far from experienced, and wrote me fully ten pages of slush about the goddess he had discovered. If I'd only realised his simplicity I might have done something, but I never thought a puppy infatuation like that could mean much. I felt absurdly sure that Denis' touchy personal honour and family pride would always keep him out of the most serious complications.

"As time went on, though, his letters began to make me nervous. He mentioned this Marceline more and more, and his friends less and less; and began talking about the 'cruel and silly way' they declined to introduce her to their mothers and sisters. He seems to have asked her no questions about herself, and I don't doubt but that she filled him full of romantic legendry concerning her origin and divine revelations and the way people slighted her. At length I could see that Denis was altogether cutting his own crowd and spending the bulk of his time with this alluring priestess. At her especial request he never told the old crowd of their continual meetings; so nobody over there tried to break the affair up.

"I suppose she thought he was fabulously rich; for he

had the air of a patrician, and people of a certain class think all aristocratic Americans are wealthy. In any case, she probably thought this a rare chance to contract a genuine right-handed alliance with a really eligible young man. By the time my nervousness burst into open advice, it was too late. The boy had lawfully married her, and wrote that he was dropping his studies and bringing the woman home to Riverside. He said she had made a great sacrifice and resigned her leadership of the magical cult, and that henceforward she would be merely a private gentlewoman—the future mistress of Riverside, and mother of de Russys to come.

"Well, sir, I took it the best way I could. I knew that sophisticated Continentals have different standards from our old American ones—and anyway, I really knew nothing against the woman. A charlatan, perhaps, but why necessarily any worse? I suppose I tried to keep as naive as possible about such things in those days, for the boy's sake. Clearly, there was nothing for a man of sense to do but to let Denis alone so long as his new wife conformed to de Russy ways. Let her have a chance to prove herself—perhaps she wouldn't hurt the family as much as some might fear. So I didn't raise any objections or ask any penitence. The thing was done, and I stood ready to welcome the boy back, whatever he brought with him.

"They got here three weeks after the telegram telling of the marriage. Marceline was beautiful—there was no denying that—and I could see how the boy might very well get foolish about her. She did have an air of breeding, and I think to this day she must have had some strains of good blood in her. She was apparently not much over twenty; of medium size, fairly slim, and as graceful as a tigress in posture and motions. Her complexion was a deep olive—like old ivory—and her eyes were large and very dark. She had small, classically regular features—though not quite clean-cut enough to suit my taste—and the most singular head of jet black hair that I ever saw.

"I didn't wonder that she had dragged the subject of hair into her magical cult, for with that heavy profusion of it the idea must have occurred to her naturally. Coiled up, it made her look like some Oriental princess in a drawing of Aubrey Beardsley's.[11] Hanging down her back, it came well below her knees and shone in the light as if it had possessed some separate, unholy vitality of its own. I would almost have thought of Medusa or Berenice myself—without having such things suggested to me—upon seeing and studying that hair.

"Sometimes I thought it moved slightly of itself, and tended to arrange itself in distinct ropes or strands, but this may have been sheer illusion. She brushed it incessantly, and seemed to use some sort of preparation on it. I got the notion once—a curious, whimsical notion—that it was a living thing which she had to feed in some strange way. All nonsense—but it added to my feeling of constraint about her and her hair.

"For I can't deny that I failed to like her wholly, no matter how hard I tried. I couldn't tell what the trouble was, but it was there. Something about her repelled me very subtly, and I could not help weaving morbid and macabre associations about everything connected with her. Her complexion called up thoughts of Babylon, Atlantis, Lemuria,[12] and the terrible forgotten dominations of an elder world; her eyes struck me sometimes as the eyes of some unholy forest creature or animal-goddess too immeasurably ancient to be fully human; and her hair—that dense, exotic, overnourished growth of oily inkiness—made one shiver as a great black python might have done. There was no doubt but that she realised my involuntary attitude—though I tried to hide it, and she tried to hide the fact that she noticed it.

"Yet the boy's infatuation lasted. He positively fawned on her, and overdid all the little gallantries of daily life to a sickening degree. She appeared to return the feeling, though I could see it took a conscious effort to make her duplicate his enthusiasms and extravagances. For one thing, I think she was piqued to learn that we weren't as wealthy as she had expected.

"It was a bad business all told. I could see that sad undercurrents were arising. Denis was half-hypnotised with puppy-love, and began to grow away from me as he felt my shrinking from his wife. This kind of thing went on for months, and I saw that I was losing my only son—the boy who had formed the centre of all my thoughts and acts for the past quarter century. I'll own that I felt bitter about it—what father wouldn't? And yet I could do nothing.

"Marceline seemed to be a good wife enough in those early months, and our friends received her without any quibbling or questioning. I was always nervous, though, about what some of the young fellows in Paris might write home to their relatives after the news of the marriage spread around. Despite the woman's love of secrecy, it couldn't remain hidden forever—indeed, Denis had written a few of his closest friends, in strict confidence, as soon as he was settled with her at Riverside.

"I got to staying alone in my room more and more, with my failing health as an excuse. It was about that time that my present spinal neuritis began to develop—which made the excuse a pretty good one. Denis didn't seem to notice the trouble, or take any interest in me and my habits and affairs; and it hurt me to see how callous he was getting.

30

I began to get sleepless, and often racked my brain in the night to try to find out what really was the matter—what it really was that made my new daughter-in-law so repulsive and even dimly horrible to me. It surely wasn't her old mystical nonsense, for she had left all the past behind her and never mentioned it once. She didn't even do any painting, although I understood that she had once dabbled in art.

"Oddly, the only ones who seemed to share my uneasiness were the servants. The darkies around the house seemed very sullen in their attitude toward her, and in a few weeks all save the few who were strongly attached to our family had left. These few—old Scipio and his wife Sarah, the cook Delilah,[13] and Mary, Scipio's daughter—were as civil as possible; but plainly revealed that their new mistress commanded their duty rather than their affection. They stayed in their own remote part of the house as much as possible. McCabe, our white chauffeur, was insolently admiring rather than hostile; and another exception was a very old Zulu woman, said to have come from Africa over a hundred years before, who had been a sort of leader in her small cabin as a kind of family pensioner. Old Sophonisba always shewed reverence whenever Marceline came near her, and one time I saw her kiss the ground where her mistress had walked. Blacks are superstitious animals, and I wondered whether Marceline had been talking any of her mystical nonsense to our hands in order to overcome their evident dislike."

III

"Well, that's how we went on for nearly half a year. Then, in the summer of 1916, things began to happen. Toward the middle of June Denis got a note from his old friend Frank Marsh, telling of a sort of nervous breakdown which made him want to take a rest in the country. It was postmarked New Orleans—for Marsh had gone home from Paris when he felt the collapse coming on—and seemed a very plain though polite bid for an invitation from us. Marsh, of course, knew that Marceline was here; and asked very courteously after her. Denis was sorry to hear of his trouble and told him at once to come along for an indefinite visit.

"Marsh came—and I was shocked to notice how he had changed since I had seen him in his earlier days. He was a smallish, lightish fellow, with blue eyes and an undecided chin; and now I could see the effects of drink and I don't know what else in his puffy eyelids, enlarged nose-pores, and heavy lines around the mouth. I reckon he had taken his pose of decadence pretty seriously, and set out to be as much of a Rimbaud, Baudelaire, or Lautréamont as he could.[14] And yet he was delightful to talk to—for like all decadents he was exquisitely sensitive to the colour and atmosphere and names of things; admirably, thoroughly alive, and with whole records of conscious experience in obscure, shadowy fields of living and feeling which most of us pass over without knowing they exist. Poor young devil—if only his father had lived longer and taken him in hand! There was great stuff in the boy!

"I was glad of the visit, for I felt it would help to set up a normal atmosphere in the house again. And that's what it really seemed to do at first; for as I said, Marsh was a delight to have around. He was as sincere and profound an artist as I ever saw in my life, and I certainly believe that nothing on earth mattered to him except the perception and expression of beauty. When he saw an exquisite thing, or was creating one, his eyes would dilate until the light irises went nearly out of sight—leaving two mystical black pits in that weak, delicate, chalk-like face; black pits opening on strange worlds which none of us could guess about.

"When he reached here, though, he didn't have many chances to shew this tendency; for he had, as he told Denis, gone quite stale. It seems he had been very successful as an artist of a bizarre kind—like Fuseli or Goya or Sime or Clark Ashton Smith[15]—but had suddenly become played out. The world of ordinary things around him had ceased to hold anything he could recognise as beauty—beauty, that is, of enough force and poignancy to arouse his creative faculty. He had often been this way before—all decadents are—but this time he could not invent any new, strange, or outré sensation or experience which would supply the needed illusion of fresh beauty or stimulatingly adventurous expectancy. He was like a Durtal or a des Esseintes at the most jaded point of his curious orbit.[16]

"Marceline was away when Marsh arrived. She hadn't been enthusiastic about his coming, and had refused to decline an invitation from some of our friends in St. Louis which came about that time for her and Denis. Denis, of course, stayed to receive his guest; but Marceline had gone on alone. It was the first time they had ever been separated, and I hoped the interval would help to dispel the sort of dazed [_____] that was making such a fool of the boy. Marceline shewed no hurry to get back, but seemed to me to prolong her absence as much as she could. Denis stood it better than one would have expected from such a doting husband, and seemed more like his old self as he talked over other days with Marsh and tried to cheer the listless aesthete up.

"It was Marsh who seemed most impatient to see the woman; perhaps because he thought her strange beauty, or some phase of the mysticism which had gone into her one-time magical cult, might help to reawaken his interest in things and give him another start toward artistic creation. That there was no baser reason, I was absolutely certain from what I knew of Marsh's character. With all his weaknesses, he was a gentleman—and it had indeed relieved me when I first learned that he wanted to come here because his willingness to accept Denis' hospitality proved that there was no reason why he shouldn't.

"When, at last, Marceline did return, I could see that Marsh was tremendously affected. He did not attempt to make her talk of the bizarre thing which she had so definitely abandoned, but was unable to hide a powerful admiration which kept his eyes—now dilated in that curious way for the first time during his visit—riveted to her every moment she was in the room. She, however, seemed uneasy rather than pleased by his steady scrutiny—that is, she seemed so at first, though this feeling of hers wore away in a few days, and left the two on a basis of the most cordial and voluble congeniality. I could see Marsh studying her constantly when he thought no one was watching; and I wondered how long it would be that only the artist, and not the primitive man, would be aroused by her mysterious graces.

"Denis naturally felt some irritation at this turn of affairs; though he realised that his guest was a man of honour and that, as kindred mystics and aesthetes, Marceline and Marsh would naturally have things and interests to discuss in which a more or less conventional person could have no part. He didn't hold anything against anybody, but merely regretted that his own imagination was too limited and traditional to let him talk with Marceline as Marsh talked. At this stage of things I began to see more of the boy. With his wife otherwise busy, he had time to remember that he had a father—and a father who was ready to help him in any sort of perplexity or difficulty.

"We often sat together on the veranda watching Marsh and Marceline as they rode up or down the drive on horseback, or played tennis on the court that used to stretch south of the house. They talked mostly in French, which Marsh, though he hadn't more than a quarter-portion of French blood, handled more glibly than either Denis or I could speak it. Marceline's English, always academically correct, was rapidly improving in accent; but it was plain that she relished dropping back into her mother-tongue. As we looked at the congenial couple they made, I could see the boy's cheek and throat muscles tighten—though he wasn't a whit less ideal a host to Marsh, or a whit less considerate a husband to Marceline.

"All this was generally in the afternoon; for Marceline rose very late, had breakfast in bed, and took an immense amount of time preparing to come downstairs. I never knew of anyone so wrapped up in cosmetics, beauty exercises, hair-oils, unguents, and everything of that kind. It was in these morning hours that Denis and Marsh did their real visiting, and exchanged the close confidences which kept their friendship up despite the strain that jealousy imposed.

"Well, it was in one of those morning talks on the veranda that Marsh made the proposition which brought on the end. I was laid up with some of my neuritis, but had managed to get downstairs and stretch out on the front parlour sofa near the long window. Denis and Marsh were just outside; so I couldn't help hearing all they said. They had been talking about art, and the curious, capricious environmental elements needed to jolt an artist into producing the real article, when Marsh suddenly swerved from abstractions to the personal application he must have had in mind from the start.

"'I suppose,' he was saying, 'that nobody can tell just what it is in some scenes or objects that makes them aesthetic stimuli for certain individuals. Basically, of course, it must have some reference to each man's background of stored-up mental associations, for no two people have the same scale of sensitiveness and responses. We decadents are artists for whom all ordinary things have ceased to have any emotional or imaginative significance, but no one of us responds in the same way to exactly the same extraordinary thing. Now take me, for instance. . . .'

"He paused and resumed.

"'I know, Denny, that I can say these things to you because you have such a preternaturally unspoiled mind—clean, fine, direct, objective, and all that. You won't misunderstand as an oversubtilised, effete man of the world might.'

"He paused once more.

"'The fact is, I think I know what's needed to set my imagination working again. I've had a dim idea of it ever since we were in Paris, but I'm sure now. It's Marceline, old chap—that face and that hair, and the train of shadowy images they bring up. Not merely visible beauty—though God knows there's enough of that—but something peculiar and individualised, that can't exactly be explained. Do you know, in the last few days I've felt the existence of such a stimulus so keenly that I honestly think I could outdo myself—break into the real masterpiece class if I could get hold of paint and canvas at just the time when her face and hair set my fancy stirring and weaving. There's something weird and other-worldly about it—something joined up with the dim ancient thing Marceline represents. I don't

36

know how much she's told you about that side of her, but I can assure you there's plenty of it. She has some marvellous links with the outside. . . .'

"Some change in Denis' expression must have halted the speaker here, for there was a considerable spell of silence before the words went on. I was utterly taken aback, for I'd expected no such overt development as this; and I wondered what my son could be thinking. My heart began to pound violently, and I strained my ears in the frankest of intentional eavesdropping. Then Marsh resumed.

"'Of course you're jealous—I know how a speech like mine must sound—but I can swear to you that you needn't be.'

"Denis did not answer, and Marsh went on.

"'To tell the truth, I could never be in love with Marceline—I couldn't even be a cordial friend of hers in the warmest sense. Why, damn it all, I felt like a hypocrite talking with her these days as I've been doing.

"'The case simply is, that one phase of her half hypnotises me in a certain way—a very strange, fantastic, and dimly terrible way—just as another phase half hypnotises you in a much more normal way. I see something in her—or to be psychologically exact, something through her or beyond her—that you don't see at all. Something that brings up a vast pageantry of shapes from forgotten abysses, and makes me want to paint incredible things whose outlines vanish the instant I try to envisage them clearly. Don't mistake, Denny, your wife is a magnificent being, a splendid focus of cosmic forces who has a right to be called divine if anything on earth has!'

"I felt a clearing of the situation at this point, for the abstract strangeness of Marsh's expressed statement, plus the flattery he was now heaping on Marceline, could not fail to disarm and mollify one as fondly proud of his consort as Denis always was. Marsh evidently caught the change himself, for there was more confidence in his tone as he continued.

"'I must paint her, Denny—must paint that hair—and you won't regret it. There's something more than mortal about that hair—something more than beautiful—'

"He paused, and I wondered what Denis could be thinking. I wondered, indeed, what I was really thinking myself. Was Marsh's interest actually that of the artist alone, or was he merely infatuated as Denis had been? I had thought, in their schooldays, that he had envied my boy; and I dimly felt that it might be the same now. On the other hand, something in that talk of artistic stimulus had rung amazingly true; so that the more I pondered, the more I was inclined to take the stuff at face value. Denis seemed to do so, too, for although I could not catch his low-spoken reply, I could tell by the effect it produced that it must have been affirmative.

"There was a sound of someone slapping another on the back, and then a grateful speech from Marsh that I was long to remember.

"'That's great, Denny; and just as I told you, you'll never regret it. In a sense, I'm half doing it for you. You'll be a different man when you see it. I'll put you back where you used to be—give you a waking-up and a sort of salvation—but you can't see what I mean as yet. Just remember old friendship, and don't get the idea that I'm not the same old bird!'

"I rose perplexedly as I saw the two stroll off across the lawn, arm in arm, and smoking in unison. What could Marsh have meant by his strange and almost ominous reassurance? The more my fears were quieted in one direction, the more they were aroused in another. Look at in any way I could, it seemed to be rather a bad business.

"But matters got started just the same. Denis fixed up an attic room with skylights, and Marsh sent for all sorts of painting equipment. Everyone was rather excited about the new venture, and I was at least glad that something was on foot to break the brooding tension. Soon the sittings began, and we all took them quite seriously—for we could see that Marsh regarded them as important artistic events. Denny and I used to go quietly about the house as though something sacred were occurring, and we knew that it was sacred so far as Marsh was concerned.

"With Marceline, though, it was a different matter, as I began to see at once. Whatever Marsh's reactions to the sittings may have been, hers were painfully obvious. Every possible way she betrayed a frank and commonplace infatuation for the artist, and would repulse Denis' marks of affection whenever she dared. Oddly, I noticed this more vividly than Denis himself, and tried to devise some plan for keeping the boy's mind easy until the matter could be straightened out. There was no use in having him excited about it if it could be helped.

"In the end I decided that Denis had better be away while the disagreeable situation existed. I could represent his interests well enough at this end, and sooner or later Marsh would finish the picture and go. My view of Marsh's honour was such that I did not look for any worse developments. When the matter had blown over, and Marceline had forgotten about her new infatuation, it would be time enough to have Denis on hand again.

"So I wrote a long letter to my marketing and financial agent in New York, and cooked up a plan to have the boy summoned there for an indefinite time. I had the agent write him that our affairs absolutely required one of us to go East, and of course my illness made it clear that I could not be the one. It was arranged that when Denis got to New York he would find enough plausible matters to keep him busy as long as I thought he ought to be away.

"The plan worked perfectly, and Denis started for New York without the least suspicion; Marceline and Marsh going with him in the car to Cape Girardeau, where he caught the afternoon train to St. Louis. They returned about dark, and as McCabe drove the car back to the stables I could hear them talking on the veranda—in those same chairs near the long parlour window where Marsh and Denis had sat when I overheard them talk about the portrait. This time I resolved to do some intentional eavesdropping, so quietly went down to the front parlour and stretched out on the sofa near the window.

"At first I could not hear anything, but very shortly there came a sound as of a chair being shifted, followed by a short, sharp breath and a sort of inarticulately hurt exclamation from Marceline. Then I heard Marsh speaking in a strained, almost formal voice.

"'I'd enjoy working tonight if you're not too tired.'

"Marceline's reply was in the same hurt tone which had marked her exclamation. She used English as he had done.

"'Oh, Frank, is that really all you care about? Forever working! Can't we just sit out in this glorious moonlight?'

"He answered impatiently, his voice shewing a certain contempt beneath the dominant quality of artistic enthusiasm.

"'Moonlight! Good God, what cheap sentimentality! For a supposedly sophisticated person you surely do hang on to some of the crudest claptrap that ever escaped from the dime novels! With art at your elbow, you have to think of the moon—cheap as a spotlight at the varieties! Or perhaps it makes you think of the Roodmas dance around the stone pillars at Auteuil.[17] Hell, how you used to make those goggle-eyed yaps stare! But no—I suppose you've dropped all that now. No more Atlantean magic or hair-snake rites for Madame de Russy! I'm the only one to remember the old things—the things that came down through the temples of Tanit and echoed on the ramparts of Zimbabwe. But I won't be cheated of that remembrance—all that is weaving itself into the thing on my canvas—the thing that is going to capture wonder and crystallise the secrets of 75,000 years. . . .'

"Marceline interrupted in a voice full of mixed emotions.

"'It's you who are cheaply sentimental now! You know well that the old things had better be let alone. All of you had better look out if ever I chant the old rites or try to call up what lies hidden in Yuggoth, Zimbabwe, and R'lyeh.[18] I thought you had more sense!

"'You lack logic. You want me to be interested in this precious painting of yours, yet you never let me see what you're doing. Always that black cloth over it! It's of me—I shouldn't think it would matter if I saw it. . . .'

"Marsh was interrupting this time, his voice curiously hard and strained.

"'No. Not now. You'll see it in due course of time. You say it's of you—yes, it's that, but it's more. If you knew, you mightn't be so impatient. Poor Denis! My God, it's a shame!'

"My throat went suddenly dry as the words rose to an almost febrile pitch. What could Marsh mean? Suddenly I saw that he had stopped and was entering the house alone.

I heard the front door slam, and listened as his footsteps ascended the stairs. Outside on the veranda I could still hear Marceline's heavy, angry breathing. I crept away sick at heart, feeling that there were grave things to ferret out before I could safely let Denis come back.

"After that evening the tension around the place was even worse than before. Marceline had always lived on flattery and fawning, and the shock of those few blunt words from Marsh was too much for her temperament. There was no living in the house with her any more, for with poor Denis gone she took out her abusiveness on everybody. When she could find no one indoors to quarrel with she would go out to Sophonisba's cabin and spend hours talking with the queer old Zulu woman. Aunt Sophy was the only person who would fawn abjectly enough to suit her, and when I tried once to overhear their conversation I found Marceline whispering about 'elder secrets' and 'unknown Kadath'[19] while the negress rocked to and fro in her chair, making inarticulate sounds of reverence and admiration every now and then.

"But nothing could break her dog-like infatuation for Marsh. She would talk bitterly and sullenly to him, yet was getting more and more obedient to his wishes. It was very convenient for him, since he now became able to make her pose for the picture whenever he felt like painting. He tried to shew gratitude for this willingness, but I thought I could detect a kind of contempt or even loathing beneath his careful politeness. For my part, I frankly hated Marceline! There was no use in calling my attitude anything as mild as mere dislike these days. Certainly, I was glad Denis was away. His letters, not nearly so frequent as I wished, shewed signs of strain and worry.

"As the middle of August went by I gathered from

Marsh's remarks that the portrait was nearly done. His mood seemed increasingly sardonic, though Marceline's temper improved a bit as the prospect of seeing the thing tickled her vanity. I can still recall the day when Marsh said he'd have everything finished within a week. Marceline brightened up perceptibly, though not without a venomous look at me. It seemed as if her coiled hair visibly tightened about her head.

"'I'm to be the first to see it!' she snapped. Then, smiling at Marsh, she said, 'And if I don't like it I shall slash it to pieces!'

"Marsh's face took on the most curious look I have ever seen it wear as he answered her.

"'I can't vouch for your taste, Marceline, but I swear it will be magnificent! Not that I want to take much credit—art creates itself—and this thing had to be done. Just wait!'

"During the next few days I felt a queer sense of foreboding, as if the completion of the picture meant a kind of catastrophe instead of a relief. Denis, too, had not written me, and my agent in New York said he was planning some trip to the country. I wondered what the outcome of the whole thing would be. What a queer mixture of elements—Marsh and Marceline, Denis and I! How would all these ultimately react on one another? When my fears grew too great I tried to lay them all to my infirmity, but that explanation never quite satisfied me."

IV

"Well, the thing exploded on Tuesday, the twenty-sixth of August. I had risen at my usual time and had breakfast, but was not good for much because of the pain in my spine. It had been troubling me badly of late, and forcing me to take opiates when it got too unbearable; nobody else was downstairs except the servants, though I could hear Marceline moving about in her room. Marsh slept in the attic next his studio, and had begun to keep such late hours that he was seldom up till noon. About ten o'clock the pain got the better of me, so that I took a double dose of my opiate and lay down on the parlour sofa. The last I heard was Marceline's pacing overhead. Poor creature—if I had known! She must have been walking before the long mirror admiring herself. That was like her. Vain from start to finish—revelling in her own beauty, just as she revelled in all the little luxuries Denis was able to give her.

"I didn't wake up till near sunset, and knew instantly how long I had slept from the golden light and long shadows outside the long window. Nobody was about, and a sort of unnatural stillness seemed to be hovering over everything. From afar, though, I thought I could sense a faint howling, wild and intermittent, whose quality had a slight but baffling familiarity about it. I'm not much for psychic premonitions, but I was frightfully uneasy from the start. There had been dreams—even worse than the ones I had been dreaming in the weeks before—and this time they seemed hideously linked to some black and festering reality. The whole place had a poisonous air. Afterward I reflected that certain sounds must have filtered through to my unconscious brain during those hours of drugged sleep. My pain, though, was very much eased; and I rose and walked without difficulty.

"Soon enough I began to see that something was wrong. Marsh and Marceline might have been riding, but someone ought to have been getting dinner in the kitchen. Instead, there was only silence, except for that faint distant howl or wail; and nobody answered when I pulled the old-fashioned bell-cord to summon Scipio. Then, chancing to look up, I saw the spreading stain on the ceiling—the bright red stain, that must have come through the floor of Marceline's room.[20]

"In an instant I forgot my crippled back and hurried upstairs to find out the worst. Everything under the sun raced through my mind as I struggled with the dampness-warped door of that silent chamber, and most hideous of all was a terrible sense of malign fulfilment and fatal ex-pectedness. I had, it struck me, known all along that name-less horrors were gathering; that something profoundly and cosmically evil had gained a foot-hold under my roof from which only blood and tragedy could result.

"The door gave at last, and I stumbled into the large room beyond—all dim from the branches of the great trees outside the windows. For a moment I could do nothing but flinch at the faint evil odour that immediately struck my nostrils. Then, turning on the electric light and glanc-ing around, I glimpsed a nameless blasphemy on the yellow and blue rug.

"It lay face down in a great pool of dark, thickened blood, and had the gory print of a shod human foot in the middle of its naked back. Blood was spattered every-where—on the walls, furniture, and floor. My knees gave way as I took in the sight, so that I had to stumble to a chair and slump down. The thing had obviously been a human being, though its identity was not easy to establish at first; since it was without clothes, and had most of its hair hacked and torn from the scalp in a very crude way. It was of a deep ivory colour, and I knew that it must have been Marceline. The shoe-print on the back made the thing seem all the more hellish. I could not even picture the strange, loath-some tragedy which must have taken place while I slept in the room below. When I raised my hand to wipe my dripping forehead I saw that my fingers were sticky with blood. I shuddered, then realised that it must have come from the knob of the door which the unknown murderer had forced shut behind him as he left. He had taken his weapon with him, it seemed, for no instrument of death was visible here.

"As I studied the floor I saw that a line of sticky footprints like the one on the body led away from the horror to the door. There was another blood-trail, too, and of a less easily explainable kind; a broadish, continuous line, as if marking the path of some huge snake. At first I concluded it must be due to something the murderer had dragged after him. Then, noting the way some of the footprints seemed to be superimposed on it, I was forced to believe that it had been there when the murderer left. But what crawling entity could have been in that room with the victim and her assassin, leaving before the killer when the deed was done? As I asked myself this question I thought I heard fresh bursts of that faint, distant wailing.

"Finally, rousing myself from a lethargy of horror, I got on my feet again and began following the footprints. Who the murderer was, I could not even faintly guess, nor could I try to explain the absence of the servants. I vaguely felt that I ought to go up to Marsh's attic quarters, but before I had fully formulated the idea I saw that the bloody trail was indeed taking me there. Was he himself the murderer? Had he gone mad under the strain of the morbid situation and suddenly run amok?

"In the attic corridor the trail became faint, the prints almost ceasing as they merged with the dark carpet. I could still, however, discern the strange single path of the entity who had gone first; and this led straight to the closed door of Marsh's studio, disappearing beneath it at a point about half way from side to side. Evidently it had crossed the threshold at a time when the door was wide open.

"Sick at heart, I tried the knob and found the door unlocked. Opening it, I paused in the waning north light to see what fresh nightmare might be awaiting me. There was certainly something human on the floor, and I reached for the switch to turn on the chandelier.

"But as the light flashed up my gaze left the floor and its horror—that was Marsh, poor devil—to fix itself frantically and incredulously upon the living thing that cowered and stared in the open doorway leading to Marsh's bedroom. It was a tousled, wild-eyed thing, crusted with dried blood and carrying in its hand a wicked machete which had been one of the ornaments of the studio wall. Yet even in that awful moment I recognised it as one whom I had thought more than a thousand miles away. It was my own boy Denis—or the maddened wreck which had once been Denis.

"The sight of me seemed to bring back a trifle of sanity—or at least of memory—in the poor boy. He straightened up and began to toss his head about as if trying to shake free from some enveloping influence. I could not speak a word, but moved my lips in an effort to get back my voice. My eyes wandered for a moment to the figure on the floor in front of the heavily draped easel—the figure toward which the strange blood-trail led, and which seemed to be tangled in the coils of some dark, ropy object. The shifting of my glance apparently produced some impression in the twisted brain of the boy, for suddenly he began to mutter in a hoarse whisper whose purport I was soon able to catch.

"'I had to exterminate her—she was the devil—the summit of [_____] and high-priestess of all evil—the spawn of the pit—Marsh knew, and tried to warn me.

Good old Frank—I didn't kill him, though I was ready to before I realised. But I went down there and killed her—then that cursed hair—'

"I listened in horror as Denis choked, paused, and began again.

"'You didn't know—her letters got queer and I knew she was in love with Marsh. Then she nearly stopped writing. He never mentioned her—I felt something was wrong, and thought I ought to come back and find out. Couldn't tell you—your manner would have given it away. Wanted to surprise them. Got here about noon today—came in a cab and sent the house-servants all off—let the field hands alone, for their cabins are all out of earshot. Told McCabe to get me some things in Cape Girardeau and not bother to come back till tomorrow. Had all the niggers take the old car and let Mary drive them to Bend Village for a vacation—told 'em we were all going on some sort of outing and wouldn't need help. Said they'd better stay all night with Uncle Scip's cousin, who keeps that nigger boarding-house.'

"Denis was getting very incoherent now, and I strained my ears to grasp every word. Again I thought I heard that wild, far-off wail, but the story had first place for the present.

"'Saw you sleeping in the parlour, and took a chance you wouldn't wake up. Then went upstairs on the quiet to hunt up Marsh and . . . that woman!'

"The boy shuddered as he avoided pronouncing Marceline's name. At the same time I saw his eyes dilate in unison with a bursting of the distant crying, whose vague familiarity had now become very great.

"'She was not in her room, so I went up to the studio. Door was shut, and I could hear voices inside. Didn't

48

knock—just burst in and found her posing for the picture. Nude, but with that hellish hair all draped around her. And making all sorts of sheep's eyes at Marsh. He had the easel turned half away from the door, so I couldn't see the picture. Both of them were pretty well jolted when I shewed up, and Marsh dropped his brush. I was in a rage and told him he'd have to shew me the portrait, but he got calmer every minute. Told me it wasn't quite done, but would be in a day or two—said I could see it then—she—hadn't seen it.

"'But that didn't go with me. I stepped up, and he dropped a velvet curtain over the thing before I could see it. He was ready to fight before letting me see it, but that—that—she—stepped up and sided with me. Said we ought to see it. Frank got horribly worked up, and gave me a punch when I tried to get at the curtain. I punched back and seemed to have knocked him out. Then I was almost knocked out myself by the shriek that—that creature—gave. She'd drawn aside the hangings herself, and had caught a look at what Marsh had been painting. I wheeled around and saw her rushing like mad out of the room—*then I saw the picture.'*

"Madness flared up in the boy's eyes again as he got to this place, and I thought for a minute he was going to spring at me with his machete. But after a pause he partly steadied himself.

"'Oh, God—that thing! Don't ever look at it! Burn it with the hangings around it and throw the ashes into the river! Marsh knew—and was warning me. He knew what it was—what that woman—that leopardess, or gorgon, or lamia, or whatever she was—actually represented. He'd tried to hint to me ever since I met her in his Paris studio, but it couldn't be told in words. I thought they all wronged her when they whispered horrors about her—she had me hypnotised so that I couldn't believe the plain facts—but this picture has caught the whole secret—the whole monstrous background!

"'God, but Frank is an artist! That thing is the greatest piece of work any living soul has produced since Rembrandt! It's a crime to burn it—but it would be a greater crime to let it exist—just as it would have been an abhorrent sin to let—that she-daemon—exist any longer. The minute I saw it I understood what—she—was, and what part she played in the frightful secret that has come down from the days of Cthulhu and the Elder Ones[21]—the secret that was nearly wiped out when Atlantis sank, but that kept half alive in hidden traditions and allegorical myths and furtive, midnight cult-practices. For you know she was the real thing. It wasn't any fake. It would have been merciful if it had been a fake. It was the old, hideous shadow that philosophers never dared mention—the thing hinted at in the *Necronomicon* and symbolised in the Easter Island colossi.[22]

"'She thought we couldn't see through—that the false front would hold till we had bartered away our immortal souls. And she was half right—she'd have got me in the end. She was only—waiting. But Frank—good old Frank—was too much for me. *He knew what it all meant, and painted it.* I don't wonder she shrieked and ran off when she saw it. It wasn't quite done, but God knows *enough was there.*

"'Then I knew I'd got to kill her—kill her, and everything connected with her. It was a taint that wholesome human blood couldn't bear. There was something else, too—but you'll never know that if you burn the picture without looking. I staggered down to her room with this machete that I got off the wall here, leaving Frank still knocked out. He was breathing, though, and I knew and thanked heaven that I hadn't killed him.

50

"'I found her in front of the mirror braiding that accursed hair. She turned on me like a wild beast, and began spitting out her hatred of Marsh. The fact that she'd been in love with him—and I knew she had—only made it worse. For a minute I couldn't move, and she came within an ace of completely hypnotising me. Then I thought of the picture, and the spell broke. She saw the breaking in my eyes, and must have noticed the machete, too. I never saw anything give such a wild jungle beast look as she did then. She sprang for me with claws out like a leopard's, but I was too quick. I swung the machete, and it was all over.'

"Denis had to stop again there, and I saw the perspiration running down his forehead through the spattered blood. But in a moment he hoarsely resumed.

"'I said it was all over—but God! some of it had only just begun! I felt I had fought the legions of Satan, and put my foot on the back of the thing I had annihilated. *Then I saw that blasphemous braid of coarse black hair begin to twist and squirm of itself.*

"'I might have known it. It was all in the old tales. That damnable hair had a life of its own, that couldn't be ended by killing the creature itself. I knew I'd have to burn it, so I started to hack it off with the machete. God, but it was devilish work! Tough—like iron wires—but I managed to do it. And it was loathsome the way the big braid writhed and struggled in my grasp.

"'About the time I had the last strand cut or pulled off I heard that eldritch wailing from behind the house. You know—it's still going off and on. I don't know what it is, but it must be something springing from this hellish business. It half seems like something I ought to know but can't quite place. It got my nerves the first time I heard it, and I dropped the severed braid in my fright. Then, I got a worse fright—for in another second the braid had turned on me and began to strike venomously with one of its ends which had knotted itself up like a sort of grotesque head. I struck out with the machete, and it turned away. Then, when I had my breath again, I saw that the monstrous thing was crawling along the floor by itself like a great black snake. I couldn't do anything for a while, but when it vanished through the door I managed to pull myself together and stumble after it. I could follow the broad, bloody trail, and I saw it led upstairs. It brought me here—and may heaven curse me if I didn't see it through the doorway, striking at poor dazed Marsh like a maddened rattler as it had struck at me, finally coiling around him as a python would. He had begun to come to, but that abominable serpent thing got him before he was on his feet. I knew that all of that woman's hatred was behind it, but I hadn't the power to pull it off. I tried, but it was too much for me. Even the machete was no good—I couldn't swing it freely or it would have slashed Frank to pieces. So I saw those monstrous coils tighten—saw poor Frank crushed to death before my eyes—and all the time that awful faint howling came from somewhere beyond the fields.

"'That's all. I pulled the velvet cloth over the picture and hope it'll never be lifted. The thing must be burnt. I couldn't pry the coils off poor, dead Frank—they cling to him like a leech, and seem to have lost their motion altogether. It's as if that snaky rope of hair has a kind of perverse fondness for the man it killed—it's clinging to him—embracing him. You'll have to burn poor Frank with it—but for God's sake don't forget to see it in ashes. That and the picture. They must both go. The safety of the world demands that they go.'

"Denis might have whispered more, but a fresh burst

of distant wailing cut us short. For the first time we knew what it was, for a westerly veering wind brought articulate words at last. We ought to have known long before, since sounds much like it had often come from the same source. It was wrinkled Sophonisba, the ancient Zulu witch-woman who had fawned on Marceline, keening from her cabin in a way which crowned the horrors of this nightmare tragedy. We could both hear some of the things she howled, and knew that secret and primordial bonds linked this savage sorceress with that other inheritor of elder secrets who had just been extirpated. Some of the words she used betrayed her closeness to daemonic and palaeogean traditions.

"*Iä! Iä! Shub-Niggurath!*[23] *Ya-R'lyeh! N'gagi n'bulu bwana n'lolo!* Ya, yo, pore Missy Tanit, pore Missy Isis! Marse Clooloo,[24] come up outen de water an' git yo chile—she done daid! She done daid! De hair ain' got no missus no mo', Marse Clooloo. Ol' Sophy, she know! Ol' Sophy, she done got de black stone outen Big Zimbabwe in ol' Affriky! Ol' Sophy, she done dance in de moonshine roun' de crocodile-stone befo' de N'bangus[25] cotch her and sell her to de ship folks! No mo' Tanit! No mo' Isis! No mo' witch-woman to keep de fire a-goin' in de big stone place! Ya, yo! *N'gagi n'bulu bwana n'lolo! Iä! Shub-Niggurath!* She daid! Ol' Sophy know!'

"That wasn't the end of the wailing, but it was all I could pay attention to. The expression on my boy's face shewed that it had reminded him of something frightful, and the tightening of his hand on the machete boded no good. I knew he was desperate, and sprang to disarm him if possible before he could do anything more.

"But I was too late. An old man with a bad spine doesn't count for much physically. There was a terrible struggle, but he had done for himself before many seconds were over. I'm not sure yet but that he tried to kill me, too. His last panting words were something about the need of wiping out everything that had been connected with Marceline, either by blood or marriage."

V

"I wonder to this day that I didn't go stark mad in that instant—or in the moments and hours afterward. In front of me was the slain body of my boy—the only human being I had to cherish—and ten feet away, in front of that shrouded easel, was the body of his best friend, with a nameless coil of horror wound around it. Below was the scalped corpse of that she-monster, about whom I was half-ready to believe anything. I was too dazed to analyse the probability of the hair story—and even if I had not been, that dismal howling from Aunt Sophy's cabin would have been enough to quiet doubt for the nonce.

"If I'd been wise, I'd have done just what poor Denis told me to—burned the picture and the body-grasping hair at once and without curiosity—but I was too shaken to be wise. I suppose I muttered foolish things over my boy—and then I remembered that the night was wearing on and that the servants would be back in the morning. It was plain that a matter like this could never be explained, and I knew that I must cover things up and invent a story.

"That coil of hair around Marsh was a monstrous thing. As I poked at it with a sword which I took from the wall I almost thought I felt it tighten its grip on the dead man. I didn't dare touch it—and the longer I looked at it the more horrible things I noticed about it. One thing gave me a start. I won't mention it—but it partly explained the need for feeding the hair with queer oils as Marceline had always done.

"In the end I decided to bury all three bodies in the cellar—with quicklime, which I knew we had in the storehouse. It was a night of hellish work. I dug three graves— my boy's a long way from the other two, for I didn't want him to be near either the woman's body or her hair. I was sorry I couldn't get the coil from around poor Marsh. It was terrible work getting them all down to the cellar. I used blankets in carting the woman and the poor devil with the coil around him. Then I had to get two barrels of lime from the storehouse. God must have given me strength, for I not only moved them both but filled all three graves without a hitch.

"Some of the lime I made into whitewash. I had to take a stepladder and fix over the parlour ceiling where the blood had oozed through. And I burned nearly everything in Marceline's room, scrubbing the walls and floor and heavy furniture. I washed up the attic studio, too, and the trail and footprints that led there. And all the time I could hear old Sophy's wailing in the distance. The devil must have been in that creature to let her voice go on like that. But she always was howling queer things. That's why the field niggers didn't get scared or curious that night. I locked the studio door and took the key to my room. Then I burned all my stained clothes in the fireplace. By dawn the whole house looked quite normal so far as any casual eye could tell. I hadn't dared touch the covered easel, but meant to attend to that later.

"Well, the servants came back next day, and I told them all the young folks had gone to St. Louis. None of the field hands seemed to have seen or heard anything, and old Sophonisba's wailing had stopped at the instant of sunrise. She was like a sphinx after that, and never let out a word of what had been on her brooding witch-brain the day and night before.

"Later on I pretended that Denis and Marsh and Marceline had gone back to Paris and had a certain discreet agency mail me letters from there—letters I had fixed up in forged handwriting. It took a good deal of deceit and reticence to explain things to various friends, and I know people have secretly suspected me of holding something back. I had the deaths of Marsh and Denis reported during the war, and later said Marceline had entered a convent. Fortunately Marsh was an orphan whose eccentric ways had alienated him from his people in Louisiana. Things might have been patched up a good deal better for me if I had had the sense to burn the picture, sell the plantation, and give up trying to manage things with a shaken and overstrained mind. You see what my folly has brought me to. Failing crops—hands discharged one by one—place falling to ruin—and myself a hermit and a target for dozens of queer countryside stories. Nobody will come around here after dark nowadays—or any other time if it can be helped. That's why I knew you must be a stranger.

"And why do I stay here? I can't wholly tell you that. It's bound up too closely with things at the very rim of sane reality. It wouldn't have been so, perhaps, if I hadn't looked at the picture. I ought to have done as poor Denis told me. I honestly meant to burn it when I went up to that locked studio a week after the horror, but I looked first—and that changed everything.

"No—there's no use telling what I saw. You can, in a way, see for yourself presently; though time and dampness have done their work. I don't think it can hurt you if you want to take a look, but it was different with me. I knew too much of what it all meant.

56

"Denis had been right—it was the greatest triumph of human art since Rembrandt, even though still unfinished. I grasped that at the start, and knew that poor Marsh had justified his decadent philosophy. He was to painting what Baudelaire was to poetry—and Marceline was the key that had unlocked his inmost stronghold of genius.

"The thing almost stunned me when I pulled aside the hangings—stunned me before I half knew what the whole thing was. You know, it's only partly a portrait. Marsh had been pretty literal when he hinted that he wasn't painting Marceline alone, but what he saw through her and beyond her.

"Of course she was in it—was the key to it, in a sense—but her figure only formed one point in a vast composition. She was nude except for that hideous web of hair spun around her, and was half-seated, half-reclining on a sort of bench or divan, carved in patterns unlike those of any known decorative tradition. There was a monstrously shaped goblet in one hand, from which was spilling fluid whose colour I haven't been able to place or classify to this day—I don't know where Marsh even got the pigments.

"The figure and the divan were in the left-hand foreground of the strangest sort of scene I ever saw in my life. I think there was a faint suggestion of its all being a kind of emanation from the woman's brain, yet there was also a directly opposite suggestion—as if she were just an evil image or hallucination conjured up by the scene itself.

"I can't tell you now whether it's an exterior or an interior—whether those hellish Cyclopean vaultings are seen from the outside or the inside, or whether they are indeed carven stone and not merely a morbid fungous arborescence. The geometry of the whole thing is crazy—one gets the acute and obtuse angles all mixed up.

"And God! The shapes of nightmare that float around in that perpetual daemon twilight! The blasphemies that lurk and leer and hold a Witches' Sabbat with that woman as a high-priestess! The black shaggy entities that are not quite goats—the crocodile-headed beast with three legs and a dorsal row of tentacles—and the flat-nosed aegipans[26] dancing in a pattern that Egypt's priests knew and called accursed!

"But the scene wasn't Egypt—it was *behind* Egypt; behind even Atlantis; behind fabled Mu, and myth-whispered Lemuria. It was the ultimate fountain-head of all horror on this earth, and the symbolism shewed only too clearly how integral a part of it Marceline was. I think it must be the unmentionable R'lyeh, that was not built by any creatures of this planet—the thing Marsh and Denis used to talk about in the shadows with hushed voices. In the picture it appears that the whole scene is deep under water—though everybody seems to be breathing freely.

"Well—I couldn't do anything but look and shudder, and finally I saw that Marceline was watching me craftily out of those monstrous, dilated eyes on the canvas. It was no mere superstition—Marsh had actually caught something of her horrible vitality in his symphonies of line and colour, so that she still brooded and stared and hated, just as if most of her weren't down in the cellar under quicklime. *And it was worst of all when some of those Hecateborn*[27] *snaky strands of hair began to lift themselves up from the surface and grope out into the room toward me.*

"Then it was that I knew the last final horror, and realised I was a guardian and a prisoner forever. She was the thing from which the first dim legends of Medusa and the Gorgons had sprung, and something in my shaken will had been captured and turned to stone at last. Never again would I be safe from those coiling snaky strands—the strands in the picture, and those that lay brooding under the lime near the wine casks. All too late I recalled the tales of the virtual indestructibility, even through centuries of burial, of the hair of the dead.

"My life since has been nothing but horror and slavery. Always there had lurked the fear of what broods down in the cellar. In less than a month the niggers began whispering about the great black snake that crawled around near the wine casks after dark, and about the curious way its trail would lead to another spot six feet away. Finally I had to move everything to another part of the cellar, for not a darky could be induced to go near the place where the snake was seen.

"Then the field hands began talking about the black snake that visited old Sophonisba's cabin every night after midnight. One of them shewed me its trail—and not long afterward I found out that Aunt Sophy herself had begun to pay strange visits to the cellar of the big house, lingering and muttering for hours in the very spot where none of the other blacks would go near. God, but I was glad when that old witch died! I honestly believe she had been a priestess of some ancient and terrible tradition back in Africa. She must have lived to be almost a hundred and fifty years old.

"Sometimes I think I hear something gliding around the house at night. There will be a queer noise on the stairs, where the boards are loose, and the latch of my room will rattle as if with an inward pressure. I always keep my door locked, of course. Then there are certain mornings when I seem to catch a sickish musty odour in the corridors, and notice a faint, ropy trail through the dust of the floors. I know I must guard the hair in the picture, for if anything were to happen to it, there are entities in this house which would take a sure and terrible revenge. I don't even dare to die—for life and death are all one to those in the clutch of what came out of R'lyeh. Something would be on hand to punish my neglect. Medusa's coil has got me, and it will always be the same. Never mix up with secret and ultimate horror, young man, if you value your immortal soul."

VI

As the old man finished his story I saw that the small lamp had long since burned dry, and that the large one was nearly empty. It must, I knew, be near dawn; and my ears told me that the storm was over. The tale had held me in a half-daze, and I almost feared to glance at the door lest it reveal an inward pressure from some unnamable source. It would be hard to say which had the greatest hold on me— stark horror, incredulity, or a kind of morbid fantastic curiosity. I was wholly beyond speech and had to wait for my strange host to break the spell.

"Do you want to see—the thing?"

His voice was very low and hesitant, and I saw he was tremendously in earnest. Of my various emotions, curiosity gained the upper hand; and I nodded silently. He rose, lighting a candle on a nearby table and holding it high before him as he opened the door.

"Come with me—upstairs."

I dreaded to brave those musty corridors again, but fascination downed all my qualms. The boards creaked beneath our feet, and I trembled once when I thought I saw a faint, rope-like line traced in the dust near the staircase.

The steps of the attic were noisy and rickety, with several of the treads missing. I was just glad of the need of looking sharply to my footing, for it gave me an excuse

60

not to glance about. The attic corridor was pitch-black and heavily cobwebbed, and inch-deep with dust except where a beaten trail led to a door on the left at the farther end. As I noticed the rotting remains of a thick carpet I thought of the other feet which had pressed it in bygone decades—of these, and of one thing which did not have feet.

The old man took me straight to the door at the end of the beaten path, and fumbled a second with the rusty latch. I was acutely frightened now that I knew the picture was so close, yet dared not retreat at this stage. In another moment my host was ushering me into the deserted studio.

The candle light was very faint, yet served to shew most of the principal features. I noticed the low, slanting roof, the huge enlarged dormer, the curios and trophies hung on the walls—and most of all, the great shrouded easel in the centre of the floor. To that easel de Russy now walked, drawing aside the dusty velvet hangings on the side turned away from me, and motioning me silently to approach. It took a good deal of courage to make me obey, especially when I saw how my guide's eyes dilated in the wavering candle light as he looked at the unveiled canvas. But again curiosity conquered everything, and I walked around to where de Russy stood. Then I saw the damnable thing.

I did not faint—though no reader can possibly realise the effort it took to keep me from doing so. I did cry out, but stopped short when I saw the frightened look on the old man's face. As I had expected, the canvas was warped, mouldy, and scabrous from dampness and neglect; but for all that I could trace the monstrous hints of evil cosmic outsideness that lurked all through the nameless scene's morbid content and perverted geometry.

It was as the old man had said—a vaulted, columned hell of mingled Black Masses and Witches' Sabbats—and what perfect completion could have added to it was beyond my power to guess. Decay had only increased the utter hideousness of its wicked symbolism and diseased suggestion, for the parts most affected by time were just those parts of the picture which in Nature—or in that extra-cosmic realm that mocked Nature—would be apt to decay or disintegrate.

The utmost horror of all, of course, was Marceline—and as I saw the bloated, discoloured flesh I formed the odd fancy that perhaps the figure on the canvas had some obscure, occult linkage with the figure which lay in quicklime under the cellar floor. Perhaps the lime had preserved the corpse instead of destroying it—but could it have preserved those black, malign eyes that glared and mocked at me from their painted hell?

And there was something else about the creature which I could not fail to notice—something which de Russy had not been able to put into words, but which perhaps had something to do with Denis' wish to kill all those of his blood who had dwelt under the same roof with her. Whether Marsh knew, or whether the genius in him painted it without his knowing, none could say. But Denis and his father could not have known till they saw the picture.

Surpassing all in horror was the streaming black hair—which covered the rotting body, *but which was itself not even slightly decayed.* All I had heard of it was amply verified. It was nothing human, this ropy, sinuous, half-oily, half-crinkly flood of serpent darkness. Vile, independent life proclaimed itself at every unnatural twist and convolution, and the suggestion of numberless *reptilian heads* at the out-turned ends was far too marked to be illusory or accidental.

The blasphemous thing held me like a magnet. I was

helpless, and did not wonder at the myth of the gorgon's glance which turned all beholders to stone. Then I thought I saw a change come over the thing. The leering features perceptibly moved, so that the rotting jaw fell, allowing the thick, beast-like lips to disclose a row of pointed yellow fangs. The pupils of the fiendish eyes dilated, and the eyes themselves seemed to bulge outward. And the hair—that accursed hair! *It had begun to rustle and wave perceptibly, the snake-heads all turning toward de Russy and vibrating as if to strike!*

Reason deserted me altogether, and before I knew what I was doing I drew my automatic and sent a shower of twelve steel-jacketed bullets through the shocking canvas. The whole thing at once fell to pieces, even the frame toppling from the easel and clattering to the dust-covered floor. But though this horror was shattered, another had risen before me in the form of de Russy himself, whose maddened shrieks as he saw the picture vanish were almost as terrible as the picture itself had been.

With a half-articulate scream of "God, now you've done it!" the frantic old man seized me violently by the arm and commenced to drag me out of the room and down the rickety stairs. He had dropped the candle in his panic; but dawn was near, and some faint grey light was filtering in through the dust-covered windows. I tripped and stumbled repeatedly, but never for a moment would my guide slacken his pace.

"Run!" he shrieked, "run for your life! You don't know what you've done! I never told you the whole thing! There were things I had to do—*the picture talked to me and told me.* I had to guard and keep it—now the worst will happen! *She and that hair will come up out of their graves, for God knows what purpose!*

63

"Hurry, man! For God's sake let's get out of here while there's time. If you have a car take me along to Cape Girardeau with you. It may get me in the end, anywhere, but I'll give it a run for its money. Out of here—quick!"

As we reached the ground floor I became aware of a slow, curious thumping from the rear of the house, followed by a sound of a door shutting. De Russy had not heard the thumping, but the other noise caught his ear and drew from him the most terrible shriek that ever sounded in human throat.

"Oh, God—great God—that was the cellar door—she's coming—"

By this time I was desperately wrestling with the rusty latch and sagging hinges of the great front door—almost as frantic as my host now that I heard the slow, thumping tread approaching from the unknown rear rooms of the accursed mansion. The night's rain had warped the oaken planks, and the heavy door stuck and resisted even more strongly than it had when I forced an entrance the evening before.

Somewhere a plank creaked beneath the foot of whatever was walking, and the sound seemed to snap the last cord of sanity in the poor old man. With a roar like that of a maddened bull he released his grip on me and made a plunge to the right, through the open door of a room which I judged had been a parlour. A second later, just as I got the front door open and was making my own escape, I heard the tinkling clatter of broken glass and knew he had leapt through a window. And as I bounded off the sagging porch to commence my mad race down the long, weed-grown drive I thought I could catch the thud of dead, dogged footfalls which did not follow me, but which kept leadenly on through the door of the cobwebbed parlour.

I looked backward only twice as I plunged heedlessly through the burrs and briers of that abandoned drive, past the dying lindens and grotesque scrub-oaks, in the grey pallor of a cloudy November dawn. The first time was when an acrid smell overtook me, and I thought of the candle de Russy had dropped in the attic studio. By then I was comfortably near the road, on the high place from which the roof of the distant house was clearly visible above its encircling trees; and just as I expected, thick clouds of smoke were billowing out of the attic dormers and curling upward into the leaden heavens. I thanked the powers of creation that an immemorial curse was about to be purged by fire and blotted from the earth.

But in the next instant came that second backward look in which I glimpsed two other things—things that cancelled most of the relief and gave me a supreme shock from which I shall never recover. I have said that I was on a high part of the drive, from which much of the plantation behind me was visible. This vista included not only the house and its trees but some of the abandoned and partly flooded flat land beside the river, and several bends of the weed-choked drive I had been so hastily traversing. In both of these latter places I now beheld sights—or suspicions of sights—which I wish devoutly I could deny.

It was a faint, distant scream which made me turn back again, and as I did so I caught a trace of motion on the dull grey marshy plain behind the house. At that distance human figures are very small, yet I thought the motion resolved itself into two of these—pursuer and pursued. I even thought I saw the dark-clothed leading figure overtaken and seized by the bald, naked figure in the rear—overtaken, seized, and dragged violently in the direction of the now burning house.

But I could not watch the outcome, for at once a nearer sight obtruded itself—a suggestion of motion among the underbrush at a point some distance back along the deserted drive. *Unmistakably, the weeds and bushes and briers were swaying as no wind could sway them; swaying as if some large, swift serpent were wriggling purposefully along on the ground in pursuit of me.*

That was all I could stand. I scrambled along madly for the gate, heedless of torn clothing and bleeding scratches, and jumped into the roadster parked under the great evergreen tree. It was a bedraggled, rain-drenched sight; but the works were unharmed and I had no trouble in starting the thing. I went on blindly in the direction the car was headed for; nothing was in my mind but to get away from that frightful region of nightmares and cacodaemons—to get away as quickly and as far as gasoline could take me.

About three or four miles along the road a farmer hailed me—a kindly, drawling fellow of middle age and considerable native intelligence. I was glad to slow down and ask directions, though I knew I must present a strange enough aspect. The man readily told me the way to Cape Girardeau, and inquired where I had come from in such a state at such an early hour. Thinking it best to say little, I merely mentioned that I had been caught in the night's rain and had taken shelter at a nearby farmhouse, afterward losing my way in the underbrush trying to find my car.

"At a farmhouse, eh? Wonder whose it could a ben. Ain't nothin' standin' this side o' Jim Ferris' place acrost Barker's Crick, an' that's all o' twenty miles by the rud."

I gave a start, and wondered what fresh mystery this portended. Then I asked my informant if he had overlooked the large ruined plantation house whose ancient gate bordered the road not far back.

"Funny ye sh'd recolleck that, stranger! Must a ben here afore some time. But that house ain't there now. Burnt down five or six years ago—and they did tell some queer stories about it."

I shuddered.

"You mean Riverside—ol' man de Russy's place. Queer goin's on there fifteen or twenty years ago. Ol' man's boy married a gal from abroad, and some folks thought she was a mighty odd sort. Didn't like the looks of her. Then she and the boy went off sudden, and later on the ol' man said he was kilt in the war. But some o' the niggers hinted queer things. Got around at last that the ol' fellow fell in love with the gal himself and kilt her and the boy. That place was sure enough haunted by a black snake, mean that what it may.

"Then five or six years ago the ol' man disappeared and the house burned down. Some do say he was burnt up in it. It was a mornin' after a rainy night just like this, when lots o' folks heard an awful yellin' acrost the fields in old de Russy's voice. When they stopped and looked, they see the house goin' up in smoke quick as a wink—that place was all like tinder anyhow, rain or no rain. Nobody never seen the ol' man agin, but onct in a while they tell of the ghost of that big black snake glidin' aroun'.

"What d'ye make of it, anyhow? You seem to hev knowed the place. Didn't ye ever hear tell of the de Russys? What d'ye reckon was the trouble with that gal young Denis married? She kinder made everybody shiver and feel hateful, though ye couldn't never tell why."

I was trying to think, but that process was almost beyond me now. The house burned down years ago? Then where, and under what conditions, had I passed the night? And why did I know what I knew of these things? Even as

67

I pondered I saw a hair on my coat sleeve—the short, grey hair of an old man.

In the end I drove on without telling anything. But I did hint that gossip was wronging the poor old planter who had suffered so much. I made it clear—as if from distant but authentic reports wafted among friends—that if anyone was to blame for the trouble at Riverside it was the woman, Marceline. She was not suited to Missouri ways, I said, and it was too bad that Denis had ever married her.

More I did not intimate, for I felt that the de Russys, with their proudly cherished honour and high, sensitive spirits, would not wish me to say more. They had borne enough, God knows, without the countryside guessing what a daemon of the pit—what a gorgon of the elder blasphemies—had come to flaunt their ancient and stainless name.

Nor was it right that the neighbours should know that other horror which my strange host of the night could not bring himself to tell me—that horror which he must have learned, as I learned it, from details in the lost masterpiece of poor Frank Marsh.

It would be too hideous if they knew that the one-time heiress of Riverside—the accursed gorgon or lamia whose hateful crinkly coil of serpent-hair must even now be brooding and twining vampirically around an artist's skeleton in a lime-packed grave beneath a charred foundation—was faintly, subtly, yet to the eyes of genius unmistakably the scion of Zimbabwe's most primal grovellers. No wonder she owned a link with that old witch-woman Sophonisba—for, though in deceitfully slight proportion, Marceline was a negress.

The Trap

With Henry S. Whitehead

t was on a certain Thursday morning in December that the whole thing began with that unaccountable motion I thought I saw in my antique Copenhagen mirror. Something, it seemed to me, stirred—something reflected in the glass, though I was alone in my quarters. I paused and looked intently, then, deciding that the effect must be a pure illusion, resumed the interrupted brushing of my hair.

I had discovered the old mirror, covered with dust and cobwebs, in an outbuilding of an abandoned estate-house in Santa Cruz's sparsely settled Northside territory, and had brought it to the United States from the Virgin Islands. The venerable glass was dim from more than two hundred years' exposure to a tropical climate, and the graceful ornamentation along the top of the gilt frame had been badly smashed. I had had the detached pieces set back into the frame before placing it in storage with my other belongings.

Now, several years later, I was staying half as a guest and half as a tutor at the private school of my old friend

Browne on a windy Connecticut hillside—occupying an unused wing in one of the dormitories, where I had two rooms and a hallway to myself. The old mirror, stowed securely in mattresses, was the first of my possessions to be unpacked on my arrival; and I had set it up majestically in the living-room, on top of an old rosewood console which had belonged to my great-grandmother.

The door of my bedroom was just opposite that of the living-room, with a hallway between; and I had noticed that by looking into my chiffonier glass I could see the larger mirror through the two doorways—which was exactly like glancing down an endless, though diminishing, corridor. On this Thursday morning I thought I saw a curious suggestion of motion down that normally empty corridor—but, as I have said, soon dismissed the notion.

When I reached the dining-room I found everyone complaining of the cold, and learned that the school's heating-plant was temporarily out of order. Being especially sensitive to low temperatures, I was myself an acute sufferer; and at once decided not to brave any freezing schoolroom that day. Accordingly I invited my class to come over to my living-room for an informal session around my grate-fire— a suggestion which the boys received enthusiastically.

After the session one of the boys, Robert Grandison, asked if he might remain; since he had no appointment for the second morning period. I told him to stay, and welcome. He sat down to study in front of the fireplace in a comfortable chair.

It was not long, however, before Robert moved to another chair somewhat farther away from the freshly replenished blaze, this change bringing him directly opposite the old mirror. From my own chair in another part of the room I noticed how fixedly he began to look at the dim, cloudy glass, and, wondering what so greatly interested him, was reminded of my own experience earlier that morning. As time passed he continued to gaze, a slight frown knitting his brows.

At last I quietly asked him what had attracted his attention. Slowly, and still wearing the puzzled frown, he looked over and replied rather cautiously:

"It's the corrugations in the glass—or whatever they are, Mr. Canevin. I was noticing how they all seem to run from a certain point. Look—I'll show you what I mean."

The boy jumped up, went over to the mirror, and placed his finger on a point near its lower left-hand corner.

"It's right here, sir," he explained, turning to look toward me and keeping his finger on the chosen spot.

His muscular action in turning may have pressed his finger against the glass. Suddenly he withdrew his hand as though with some slight effort, and with a faintly muttered "Ouch." Then he looked at the glass in obvious mystification.

"What happened?" I asked, rising and approaching.

"Why—it—" He seemed embarrassed. "It—I—felt—well, as though it were pulling my finger into it. Seems—er—perfectly foolish, sir, but—well—it was a most peculiar sensation." Robert had an unusual vocabulary for his fifteen years.

I came over and had him show me the exact spot he meant.

"You'll think I'm rather a fool, sir," he said shamefacedly, "but—well, from right here I can't be absolutely sure. From the chair it seemed to be clear enough."

Now thoroughly interested, I sat down in the chair Robert had occupied and looked at the spot he selected on the mirror. Instantly the thing "jumped out at me." Un-

71

mistakably, from that particular angle, all the many whorls in the ancient glass appeared to converge like a large number of spread strings held in one hand and radiating out in streams.

Getting up and crossing to the mirror, I could no longer see the curious spot. Only from certain angles, apparently, was it visible. Directly viewed, that portion of the mirror did not even give back a normal reflection—for I could not see my face in it. Manifestly I had a minor puzzle on my hands.

Presently the school gong sounded, and the fascinated Robert Grandison departed hurriedly, leaving me alone with my odd little problem in optics. I raised several window-shades, crossed the hallway, and sought for the spot in the chiffonier mirror's reflection. Finding it readily, I looked very intently and thought I again detected something of the "motion." I craned my neck, and at last, at a certain angle of vision, the thing again "jumped out at me."

The vague "motion" was now positive and definite—an appearance of torsional movement, or of whirling; much like a minute yet intense whirlwind or waterspout, or a huddle of autumn leaves dancing circularly in an eddy of wind along a level lawn. It was, like the earth's, a double motion—around and around, and at the same time *inward,* as if the whorls poured themselves endlessly toward some point inside the glass. Fascinated, yet realizing that the thing must be an illusion, I grasped an impression of quite distinct *suction,* and thought of Robert's embarrassed explanation: *"I felt as though it were pulling my finger into it."*

A kind of slight chill ran suddenly up and down my backbone. There was something here distinctly worth looking into. And as the idea of investigation came to me, I recalled the rather wistful expression of Robert Grandison when the gong called him to class. I remembered how he had looked back over his shoulder as he walked obediently out into the hallway, and resolved that he should be included in whatever analysis I might make of this little mystery.

Exciting events connected with that same Robert, however, were soon to chase all thoughts of the mirror from my consciousness for a time. I was away all that afternoon, and did not return to the school until the five-fifteen "Call-Over"—a general assembly at which the boys' attendance was compulsory. Dropping in at this function with the idea of picking Robert up for a session with the mirror, I was astonished and pained to find him absent—a very unusual and unaccountable thing in his case. That evening Browne told me that the boy had actually disappeared, a search in his room, in the gymnasium, and in all other accustomed places being unavailing, though all his belongings—including his outdoor clothing—were in their proper places.

He had not been encountered on the ice or with any of the hiking groups that afternoon, and telephone calls to all the school-catering merchants of the neighborhood were in vain. There was, in short, no record of his having been seen since the end of the lesson periods at two-fifteen; when he had turned up the stairs toward his room in Dormitory Number Three.

When the disappearance was fully realized, the resulting sensation was tremendous throughout the school. Browne, as headmaster, had to bear the brunt of it; and such an unprecedented occurrence in his well-regulated, highly organized institution left him quite bewildered. It was learned that Robert had not run away to his home in western Pennsylvania, nor did any of the searching-parties of boys and masters find any trace of him in the snowy countryside around the school. So far as could be seen, he had simply vanished.

Robert's parents arrived on the afternoon of the second day after his disappearance. They took their trouble quietly, though, of course, they were staggered by this unexpected disaster. Browne looked ten years older for it, but there was absolutely nothing that could be done. By the fourth day the case had settled down in the opinion of the school as an insoluble mystery. Mr. and Mrs. Grandison went reluctantly back to their home, and on the following morning the ten days' Christmas vacation began.

Boys and masters departed in anything but the usual holiday spirit; and Browne and his wife were left, along with the servants, as my only fellow-occupants of the big place. Without the masters and boys it seemed a very hollow shell indeed.

That afternoon I sat in front of my grate-fire thinking about Robert's disappearance and evolving all sorts of fantastic theories to account for it. By evening I had acquired a bad headache, and ate a light supper accordingly. Then, after a brisk walk around the massed buildings, I returned to my living-room and took up the burden of thought once more.

A little after ten o'clock I awakened in my armchair, stiff and chilled, from a doze during which I had let the fire go out. I was physically uncomfortable, yet mentally aroused by a peculiar sensation of expectancy and possible hope. Of course it had to do with the problem that was harassing me. For I had started from that inadvertent nap with a curious, persistent idea—the odd idea that a tenuous, hardly recognizable Robert Grandison had been trying desperately to communicate with me. I finally went to bed with one conviction unreasoningly strong in my mind. Somehow I was sure that young Robert Grandison was still alive.

That I should be receptive of such a notion will not seem strange to those who know my long residence in the West Indies and my close contact with unexplained happenings there. It will not seem strange, either, that I fell asleep with an urgent desire to establish some sort of mental communication with the missing boy. Even the most prosaic scientists affirm, with Freud, Jung, and Adler,[1] that the subconscious mind is most open to external impressions in sleep; though such impressions are seldom carried over intact into the waking state.

Going a step further and granting the existence of telepathic forces, it follows that such forces must act most strongly on a sleeper; so that if I were ever to get a definite message from Robert, it would be during a period of profoundest slumber. Of course, I might lose the message in waking; but my aptitude for retaining such things has been sharpened by types of mental discipline picked up in various obscure corners of the globe.

I must have dropped asleep instantaneously, and from the vividness of my dreams and the absence of wakeful intervals I judge that my sleep was a very deep one. It was six-forty-five when I awakened, and there still lingered with me certain impressions which I knew were carried over from the world of somnolent cerebration. Filling my mind was the vision of Robert Grandison strangely transformed to a boy of a dull greenish dark-blue color; Robert desperately endeavoring to communicate with me by means of speech, yet finding some almost insuperable difficulty in so doing. A wall of curious spatial separation seemed to stand between him and me—a mysterious, invisible wall which completely baffled us both.

I had seen Robert as though at some distance, yet

queerly enough he seemed at the same time to be just beside me. He was both larger and smaller than in real life, his apparent size varying *directly,* instead of *inversely,* with the distance as he advanced and retreated in the course of conversation. That is, he grew larger instead of smaller to my eye when he stepped away or backwards, and vice versa; as if the laws of perspective in his case had been wholly reversed. His aspect was misty and uncertain—as if he lacked sharp or permanent outlines; and the anomalies of his coloring and clothing baffled me utterly at first.

At some point in my dream Robert's vocal efforts had finally crystallized into audible speech—albeit speech of an abnormal thickness and dullness. I could not for a time understand anything he said, and even in the dream racked my brain for a clue to where he was, what he wanted to tell, and why his utterance was so clumsy and unintelligible. Then little by little I began to distinguish words and phrases, the very first of which sufficed to throw my dreaming self into the wildest excitement and to establish a certain mental connection which had previously refused to take conscious form because of the utter incredibility of what it implied.

I do not know how long I listened to those halting words amidst my deep slumber, but hours must have passed while the strangely remote speaker struggled on with his tale. There was revealed to me such a circumstance as I cannot hope to make others believe without the strongest corroborative evidence, yet which I was quite ready to accept as truth—both in the dream and after waking—because of my former contacts with uncanny things. The boy was obviously watching my face—mobile in receptive sleep—as he choked along; for about the time I began to comprehend him, his own expression brightened and gave signs of gratitude and hope.

Any attempt to hint at Robert's message, as it lingered in my ears after a sudden awakening in the cold, brings this narrative to a point where I must choose my words with the greatest care. Everything involved is so difficult to record that one tends to flounder helplessly. I have said that the revelation established in my mind a certain connection which reason had not allowed me to formulate consciously before. This connection, I need no longer hesitate to hint, had to do with the old Copenhagen mirror whose suggestions of motion had so impressed me on the morning of the disappearance, and whose whorl-like contours and apparent illusions of suction had later exerted such a disquieting fascination on both Robert and me.

Resolutely, though my outer consciousness had previously rejected what my intuition would have liked to imply, it could reject that stupendous conception no longer. What was fantasy in the tale of "Alice" now came to me as a grave and immediate reality. That looking-glass had indeed possessed a malign, abnormal suction; and the struggling speaker in my dream made clear the extent to which it violated all the known precedents of human experience and all the age-old laws of our three sane dimensions. It was more than a mirror—it was a gate; a trap; a link with spatial recesses not meant for the denizens of our visible universe, and realizable only in terms of the most intricate non-Euclidean mathematics.[2] *And in some outrageous fashion Robert Grandison had passed out of our ken into the glass and was there immured, waiting for release.*

It is significant that upon awakening I harbored no genuine doubt of the reality of the revelation. That I had actually held conversation with a trans-dimensional Robert, rather than evoked the whole episode from my broodings about his disappearance and about the old illusions of the mirror, was as certain to my utmost instincts as any of the instinctive certainties commonly recognized as valid.

The tale thus unfolded to me was of the most incredibly bizarre character. As had been clear on the morning of his disappearance, Robert was intensely fascinated by the ancient mirror. All through the hours of school, he had it in mind to come back to my living-room and examine it further. When he did arrive, after the close of the school day, it was somewhat later than two-twenty, and I was absent in town. Finding me out and knowing that I would not mind, he had come into my living-room and gone straight to the mirror; standing before it and studying the place where, as we had noted, the whorls appeared to converge.

Then, quite suddenly, there had come to him an over-powering urge to place his hand upon this whorl-center. Almost reluctantly, against his better judgment, he had done so; and upon making the contact had felt at once the strange, almost painful suction which had perplexed him that morning. Immediately thereafter—quite without warning, but with a wrench which seemed to twist and tear every bone and muscle in his body and to bulge and press and cut at every nerve—he had been abruptly *drawn through* and found himself *inside*.

Once through, the excruciatingly painful stress upon his entire system was suddenly released. He felt, he said, as though he had just been born—a feeling that made itself evident every time he tried to do anything; walk, stoop, turn his head, or utter speech. Everything about his body seemed a misfit.

These sensations wore off after a long while, Robert's body becoming an organized whole rather than a number of protesting parts. Of all the forms of expression, speech remained the most difficult; doubtless because it is complicated, bringing into play a number of different organs, muscles, and tendons. Robert's feet, on the other hand, were the first members to adjust themselves to the new conditions within the glass.

During the morning hours I rehearsed the whole reason-defying problem; correlating everything I had seen and heard, dismissing the natural scepticism of a man of sense, and scheming to devise possible plans for Robert's release from his incredible prison. As I did so a number of originally perplexing points became clear—or at least, clearer—to me.

There was, for example, the matter of Robert's coloring. His face and hands, as I have indicated, were a kind of dull greenish dark-blue; and I may add that his familiar blue Norfolk jacket had turned to a pale lemon-yellow while his trousers remained a neutral gray as before. Reflecting on this after waking, I found the circumstance closely allied to the reversal of perspective which made Robert seem to grow larger when receding and smaller when approaching. Here, too, was a physical *reversal*—for every detail of his coloring in the unknown dimension was the exact reverse or complement of the corresponding color detail in normal life. In physics the typical complementary colors are blue and yellow, and red and green. These pairs are opposites, and when mixed yield gray. Robert's natural color was a pinkish-buff, the opposite of which is the greenish-blue I saw. His blue coat had become yellow, while the gray trousers remained gray. This latter point baffled me until I remembered that gray is itself a mixture of opposites. There is no opposite for gray—or rather, it is its own opposite.

Another clarified point was that pertaining to Robert's curiously dulled and thickened speech—as well as to the general awkwardness and sense of misfit bodily parts of which he complained. This, at the outset, was a puzzle indeed; though after long thought the clue occurred to me. Here again was the same *reversal* which affected perspective and coloration. Anyone in the fourth dimension must necessarily be reversed in just this way—hands and feet, as well as colors and perspectives, being changed about. It would be the same with all the other dual organs, such as nostrils, ears, and eyes. Thus Robert had been talking with a reversed tongue, teeth, vocal cords, and kindred speech-apparatus; so that his difficulties in utterance were little to be wondered at.

As the morning wore on, my sense of the stark reality and maddening urgency of the dream-disclosed situation increased rather than decreased. More and more I felt that something must be done, yet realized that I could not seek advice or aid. Such a story as mine—a conviction based upon mere dreaming—could not conceivably bring me anything but ridicule or suspicions as to my mental state. And what, indeed, could I do, aided or unaided, with as little working data as my nocturnal impressions had provided? I must, I finally recognized, have more information before I could even think of a possible plan for releasing Robert. This could come only through the receptive conditions of sleep, and it heartened me to reflect that according to every probability my telepathic contact would be resumed the moment I fell into deep slumber again.

I accomplished sleeping that afternoon, after a midday dinner at which, through rigid self-control, I succeeded in concealing from Browne and his wife the tumultuous thoughts that crashed through my mind. Hardly had my eyes closed when a dim telepathic image began to appear; and I soon realized to my infinite excitement that it was identical with what I had seen before. If anything, it was more distinct; and when it began to speak I seemed able to grasp a greater proportion of the words.

During this sleep I found most of the morning's deductions confirmed, though the interview was mysteriously cut off long prior to my awakening. Robert had seemed apprehensive just before communication ceased, but had already told me that in his strange fourth-dimensional prison colors and spatial relationships were indeed reversed—black being white, distance increasing apparent size, and so on.

He had also intimated that, notwithstanding his possession of full physical form and sensations, most human vital properties seemed curiously suspended. Nutriment, for example, was quite unnecessary—a phenomenon really more singular than the omnipresent reversal of objects and attributes, since the latter was a reasonable and mathematically indicated state of things. Another significant piece of information was that the only exit from the glass to the world was the entrance-way, and that this was permanently barred and impenetrably sealed, so far as egress was concerned.

That night I had another visitation from Robert; nor did such impressions, received at odd intervals while I slept receptively minded, cease during the entire period of his incarceration. His efforts to communicate were desperate and often pitiful; for at times the telepathic bond would weaken, while at other times fatigue, excitement, or fear of interruption would hamper and thicken his speech.

I may as well narrate as a continuous whole all that Robert told me throughout the whole series of transient mental contacts—perhaps supplementing it at certain points with facts directly related after his release. The telepathic information was fragmentary and often nearly inarticulate, but I studied it over and over during the waking intervals of three intense days; classifying and cogitating with feverish diligence, since it was all that I had to go upon if the boy were to be brought back into our world.

The fourth-dimensional region in which Robert found himself was not, as in scientific romance, an unknown and infinite realm of strange sights and fantastic denizens; but was rather a projection of certain limited parts of our own terrestrial sphere within an alien and normally inaccessible aspect or direction of space. It was a curiously fragmentary, intangible, and heterogeneous world—a series of apparently dissociated scenes merging indistinctly one into the other; their constituent details having an obviously different status from that of an object drawn into the ancient mirror as Robert had been drawn. These scenes were like dream-vistas or magic-lantern[3] images—elusive visual impressions of which the boy was not really a part, but which formed a sort of panoramic background or ethereal environment against which or amidst which he moved.

He could not touch any of the parts of these scenes—walls, trees, furniture, and the like—but whether this was because they were truly non-material, or because they always receded at his approach, he was singularly unable to determine. Everything seemed fluid, mutable, and unreal. When he walked, it appeared to be on whatever lower surface the visible scene might have—floor, path, greensward, or such; but upon analysis he always found that the contact was an illusion. There was never any difference in the resisting force met by his feet—and by his hands when he would stoop experimentally—no matter what changes of apparent surface might be involved. He could not describe this foundation or limiting plane on which he walked as anything more definite than a virtually abstract pressure balancing his gravity. Of definite tactile distinctiveness it had none, and supplementing it there seemed to be a kind of restricted levitational force which accomplished transfers of altitude. He could never actually climb stairs, yet would gradually walk up from a lower level to a higher.

Passage from one definite scene to another involved a sort of gliding through a region of shadow or blurred focus where the details of each scene mingled curiously. All the vistas were distinguished by the absence of transient objects, and the indefinite or ambiguous appearance of such semi-transient objects as furniture or details of vegetation. The lighting of every scene was diffuse and perplexing, and of course the scheme of reversed colors—bright red grass, yellow sky with confused black and gray cloud-forms, white tree-trunks, and green brick walls—gave to everything an air of unbelievable grotesquerie. There was an alteration of day and night, which turned out to be a reversal of the normal hours of light and darkness at whatever point on the earth the mirror might be hanging.

This seemingly irrelevant diversity of the scenes puzzled Robert until he realized that they comprised merely such places as had been reflected for long continuous periods in the ancient glass. This also explained the odd absence of transient objects, the generally arbitrary boundaries of vision, and the fact that all exteriors were framed by the outlines of doorways or windows. The glass, it appeared, had power to store up these intangible scenes through long exposure; though it could never absorb anything corporeally, as Robert had been absorbed, except by a very different and particular process.

But—to me at least—the most incredible aspect of the mad phenomenon was the monstrous subversion of our known laws of space involved in the relation of various illusory scenes to the actual terrestrial regions represented. I have spoken of the glass as storing up the images of these regions, but this is really an inexact definition. In truth, each of the mirror scenes formed a true and quasi-permanent fourth-dimensional projection of the corresponding mundane region; so that whenever Robert moved to a certain part of a certain scene, as he moved into the image of my room when sending his telepathic messages, *he was actually in that place itself, on earth*—though under spatial conditions which cut off all sensory communication, in either direction, between him and the present tri-dimensional aspect of the place.

Theoretically speaking. a prisoner in the glass could in a few moments go anywhere on our planet—into any place, that is, which had ever been reflected in the mirror's surface. This probably applied even to places where the mirror had not hung long enough to produce a clear illusory scene; the terrestrial region being then represented by a zone of more or less formless shadow. Outside the definite scenes was a seemingly limitless waste of neutral gray shadow about which Robert could never be certain, and into which he never dared stray far lest he become hopelessly lost to the real and mirror worlds alike.

Among the earliest particulars which Robert gave, was the fact that he was not alone in his confinement. Various others, all in antique garb, were in there with him—a corpulent middle-aged gentleman with tied queue and velvet knee-breeches who spoke English fluently though with a marked Scandinavian accent; a rather beautiful small girl with very blonde hair which appeared a glossy dark blue; two apparently mute Negroes whose features contrasted grotesquely with the pallor of their reversed-colored skins; three young men; one young woman; a very small child,

84

almost an infant; and a lean, elderly Dane of extremely distinctive aspect and a kind of half-malign intellectuality of countenance.

This last-named individual—Axel Holm, who wore the satin small-clothes, flared-skirted coat, and voluminous full-bottomed periwig of an age more than two centuries in the past—was notable among the little band as being the one responsible for the presence of them all. He it was who, skilled equally in the arts of magic and glass working, had long ago fashioned this strange dimensional prison in which himself, his slaves, and those whom he chose to invite or allure thither were immured unchangingly for as long as the mirror might endure.

Holm was born early in the seventeenth century, and had followed with tremendous competence and success the trade of a glass-blower and molder in Copenhagen. His glass, especially in the form of large drawing-room mirrors, was always at a premium. But the same bold mind which had made him the first glazier of Europe also served to carry his interests and ambitions far beyond the sphere of mere material craftsmanship. He had studied the world around him, and chafed at the limitations of human knowledge and capability. Eventually he sought for dark ways to overcome those limitations, and gained more success than is good for any mortal.

He had aspired to enjoy something like eternity, the mirror being his provision to secure this end. Serious study of the fourth dimension was far from beginning with Einstein in our own era; and Holm, more than erudite in all the methods of his day, knew that a bodily entrance into that hidden phase of space would prevent him from dying in the ordinary physical sense. Research showed him that the principle of reflection undoubtedly forms the chief gate to all dimensions beyond our familiar three; and chance placed in his hands a small and very ancient glass whose cryptic properties he believed he could turn to advantage. Once "inside" this mirror according to the method he had envisaged, he felt that "life" in the sense of form and consciousness would go on virtually forever, provided the mirror could be preserved indefinitely from breakage or deterioration.

Holm made a magnificent mirror, such as would be prized and carefully preserved; and in it deftly fused the strange whorl-configured relic he had acquired. Having thus prepared his refuge and his trap, he began to plan his mode of entrance and conditions of tenancy. He would have with him both servitors and companions; and as an experimental beginning he sent before him into the glass two dependable Negro slaves brought from the West Indies. What his sensations must have been upon beholding this first concrete demonstration of his theories, only imagination can conceive.

Undoubtedly a man of his knowledge realized that absence from the outside world, if deferred beyond the natural span of life of those within, must mean instant dissolution at the first attempt to return to that world. But, barring that misfortune or accidental breakage, those within would remain forever as they were at the time of entrance. They would never grow old, and would need neither food nor drink.

To make his prison tolerable he sent ahead of him certain books and writing materials, a chair and table of stoutest workmanship, and a few other accessories. He knew that the images which the glass would reflect or absorb would not be tangible, but would merely extend around him like a background of dream. His own transition in 1687 was a momentous experience; and must have been attended by mixed sensations of triumph and terror. Had anything gone wrong, there were frightful possibilities of being lost in dark and inconceivable multiple dimensions.

For over fifty years he had been unable to secure any additions to the little company of himself and slaves, but later on he had perfected his telepathic method of visualizing small sections of the outside world close to the glass, and attracting certain individuals in those areas through the mirror's strange entrance. Thus Robert, influenced into a desire to press upon the "door," had been lured within. Such visualizations depended wholly on telepathy, since no one inside the mirror could see out into the world of men.

It was, in truth, a strange life that Holm and his company had lived inside the glass. Since the mirror had stood for fully a century with its face to the dusty stone wall of the shed where I found it, Robert was the first being to enter this limbo after all that interval. His arrival was a gala event, for he brought news of the outside world which must have been of the most startling impressiveness to the more thoughtful of those within. He, in his turn—young though he was—felt overwhelmingly the weirdness of meeting and talking with persons who had been alive in the seventeenth and eighteenth centuries.

The deadly monotony of life for the prisoners can only be vaguely conjectured. As mentioned, its extensive spatial variety was limited to localities which had been reflected in the mirror for long periods; and many of these had become dim and strange as tropical climates had made inroads on the surface. Certain localities were bright and beautiful, and in these the company usually gathered. But no scene could be fully satisfying; since the visible objects were all unreal and intangible, and often of perplexingly indefinite outline. When the tedious periods of darkness came, the general custom was to indulge in memories, reflections, or conversations. Each one of that strange, pathetic group had retained his or her personality unchanged and unchangeable, since becoming immune to the time effects of outside space.

The number of inanimate objects within the glass, aside from the clothing of the prisoners, was very small; being largely limited to the accessories Holm had provided for himself. The rest did without even furniture, since sleep and fatigue had vanished along with most other vital attributes. Such inorganic things as were present, seemed as exempt from decay as the living beings. The lower forms of animal life were wholly absent.

Robert derived most of his information from Herr Thiele, the gentleman who spoke English with a Scandinavian accent. This portly Dane had taken a fancy to him, and talked at considerable length. The others, too, had received him with courtesy and goodwill; Holm himself, seeming well-disposed, had told him about various matters including the door of the trap.

The boy, as he told me later, was sensible enough never to attempt communication with me when Holm was nearby. Twice, while thus engaged, he had seen Holm appear; and had accordingly ceased at once. At no time could I see the world behind the mirror's surface. Robert's visual image, which included his bodily form and the clothing connected with it, was—like the aural image of his halting voice and like his own visualization of myself—a case of purely telepathic transmission; and did not involve true interdimensional sight. However, had Robert been as trained a telepathist as Holm, he might have transmitted a few strong images apart from his immediate person.

Throughout this period of revelation I had, of course, been desperately trying to devise a method for Robert's release. On the fourth day—the ninth after the disappearance—I hit on a solution. Everything considered, my laboriously formulated process was not a very complicated one; though I could not tell beforehand how it would work, while the possibility of ruinous consequences in case of a slip was appalling. This process depended, basically, on the fact that there was no possible exit from inside the glass. If Holm and his prisoners were permanently sealed in, then release must come wholly from outside. Other considerations included the disposal of the other prisoners, if any survived, and especially of Axel Holm. What Robert had told me of him was anything but reassuring; and I certainly did not wish him loose in my apartment, free once more to work his evil will upon the world. The telepathic messages had not made fully clear the effect of liberation on those who had entered the glass so long ago.

There was, too, a final though minor problem in case of success—that of getting Robert back into the routine of school life without having to explain the incredible. In case of failure, it was highly inadvisable to have witnesses present at the release operations—and lacking these, I simply could not attempt to relate the actual facts if I should succeed. Even to me the reality seemed a mad one whenever I let my mind turn from the data so compellingly presented in that tense series of dreams.

When I had thought these problems through as far as possible, I procured a large magnifying-glass from the school laboratory and studied minutely every square millimeter of that whorl-center which presumably marked the extent of the original ancient mirror used by Holm. Even with this aid I could not quite trace the exact boundary between the old area and the surface added by the Danish wizard; but after a long study decided on a conjectural oval boundary which I outlined very precisely with a soft blue pencil. I then made a trip to Stamford, where I procured a heavy glass-cutting tool; for my primary idea was to remove the ancient and magically potent mirror from its later setting.

My next step was to figure out the best time of day to make the crucial experiment. I finally settled on two-thirty a.m.—both because it was a good season for uninterrupted work, and because it was the "opposite" of two-thirty p.m., the probable moment at which Robert had entered the mirror. This form of "oppositeness" may or may not have been relevant, but I knew at least that the chosen hour was as good as any—and perhaps better than most.

I finally set to work in the early morning of the eleventh day after the disappearance, having drawn all the shades of my living-room and closed and locked the door into the hallway. Following with breathless care the elliptical line I had traced, I worked around the whorl-section with my steel-wheeled cutting tool. The ancient glass, half an inch thick, crackled crisply under the firm, uniform pressure; and upon completing the circuit I cut around it a second time, crunching the roller more deeply into the glass.

Then, very carefully indeed, I lifted the heavy mirror down from its console and leaned it face-inward against the wall; prying off two of the thin, narrow boards nailed to the back. With equal caution I smartly tapped the cut-around space with the heavy wooden handle of the glass-cutter.

At the very first tap the whorl-containing section of glass dropped out on the Bokhara rug[4] beneath. I did not know what might happen, but was keyed up for anything, and took a deep involuntary breath. I was on my knees for convenience at the moment, with my face quite near the newly made aperture; and as I breathed there poured into my nostrils a powerful *dusty* odor—a smell not comparable to any other I have ever encountered. Then everything within my range of vision suddenly turned to a dull gray before my failing eyesight as I felt myself overpowered by an invisible force which robbed my muscles of their power to function.

I remember grasping weakly and futilely at the edge of the nearest window drapery and feeling it rip loose from its fastening. Then I sank slowly to the floor as the darkness of oblivion passed over me.

When I regained consciousness I was lying on the Bokhara rug with my legs held unaccountably up in the air. The room was full of that hideous and inexplicable dusty smell—and as my eyes began to take in definite images I saw that Robert Grandison stood in front of me. It was he—fully in the flesh and with his coloring normal—who was holding my legs aloft to bring the blood back to my head as the school's first-aid course had taught him to do with persons who had fainted. For a moment I was struck mute by the stifling odor and by a bewilderment which quickly merged into a sense of triumph. Then I found myself able to move and speak collectedly.

I raised a tentative hand and waved feebly at Robert.

"All right, old man," I murmured, "you can let my legs down now. Many thanks. I'm all right again, I think. It was the smell—I imagine—that got me. Open that farthest window, please—wide—from the bottom. That's it— thanks. No—leave the shade down the way it was."

I struggled to my feet, my disturbed circulation adjusting itself in waves, and stood upright hanging to the back of a big chair. I was still "groggy," but a blast of fresh, bitterly cold air from the window revived me rapidly. I sat down in the big chair and looked at Robert, now walking toward me.

"First," I said hurriedly, "tell me, Robert—those others—Holm? What happened to *them,* when I—opened the exit?"

Robert paused half-way across the room and looked at me very gravely.

"I saw them fade away—into nothingness—Mr. Canevin," he said with solemnity; "and with them—everything. There isn't any more 'inside,' sir—thank God, and you, sir!"

And young Robert, at last yielding to the sustained strain which he had borne through all those terrible eleven days, suddenly broke down like a little child and began to weep hysterically in great, stifling, dry sobs.

I picked him up and placed him gently on my davenport, threw a rug over him, sat down by his side, and put a calming hand on his forehead.

"Take it easy, old fellow," I said soothingly.

The boy's sudden and very natural hysteria passed as quickly as it had come on as I talked to him reassuringly about my plans for his quiet restoration to the school. The interest of the situation and the need of concealing the incredible truth beneath a rational explanation took hold of his imagination as I had expected; and at last he sat up eagerly, telling the details of his release and listening to the instructions I had thought out. He had, it seems, been in the "projected area" of my bedroom when I opened the way back, and had emerged in that actual room—hardly realizing that he was "out." Upon hearing a fall in the living-room he had hastened thither, finding me on the rug in my fainting spell.

I need mention only briefly my method of restoring Robert in a seemingly normal way—how I smuggled him out of the window in an old hat and sweater of mine, took him down the road in my quietly started car, coached him carefully in a tale I had devised, and returned to arouse Browne with the news of his discovery. He had, I explained, been walking alone on the afternoon of his disappearance; and had been offered a motor ride by two young men who, as a joke and over his protests that he could go no farther than Stamford and back, had begun to carry him past that town. Jumping from the car during a traffic stop with the intention of hitch-hiking back before Call-Over, he had been hit by another car just as the traffic was released—awakening ten days later in the Greenwich home of the people who had hit him. On learning the date, I added, he had immediately telephoned the school; and I, being the only one awake, had answered the call and hurried after him in my car without stopping to notify anyone.

Browne, who at once telephoned to Robert's parents, accepted my story without question; and forbore to interrogate the boy because of the latter's manifest exhaustion. It was arranged that he should remain at the school for a rest, under the expert care of Mrs. Browne, a former trained nurse. I naturally saw a good deal of him during the remainder of the Christmas vacation, and was thus enabled to fill in certain gaps in his fragmentary dream-story.

Now and then we would almost doubt the actuality of what had occurred; wondering whether we had not both shared some monstrous delusion born of the mirror's glittering hypnotism, and whether the tale of the ride and accident were not after all the real truth. But whenever we did so we would be brought back to belief by some monstrous and haunting memory; with me, of Robert's dream-figure and its thick voice and inverted colors; with him, of the whole fantastic pageantry of ancient people and dead scenes that he had witnessed. And then there was that joint recollection of that damnable dusty odor.... We knew what it meant: the instant dissolution of those who had entered an alien dimension a century and more ago.

There are, in addition, at least two lines of rather more positive evidence; one of which comes through my researches in Danish annals concerning the sorcerer, Axel Holm. Such a person, indeed, left many traces in folklore and written records; and diligent library sessions, plus conferences with various learned Danes, have shed much more light on his evil fame. At present I need say only that the Copenhagen glass-blower—born in 1612—was a notorious Luciferian[5] whose pursuits and final vanishing formed a matter of awed debate over two centuries ago. He had burned with a desire to know all things and to conquer every limitation of mankind—to which end he had delved deeply into occult and forbidden fields ever since he was a child.

He was commonly held to have joined a coven of the dreaded witch-cult, and the vast lore of ancient Scandinavian myth—with its Loki the Sly One and the accursed Fenris-Wolf[6]—was soon an open book to him. He had strange interests and objectives, few of which were definitely known, but some of which were recognized as intolerably evil. It is recorded that his two Negro helpers, originally slaves from the Danish West Indies, had become mute soon after their acquisition by him; and that they had disappeared not long before his own disappearance from the ken of mankind.

Near the close of an already long life the idea of a glass of immortality appears to have entered his mind. That he had acquired an enchanted mirror of inconceivable antiquity was a matter of common whispering; it being alleged that he had purloined it from a fellow-sorcerer who had entrusted it to him for polishing.

This mirror—according to popular tales a trophy as potent in its way as the better-known Aegis of Minerva or Hammer of Thor[7]—was a small oval object called "Loki's Glass," made of some polished fusible mineral and having magical properties which included the divination of the immediate future and the power to show the possessor his enemies. That it had deeper potential properties, realizable in the hands of an erudite magician, none of the common people doubted; and even educated persons attached much fearful importance to Holm's rumored attempts to incorporate it in a larger glass of immortality. Then had come the wizard's disappearance in 1687, and the final sale and dispersal of his goods amidst a growing cloud of fantastic legendry. It was, altogether, just such a story as one would laugh at if possessed of no particular key; yet to me, remembering those dream messages and having Robert Grandison's corroboration before me, it formed a positive confirmation of all the bewildering marvels that had been unfolded.

But as I have said, there is still another line of rather positive evidence—of a very different character—at my disposal. Two days after his release, as Robert, greatly improved in strength and appearance, was placing a log on my living-room fire, I noticed a certain awkwardness in his motions and was struck by a persistent idea. Summoning him to my desk I suddenly asked him to pick up an inkstand—and was scarcely surprised to note that, despite lifelong right-handedness, he obeyed unconsciously with his left hand. Without alarming him, I then asked that he unbutton his coat and let me listen to his cardiac action. What I found upon placing my ear to his chest—and what I did not tell him for some time afterward—was that *his heart was beating on his right side.*

He had gone into the glass right-handed and with all organs in their normal positions. Now he was left-handed and with organs reversed, and would doubtless continue so for the rest of his life. Clearly, the dimensional transition had been no illusion—for this physical change was tangible and unmistakable. Had there been a natural exit from the glass, Robert would probably have undergone a thorough re-reversal and emerged in perfect normality—as indeed the color-scheme of his body and clothing did emerge. The forcible nature of his release, however, undoubtedly set something awry; so that dimensions no longer had a chance to right themselves as chromatic wave-frequencies still did.

I had not merely *opened* Holm's trap; I had *destroyed* it; and at the particular stage of destruction marked by Robert's escape some of the reversing properties had perished. It is significant that in escaping Robert had felt no pain comparable to that experienced in entering. Had the destruction been still more sudden, I shiver to think of the monstrosities of color the boy would always have been forced to bear. I may add that after discovering Robert's reversal I examined the rumpled and discarded clothing he had worn in the glass, and found, as I had expected, a complete reversal of pockets, buttons, and all other corresponding details.

At this moment Loki's Glass, just as it fell on my Bokhara rug from the now patched and harmless mirror, weighs down a sheaf of papers on my writing-table here in St. Thomas, venerable capital of the Danish West Indies— now the American Virgin Islands. Various collectors of old

Sandwich glass[8] have mistaken it for an odd bit of that early American product—but I privately realize that my paperweight is an antique of far subtler and more paleogean craftsmanship. Still, I do not disillusion such enthusiasts.

The Man of Stone

With Hazel Heald

en Hayden was always a stubborn chap, and once he had heard about those strange statues in the upper Adirondacks, nothing could keep him from going to see them. I had been his closest acquaintance for years, and our Damon and Pythias friendship made us inseparable at all times. So when Ben firmly decided to go—well, I had to trot along too, like a faithful collie.

"Jack," he said, "you know Henry Jackson, who was up in a shack beyond Lake Placid[1] for that beastly spot in his lung? Well, he came back the other day nearly cured, but had a lot to say about some devilish queer conditions up there. He ran into the business all of a sudden and can't be sure yet that it's anything more than a case of bizarre sculpture; but just the same his uneasy impression sticks.

"It seems he was out hunting one day, and came across a cave with what looked like a dog in front of it. Just as he was expecting the dog to bark he looked again, and saw that the thing wasn't alive at all. It was a stone dog—such a perfect image, down to the smallest whisker, that he couldn't decide whether it was a supernaturally clever statue or a petrified animal. He was almost afraid to touch it, but when he did he realised it was surely made of stone.

"After a while he nerved himself up to go into the cave—and there he got a still bigger jolt. Only a little way in there was another stone figure—or what looked like it—but this time it was a man's. It lay on the floor, on its side, wore clothes, and had a peculiar smile on its face. This time Henry didn't stop to do any touching, but beat it straight for the village, Mountain Top, you know.[2] Of course he asked questions—but they did not get him very far. He found he was on a ticklish subject, for the natives only shook their heads, crossed their fingers, and muttered something about a 'Mad Dan'—whoever he was.

"It was too much for Jackson, so he came home weeks ahead of his planned time. He told me all about it because he knows how fond I am of strange things—and oddly enough, I was able to fish up a recollection that dovetailed pretty neatly with his yarn. Do you remember Arthur Wheeler, the sculptor who was such a realist that people began calling him nothing but a solid photographer? I think you knew him slightly. Well, as a matter of fact, he ended up in that part of the Adirondacks himself. Spent a lot of time there, and then dropped out of sight. Never heard from again. Now if stone statues that look like men and dogs are turning up around there, it looks to me as if they might be his work—no matter what the rustics say, or refuse to say, about them. Of course a fellow with Jackson's nerves might easily get flighty and disturbed over things like that; but I'd have done a lot of examining before running away.

"In fact, Jack, I'm going up there now to look things over—and you're coming along with me. It would mean a lot to find Wheeler—or any of his work. Anyhow, the mountain air will brace us both up."

So less than a week later, after a long train ride and a jolting bus trip through breathlessly exquisite scenery, we arrived at Mountain Top in the late, golden sunlight of a June evening. The village comprised only a few small houses, a hotel, and the general store at which our bus drew up; but we knew that the latter would probably prove a focus for such information. Surely enough, the usual group of idlers was gathered around the steps; and when we represented ourselves as health-seekers in search of lodgings they had many recommendations to offer.

Though we had not planned to do any investigating till the next day, Ben could not resist venturing some vague, cautious questions when he noticed the senile garrulousness of one of the ill-clad loafers. He felt, from Jackson's previous experience, that it would be useless to begin with references to the queer statues; but decided to mention Wheeler as one whom we had known, and in whose fate we consequently had a right to be interested.

The crowd seemed uneasy when Sam stopped his whittling and started talking, but they had slight occasion for alarm. Even this barefoot old mountain decadent tightened up when he heard Wheeler's name, and only with difficulty could Ben get anything coherent out of him.

"Wheeler?" he had finally wheezed. "Oh, yeh—that feller as was all the time blastin' rocks and cuttin' 'em up into statues. So yew knowed him, hey? Wal, they ain't much we kin tell ye, and mebbe that's too much. He stayed out to Mad Dan's cabin in the hills—but not so very long. Got so he wa'n't wanted no more . . . by Dan, that is. Kinder soft-spoken and got around Dan's wife till the old devil took notice. Pretty sweet on her, I guess. But he took the trail sudden, and nobody's seen hide nor hair of him since. Dan must a told him sumthin' pretty plain—bad feller to get agin ye, Dan is! Better keep away from thar, boys, for they ain't no good in that part of the hills. Dan's ben workin' up a worse and worse mood, and ain't seen about no more. Nor his wife, neither. Guess he's penned her up so's nobody else kin make eyes at her!"

As Sam resumed his whittling after a few more observations, Ben and I exchanged glances. Here, surely, was a new lead which deserved intensive following up. Deciding to lodge at the hotel, we settled ourselves as quickly as possible; planning for a plunge into the wild hilly country on the next day.

At sunrise we made our start, each bearing a knapsack laden with provisions and such tools as we thought we might need. The day before us had an almost stimulating air of invitation—through which only a faint undercurrent of the sinister ran. Our rough mountain road quickly became steep and winding, so that before long our feet ached considerably.

After about two miles we left the road—crossing a stone wall on our right near a great elm and striking off diagonally toward a steeper slope according to the chart and directions which Jackson had prepared for us. It was rough and briery travelling, but we knew that the cave could not be far off. In the end we came upon the aperture quite suddenly—a black, bush-grown crevice where the ground shot abruptly upward, and beside it, near a shallow rock pool, a small, still figure stood rigid—as if rivalling its own uncanny petrification.

It was a grey dog—or a dog's statue—and as our simultaneous gasp died away we scarcely knew what to think. Jackson had exaggerated nothing, and we could not believe that any sculptor's hand had succeeded in producing such perfection. Every hair of the animal's magnificent coat seemed distinct, and those on the back were bristled up as if some unknown thing had taken him unaware. Ben, at last half-kindly touching the delicate stony fur, gave vent to an exclamation.

"Good God, Jack, but this can't be any statue! Look at it—all the little details, and the way the hair lies! None of Wheeler's technique here! This is a real dog—though heaven only knows how he ever got in this state. Just like stone—feel for yourself. Do you suppose there's any strange gas that sometimes comes out of the cave and does this to animal life? We ought to have looked more into the local legends. And if this is a real dog—or was a real dog—then that man inside must be the real thing too."

It was with a good deal of genuine solemnity—almost dread—that we finally crawled on hands and knees through the cave-mouth, Ben leading. The narrowness looked hardly three feet, after which the grotto expanded in every direction to form a damp, twilight chamber floored with rubble and detritus. For a time we could make out very little, but as we rose to our feet and strained our eyes we began slowly to descry a recumbent figure amidst the greater darkness ahead. Ben fumbled with his flashlight, but hesitated for a moment before turning it on the prostrate figure. We had little doubt that the stony thing was what had once been a man, and something in the thought unnerved us both.

When Ben at last sent forth the electric beam we saw that the object lay on its side, back toward us. It was clearly of the same material as the dog outside, but was dressed in the mouldering and unpetrified remains of rough sport clothing. Braced as we were for a shock, we approached quite calmly to examine the thing; Ben going around to the other side to glimpse the averted face. Neither could possibly have been prepared for what Ben saw when he flashed the light on those stony features. His cry was wholly excusable, and I could not help echoing it as I leaped to his side and shared the sight. Yet it was nothing hideous or intrinsically terrifying. It was merely a matter of recognition, for beyond the least shadow of a doubt this chilly rock figure with its half-frightened, half-bitter expression had at one time been our old acquaintance, Arthur Wheeler.

Some instinct sent us staggering and crawling out of the cave, and down the tangled slope to a point whence we could not see the ominous stone dog. We hardly knew what to think, for our brains were churning with conjectures and apprehensions. Ben, who had known Wheeler well, was especially upset; and seemed to be piecing together some threads I had overlooked.

Again and again as we paused on the green slope he repeated "Poor Arthur, poor Arthur!" but not till he muttered the name "Mad Dan" did I recall the trouble into which, according to old Sam Poole, Wheeler had run just before his disappearance. Mad Dan, Ben implied, would doubtless be glad to see what had happened. For a moment it flashed over both of us that the jealous host might have been responsible for the sculptor's presence in this evil cave, but the thought went as quickly as it came.

The thing that puzzled us most was to account for the phenomenon itself. What gaseous emanation or mineral vapour could have wrought this change in so relatively short a time was utterly beyond us. Normal petrification, we know, is a slow chemical replacement process requiring vast ages for completion; yet here were two stone images which had been living things—or at least Wheeler had—only a few weeks before. Conjecture was useless. Clearly, nothing remained but to notify the authorities and let them guess what they might; and yet at the back of Ben's head that no-tion about Mad Dan still persisted. Anyhow, we clawed our way back to the road, but Ben did not turn toward the vil-lage, but looked along upward toward where old Sam had said Dan's cabin lay. It was the second house from the vil-lage, the ancient loafer had wheezed, and lay on the left far back from the road in a thick copse of scrub oaks. Before I knew it Ben was dragging me up the sandy highway past a dingy farmstead and into a region of increasing wildness.

It did not occur to me to protest, but I felt a certain sense of mounting menace as the familiar marks of agri-culture and civilisation grew fewer and fewer. At last the beginning of a narrow, neglected path opened up on our left, while the peaked roof of a squalid, unpainted build-ing shewed itself beyond a sickly growth of half-dead trees. This, I knew, must be Mad Dan's cabin; and I wondered that Wheeler had ever chosen so unprepossessing a place for his headquarters. I dreaded to walk up that weedy, un-inviting path, but could not lag behind when Ben strode determinedly along and began a vigorous rapping at the rickety, musty-smelling door.

There was no response to the knock, and something in its echoes sent a series of shivers through one. Ben, how-ever, was quite unperturbed; and at once began to circle the house in quest of unlocked windows. The third that he tried—in the rear of the dismal cabin—proved capable of opening, and after a boost and a vigorous spring he was safely inside and helping me after him.

The room in which we landed was full of limestone and granite blocks, chiselling tools and clay models, and we realised at once that it was Wheeler's erstwhile studio. So far we had not met with any sign of life, but over everything hovered a damnably ominous dusty odour. On our left was

104

an open door evidently leading to a kitchen on the chimney side of the house, and through this Ben started, intent on finding anything he could concerning his friend's last habitat. He was considerably ahead of me when he crossed the threshold, so that I could not see at first what brought him up short and wrung a low cry of horror from his lips.

In another moment, though, I did see—and repeated his cry as instinctively as I had done in the cave. For here in this cabin—far from any subterranean depths which could breed strange gases and work strange mutations—were two stony figures which I knew at once were no products of Arthur Wheeler's chisel. In a rude armchair before the fireplace, bound in position by the lash of a long rawhide whip, was the form of a man—unkempt, elderly, and with a look of fathomless horror on its evil, petrified face.

On the floor beside it lay a woman's figure; graceful, and with a face betokening considerable youth and beauty. Its expression seemed to be one of sardonic satisfaction, and near its outflung right hand was a large tin pail, somewhat stained on the inside, as with a darkish sediment.

We made no move to approach those inexplicably petrified bodies, nor did we exchange any but the simplest conjectures. That this stony couple had been Mad Dan and his wife we could not well doubt, but how to account for their present condition was another matter. As we looked horrifiedly around we saw the suddenness with which the final development must have come—for everything about us seemed, despite a heavy coating of dust, to have been left in the midst of commonplace household activities.

The only exception to this rule of casualness was on the kitchen table; in whose cleared centre, as if to attract attention, lay a thin, battered blank-book weighted down by a sizeable tin funnel. Crossing to read the thing, Ben saw that it was a kind of diary or set of dated entries, written in a somewhat cramped and none too practiced hand. The very first words riveted my attention, and before ten seconds had elapsed he was breathlessly devouring the halting text—I avidly following as I peered over his shoulder. As we read on—moving as we did so into the less loathsome atmosphere of the adjoining room—many obscure things became terribly clear to us, and we trembled with a mixture of complex emotions.

This is what we read—and what the coroner read later on. The public has seen a highly twisted and sensationalised version in the cheap newspapers, but not even that has more than a fraction of the genuine terror which the simple original held for us as we puzzled it out alone in that musty cabin among the wild hills, with two monstrous stone abnormalities lurking in the death-like silence of the next room. When we had finished Ben pocketed the book with a gesture half of repulsion, and his first words were "Let's get out of here."

Silently and nervously we stumbled to the front of the house, unlocked the door, and began the long tramp back to the village. There were many statements to make and questions to answer in the days that followed, and I do not think that either Ben or I can ever shake off the effects of the whole harrowing experience. Neither can some of the local authorities and city reporters who flocked around—even though they burned a certain book and many papers found in attic boxes, and destroyed considerable apparatus in the deepest part of that sinister hillside cave. But here is the text itself:

"Nov. 5—My name is Daniel Morris. Around here they call me 'Mad Dan' because I believe in powers that nobody else believes in nowadays. When I go up on Thunder

Hill to keep the Feast of the Foxes they think I am crazy—all except the back country folks that are afraid of me. They try to stop me from sacrificing the Black Goat[3] at Hallow Eve, and always prevent my doing the Great Rite that would open the gate. They ought to know better, for they know I am a Van Kauran on my mother's side, and anybody this side of the Hudson can tell what the Van Kaurans have handed down. We come from Nicholas Van Kauran, the wizard, who was hanged in Wijtgaart in 1587,[4] and everybody knows he had made the bargain with the Black Man.

"The soldiers never got his *Book of Eibon*[5] when they burned his house, and his grandson, William Van Kauran, brought it over when he came to Rensselaerwyck and later crossed the river to Esopus.[6] Ask anybody in Kingston or Hurley about what the William Van Kauran line could do to people that got in their way. Also, ask them if my Uncle Hendrik didn't manage to keep hold of the *Book of Eibon* when they ran him out of town and he went up the river to this place with his family.

"I am writing this—and am going to keep writing this—because I want people to know the truth after I am gone. Also, I am afraid I shall really go mad if I don't set things down in plain black and white. Everything is going against me, and if it keeps up I shall have to use the secrets in the *Book* and call in certain Powers. Three months ago that sculptor Arthur Wheeler came to Mountain Top, and they sent him up to me because I am the only man in the place who knows anything except farming, hunting, and fleecing summer boarders. The fellow seemed to be interested in what I had to say, and made a deal to stop here for $13.00 a week with meals. I gave him the back room beside the kitchen for his lumps of stone and his chiselling, and arranged with Nate Williams to tend to his rock blasting and haul his big pieces with a drag and yoke of oxen.

"That was three months ago. Now I know why that cursed son of hell took so quick to the place. It wasn't my talk at all, but the looks of my wife Rose, that is Osborne Chandler's oldest girl. She is sixteen years younger than I am, and is always casting sheep's eyes at the fellows in town. But we always managed to get along fine enough till this dirty rat shewed up, even if she did balk at helping me with the Rites on Roodmas and Hallowmass. I can see now that Wheeler is working on her feelings and getting her so fond of him that she hardly looks at me, and I suppose he'll try to elope with her sooner or later.

"But he works slow like all sly, polished dogs, and I've got plenty of time to think up what to do about it. They don't either of them know I suspect anything, but before long they'll both realise it doesn't pay to break up a Van Kauran's home. I promise them plenty of novelty in what I'll do.

"Nov. 25—Thanksgiving Day! That's a pretty good joke! But at that I'll have something to be thankful for when I finish what I've started. No question but that Wheeler is trying to steal my wife. For the time being, though, I'll let him keep on being a star boarder. Got the *Book of Eibon* down from Uncle Hendrik's old trunk in the attic last week, and am looking up something good which won't require sacrifices that I can't make around here. I want something that'll finish these two sneaking traitors, and at the same time get me into no trouble. If it has a twist of drama in it, so much the better. I've thought of calling in the emanation of Yoth,[7] but that needs a child's blood and I must be careful about the neighbours. The Green Decay looks promising, but that would be a bit unpleasant for me as well as for them. I don't like certain sights and smells.

"Dec. 10—*Eureka!* I've got the very thing at last! Revenge is sweet—and this is the perfect climax! Wheeler, the sculptor—this is too good! Yes, indeed, that damned sneak is going to produce a statue that will sell quicker than any of the things he's been carving these past weeks! A realist, eh? Well—the new statuary won't lack any realism! I found the formula in a manuscript insert opposite page 679 of the *Book*. From the handwriting I judge it was put there by my great-grandfather Bareut Picterse Van Kauran—the one who disappeared from New Paltz in 1839. *Iä! Shub-Niggurath!* The Goat with a Thousand Young!

"To be plain, I've found a way to turn those wretched rats into stone statues. It's absurdly simple, and really depends more on plain chemistry than on the Outer Powers. If I can get hold of the right stuff I can brew a drink that'll pass for home-made wine, and one swig ought to finish any ordinary being short of an elephant. What it amounts to is a kind of petrification infinitely speeded up. Shoots the whole system full of calcium and barium salts and replaces living cells with mineral matter so fast that nothing can stop it. It must have been one of those things great-grandfather got at the Great Sabbat on Sugar-Loaf in the Catskills.[8] Queer things used to go on there. Seems to me I heard of a man in New Paltz—Squire Hasbrouck—turned to stone or something like that in 1834. He was an enemy of the Van Kaurans. First thing I must do is order the five chemicals I need from Albany and Montreal. Plenty of time later to experiment. When everything is over I'll round up all the statues and sell them as Wheeler's work to pay for his overdue board bill! He always was a realist and an egoist—wouldn't it be natural for him to make a self-portrait in stone, and to use my wife for another model—as indeed he's really been doing for the past fortnight? Trust the dull public not to ask *what quarry* the queer stone came from!

"Dec. 25—Christmas. Peace on earth, and so forth! These two swine are goggling at each other as if I didn't exist. They must think I'm deaf, dumb, and blind! Well, the barium sulphate and calcium chloride came from Albany last Thursday, and the acids, catalytics, and instruments are due from Montreal any day now. The mills of the gods—and all that![9] I'll do the work in Allen's Cave near the lower wood lot, and at the same time will be openly making some wine in the cellar here. There ought to be some excuse for offering a new drink—though it won't take much planning to fool those moonstruck nincompoops. The trouble will be to make Rose take wine, for she pretends not to like it. Any experiments that I make on animals will be down at the cave, and nobody ever thinks of going there in winter. I'll do some wood-cutting to account for my time away. A small load or two brought in will keep him off the track.

"Jan. 20—It's harder work than I thought. A lot depends on the exact proportions. The stuff came from Montreal, but I had to send again for some better scales and an acetylene lamp. They're getting curious down at the village. Wish the express office weren't in Steenwyck's store. Am trying various mixtures on the sparrows that drink and bathe in the pool in front of the cave—when it's melted. Sometimes it kills them, but sometimes they fly away. Clearly, I've missed some important reaction. I suppose Rose and that upstart are making the most of my absence—but I can afford to let them. There can be no doubt of my success in the end.

"Feb. 11—Have got it at last! Put a fresh lot in the little pool—which is well melted today—and the first bird that drank toppled over as if he were shot. I picked him up a second later, and he was a perfect piece of stone, down to the smallest claws and feather. Not a muscle changed since he was poised for drinking, so he must have died the instant any of the stuff got to his stomach. I didn't expect the petrification to come so soon. But a sparrow isn't a fair test of the way the thing would act with a large animal. I must get something bigger to try it on, for it must be the right strength when I give it to those swine. I guess Rose's dog Rex will do. I'll take him along the next time and say a timber wolf got him. She thinks a lot of him, and I shan't be sorry to give her something to sniffle over before the big reckoning. I must be careful where I keep this book. Rose sometimes pries around in the queerest places.

"Feb. 15—Getting warm! Tried it on Rex and it worked like a charm with only double the strength. I fixed the rock pool and got him to drink. He seemed to know something queer had hit him, for he bristled and growled, but he was a piece of stone before he could turn his head. The solution ought to have been stronger, and for a human being ought to be very much stronger. I think I'm getting the hang of it now, and am about ready for that cur Wheeler. The stuff seems to be tasteless, but to make sure I'll flavour it with the new wine I'm making up at the house. Wish I were surer about the tastelessness, so I could give it to Rose in water without trying to urge wine on her. I'll get the two separately––Wheeler out here and Rose at home. Have just fixed a strong solution and cleared away all strange objects in front of the cave. Rose whimpered like a puppy when I told her a wolf had got Rex, and Wheeler gurgled a lot of sympathy.

"March 1—*Iä R'lyeh!* Praise the Lord Tsathoggua![10] I've got the son of hell at last! Told him I'd found a new ledge of friable limestone down this way, and he trotted af-ter me like the yellow cur he is! I had the wine-flavoured stuff in a bottle on my hip, and he was glad of a swig when we got here. Gulped it down without a wink—and dropped in his tracks before you could count three. But he knows I've had my vengeance, for I made a face at him that he couldn't miss. I saw the look of understanding come into his face as he keeled over. In two minutes he was solid stone.

"I dragged him into the cave and put Rex's figure outside again. That bristling dog shape will help to scare people off. It's getting time for the spring hunters, and besides, there's a damned 'lunger'[11] named Jackson in a cabin over the hill who does a lot of snooping around in the snow. I wouldn't want my laboratory and storeroom to be found just yet! When I got home I told Rose that Wheeler had found a telegram at the village summoning him suddenly home. I don't know whether she believed me or not but it doesn't matter. For form's sake, I packed Wheeler's things and took them down the hill, telling her I was going to ship them after him. I put them in the dry well at the abandoned Rapelye place. Now for Rose!

"March 3—Can't get Rose to drink any wine. I hope that stuff is tasteless enough to go unnoticed in water. I tried it in tea and coffee, but it forms a precipitate and can't be used that way. If I use it in water I'll have to cut down the dose and trust to a more gradual action. Mr. and Mrs. Hoog[12] dropped in this noon, and I had hard work keeping the conversation away from Wheeler's departure. It mustn't get around that we say he was called back to New York when everybody at the village knows no telegram came, and that he didn't leave on the bus. Rose is acting damned queer about the whole thing. I'll have to pick a quarrel with her and keep her locked in the attic. The best way is to try to make her drink that doctored wine—and if she does give in, so much better.

"March 7—Have started in on Rose. She wouldn't drink the wine so I took a whip to her and drove her up in the attic. She'll never come down alive. I pass her a platter of salty bread and salt meat, and a pail of slightly doctored water, twice a day. The salt food ought to make her drink a lot, and it can't be long before the action sets in. I don't like the way she shouts about Wheeler when I'm at the door. The rest of the time she is absolutely silent.

"March 9—It's damned peculiar how slow that stuff is in getting hold of Rose. I'll have to make it stronger—probably she'll never taste it with all the salt I've been feeding her. Well, if it doesn't get her there are plenty of other ways to fall back on. But I would like to carry this neat statue plan through! Went to the cave this morning and all is well there. I sometimes hear Rose's steps on the ceiling overhead, and I think they're getting more and more dragging. The stuff is certainly working, but it's too slow. Not strong enough. From now on I'll rapidly stiffen up the dose.

"March 11—It is very queer. She is still alive and moving. Tuesday night I heard her piggling[13] with a window, so went up and gave her a rawhiding. She acts more sullen than frightened, and her eyes look swollen. But she could never drop to the ground from that height and there's nowhere she could climb down. I have had dreams at night, for her slow, dragging pacing on the floor above gets on my nerves. Sometimes I think she works at the lock on the door.

"March 15—Still alive, despite all the strengthening of the dose. There's something queer about it. She crawls now, and doesn't pace very often. But the sound of her crawling is horrible. She rattles the windows, too, and fumbles with the door. I shall have to finish her off with the rawhide if this keeps up. I'm getting very sleepy. Wonder if Rose has got on her guard somehow. But she must be drinking the stuff. This sleepiness is abnormal—I think the strain is telling on me. I'm sleepy. . . ."

(Here the cramped handwriting trails out in a vague scrawl, giving place to a note in a firmer, evidently feminine handwriting, indicative of great emotional tension.)

"March 16—4 a.m.—This is added by Rose C. Morris, about to die. Please notify my father, Osborne E. Chandler, Route 2, Mountain Top, N.Y. I have just read what the beast has written. I felt sure he had killed Arthur Wheeler, but did not know how till I read this terrible notebook. Now I know what I escaped. I noticed the water tasted queer, so took none of it after the first sip. I threw it all out of the window. That one sip has half paralysed me, but I can still get about. The thirst was terrible, but I ate as little as possible of the salty food and was able to get a little water by setting some old pans and dishes that were up here under places where the roof leaked.

"There were two great rains. I thought he was trying to poison me, though I didn't know what the poison was like. What he has written about himself and me is a lie. We were never happy together and I think I married him only under one of those spells that he was able to lay on people. I guess he hypnotised both my father and me, for he was always hated and feared and suspected of dark dealings with the devil. My father once called him The Devil's Kin, and he was right.

"No one will ever know what I went through as his wife. It was not simply common cruelty—though God knows he was cruel enough, and beat me often with a leather whip. It was more—more than anyone in this age can ever understand. He was a monstrous creature, and practiced all sorts of hellish ceremonies handed down by his mother's people. He tried to make me help in the rites—and I don't dare even hint what they were. I would not, so he beat me. It would be blasphemy to tell what he tried to make me do. I can say he was a murderer even then, for I know what he sacrificed one night on Thunder Hill. He was surely the Devil's Kin. I tried four times to run away, but he always caught and beat me. Also, he had a sort of hold over my mind, and even over my father's mind.

"About Arthur Wheeler I have nothing to be ashamed of. We did come to love each other, but only in an honourable way. He gave me the first kind treatment I had ever had since leaving my father's, and meant to help me get out of the clutches of that fiend. He had several talks with my father, and was going to help me get out west. After my divorce we would have been married.

"Ever since that brute locked me in the attic I have planned to get out and finish him. I always kept the poison overnight in case I could escape and find him asleep and give it to him somehow. At first he waked easily when I worked on the lock of the door and tested the conditions at the windows, but later he began to get more tired and sleep sounder. I could always tell by his snoring when he was asleep.

"Tonight he was so fast asleep I forced the lock without waking him. It was hard work getting downstairs with my partial paralysis, but I did. I found him here with the lamp burning—asleep at the table, where he had been writing in this book. In the corner was the long rawhide whip he had so often beaten me with. I used it to tie him to the chair so he could not move a muscle. I lashed his neck so that I could pour anything down his throat without his resisting.

"He waked up just as I was finishing and I guess he saw right off that he was done for. He shouted frightful things and tried to chant mystical formulas, but I choked him off with a dish towel from the sink. Then I saw this book he had been writing in, and stopped to read it. The shock was terrible, and I almost fainted four or five times. My mind was not ready for such things. After that I talked to that fiend for two or three hours steady. I told him everything I had wanted to tell him through all the years I had been his slave, and a lot of other things that had to do with what I had read in this awful book.

"He looked almost purple when I was through, and I think he was half delirious. Then I got a funnel from the cupboard and jammed it into his mouth after taking out the gag. He knew what I was going to do, but was helpless. I had brought down the pail of poisoned water, and without a qualm, I poured a good half of it into the funnel.

"It must have been a very strong dose, for almost at once I saw that brute begin to stiffen and turn a dull stony grey. In ten minutes I knew he was solid stone. I could not bear to touch him, but the tin funnel *clinked* horribly when I pulled it out of his mouth. I wish I could have given that Kin of the Devil a more painful, lingering death, but surely this was the most appropriate he could have had.

"There is not much more to say. I am half-paralysed, and with Arthur murdered I have nothing to live for. I shall make things complete by drinking the rest of the poison after placing this book where it will be found. In a quarter of an hour I shall be a stone statue. My only wish is to be buried beside the statue that was Arthur—when it is found in that cave where the fiend left it. Poor trusting Rex ought to lie at our feet. I do not care what becomes of the stone devil tied in the chair. . . ."

Winged Death

With Hazel Heald

he Orange Hotel stands in High Street near the railway station in Bloemfontein, South Africa.[1] On Sunday, January 24, 1932, four men sat shivering from terror in a room on its third floor. One was George C. Titteridge, proprietor of the hotel; another was police constable Ian De Witt of the Central Station; a third was Johannes Bogaert, the local coroner; the fourth, and apparently the least disorganised of the group, was Dr. Cornelius Van Keulen, the coroner's physician.

On the floor, uncomfortably evident amidst the stifling summer heat, was the body of a dead man—but this was not what the four were afraid of. Their glances wandered from the table, on which lay a curious assortment of things, to the ceiling overhead, across whose smooth whiteness a series of huge, faltering alphabetical characters had somehow been scrawled in ink; and every now and then Dr. Van Keulen would glance half-furtively at a worn leather blank-book which he held in his left hand. The horror of the four seemed about equally divided among the blank-book, the scrawled words on the ceiling, and a dead fly of peculiar aspect which floated in a bottle of ammonia on the table. Also on the table were an open inkwell, a pen and writing-pad, a physician's medical case, a bottle of hydrochloric acid, and a tumbler about a quarter full of black oxide of manganese.

The worn leather book was the journal of the dead man on the floor, and had at once made it clear that the name "Frederick N. Mason, Mining Properties, Toronto, Canada", signed in the hotel register, was a false one. There were other things—terrible things—which it likewise made clear; and still other things of far greater terror at which it hinted hideously without making them clear or even fully believable. It was the half-belief of the four men, fostered by lives spent close to the black, settled secrets of brooding Africa, which made them shiver so violently in spite of the searing January heat.

The blank-book was not a large one, and the entries were in a fine handwriting, which, however, grew careless and nervous-looking toward the last. It consisted of a series of jottings at first rather irregularly spaced, but finally becoming daily. To call it a diary would not be quite correct, for it chronicled only one set of its writer's activities. Dr. Van Keulen recognised the name of the dead man the moment he opened the cover, for it was that of an eminent member of his own profession who had been largely connected with African matters. In another moment he was horrified to find this name linked with a dastardly crime, officially unsolved, which had filled the newspapers some four months before. And the farther he read, the deeper grew his horror, awe, and sense of loathing and panic.

Here, in essence, is the text which the doctor read aloud in that sinister and increasingly noisome room while the three men around him breathed hard, fidgeted in their chairs, and darted frightened glances at the ceiling, the table, the thing on the floor, and one another:

JOURNAL OF
THOMAS SLAUENWITE, M.D.

Touching punishment of Henry Sargent Moore, Ph.D., of Brooklyn, New York, Professor of Invertebrate Biology in Columbia University, New York, N.Y. Prepared to be read after my death, for the satisfaction of making public the accomplishment of my revenge, which may otherwise never be imputed to me even if it succeeds.

January 5, 1929—I have now fully resolved to kill Dr. Henry Moore, and a recent incident has shewn me how I shall do it. From now on, I shall follow a consistent line of action; hence the beginning of this journal.

It is hardly necessary to repeat the circumstances which have driven me to this course, for the informed part of the public is familiar with all the salient facts. I was born in Trenton, New Jersey, on April 12, 1885, the son of Dr. Paul Slauenwite, formerly of Pretoria, Transvaal, South Africa. Studying medicine as part of my family tradition, I was led by my father (who died in 1916, while I was serving in France in a South African regiment)[2] to specialise in African fevers; and after my graduation from Columbia spent much time in researches which took me from Durban, in Natal, up to the equator itself.

In Mombasa[3] I worked out my new theory of the transmission and development of remittent fever, aided only slightly by the papers of the late government physician, Sir Norman Sloane, which I found in the house I occupied. When I published my results I became at a single stroke a famous authority. I was told of the probability of an almost supreme position in the South African health service, and even a probable knighthood, in the event of my becoming a naturalised citizen, and accordingly I took the necessary steps.

Then occurred the incident for which I am about to kill Henry Moore. This man, my classmate and friend of years in America and Africa, chose deliberately to undermine my claim to my own theory; alleging that Sir Norman Sloane had anticipated me in every essential detail, and implying that I had probably found more of his papers than I had stated in my account of the matter. To buttress this absurd accusation he produced certain personal letters from Sir Norman which indeed shewed that the older man had been over my ground, and that he would have published his results very soon but for his sudden death. This much I could only admit with regret. What I could not excuse was the jealous suspicion that I had stolen the theory from Sir Norman's papers. The British government, sensibly enough, ignored these aspersions, but withheld the half-promised appointment and knighthood on the ground that my theory, while original with me, was not in fact new.

I could soon see that my career in Africa was perceptibly checked; though I had placed all my hopes on such a career, even to the point of resigning American citizenship. A distinct coolness toward me had arisen among the Government set in Mombasa, especially among those who had known Sir Norman. It was then that I resolved to be even with Moore sooner or later, though I did not know how. He had been jealous of my early celebrity, and had taken advantage of his old correspondence with Sir Norman to ruin me. This from the friend whom I had myself led to take an interest in Africa—whom I had coached and inspired till he achieved his present moderate fame as an authority on African entomology. Even now, though, I will not deny that his attainments are profound. I made him, and in return he has ruined me. Now—some day—I shall destroy him.

When I saw myself losing ground in Mombasa, I applied for my present situation in the interior—at M'gonga,[4] only fifty miles from the Uganda line. It is a cotton and ivory trading-post, with only eight white men besides myself. A beastly hole, almost on the equator, and full of every sort of fever known to mankind. Poisonous snakes and insects everywhere, and niggers with diseases nobody ever heard of outside medical college. But my work is not hard, and I have always had plenty of time to plan things to do to Henry Moore. It amuses me to give his *Diptera of Central and Southern Africa*[5] a prominent place on my shelf. I suppose it actually is a standard manual—they use it at Columbia, Harvard, and the U. of Wis.—but my own suggestions are really responsible for half its strong points.

Last week I encountered the thing which decided me how to kill Moore. A party from Uganda brought in a black with a queer illness which I can't yet diagnose. He was lethargic, with a very low temperature, and shuffled in a peculiar way. Most of the others were afraid of him and said he was under some kind of witch-doctor spell; but Gobo, the interpreter, said he had been bitten by an insect. What it was, I can't imagine—for there is only a slight puncture on the arm. It is bright red, though, with a purple ring around it. Spectral-looking—I don't wonder the boys lay it to black magic. They seem to have seen cases like it before, and say there's really nothing to do about it.

Old N'Kuru, one of the Galla[6] boys at the post, says it must be the bite of a devil-fly, which makes its victim waste away gradually and die, and then takes hold of his soul and personality if it is still alive itself—flying around with all his likes, dislikes, and consciousness. A queer legend—and I don't know of any local insect deadly enough to account for it. I gave this sick black—his name is Mevana—a good shot of quinine and took a sample of his blood for testing, but haven't made much progress. There is certainly a strange germ present, but I can't even remotely identify it. The nearest thing to it is the bacillus one finds in oxen, horses, and dogs that the tsetse-fly has bitten; but tsetse-flies don't infect human beings, and this is too far north for them anyway.

However—the important thing is that I've decided how to kill Moore. If this interior region has insects as poisonous as the natives say, I'll see that he gets a shipment of them from a source he won't suspect, and with plenty of assurances that they are harmless. Trust him to throw overboard all caution when it comes to studying an unknown species—and then we'll see how Nature takes its course! It ought not to be hard to find an insect that scares the blacks so much. First to see how poor Mevana turns out—and then to find my envoy of death.

Jan. 7—Mevana is no better, though I have injected all the antitoxins I know of. He has fits of trembling, in which he rants affrightedly about the way his soul will pass when he dies into the insect that bit him, but between them he remains in a kind of half-stupor. Heart action still strong, so I may pull him through. I shall try to, for he can probably guide me better than anyone else to the region where he was bitten.

Meanwhile I'll write to Dr. Lincoln, my predecessor here, for Allen, the head factor, says he had a profound knowledge of the local sicknesses. He ought to know about the death-fly if any white man does. He's at Nairobi now, and a black runner ought to get me a reply in a week—using the railway for half the trip.

Jan. 10—Patient unchanged, but I have found what I want! It was in an old volume of the local health records, which I've been going over diligently while waiting to hear from Lincoln. Thirty years ago there was an epidemic that killed off thousands of natives in Uganda, and it was definitely traced to a rare fly called *Glossina palpalis*—a sort of cousin of the *Glossina marsitans,* or tsetse.[7] It lives in the bushes on the shores of lakes and rivers, and feeds on the blood of crocodiles, antelopes, and large mammals. When these food animals have the germ of trypanosomiasis, or sleeping-sickness, it picks it up and develops acute infectivity after an incubation period of thirty-one days. Then for seventy-five days it is sure death to anyone or anything it bites.

Without doubt, this must be the "devil-fly" the niggers talk about. Now I know what I'm heading for. Hope Mevana pulls through. Ought to hear from Lincoln in four or five days—he has a great reputation for success in things like this. My worst problem will be to get the flies to Moore without his recognising them. With his cursed plodding scholarship it would be just like him to know all about them since they're actually on record.

Jan. 15—Just heard from Lincoln, who confirms all that the records say about *Glossina palpalis.* He has a remedy for sleeping-sickness which has succeeded in a great number of cases when not given too late. Intermuscular injections of tryparsamide.[8] Since Mevana was bitten about two months ago, I don't know how it will work—but Lincoln says that cases have been known to drag on eighteen months, so possibly I'm not too late. Lincoln sent over some of his stuff, so I've just given Mevana a stiff shot. In a stupor now. They've brought his principal wife from the village, but he doesn't even recognise her. If he recovers, he can certainly shew me where the flies are. He's a great crocodile hunter, according to report, and knows all Uganda like a book. I'll give him another shot tomorrow.

Jan. 16—Mevana seems a little brighter today, but his heart action is slowing up a bit. I'll keep up the injections, but not overdo them.

Jan. 17—Recovery really pronounced today. Mevana opened his eyes and shewed signs of actual consciousness, though dazed, after the injection. Hope Moore doesn't know about tryparsamide. There's a good chance he won't, since he never leaned much toward medicine. Mevana's tongue seemed paralysed, but I fancy that will pass off if I can only wake him up. Wouldn't mind a good sleep myself, but not of this kind!

Jan. 25—Mevana nearly cured! In another week I can let him take me into the jungle. He was frightened when he first came to—about having the fly take his personality after he died—but brightened up finally when I told him he was going to get well. His wife, Ugowe, takes good care of him now, and I can rest a bit. Then for the envoys of death!

Feb. 3—Mevana is well now, and I have talked with him about a hunt for flies. He dreads to go near the place where they got him, but I am playing on his gratitude. Besides, he has an idea that I can ward off disease as well as cure it. His pluck would shame a white man—there's no doubt that he'll go. I can get off by telling the head factor the trip is in the interest of local health work.

March 12—In Uganda at last! Have five boys besides Mevana, but they are all Gallas. The local blacks couldn't be hired to come near the region after the talk of what had happened to Mevana. This jungle is a pestilential place—

124

steaming with miasmal vapours. All the lakes look stagnant. In one spot we came upon a trace of Cyclopean ruins which made even the Gallas run past in a wide circle. They say these megaliths are older than man, and that they used to be a haunt or outpost of "The Fishers from Outside"[9]—whatever that means—and of the evil gods Tsadogwa and Clulu.[10] To this day they are said to have a malign influence, and to be connected somehow with the devil-flies.

March 15—Struck Lake Mlolo[11] this morning—where Mevana was bitten. A hellish, green-scummed affair, full of crocodiles. Mevana has fixed up a fly-trap of fine wire netting baited with crocodile meat. It has a small entrance, and once the quarry get in, they don't know enough to get out. As stupid as they are deadly, and ravenous for fresh meat or a bowl of blood. Hope we can get a good supply. I've decided that I must experiment with them—finding a way to change their appearance so that Moore won't recognise them. Possibly I can cross them with some other species, producing a strange hybrid whose infection-carrying capacity will be undiminished. We'll see. I must wait, but am in no hurry now. When I get ready I'll have Mevana get me some infected meat to feed my envoys of death—and then for the post-office. Ought to be no trouble getting infection, for this country is a veritable pest-hole.

March 16—Good luck. Two cages full. Five vigorous specimens with wings glistening like diamonds. Mevana is emptying them into a large can with a tightly meshed top, and I think we caught them in the nick of time. We can get them to M'gonga without trouble. Taking plenty of crocodile meat for their food. Undoubtedly all or most of it is infected.

April 20—Back at M'gonga and busy in the laboratory. Have sent to Dr. Joost in Pretoria for some tsetse-flies for hybridisation experiments. Such a crossing, if it will work at all, ought to produce something pretty hard to recognise yet at the same time just as deadly as the *palpalis*. If this doesn't work, I shall try certain other diptera from the interior, and I have sent to Dr. Vandervelde at Nyangwe[12] for some of the Congo types. I shan't have to send Mevana for more tainted meat after all; for I find I can keep cultures of the germ *Trypanosoma gambiense,*[13] taken from the meat we got last month, almost indefinitely in tubes. When the time comes, I'll taint some fresh meat and feed my winged envoys a good dose—then *bon voyage* to them!

June 18—My tsetse-flies from Joost came today. Cages for breeding were all ready long ago, and I am now making selections. Intend to use ultra-violet rays to speed up the life-cycle. Fortunately I have the needed apparatus in my regular equipment. Naturally I tell no one what I'm doing. The ignorance of the few men here makes it easy for me to conceal my aims and pretend to be merely studying existing species for medical reasons.

June 29—The crossing is fertile! Good deposits of eggs last Wednesday, and now I have some excellent larvae. If the mature insects look as strange as these do, I need do nothing more. Am preparing separate numbered cages for the different specimens.

July 7—New hybrids are out! Disguise is excellent as to shape, but sheen of wings still suggests *palpalis*. Thorax has faint suggestions of the stripes of the tsetse. Slight variation in individuals. Am feeding them all on tainted crocodile meat, and after infectivity develops will try them on some of the blacks—apparently, of course, by accident. There are so many mildly venomous flies around here that it can easily be done without exciting suspicion. I shall loose an insect in my tightly screened dining-room when

Batta, my house-boy, brings in breakfast—keeping well on guard myself. When it has done its work I'll capture or swat it—an easy thing because of its stupidity—or asphyxiate it by filling the room with chlorine gas. If it doesn't work the first time, I'll try again until it does. Of course, I'll have the tryparsamide handy in case I get bitten myself—but I shall be careful to avoid biting, for no antidote is really certain.

Aug. 10—Infectivity mature, and managed to get Batta stung in fine shape. Caught the fly on him, returning it to its cage. Eased up the pain with iodine, and the poor devil is quite grateful for the service. Shall try a variant specimen on Gamba, the factor's messenger, tomorrow. That will be all the tests I shall dare to make here, but if I need more I shall take some specimens to Ukala[14] and get additional data.

Aug. 11—Failed to get Gamba, but recaptured the fly alive. Batta still seems as well as usual, and has no pain in the back where he was stung. Shall wait before trying to get Gamba again.

Aug. 14—Shipment of insects from Vandervelde at last. Fully seven distinct species, some more or less poisonous. Am keeping them well fed in case the tsetse crossing doesn't work. Some of these fellows look very unlike the *palpalis*, but the trouble is that they may not make a fertile cross with it.

Aug. 17—Got Gamba this afternoon, but had to kill the fly on him. It nipped him in the left shoulder. I dressed the bite, and Gamba is as grateful as Batta was. No change in Batta.

Aug. 20—Gamba unchanged so far—Batta too. Am experimenting with a new form of disguise to supplement the hybridisation—some sort of dye to change the telltale glitter of the *palpalis'* wings. A bluish tint would be best—

something I could spray on a whole batch of insects. Shall begin by investigating things like Prussian and Turnbull's blue[15]—iron and cyanogen salts.

Aug. 25—Batta complained of a pain in his back to-day—things may be developing.

Sept. 3—Have made fair progress in my experiments. Batta shews signs of lethargy, and says his back aches all the time. Gamba beginning to feel uneasy in his bitten shoulder.

Sept. 24—Batta worse and worse, and beginning to get frightened about his bite. Thinks it must be a devil-fly, and entreated me to kill it—for he saw me cage it—until I pretended to him that it had died long ago. Said he didn't want his soul to pass into it upon his death. I give him shots of plain water with a hypodermic to keep his morale up. Evidently the fly retains all the properties of the *palpalis*. Gamba down, too, and repeating all of Batta's symptoms. I may decide to give him a chance with tryparsamide, for the effect of the fly is proved well enough. I shall let Batta go on, however, for I want a rough idea of how long it takes to finish a case.

Dye experiments coming along finely. An isomeric form of ferrous ferrocyanide, with some admixture of potassium salts, can be dissolved in alcohol and sprayed on the insects with splendid effect. It stains the wings blue without affecting the dark thorax much, and doesn't wear off when I sprinkle the specimens with water. With this disguise, I think I can use the present tsetse hybrids and avoid bothering with any more experiments. Sharp as he is, Moore couldn't recognise a blue-winged fly with a half-tsetse thorax. Of course, I keep all this dye business strictly under cover. Nothing must ever connect me with the blue flies later on.

Oct. 9—Batta is lethargic and has taken to his bed. Have been giving Gamba tryparsamide for two weeks, and fancy he'll recover.

Oct. 25—Batta very low, but Gamba nearly well.

Nov. 18—Batta died yesterday, and a curious thing happened which gave me a real shiver in view of the native legends and Batta's own fears. When I returned to the laboratory after the death I heard the most singular buzzing and thrashing in cage 12, which contained the fly that bit Batta. The creature seemed frantic, but stopped still when I appeared—lighting on the wire netting and looking at me in the oddest way. It reached its legs through the wires as if it were bewildered. When I came back from dining with Allen, the thing was dead. Evidently it had gone wild and beaten its life out on the sides of the cage.

It certainly is peculiar that this should happen just as Batta died. If any black had seen it, he'd have laid it at once to the absorption of the poor devil's soul. I shall start my blue-stained hybrids on their way before long now. The hybrid's rate of killing seems a little ahead of the pure *palpalis'* rate, if anything. Batta died three months and eight days after infection—but of course there is always a wide margin of uncertainty. I almost wish I had let Gamba's case run on.

Dec. 5—Busy planning how to get my envoys to Moore. I must have them appear to come from some disinterested entomologist who has read his *Diptera of Central and Southern Africa* and believes he would like to study this "new and unidentifiable species". There must also be ample assurances that the blue-winged fly is harmless, as proved by the natives' long experience. Moore will be off his guard, and one of the flies will surely get him sooner or later—though one can't tell just when.

I'll have to rely on the letters of New York friends—

they still speak of Moore from time to time—to keep me informed of early results, though I dare say the papers will announce his death. Above all, I must shew no interest in his case. I shall mail the flies while on a trip, but must not be recognised when I do it. The best plan will be to take a long vacation in the interior, grow a beard, mail the package at Ukala while passing as a visiting entomologist, and return here after shaving off the beard.

April 12, 1930—Back in M'gonga after my long trip. Everything has come off finely—with clockwork precision. Have sent the flies to Moore without leaving a trace. Got a Christmas vacation Dec. 15th, and set out at once with the proper stuff. Made a very good mailing container with room to include some germ-tainted crocodile meat as food for the envoys. By the end of February I had beard enough to shape into a close Vandyke.

Shewed up at Ukala March 9th and typed a letter to Moore on the trading-post machine. Signed it "Nevil Wayland-Hall"[16]—supposed to be an entomologist from London. Think I took just the right tone—interest of a brother-scientist, and all that. Was artistically casual in emphasising the "complete harmlessness" of the specimens. Nobody suspected anything. Shaved the beard as soon as I hit the bush, so that there wouldn't be any uneven tanning by the time I got back here. Dispensed with native bearers except for one small stretch of swamp—I can do wonders with one knapsack, and my sense of direction is good. Lucky I'm used to such travelling. Explained my protracted absence by pleading a touch of fever and some mistakes in direction when going through the bush.

But now comes the hardest part psychologically—waiting for news of Moore without shewing the strain. Of course, he may possibly escape a bite until the venom is played out—but with his recklessness the chances are one hundred to one against him. I have no regrets; after what he did to me, he deserves this and more.

June 30, 1930—Hurrah! The first step worked! Just heard casually from Dyson of Columbia that Moore had received some new blue-winged flies from Africa, and that he is badly puzzled over them! No word of any bite—but if I know Moore's slipshod ways as I think I do, there'll be one before long!

August 27, 1930—Letter from Morton[17] in Cambridge. He says Moore writes of feeling very run-down, and tells of an insect bite on the back of his neck—from a curious new specimen that he received about the middle of June. Have I succeeded? Apparently Moore doesn't connect the bite with his weakness. If this is the real stuff, then Moore was bitten well within the insect's period of infectivity.

Sept. 12, 1930—Victory! Another line from Dyson says that Moore is really in an alarming shape. He now traces his illness to the bite, which he received around noon on June 19, and is quite bewildered about the identity of the insect. Is trying to get in touch with the "Nevil Wayland-Hall" who sent him the shipment. Of the hundred-odd that I sent, about twenty-five seem to have reached him alive. Some escaped at the time of the bite, but several larvae have appeared from eggs laid since the time of mailing. He is, Dyson says, carefully incubating these larvae. When they mature I suppose he'll identify the tsetse-*palpalis* hybridisation—but that won't do him much good now. He'll wonder, though, why the blue wings aren't transmitted by heredity!

Nov. 8, 1930—Letters from half a dozen friends tell of Moore's serious illness. Dyson's came today. He says Moore is utterly at sea about the hybrids that came from the larvae and is beginning to think that the parents got their blue wings in some artificial way. Has to stay in bed most of the time now. No mention of using tryparsamide.

Feb. 13, 1931—Not so good! Moore is sinking, and seems to know no remedy, but I think he suspects me. Had a very chilly letter from Morton last month, which told nothing of Moore; and now Dyson writes—also rather constrainedly—that Moore is forming theories about the whole matter. He's been making a search for "Wayland-Hall" by telegraph—at London, Ukala, Nairobi, Mombasa, and other places—and of course finds nothing. I judge that he's told Dyson whom he suspects, but that Dyson doesn't believe it yet. Fear Morton does believe it.

I see that I'd better lay plans for getting out of here and effacing my identity for good. What an end to a career that started out so well! More of Moore's work—but this time he's paying for it in advance! Believe I'll go back to South Africa—and meanwhile will quietly deposit funds there to the credit of my new self—"Frederick Nasmyth Mason of Toronto, Canada, broker in mining properties". Will establish a new signature for identification. If I never have to take the step, I can easily re-transfer the funds to my present self.

Aug. 15, 1931—Half a year gone, and still suspense. Dyson and Morton—as well as several other friends—seem to have stopped writing me. Dr. James of San Francisco hears from Moore's friends now and then, and says Moore is in an almost continuous coma. He hasn't been able to walk since May. As long as he could talk he complained of being cold. Now he can't talk, though it is thought he still has glimmers of consciousness. His breathing is short and quick, and can be heard some distance away. No question

but that *Trypanosoma gambiense* is feeding on him—but
he holds out better than the niggers around here. Three
months and eight days finished Batta, and here Moore is
alive over a year after his biting. Heard rumours last month
of an intensive search around Ukala for "Wayland-Hall".
Don't think I need to worry yet, though, for there's absolutely nothing in existence to link me with this business.

Oct. 7, 1931—It's over at last! News in the *Mombasa
Gazette*. Moore died September 20 after a series of trembling fits and with a temperature vastly below normal. So
much for that! I said I'd get him, and I did! The paper had
a three-column report of his long illness and death, and of
the futile search for "Wayland-Hall". Obviously, Moore was
a bigger character in Africa than I had realised. The insect
that bit him has now been fully identified from the surviving specimens and developed larvae, and the wing-staining
is also detected. It is universally realised that the flies were
prepared and shipped with intent to kill. Moore, it appears,
communicated certain suspicions to Dyson, but the latter—and the police—are maintaining secrecy because of
absence of proof. All of Moore's enemies are being looked
up, and the Associated Press hints that "an investigation,
possibly involving an eminent physician now abroad, will
follow".

One thing at the very end of the report—undoubtedly, the cheap romancing of a yellow journalist—gives
me a curious shudder in view of the legends of the blacks
and the way the fly happened to go wild when Batta died.
It seems that an odd incident occurred on the night of
Moore's death; Dyson having been aroused by the buzzing of a blue-winged fly—which immediately flew out the
window—just before the nurse telephoned the death news
from Moore's home, miles away in Brooklyn.

But what concerns me most is the African end of the matter. People at Ukala remember the bearded stranger who typed the letter and sent the package, and the constabulary are combing the country for any blacks who may have carried him. I didn't use many, but if officers question the Ubandes who took me through N'Kini jungle belt[18] I'll have more to explain than I like. It looks as if the time has come for me to vanish; so tomorrow I believe I'll resign and prepare to start for parts unknown.

Nov. 9, 1931—Hard work getting my resignation acted on, but release came today. I didn't want to aggravate suspicion by decamping outright. Last week I heard from James about Moore's death—but nothing more than is in the papers. Those around him in New York seem rather reticent about details, though they all talk about a searching investigation. No word from any of my friends in the East. Moore must have spread some dangerous suspicions around before he lost consciousness—but there isn't an iota of proof he could have adduced.

Still, I am taking no chances. On Thursday I shall start for Mombasa, and when there will take a steamer down the coast to Durban. After that I shall drop from sight—but soon afterward the mining properties' broker Frederick Nasmyth Mason, from Toronto, will turn up in Johannesburg.

Let this be the end of my journal. If in the end I am not suspected, it will serve its original purpose after my death and reveal what would otherwise not be known. If, on the other hand, these suspicions do materialise and persist, it will confirm and clarify the vague charges, and fill in many important and puzzling gaps. Of course, if danger comes my way I shall have to destroy it.

Well, Moore is dead—as he amply deserves to be.

Now Dr. Thomas Slauenwite is dead, too. And when the body formerly belonging to Thomas Slauenwite is dead, the public may have this record.

II

Jan. 15, 1932—A new year—and a reluctant reopening of this journal. This time I am writing solely to relieve my mind, for it would be absurd to fancy that the case is not definitely closed. I am settled in the Vaal Hotel, Johannesburg, under my new name, and no one has so far challenged my identity. Have had some inconclusive business talks to keep up my part as a mine broker, and believe I may actually work myself into that business. Later I shall go to Toronto and plant a few evidences for my fictitious past.

But what is bothering me is an insect that invaded my room around noon today. Of course I have had all sorts of nightmares about blue flies of late, but those were only to be expected in view of my prevailing nervous strain. This thing, however, was a waking actuality, and I am utterly at a loss to account for it. It buzzed around my bookshelf for fully a quarter of an hour, and eluded every attempt to catch or kill it. The queerest thing was its colour and aspect—for it had blue wings and was in every way a duplicate of my hybrid envoys of death. How it could possibly be one of these, in fact, I certainly don't know. I disposed of all the hybrids—stained and unstained—that I didn't send to Moore, and can't recall any instance of escape.

Can this be wholly an hallucination? Or could any of the specimens that escaped in Brooklyn when Moore was bitten have found their way back to Africa? There was that absurd story of the blue fly that waked Dyson when Moore died—but after all, the survival and return of some of the things is not impossible. It is perfectly plausible that the blue should stick to their wings, too, for the pigment I devised was almost as good as tattooing for permanence. By elimination, that would seem to be the only rational explanation for this thing; though it is very curious that the fellow has come as far south as this. Possibly it's some hereditary homing instinct inherent in the tsetse strain. After all, that side of him belongs to South Africa.

I must be on my guard against a bite. Of course the original venom—if this is actually one of the flies that escaped from Moore—was worn out ages ago; but the fellow must have fed as he flew back from America, and he may well have come through Central Africa and picked up a fresh infectivity. Indeed, that's more probable than not; for the *palpalis* half of his heredity would naturally take him back to Uganda, and all the trypanosomiasis germs. I still have some of the tryparsamide left—I couldn't bear to destroy my medicine case, incriminating though it may be—but since reading up on the subject I am not so sure about the drug's action as I was. It gives one a fighting chance—certainly it saved Gamba—but there's always a large probability of failure.

It's devilish queer that this fly should have happened to come into my room—of all places in the wide expanse of Africa! Seems to strain coincidence to the breaking-point. I suppose that if it comes again, I shall certainly kill it. I'm surprised that it escaped me today, for ordinarily these fellows are extremely stupid and easy to catch. Can it be a pure illusion after all? Certainly the heat is getting me of late as it never did before—even up around Uganda.

Jan. 16—Am I going insane? The fly came again this noon, and acted so anomalously that I can't make head or tail of it. Only delusion on my part could account for what that buzzing pest seemed to do. It appeared from nowhere, and went straight to my bookshelf—circling again and again to front a copy of Moore's *Diptera of Central and Southern Africa.* Now and then it would light on top or back of the volume, and occasionally it would dart forward toward me and retreat before I could strike at it with a folded paper. Such cunning is unheard of among the notoriously stupid African diptera. For nearly half an hour I tried to get the cursed thing, but at last it darted out the window through a hole in the screen that I hadn't noticed. At times I fancied it deliberately mocked me by coming within reach of my weapon and then skilfully sidestepping as I struck out. I must keep a tight hold of my consciousness.

Jan. 17—Either I am mad or the world is in the grip of some sudden suspension of the laws of probability as we know them. That damnable fly came in from somewhere just before noon and commenced buzzing around the copy of Moore's *Diptera* on my shelf. Again I tried to catch it, and again yesterday's experience was repeated. Finally the pest made for the open inkwell on my table and dipped itself in—just the legs and thorax, keeping its wings clear. Then it sailed up to the ceiling and lit—beginning to crawl around in a curved patch and leaving a trail of ink. After a time it hopped a bit and made a single ink spot unconnected with the trail—then it dropped squarely in front of my face, and buzzed out of sight before I could get it.

Something about this whole business struck me as monstrously sinister and abnormal—more so than I could explain to myself. When I looked at the ink-trail on the ceiling from different angles, it seemed more and more familiar to me, and it dawned on me suddenly that it formed an absolutely perfect question-mark. What device could be more malignly appropriate? It is a wonder that I did not faint. So far the hotel attendants have not noticed it. Have not seen the fly this afternoon and evening, but am keeping my inkwell securely closed. I think my extermination of Moore must be preying on me, and giving me morbid hallucinations. Perhaps there is no fly at all.

Jan. 18—Into what strange hell of living nightmare am I plunged? What occurred today is something which could not normally happen—*and yet an hotel attendant has seen the marks on the ceiling and concedes their reality.* About eleven o'clock this morning, as I was writing on a manuscript, something darted down to the inkwell for a second and flashed aloft again before I could see what it was. Looking up, I saw that hellish fly on the ceiling as it had been before—crawling along and tracing another trail of curves and turns. There was nothing I could do, but I folded a newspaper in readiness to get the creature if it should fly near enough. When it had made several turns on the ceiling it flew into a dark corner and disappeared, and as I looked upward at the doubly defaced plastering I saw that the new ink-trail was that of a huge and unmistakable figure 5!

For a time I was almost unconscious from a wave of nameless menace for which I could not fully account. Then I summoned up my resolution and took an active step. Going out to a chemist's shop I purchased some gum and other things necessary for preparing a sticky trap—also a duplicate inkwell. Returning to my room, I filled the new inkwell with the sticky mixture and set it where the old one had been, leaving it open. Then I tried to concentrate my mind on some reading. About three o'clock I heard the accursed insect again, and saw it circling around the new inkwell. It descended to the sticky surface but did not touch it, and afterward sailed straight toward me—retreating before

138

I could hit it. Then it went to the bookshelf and circled around Moore's treatise. There is something profound and diabolic about the way the intruder hovers near that book.

The worst part was the last. Leaving Moore's book, the insect flew over to the open window and began beating itself rhythmically against the wire screen. There would be a series of beats and then a series of equal length and another pause, and so on. Something about this performance held me motionless for a couple of moments, but after that I went over to the window and tried to kill the noxious thing. As usual, no use. It merely flew across the room to a lamp and began beating the same tattoo on the stiff cardboard shade. I felt a vague desperation, and proceeded to shut all the doors as well as the window whose screen had the imperceptible hole. It seemed very necessary to kill this persistent being, whose hounding was rapidly unseating my mind. Then, unconsciously counting, I began to notice that each of its series of beatings contained just *five* strokes.

Five—the same number that the thing had traced in ink on the ceiling in the morning! Could there be any conceivable connexion? The notion was maniacal, for that would argue a human intellect and a knowledge of written figures in the hybrid fly. A human intellect—did not that take one back to the most primitive legends of the Uganda blacks? And yet there was that infernal cleverness in eluding me as contrasted with the normal stupidity of the breed. As I laid aside my folded paper and sat down in growing horror, the insect buzzed aloft and disappeared through a hole in the ceiling where the radiator pipe went to the room above.

The departure did not soothe me, for my mind had started on a train of wild and terrible reflections. If this fly had a human intelligence, where did that intelligence come from? Was there any truth in the native notion that these creatures acquire the personality of their victims after the latter's death? If so, whose personality did this fly bear? I had reasoned out that it must be one of those which escaped from Moore at the time he was bitten. *Was this the envoy of death which had bitten Moore? If so, what did it want with me?* What did it want with me anyway? In a cold perspiration I remembered the actions of the fly that had bitten Batta when Batta died. Had its own personality been displaced by that of its dead victim? Then there was that sensational news account of the fly that waked Dyson when Moore died. As for that fly that was hounding me— could it be that a vindictive human personality drove it on? How it hovered around Moore's book!—I refused to think any farther than that. All at once I began to feel sure that the creature was indeed infected, and in the most virulent way. With a malign deliberation so evident in every act, it must surely have charged itself on purpose with the deadliest bacilli in all Africa. My mind, thoroughly shaken, was now taking the thing's human qualities for granted.

I now telephoned the clerk and asked for a man to stop up the radiator pipehole and other possible chinks in my room. I spoke of being tormented by flies, and he seemed to be quite sympathetic. When the man came, I shewed him the ink-marks on the ceiling, which he recognised without difficulty. So they are real! The resemblance to a question-mark and a figure 5 puzzled and fascinated him. In the end he stopped up all the holes he could find, and mended the window-screen, so that I can now keep both windows open. He evidently thought me a bit eccentric, especially since no insects were in sight while he was here. But I am past minding that. So far the fly has not appeared this evening. God knows what it is, what it wants, or what will become of me!

Jan. 19—I am utterly engulfed in horror. *The thing has touched me.* Something monstrous and daemoniac is at work around me, and I am a helpless victim. In the morning, when I returned from breakfast, that winged fiend from hell brushed into the room over my head, and began beating itself against the window-screen as it did yesterday. This time, though, each series of beats contained only *four* strokes. I rushed to the window and tried to catch it, but it escaped as usual and flew over to Moore's treatise, where it buzzed around mockingly. Its vocal equipment is limited, but I noticed that its spells of buzzing came in groups of four.

By this time I was certainly mad, for I called out to it, *"Moore, Moore, for God's sake, what do you want?"* When I did so, the creature suddenly ceased its circling, flew toward me, and made a low, graceful dip in the air, somehow suggestive of a bow. Then it flew back to the book. At least, I seemed to see it do all this—though I am trusting my senses no longer.

And then the worst thing happened. I had left my door open, hoping the monster would leave if I could not catch it; but about 11:30 I shut the door, concluding it had gone. Then I settled down to read. Just at noon I felt a tickling on the back of my neck, but when I put my hand up nothing was there. In a moment I felt the tickling again—and before I could move, that nameless spawn of hell sailed into view from behind, did another of those mocking, graceful dips in the air, and flew out through the keyhole—which I had never dreamed was large enough to allow its passage.

That the thing had touched me, I could not doubt. It had touched me without injuring me—and then I remembered in a sudden cold fright that Moore had been bitten *on the back of the neck at noon.* No invasion since then—

but I have stuffed all the keyholes with paper and shall have a folded paper ready for use whenever I open the door to leave or enter.

Jan. 20—I cannot yet believe fully in the supernatural, yet I fear none the less that I am lost. The business is too much for me. Just before noon today that devil appeared *outside* the window and repeated its beating operations; but this time in series of *three*. When I went to the window it flew off out of sight. I still have resolution enough to take one more defensive step. Removing both window-screens, I coated them with my sticky preparation—the one I used in the inkwell—outside and inside, and set them back in place. If that creature attempts another tattoo, it will be its last!

Rest of the day in peace. Can I weather this experience without becoming a maniac?

Jan. 21—On board train for Bloemfontein.

I am routed. The thing is winning. It has a diabolic intelligence against which all my devices are powerless. It appeared outside the window this morning, *but did not touch the sticky screen.* Instead, it sheered off without lighting and began buzzing around in circles—*two at a time,* followed by a pause in the air. After several of these performances it flew off out of sight over the roofs of the city. My nerves are just about at the breaking-point, for these *suggestions of numbers* are capable of a hideous interpretation. Monday the thing dwelt on the figure *five;* Tuesday it was *four;* Wednesday it was *three;* and now today it is *two. Five, four, three, two*—what can this be save some monstrous and unthinkable *counting-off of days?* For what purpose, only the evil powers of the universe can know. I spent all the afternoon packing and arranging about my trunks, and now I have taken the night express for Bloemfontein. Flight may be useless, but what else can one do?

Jan. 22—Settled at the Orange Hotel, Bloemfontein—a comfortable and excellent place—but the horror followed me. I had shut all the doors and windows, stopped all the keyholes, looked for any possible chinks, and pulled down all the shades—but just before noon I heard a dull tap on one of the window-screens. I waited—and after a long pause another tap came. A second pause, and still another single tap. Raising the shade, I saw that accursed fly, as I had expected. It described one large, slow circle in the air, and then flew out of sight. I was left as weak as a rag, and had to rest on the couch. *One!* This was clearly the burden of the monster's present message. *One* tap, *one* circle. Did this mean *one* more day for me before some unthinkable doom? Ought I to flee again, or entrench myself here by sealing up the room?

After an hour's rest I felt able to act, and ordered a large reserve supply of canned and packaged food—also linen and towels—sent in. Tomorrow I shall not under any circumstances open any crevice of door or window. When the food and linen came the black looked at me queerly, but I no longer care how eccentric—or insane—I may appear. I am hounded by powers worse than the ridicule of mankind. Having received my supplies, I went over every square millimeter of the walls, and stopped up every microscopic opening I could find. At last I feel able to get real sleep.

[*Handwriting here becomes irregular, nervous, and very difficult to decipher.*]

Jan. 23—It is just before noon, and I feel that something very terrible is about to happen. Didn't sleep as late as I expected, even though I got almost no sleep on the train the night before. Up early, and have had trouble getting concentrated on anything—reading or writing. That slow, deliberate counting-off of days is too much for me. I don't know which has gone wild—Nature or my head. Until about eleven I did very little except walk up and down the room.

Then I heard a rustle among the food packages brought in yesterday, and that daemoniac fly crawled out before my eyes. I grabbed something flat and made passes at the thing despite my panic fear, but with no more effect than usual. As I advanced, that blue-winged horror retreated as usual to the table where I had piled my books, and lit for a second on Moore's *Diptera of Central and Southern Africa*. Then as I followed, it flew over to the mantel clock and lit on the dial near the figure 12. Before I could think up another move it had begun to crawl around the dial very slowly and deliberately—in the direction of the hands. It passed under the minute hand, curved down and up, passed under the hour hand, and finally came to a stop exactly at the figure 12. As it hovered there it fluttered its wings with a buzzing noise.

Is this a portent of some sort? I am getting as superstitious as the blacks. The hour is now a little after eleven. Is twelve the end? I have just one last resort, brought to my mind through utter desperation. Wish I had thought of it before. Recalling that my medicine case contains both of the substances necessary to generate chlorine gas, I have resolved to fill the room with that lethal vapour—asphyxiating the fly while protecting myself with an ammonia-sealed handkerchief tied over my face. Fortunately I have a good supply of ammonia. This crude mask will probably neutralise the acrid chlorine fumes till the insect is dead—or at least helpless enough to crush. But I must be quick. How can I be sure that the thing will not suddenly dart for me before my preparations are complete? I ought not to be stopping to write in this journal.

Later—Both chemicals—hydrochloric acid and manganese dioxide—on the table all ready to mix. I've tied the handkerchief over my nose and mouth, and have a bottle of ammonia ready to keep it soaked until the chlorine is gone. Have battened down both windows. But I don't like the actions of that hybrid daemon. It stays on the clock, but is very slowly crawling around backward from the 12 mark to meet the gradually advancing minute-hand.

Is this to be my last entry in this journal? It would be useless to try to deny what I suspect. Too often a grain of incredible truth lurks behind the wildest and most fantastic of legends. Is the personality of Henry Moore trying to get at me through this blue-winged devil? Is this the fly that bit him, and that in consequence absorbed his consciousness when he died? If so, and if it bites me, will my own personality displace Moore's and enter that buzzing body when I die of the bite later on? Perhaps, though, I need not die even if it gets me. There is always a chance with tryparsamide. And I regret nothing. Moore had to die, be the outcome what it will.

Slightly later.

The fly has paused on the clock-dial near the 45-minute mark. It is now 11:30. I am saturating the handkerchief over my face with ammonia, and keeping the bottle handy for further applications. This will be the final entry before I mix the acid and manganese and liberate the chlorine. I ought not to be losing time, but it steadies me to get things down on paper. But for this record, I'd have lost all my reason long ago. The fly seems to be getting restless, and the minute-hand is approaching it. Now for the chlorine. . . .

[*End of the journal*]

On Sunday, Jan. 24, 1932, after repeated knocking had failed to gain any response from the eccentric man in Room 303 of the Orange Hotel, a black attendant entered with a pass key and at once fled shrieking downstairs to tell the clerk what he had found. The clerk, after notifying the police, summoned the manager; and the latter accompanied Constable De Witt, Coroner Bogaert, and Dr. Van Keulen to the fatal room.

The occupant lay dead on the floor—his face upward, and bound with a handkerchief which smelled strongly of ammonia. Under this covering the features shewed an expression of stark, utter fear which transmitted itself to the observers. On the back of the neck Dr. Van Keulen found a virulent insect bite—dark red, with a purple ring around it—which suggested a tsetse-fly or something less innocuous. An examination indicated that death must be due to heart-failure induced by sheer fright rather than to the bite—though a subsequent autopsy indicated that the germ of trypanosomiasis had been introduced into the system.

On the table were several objects—a worn leather blank-book containing the journal just described, a pen, writing-pad, and open inkwell, a doctor's medicine case with the initials "T. S." marked in gold, bottles of ammonia and hydrochloric acid, and a tumbler about a quarter full of black manganese dioxide. The ammonia bottle demanded a second look because something besides the fluid seemed to be in it. Looking closer, Coroner Bogaert saw that the alien occupant was a fly.

It seemed to be some sort of hybrid with vague tsetse affiliations, but its wings—shewing faintly blue despite the action of the strong ammonia—were a complete puzzle.

Something about it waked a faint memory of newspaper reading in Dr. Van Keulen—a memory which the journal was soon to confirm. Its lower parts seemed to have been stained with ink, so thoroughly that even the ammonia had not bleached them. Possibly it had fallen at one time into the inkwell, though the wings were untouched. But how had it managed to fall into the narrow-necked ammonia bottle? It was as if the creature had deliberately crawled in and committed suicide!

But the strangest thing of all was what Constable De Witt noticed on the smooth white ceiling overhead as his eyes roved about curiously. At his cry the other three followed his gaze—even Dr. Van Keulen, who had for some time been thumbing through the worn leather book with an expression of mixed horror, fascination, and incredulity. The thing on the ceiling was a series of shaky, straggling ink-tracks, such as might have been made by the crawling of some ink-drenched insect. At once everyone thought of the stains on the fly so oddly found in the ammonia bottle.

But these were no ordinary ink-tracks. Even a first glance revealed something hauntingly familiar about them, and closer inspection brought gasps of startled wonder from all four observers. Coroner Bogaert instinctively looked around the room to see if there were any conceivable instrument or arrangement of piled-up furniture which could make it possible for those straggling marks to have been drawn by human agency. Finding nothing of the sort, he resumed his curious and almost awestruck upward glance.

For beyond a doubt these inky smudges formed definite letters of the alphabet—letters coherently arranged in English words. The doctor was the first to make them out clearly, and the others listened breathlessly as he recited the insane-sounding message so incredibly scrawled in a place no human hand could reach:

"SEE MY JOURNAL—*IT* GOT ME FIRST—I DIED—THEN I SAW I WAS IN *IT*—THE BLACKS ARE RIGHT—STRANGE POWERS IN NATURE—NOW I WILL DROWN WHAT IS LEFT—"

Presently, amidst the puzzled hush that followed, Dr. Van Keulen commenced reading aloud from the worn leather journal.

The Horror in the Museum

With Hazel Heald

I

t was languid curiosity which first brought
Stephen Jones to Rogers' Museum. Someone had told him
about the queer underground place in Southwark Street
across the river, where waxen things so much more horrible
than the worst effigies at Madame Tussaud's[1] were shewn,
and he had strolled in one April day to see how disappointing he would find it. Oddly, he was not disappointed. There
was something different and distinctive here, after all. Of
course, the usual gory commonplaces were present—Landru, Dr. Crippen, Madame Demers, Rizzio, Lady Jane Grey,[2]
endless maimed victims of war and revolution, and monsters like Gilles de Rais and Marquis de Sade[3]—but there
were other things which had made him breathe faster and
stay till the ringing of the closing bell. The man who had
fashioned this collection could be no ordinary mounte-
bank. There was imagination—even a kind of diseased genius—in some of this stuff.

Later he had learned about George Rogers. The man had been on the Tussaud staff, but some trouble had developed which led to his discharge. There were aspersions on his sanity and tales of his crazy forms of secret worship—though latterly his success with his own basement museum had dulled the edge of some criticisms while sharpening the insidious point of others. Teratology and the iconography of nightmare were his hobbies, and even he had had the prudence to screen off some of his worst effigies in a special alcove for adults only. It was this alcove which had fascinated Jones so much. There were lumpish hybrid things which only fantasy could spawn, moulded with devilish skill, and coloured in a horribly life-like fashion.

Some were the figures of well-known myth—gorgons, chimaeras, dragons, cyclops, and all their shuddersome congeners. Others were drawn from darker and more furtively whispered cycles of subterranean legend—black, formless Tsathoggua, many-tentacled Cthulhu, proboscidian Chaugnar Faugn,[4] and other rumoured blasphemies from forbidden books like the *Necronomicon,* the *Book of Eibon,* or the *Unaussprechlichen Kulten* of von Junzt.[5] But the worst were wholly original with Rogers, and represented shapes which no tale of antiquity had ever dared to suggest. Several were hideous parodies on forms of organic life we know, while others seemed taken from feverish dreams of other planets and other galaxies. The wilder paintings of Clark Ashton Smith might suggest a few—but nothing could suggest the effect of poignant, loathsome terror created by their great size and fiendishly cunning workmanship, and by the diabolically clever lighting conditions under which they were exhibited.

Stephen Jones, as a leisurely connoisseur of the bizarre in art, had sought out Rogers himself in the dingy office and workroom behind the vaulted museum chamber—an evil-looking crypt lighted dimly by dusty windows set slit-like and horizontal in the brick wall on a level with the ancient cobblestones of a hidden courtyard. It was here that the images were repaired—here, too, where some of them had been made. Waxen arms, legs, heads, and torsos lay in grotesque array on various benches, while on high tiers of shelves matted wigs, ravenous-looking teeth, and glassy, staring eyes were indiscriminately scattered. Costumes of all sorts hung from hooks, and in one alcove were great piles of flesh-coloured wax-cakes and shelves filled with paint-cans and brushes of every description. In the centre of the room was a large melting-furnace used to prepare the wax for moulding, its fire-box topped by a huge iron container on hinges, with a spout which permitted the pouring of melted wax with the merest touch of a finger.

Other things in the dismal crypt were less describable—isolated parts of problematical entities whose assembled forms were the phantoms of delirium. At one end was a door of heavy plank, fastened by an unusually large padlock and with a very peculiar symbol painted over it. Jones, who had once had access to the dreaded *Necronomicon,* shivered involuntarily as he recognised that symbol. This showman, he reflected, must indeed be a person of disconcertingly wide scholarship in dark and dubious fields.

Nor did the conversation of Rogers disappoint him. The man was tall, lean, and rather unkempt, with large black eyes which gazed combustively from a pallid and usually stubble-covered face. He did not resent Jones's intrusion, but seemed to welcome the chance of unburdening himself to an interested person. His voice was of singular depth and resonance, and harboured a sort of repressed intensity bordering on the feverish. Jones did not wonder that many had thought him mad.

With every successive call—and such calls became a habit as the weeks went by—Jones had found Rogers more communicative and confidential. From the first there had been hints of strange faiths and practices on the showman's part, and later on these hints expanded into tales—despite a few odd corroborative photographs—whose extravagance was almost comic. It was some time in June, on a night when Jones had brought a bottle of good whiskey and plied his host somewhat freely, that the really demented talk first appeared. Before that there had been wild enough stories—accounts of mysterious trips to Thibet, the African interior, the Arabian desert, the Amazon valley, Alaska, and certain little-known islands of the South Pacific, plus claims of having read such monstrous and half-fabulous books as the prehistoric Pnakotic fragments and the Dhol chants attributed to malign and non-human Leng[6]—but nothing in all this had been so unmistakably insane as what had cropped out that June evening under the spell of the whiskey.

To be plain, Rogers began making vague boasts of having found certain things in Nature that no one had found before, and of having brought back tangible evidences of such discoveries. According to his bibulous harangue, he had gone farther than anyone else in interpreting the obscure and primal books he studied, and had been directed by them to certain remote places where strange survivals are hidden—survivals of aeons and life-cycles earlier than mankind, and in some cases connected with other dimensions and other worlds, communication with which was frequent in the forgotten pre-human days. Jones marvelled at the fancy which could conjure up such notions, and wondered just what Rogers' mental history had been. Had his work amidst the morbid grotesqueries of Madame Tussaud's been the start of his imaginative flights, or was the tendency innate, so that his choice of occupation was merely one of its manifestations? At any rate, the man's work was very closely linked with his notions. Even now there was no mistaking the trend of his blackest hints about the nightmare monstrosities in the screened-off "Adults only" alcove. Heedless of ridicule, he was trying to imply that not all of these daemoniac abnormalities were artificial.

It was Jones's frank scepticism and amusement at these irresponsible claims which broke up the growing cordiality. Rogers, it was clear, took himself very seriously; for he now became morose and resentful, continuing to tolerate Jones only through a dogged urge to break down his wall of urbane and complacent incredulity. Wild tales and suggestions of rites and sacrifices to nameless elder gods continued, and now and then Rogers would lead his guest to one of the hideous blasphemies in the screened-off alcove and point out features difficult to reconcile with even the finest human craftsmanship. Jones continued his visits through sheer fascination, though he knew he had forfeited his host's regard. At times he would try to humour Rogers with pretended assent to some mad hint or assertion, but the gaunt showman was seldom to be deceived by such tactics.

The tension came to a head later in September. Jones had casually dropped into the museum one afternoon, and was wandering through the dim corridors whose horrors were now so familiar, when he heard a very peculiar sound from the general direction of Rogers' workroom. Others heard it, too, and started nervously as the echoes reverberated through the great vaulted basement. The three attendants exchanged odd glances; and one of them, a dark, taciturn, foreign-looking fellow who always served Rogers as a repairer and assistant designer, smiled in a way which seemed to puzzle his colleagues and which grated very harshly on some facet of Jones's sensibilities. It was the yelp or scream of a dog, and was such a sound as could be made only under conditions of the utmost fright and agony combined. Its stark, anguished frenzy was appalling to hear, and in this setting of grotesque abnormality it held a double hideousness. Jones remembered that no dogs were allowed in the museum.

He was about to go to the door leading into the workroom, when the dark attendant stopped him with a word and a gesture. Mr. Rogers, the man said in a soft, somewhat accented voice at once apologetic and vaguely sardonic, was out, and there were standing orders to admit no one to the workroom during his absence. As for that yelp, it was undoubtedly something out in the courtyard behind the museum. This neighbourhood was full of stray mongrels, and their fights were sometimes shockingly noisy. There were no dogs in any part of the museum. But if Mr. Jones wished to see Mr. Rogers he might find him just before closing-time.

After this Jones climbed the old stone steps to the street outside and examined the squalid neighbourhood curiously. The leaning, decrepit buildings—once dwellings but now largely shops and warehouses—were very ancient indeed. Some of them were of a gabled type seeming to go back to Tudor times, and a faint miasmatic stench hung subtly about the whole region. Beside the dingy house whose basement held the museum was a low archway pierced by a dark cobbled alley, and this Jones entered in a vague wish to find the courtyard behind the workroom and settle the affair of the dog more comfortably in his mind. The courtyard was dim in the late afternoon light, hemmed in by rear walls even uglier and more intangibly menacing than the crumbling street facades of the evil old houses. Not a dog was in sight, and Jones wondered how the aftermath of such a frantic turmoil could have completely vanished so soon.

Despite the assistant's statement that no dog had been in the museum, Jones glanced nervously at the three small windows of the basement workroom—narrow, horizontal rectangles close to the grass-grown pavement, with grimy panes that stared repulsively and incuriously like the eyes of dead fish. To their left a worn flight of steps led to an opaque and heavily bolted door. Some impulse urged him to crouch low on the damp, broken cobblestones and peer in, on the chance that the thick green shades, worked by long cords that hung down to a reachable level, might not be drawn. The outer surfaces were thick with dirt, but as he rubbed them with his handkerchief he saw there was no obscuring curtain in the way of his vision.

So shadowed was the cellar from the inside that not much could be made out, but the grotesque working paraphernalia now and then loomed up spectrally as Jones tried each of the windows in turn. It seemed evident at first that no one was within; yet when he peered through the extreme right-hand window—the one nearest the entrance alley— he saw a glow of light at the farther end of the apartment which made him pause in bewilderment. There was no reason why any light should be there. It was an inner side of the room, and he could not recall any gas or electric fixture near that point. Another look defined the glow as a large vertical rectangle, and a thought occurred to him. It was in that direction that he had always noticed the heavy plank door with the abnormally large padlock—the door which was never opened, and above which was crudely smeared that hideous cryptic symbol from the fragmentary records of forbidden elder magic. It must be open now—and there was a light inside. All his former speculations as to where that door led, and as to what lay behind it, were now renewed with trebly disquieting force.

Jones wandered aimlessly around the dismal locality till close to six o'clock, when he returned to the museum to make the call on Rogers. He could hardly tell why he wished so especially to see the man just then, but there must have been some subconscious misgivings about that terribly unplaceable canine scream of the afternoon, and about the glow of light in that disturbing and usually unopened inner doorway with the heavy padlock. The attendants were leaving as he arrived, and he thought that Orabona—the dark foreign-looking assistant—eyed him with something like sly, repressed amusement. He did not relish that look—even though he had seen the fellow turn it on his employer many times.

The vaulted exhibition room was ghoulish in its desertion, but he strode quickly through it and rapped at the door of the office and workroom. Response was slow in coming, though there were footsteps inside. Finally, in response to a second knock, the lock rattled, and the ancient six-panelled portal creaked reluctantly open to reveal the slouching, feverish-eyed form of George Rogers. From the first it was clear that the showman was in an unusual mood. There was a curious mixture of reluctance and actual gloating in his welcome, and his talk at once veered to extravagances of the most hideous and incredible sort.

Surviving elder gods—nameless sacrifices—the other than artificial nature of some of the alcove horrors—all the usual boasts, but uttered in a tone of peculiarly increasing confidence. Obviously, Jones reflected, the poor fellow's madness was gaining on him. From time to time Rogers would send furtive glances toward the heavy, padlocked inner door at the end of the room, or toward a piece of coarse burlap on the floor not far from it, beneath which some small object appeared to be lying. Jones grew more nervous as the moments passed, and began to feel as hesitant about mentioning the afternoon's oddities as he had formerly been anxious to do so.

Rogers' sepulchrally resonant bass almost cracked under the excitement of his fevered rambling.

"Do you remember," he shouted, "what I told you about that ruined city in Indo-China where the Tcho-Tchos[7] lived? You had to admit I'd been there when you saw the photographs, even if you did think I made that oblong swimmer in darkness out of wax. If you'd seen it writhing in the underground pools as I did . . .

"Well, this is bigger still. I never told you about this, because I wanted to work out the later parts before making any claim. When you see the snapshots you'll know the geography couldn't have been faked, and I fancy I have another way of proving that *It* isn't any waxed concoction of mine. You've never seen it, for the experiments wouldn't let me keep It on exhibition."

The showman glanced queerly at the padlocked door.

"It all comes from that long ritual in the eighth Pnakotic fragment. When I got it figured out I saw it could have only one meaning. There were things in the north before the land of Lomar[8]—before mankind existed—and this was one of them. It took us all the way to Alaska, and up the Noatak from Fort Morton,[9] but the thing was there as we knew it would be. Great Cyclopean ruins, acres of them. There was less left than we had hoped for, but after three million years what could one expect? And weren't the Esquimau legends all in the right direction? We couldn't get one of the beggars to go with us, and had to sledge all the way back to Nome for Americans. Orabona was no good up in that climate—it made him sullen and hateful.

"I'll tell you later how we found It. When we got the ice blasted out of the pylons of the central ruin the stairway was just as we knew it would be. Some carvings still there, and it was no trouble keeping the Yankees from following us in. Orabona shivered like a leaf—you'd never think it from the damned insolent way he struts around here. He knew enough of the Elder Lore to be properly afraid. The eternal light was gone, but our torches shewed enough. We saw the bones of others who had been before us—aeons ago, when the climate was warm. Some of these bones were of things you couldn't even imagine. At the third level down we found the ivory throne the fragments said so much about—and I may as well tell you it wasn't empty.

"The thing on that throne didn't move—and we knew then that It needed the nourishment of sacrifice. But we didn't want to wake It then. Better to get It to London first. Orabona and I went to the surface for the big box, but when we had packed it we couldn't get It up the three flights of steps. These steps weren't made for human beings, and their size bothered us. Anyway, it was devilish heavy. We had to have the Americans down to get It out. They weren't anxious to go into the place, but of course the worst thing was safely inside the box. We told them it was a batch of ivory carvings—archaeological stuff; and after seeing the carved throne they probably believed us. It's a wonder they didn't suspect hidden treasure and demand a share. They must have told queer tales around Nome later on; though I doubt if they ever went back to those ruins, even for the ivory throne."

Rogers paused, felt around in his desk, and produced an envelope of good-sized photographic prints. Extracting one and laying it face down before him, he handed the rest to Jones. The set was certainly an odd one: ice-clad hills, dog sledges, men in furs, and vast tumbled ruins against a background of snow—ruins whose bizarre outlines and enormous stone blocks could hardly be accounted for. One flashlight view shewed an incredible interior chamber with wild carvings and a curious throne whose proportion could not have been designed for a human occupant. The carvings on the gigantic masonry—high walls and peculiar vaulting overhead—were mainly symbolic, and involved both wholly unknown designs and certain hieroglyphs darkly cited in obscene legends. Over the throne loomed the same dreadful symbol which was now painted on the workroom wall above the padlocked plank door. Jones darted a nervous glance at the closed portal. Assuredly, Rogers had been to strange places and had seen strange things. Yet this mad interior picture might easily be a fraud—taken from a very clever stage setting. One must not be too credulous. But Rogers was continuing:

"Well, we shipped the box from Nome and got to London without any trouble. That was the first time we'd ever brought back anything that had a chance of coming alive. I didn't put It on display, because there were more important things to do for It. It needed the nourishment of sacrifice, for It was a god. Of course I couldn't get It the sort of sacrifices which It used to have in Its day, for such things don't exist now. But there were other things which might do. The blood is the life, you know.[10] Even the lemurs and elementals that are older than the earth will come when the blood of men or beasts is offered under the right conditions."

The expression on the narrator's face was growing very alarming and repulsive, so that Jones fidgeted involuntarily in his chair. Rogers seemed to notice his guest's nervousness, and continued with a distinctly evil smile.

"It was last year that I got It, and ever since then I've been trying rites and sacrifices. Orabona hasn't been much help, for he was always against the idea of waking It. He hates It—probably because he's afraid of what It will come to mean. He carries a pistol all the time to protect himself—fool, as if there were human protection against It! If I ever see him draw that pistol, I'll strangle him. He wanted me to kill It and make an effigy of It. But I've stuck by my plans, and I'm coming out on top in spite of all the cowards like Orabona and damned sniggering sceptics like you, Jones! I've chanted the rites and made certain sacrifices, *and last week the transition came.* The sacrifice was—received and enjoyed!"

Rogers actually licked his lips, while Jones held himself uneasily rigid. The showman paused and rose, crossing the room to the piece of burlap at which he had glanced so often. Bending down, he took hold of one corner as he spoke again.

"You've laughed enough at my work—now it's time for you to get some facts. Orabona tells me you heard a dog screaming around here this afternoon. *Do you know what that meant?*"

Jones started. For all his curiosity he would have been glad to get out without further light on the point which had so puzzled him. But Rogers was inexorable, and began to lift the square of burlap. Beneath it lay a crushed, almost shapeless mass which Jones was slow to classify. Was it a once-living thing which some agency had flattened, sucked dry of blood, punctured in a thousand places, and wrung into a limp, broken-boned heap of grotesqueness? After a moment Jones realised what it must be. It was what was left of a dog—a dog, perhaps of considerable size and whitish colour. Its breed was past recognition, for distortion had come in nameless and hideous ways. Most of the hair was burned off as by some pungent acid, and the exposed, bloodless skin was riddled by innumerable circular wounds or incisions. The form of torture necessary to cause such results was past imagining.

Electrified with a pure loathing which conquered his mounting disgust, Jones sprang up with a cry.

"You damned sadist—you madman—you do a thing like this and dare to speak to a decent man!"

Rogers dropped the burlap with a malignant sneer and faced his oncoming guest. His words held an unnatural calm.

"Why, you fool, do you think *I* did this? Let us admit that the results are unbeautiful from our limited human standpoint. What of it? It is not human and does not pretend to be. To sacrifice is merely to offer. I gave the dog to *It*. What happened is Its work, not mine. It needed the nourishment of the offering, and took it in Its own way. But let me shew you what It looks like."

As Jones stood hesitating, the speaker returned to his desk and took up the photograph he had laid face down without shewing. Now he extended it with a curious look. Jones took it and glanced at it in an almost mechanical way. After a moment the visitor's glance became sharper and more absorbed, for the utterly satanic force of the object depicted had an almost hypnotic effect. Certainly, Rogers had outdone himself in modelling the eldritch nightmare which the camera had caught. The thing was a work of sheer, infernal genius, and Jones wondered how the public would react when it was placed on exhibition. So hideous a thing had no right to exist—probably the mere contempla-

161

tion of it, after it was done, had completed the unhinging of its maker's mind and led him to worship it with brutal sacrifices. Only a stout sanity could resist the insidious suggestion that the blasphemy was—or had once been—some morbid and exotic form of actual life.

The thing in the picture squatted or was balanced on what appeared to be a clever reproduction of the monstrously carved throne in the other curious photograph. To describe it with any ordinary vocabulary would be impossible, for nothing even roughly corresponding to it has ever come within the imagination of sane mankind. It represented something meant perhaps to be roughly connected with the vertebrates of this planet—though one could not be too sure of that. Its bulk was Cyclopean, for even squatted it towered to almost twice the height of Orabona, who was shewn beside it. Looking sharply, one might trace its approximations toward the bodily features of the higher vertebrates.

There was an almost globular torso, with six long, sinuous limbs terminating in crab-like claws. From the upper end a subsidiary globe bulged forward bubble-like; its triangle of three staring, fishy eyes, its foot-long and evidently flexible proboscis, and a distended lateral system analogous to gills, suggesting that it was a head. Most of the body was covered with what at first appeared to be fur, but which on closer examination proved to be a dense growth of dark, slender tentacles or sucking filaments, each tipped with a mouth suggesting the head of an asp. On the head and below the proboscis the tentacles tended to be longer and thicker, and marked with spiral stripes—suggesting the traditional serpent-locks of Medusa. To say that such a thing could have an *expression* seems paradoxical; yet Jones felt that that triangle of bulging fish-eyes and that obliquely poised proboscis all bespoke a blend of hate, greed, and sheer cruelty incomprehensible to mankind because mixed with other emotions not of the world or this solar system. Into this bestial abnormality, he reflected, Rogers must have poured at once all his malignant insanity and all his uncanny sculptural genius. The thing was incredible—and yet the photograph proved that it existed.

Rogers interrupted his reveries.

"Well—what do you think of It? Now do you wonder what crushed the dog and sucked it dry with a million mouths? It needed nourishment—and It will need more. It is a god, and I am the first priest of Its latter-day hierarchy. Iä! Shub-Niggurath! The Goat with a Thousand Young!"

Jones lowered the photograph in disgust and pity.

"See here, Rogers, this won't do. There are limits, you know. It's a great piece of work, and all that, but it isn't good for you. Better not see it any more—let Orabona break it up, and try to forget about it. And let me tear this beastly picture up, too."

With a snarl, Rogers snatched the photograph and returned it to the desk.

"Idiot—you—and you still think It's all a fraud! You still think I made It, and you still think my figures are nothing but lifeless wax! Why, damn you, you're a worse clod than a wax image yourself! But I've got proof this time, and you're going to know! Not just now, for It is resting after the sacrifice—but later. Oh, yes—you will not doubt the power of It then."

As Rogers glanced toward the padlocked inner door Jones retrieved his hat and stick from a nearby bench.

"Very well, Rogers, let it be later. I must be going now, but I'll call around tomorrow afternoon. Think my advice over and see if it doesn't sound sensible. Ask Orabona what he thinks, too."

Rogers actually bared his teeth in wild-beast fashion.

"Must be going now, eh? Afraid, after all! Afraid, for all your bold talk! You say the effigies are only wax, and yet you run away when I begin to prove that they aren't. You're like the fellows who take my standing bet that they daren't spend the night in the museum—they come boldly enough, but after an hour they shriek and hammer to get out! Want me to ask Orabona, eh? You two—always against me! You want to break down the coming earthly reign of It!"

Jones preserved his calm.

"No, Rogers—there's nobody against you. And I'm not afraid of your figures, either, much as I admire your skill. But we're both a bit nervous tonight, and I fancy some rest will do us good."

Again Rogers checked his guest's departure.

"Not afraid, eh?—then why are you so anxious to go? Look here—do you or don't you dare to stay alone here in the dark? What's your hurry if you don't believe in It?"

Some new idea seemed to have struck Rogers, and Jones eyed him closely.

"Why, I've no special hurry—but what would be gained by my staying here alone? What would it prove? My only objection is that it isn't very comfortable for sleeping. What good would it do either of us?"

This time it was Jones who was struck with an idea. He continued in a tone of conciliation.

"See here, Rogers—I've just asked you what it would prove if I stayed, when we both know. It would prove that your effigies are just effigies, and that you oughtn't to let your imagination go the way it's been going lately. Suppose I *do* stay. If I stick it out till morning, will you agree to take a new view of things—go on a vacation for three months or so and let Orabona destroy that new thing of yours? Come, now—isn't that fair?"

The expression on the showman's face was hard to read. It was obvious that he was thinking quickly, and that of sundry conflicting emotions, malign triumph was getting the upper hand. His voice held a choking quality as he replied.

"Fair enough! *If you do stick it out,* I'll take your advice. But stick you must. We'll go out for dinner and come back. I'll lock you in the display room and go home. In the morning I'll come down ahead of Orabona—he comes half an hour before the rest—and see how you are. But don't try it unless you are *very* sure of your scepticism. Others have backed out—you have that chance. And I suppose a pounding on the outer door would always bring a constable. You may not like it so well after a while—you'll be in the same building, though not in the same room with It."

As they left the rear door into the dingy courtyard, Rogers took with him the piece of burlap—weighted with a gruesome burden. Near the centre of the court was a manhole, whose cover the showman lifted quietly, and with a shuddersome suggestion of familiarity. Burlap and all, the burden went down to the oblivion of a cloacal labyrinth. Jones shuddered, and almost shrank from the gaunt figure at his side as they emerged into the street.

By unspoken mutual consent, they did not dine together, but agreed to meet in front of the museum at eleven.

Jones hailed a cab, and breathed more freely when he had crossed Waterloo Bridge and was approaching the brilliantly lighted Strand. He dined at a quiet café, and subsequently went to his home in Portland Place to bathe and get a few things. Idly he wondered what Rogers was doing. He had heard that the man had a vast, dismal house in the Walworth Road, full of obscure and forbidden books, occult paraphernalia, and wax images which he did not choose to place on exhibition. Orabona, he understood, lived in separate quarters in the same house.

At eleven Jones found Rogers waiting by the basement door in Southwark Street. Their words were few, but each seemed taut with a menacing tension. They agreed that the vaulted exhibition room alone should form the scene of the vigil, and Rogers did not insist that the watcher sit in the special adult alcove of supreme horrors. The showman, having extinguished all the lights with switches in the work-room, locked the door of that crypt with one of the keys on his crowded ring. Without shaking hands he passed out the street door, locked it after him, and stamped up the worn steps to the sidewalk outside. As his tread receded, Jones realised that the long, tedious vigil had commenced.

II

Later, in the utter blackness of the great arched cellar, Jones cursed the childish naiveté which had brought him there. For the first half-hour he had kept flashing on his pocket-light at intervals, but now just sitting in the dark on one of the visitors' benches had become a more nerve-racking thing. Every time the beam shot out it lighted up some morbid, grotesque object—a guillotine, a nameless hybrid monster, a pasty-bearded face crafty with evil, a body with red torrents streaming from a severed throat. Jones knew that no sinister reality was attached to these things, but after that first half-hour he preferred not to see them.

Why he had bothered to humour that madman he could scarcely imagine. It would have been much simpler merely to have let him alone, or to have called in a mental specialist. Probably, he reflected, it was the fellow-feeling of one artist for another. There was so much genius in Rogers that he deserved every possible chance to be helped quietly out of his growing mania. Any man who could imagine and construct the incredibly life-like things that he had produced was surely not far from actual greatness. He had the fancy of a Sime or a Doré[11] joined to the minute, scientific craftsmanship of a Blatschka.[12] Indeed, he had done for the world of nightmare what the Blatschkas with their marvellously accurate plant models of finely wrought and coloured glass had done for the world of botany.

At midnight the strokes of a distant clock filtered through the darkness, and Jones felt cheered by the message from a still-surviving outside world. The vaulted museum chamber was like a tomb—ghastly in its utter solitude. Even a mouse would be cheering company; yet Rogers had once boasted that—for "certain reasons", as he said—no mice or even insects ever came near the place. That was very curious, yet it seemed to be true. The deadness and silence were virtually complete. If only something would make a sound! He shuffled his feet, and the echoes came spectrally out of the absolute stillness. He coughed, but there was something mocking in the staccato reverberations. He could not, he vowed, begin talking to himself. That meant nervous disintegration. Time seemed to pass with abnormal and disconcerting slowness. He could have sworn that hours had elapsed since he last flashed the light on his watch, yet here was only the stroke of midnight.

He wished that his senses were not so preternaturally keen. Something in the darkness and stillness seemed to have sharpened them, so that they responded to faint intimations hardly strong enough to be called true impressions. His ears seemed at times to catch a faint, elusive susurrus which could not *quite* be identified with the nocturnal hum of the squalid streets outside, and he thought of vague, irrelevant things like the music of the spheres and the unknown, inaccessible life of alien dimensions pressing on our own. Rogers often speculated about such things.

The floating specks of light in his blackness-drowned eyes seemed inclined to take on curious symmetries of pattern and motion. He had often wondered about those strange rays from the unplumbed abyss which scintillate before us in the absence of all earthly illumination, but he had never known any that behaved just as these were behaving. They lacked the restful aimlessness of ordinary light-specks—suggesting some will and purpose remote from any terrestrial conception.

Then there was that suggestion of odd stirrings. Nothing was open, yet in spite of the general draughtlessness Jones felt that the air was not uniformly quiet. There were intangible variations in pressure—not quite decided enough to suggest the loathsome pawings of unseen elementals. It was abnormally chilly, too. He did not like any of this. The air tasted salty, as if it were mixed with the brine of dark subterrene waters, and there was a bare hint of some odour of ineffable mustiness. In the daytime he had never noticed that the waxen figures had an odour. Even now that half-received hint was not the way wax figures ought to smell. It was more like the faint smell of specimens in a natural-history museum. Curious, in view of Rogers' claims that his figures were not all artificial—indeed, it was probably that claim which made one's imagination conjure up the olfactory suspicion. One must guard against excesses of the imagination—had not such things driven poor Rogers mad?

But the utter loneliness of this place was frightful.

Even the distant chimes seemed to come from across cosmic gulfs. It made Jones think of that insane picture which Rogers had shewed him—the wildly carved chamber with the cryptic throne which the fellow had claimed was part of a three-million-year-old ruin in the shunned and inaccessible solitudes of the Arctic. Perhaps Rogers had been to Alaska, but that picture was certainly nothing but stage scenery. It couldn't normally be otherwise, with all that carving and those terrible symbols. And that monstrous shape supposed to have been found on that throne—what a flight of diseased fancy! Jones wondered just how far he actually was from the insane masterpiece in wax—probably it was kept behind that heavy, padlocked plank door leading somewhere out of the workroom. But it would never do to brood about a waxen image. Was not the present room full of such things, some of them scarcely less horrible than the dreadful "IT"? And beyond a thin canvas screen on the left was the "Adults only" alcove with its nameless phantoms of delirium.

The proximity of the numberless waxen shapes began to get on Jones's nerves more and more as the quarter-hours wore on. He knew the museum so well that he could not get rid of their usual images even in the total darkness. Indeed, the darkness had the effect of adding to the remembered images certain very disturbing imaginative overtones. The guillotine seemed to creak, and the bearded face of Landru—slayer of his fifty wives—twisted itself into expressions of monstrous menace. From the severed throat of Madame Demers a hideous bubbling sound seemed to emanate, while the headless, legless victim of a trunk murder tried to edge closer and closer on its gory stumps. Jones began shutting his eyes to see if that would dim the images, but found it was useless. Besides, when he shut his eyes the strange,

purposeful patterns of light-specks became more disturb-
ingly pronounced.

Then suddenly he began trying to keep the hideous
images he had formerly been trying to banish. He tried
to keep them because they were giving place to still more
hideous ones. In spite of himself his memory began recon-
structing the utterly non-human blasphemies that lurked
in the obscurer corners, and these lumpish hybrid growths
oozed and wriggled toward him as though hunting him
down in a circle. Black Tsathoggua moulded itself from a
toad-like gargoyle to a long, sinuous line with hundreds of
rudimentary feet, and a lean, rubbery night-gaunt spread
its wings as if to advance and smother the watcher. Jones
braced himself to keep from screaming. He knew he was
reverting to the traditional terrors of his childhood, and resolved to use his adult reason to keep the phantoms at bay.
It helped a bit, he found, to flash the light again. Frightful
as were the images it shewed, these were not as bad as what
his fancy called out of the utter blackness.

But there were drawbacks. Even in the light of his
torch he could not help suspecting a slight, furtive trembling on the part of the canvas partition screening off the
terrible "Adults only" alcove. He knew what lay beyond,
and shivered. Imagination called up the shocking form
of fabulous Yog-Sothoth—only a congeries of iridescent
globes, yet stupendous in its malign suggestiveness.[13] What
was this accursed mass slowly floating toward him and
bumping on the partition that stood in the way? A small
bulge in the canvas far to the right suggested the sharp horn
of Gnoph-keh, the hairy myth-thing of the Greenland ice,
that walked sometimes on two legs, sometimes on four, and
sometimes on six.[14] To get this stuff out of his head Jones
walked boldly toward the hellish alcove with torch burning

steadily. Of course, none of his fears was true. Yet were not the long, facial tentacles of great Cthulhu actually swaying, slowly and insidiously? He knew they were flexible, but he had not realised that the draught caused by his advance was enough to set them in motion.

Returning to his former seat outside the alcove, he shut his eyes and let the symmetrical light-specks do their worst. The distant clock boomed a single stroke. Could it be only one? He flashed the light on his watch and saw that it was precisely that hour. It would be hard indeed waiting for morning. Rogers would be down at about eight o'clock, ahead of even Orabona. It would be light outside in the main basement long before that, but none of it could penetrate here. All the windows in this basement had been bricked up but the three small ones facing the court. A pretty bad wait, all told.

His ears were getting most of the hallucinations now—for he could swear he heard stealthy, plodding footsteps in the workroom beyond the closed and locked door. He had no business thinking of that unexhibited horror which Rogers called "It". The thing was a contamination— it had driven its maker mad, and now even its picture was calling up imaginative terrors. It could not be in the workroom—it was very obviously beyond that padlocked door of heavy planking. Those steps were certainly pure imagination.

Then he thought he heard the key turn in the workroom door. Flashing on his torch, he saw nothing but the ancient six-panelled portal in its proper position. Again he tried darkness and closed eyes, but there followed a harrowing illusion of creaking—not the guillotine this time, but the slow, furtive opening of the workroom door. He would not scream. Once he screamed, he would be lost. There was a sort of padding or shuffling audible now, and it was slowly advancing toward him. He must retain command of himself. Had he not done so when the nameless brain-shapes tried to close in on him? The shuffling crept nearer, and his resolution failed. He did not scream but merely gulped out a challenge.

"Who goes there? Who are you? What do you want?"

There was no answer, but the shuffling kept on. Jones did not know which he feared most to do—turn on his flashlight or stay in the dark while the thing crept upon him. This thing was different, he felt profoundly, from the other terrors of the evening. His fingers and throat worked spasmodically. Silence was impossible, and the suspense of utter blackness was beginning to be the most intolerable of all conditions. Again he cried out hysterically—"Halt! Who goes there?"—as he switched on the revealing beams of his torch. Then, paralysed by what he saw, he dropped the flashlight and screamed—not once but many times.

Shuffling toward him in the darkness was the gigantic, blasphemous form of a black thing not wholly ape and not wholly insect. Its hide hung loosely upon its frame, and its rugose, dead-eyed rudiment of a head swayed drunkenly from side to side. Its fore paws were extended, with talons spread wide, and its whole body was taut with murderous malignity despite its utter lack of facial expression. After the screams and the final coming of darkness it leaped, and in a moment had Jones pinned to the floor. There was no struggle, for the watcher had fainted.

Jones's fainting spell could not have lasted more than a moment, for the nameless thing was apishly dragging him through the darkness when he began recovering consciousness. What started him fully awake were the sounds which the thing was making—or rather, the voice with which it was making them. That voice was human, and it was familiar. Only one living being could be behind the hoarse, feverish accents which were chanting to an unknown horror.

"Iä! Iä!" it was howling. "I am coming, O Rhan-Tegoth, coming with the nourishment. You have waited long and fed ill, but now you shall have what was promised. That and more, for instead of Orabona it will be one of high degree who had doubted you. You shall crush and drain him, with all his doubts, and grow strong thereby. And ever after among men he shall be shewn as a monument to your glory. Rhan-Tegoth, infinite and invincible, I am your slave and high-priest. You are hungry, and I provide. I read the sign and have led you forth. I shall feed you with blood, and you shall feed me with power. Iä! Shub-Niggurath! The Goat with a Thousand Young!"

In an instant all the terrors of the night dropped from Jones like a discarded cloak. He was again master of his mind, for he knew the very earthly and material peril he had to deal with. This was no monster of fable, but a dangerous madman. It was Rogers, dressed in some nightmare covering of his own insane designing, and about to make a frightful sacrifice to the devil-god he had fashioned out of wax. Clearly, he must have entered the workroom from the rear courtyard, donned his disguise, and then advanced to seize his neatly trapped and fear-broken victim. His strength was prodigious, and if he was to be thwarted, one must act quickly. Counting on the madman's confidence in his unconsciousness he determined to take him by surprise, while his grasp was relatively lax. The feel of a threshold told him he was crossing into the pitch-black workroom.

With the strength of mortal fear Jones made a sudden spring from the half-recumbent posture in which he was being dragged. For an instant he was free of the astonished maniac's hands, and in another instant a lucky lunge in the dark had put his own hands at his captor's weirdly concealed throat. Simultaneously Rogers gripped him again, and without further preliminaries the two were locked in a desperate struggle of life and death. Jones's athletic training, without doubt, was his sole salvation; for his mad assailant, freed from every inhibition of fair play, decency, or even self-preservation, was an engine of savage destruction as formidable as a wolf or panther.

Guttural cries sometimes punctured the hideous tussle in the dark. Blood spurted, clothing ripped, and Jones at last felt the actual throat of the maniac, shorn of its spectral mask. He spoke not a word, but put every ounce of energy into the defence of his life. Rogers kicked, gouged, butted, bit, clawed, and spat—yet found strength to yelp out actual sentences at times. Most of his speech was in a ritualistic jargon full of references to "It" or "Rhan-Tegoth", and to Jones's overwrought nerves it seemed as if the cries echoed from an infinite distance of daemoniac snortings and bayings. Toward the last they were rolling on the floor, overturning benches or striking against the walls and the brick foundations of the central melting-furnace. Up to the very end Jones could not be certain of saving himself, but chance finally intervened in his favour. A jab of his knee against Rogers' chest produced a general relaxation, and a moment later he knew he had won.

Though hardly able to hold himself up, Jones rose and stumbled about the walls seeking the light-switch—for his flashlight was gone, together with most of his clothing. As he lurched along he dragged his limp opponent with him, fearing a sudden attack when the madman came to. Finding the switch-box, he fumbled till he had the right handle. Then, as the wildly disordered workroom burst into sudden

174

radiance, he set about binding Rogers with such cords and belts as he could easily find. The fellow's disguise—or what was left of it—seemed to be made of a puzzlingly queer sort of leather. For some reason it made Jones's flesh crawl to touch it, and there seemed to be an alien, rusty odour about it. In the normal clothes beneath it was Rogers' key-ring, and this the exhausted victor seized as his final passport to freedom. The shades at the small, slit-like windows were all securely drawn, and he let them remain so.

Washing off the blood of battle at a convenient sink, Jones donned the most ordinary-looking and least ill-fitting clothes he could find on the costume hooks. Testing the door to the courtyard, he found it fastened with a spring-lock which did not require a key from the inside. He kept the key-ring, however, to admit him on his return with aid—for plainly, the thing to do was to call in an alienist. There was no telephone in the museum, but it would not take long to find an all-night restaurant or chemist's shop where one could be had. He had almost opened the door to go when a torrent of hideous abuse from across the room told him that Rogers—whose visible injuries were confined to a long, deep scratch down the left cheek—had regained consciousness.

"Fool! Spawn of Noth-Yidik and effluvium of K'thun![15] Son of the dogs that howl in the maelstrom of Azathoth![16] You would have been sacred and immortal, and now you are betraying It and Its priest! Beware—for It is hungry! It would have been Orabona—that damned treacherous dog ready to turn against me and It—but I give you the first honour instead. Now you must both beware, for It is not gentle without Its priest.

"Iä! Iä! Vengeance is at hand! Do you know you would have been immortal? Look at the furnace! There is a fire ready to light, and there is wax in the kettle. I would have done with you as I have done with other once-living forms. Hei! You, who have vowed all my effigies are waxen, would have become a waxen effigy yourself! The furnace was all ready! When It had had Its fill, and you were like that dog I shewed you, I would have made your flattened, punctured fragments immortal! Wax would have done it. Haven't you said I'm a great artist? Wax in every pore—wax over every square inch of you—Iä! Iä! And ever after the world would have looked at your mangled carcass and wondered how I ever imagined and made such a thing! Hei! And Orabona would have come next, and others after him—and thus would my waxen family have grown!

"Dog—do you still think I *made* all my effigies? Why not say *preserved*? You know by this time the strange places I've been to, and the strange things I've brought back. Coward—you could never face the dimensional shambler whose hide I put on to scare you—the mere sight of it alive, or even the full-fledged thought of it, would kill you instantly with fright! Iä! Iä! It waits hungry for the blood that is the life!"

Rogers, propped against the wall, swayed to and fro in his bonds.

"See here, Jones—if I let you go will you let me go? It must be taken care of by Its high-priest. Orabona will be enough to keep It alive—and when he is finished I will make his fragments immortal in wax for the world to see. It could have been you, but you have rejected the honour. I won't bother you again. Let me go, and I will share with you the power that It will bring me. Iä! Iä! Great is Rhan-Tegoth! Let me go! Let me go! It is starving down there beyond that door, and if It dies the Old Ones can never come back. Hei! Hei! Let me go!"

Jones merely shook his head, though the hideousness of the showman's imaginings revolted him. Rogers, now staring wildly at the padlocked plank door, thumped his head again and again against the brick wall and kicked with his tightly bound ankles. Jones was afraid he would injure himself, and advanced to bind him more firmly to some stationary object. Writhing, Rogers edged away from him and set up a series of frenetic ululations whose utter, monstrous unhumanness was appalling, and whose sheer volume was almost incredible. It seemed impossible that any human throat could produce noises so loud and piercing, and Jones felt that if this continued there would be no need to telephone for aid. It could not be long before a constable would investigate, even granting that there were no listening neighbours in this deserted warehouse district.

"Wza-y'ei! Wza-y'ei!" howled the madman. *"Y'kaa haa bho—ii, Rhan-Tegoth—Cthulhu fhtagn*[17]*—Ei! Ei! Ei! Ei!—Rhan-Tegoth, Rhan-Tegoth, Rhan-Tegoth!"*

The tautly trussed creature, who had started squirming his way across the littered floor, now reached the padlocked plank door and commenced knocking his head thunderously against it. Jones dreaded the task of binding him further, and wished he were not so exhausted from the previous struggle. This violent aftermath was getting hideously on his nerves, and he began to feel a return of the nameless qualms he had felt in the dark. Everything about Rogers and his museum was so hellishly morbid and suggestive of black vistas beyond life! It was loathsome to think of the waxen masterpiece of abnormal genius which must at this very moment be lurking close at hand in the blackness beyond the heavy, padlocked door.

And now something happened which sent an additional chill down Jones's spine, and caused every hair—

177

even the tiny growth on the backs of his hands—to bristle with a vague fright beyond classification. Rogers had suddenly stopped screaming and beating his head against the stout plank door, and was straining up to a sitting posture, head cocked on one side as if listening intently for something. All at once a smile of devilish triumph overspread his face, and he began speaking intelligibly again—this time in a hoarse whisper contrasting oddly with his former stentorian howling.

"Listen, fool! Listen hard! *It* has heard me, and is coming. Can't you hear It splashing out of Its tank down there at the end of the runway? I dug it deep, because there was nothing too good for It. It is amphibious, you know—you saw the gills in the picture. It came to the earth from lead-grey Yuggoth,[18] where the cities are under the warm deep sea. It can't stand up in there—too tall—has to sit or crouch. Let me get my keys—we must let It out and kneel down before It. Then we will go out and find a dog or cat—or perhaps a drunken man—to give It the nourishment It needs."

It was not what the madman said, but the way he said it, that disorganised Jones so badly. The utter, insane confidence and sincerity in that crazed whisper were damnably contagious. Imagination, with such a stimulus, could find an active menace in the devilish wax figure that lurked unseen just beyond the heavy planking. Eyeing the door in unholy fascination, Jones noticed that it bore several distinct cracks, though no marks of violent treatment were visible on this side. He wondered how large a room or closet lay behind it, and how the waxen figure was arranged. The maniac's idea of a tank and runway was as clever as all his other imaginings.

Then, in one terrible instant, Jones completely lost the

power to draw a breath. The leather belt he had seized for Rogers' further strapping fell from his limp hands, and a spasm of shivering convulsed him from head to foot. He might have known the place would drive him mad as it had driven Rogers—and now he *was* mad. He was mad, for he now harboured hallucinations more weird than any which had assailed him earlier that night. The madman was bidding him hear the splashing of a mythical monster in a tank beyond the door—and now, God help him, *he did hear it!*

Rogers saw the spasm of horror reach Jones's face and transform it to a staring mask of fear. He cackled.

"At last, fool, you believe! At last you know! You hear It and It comes! Get me my keys, fool—we must do homage and serve It!"

But Jones was past paying attention to any human words, mad or sane. Phobic paralysis held him immobile and half-conscious, with wild images racing phantasmagorically through his helpless imagination. There *was* a splashing. There *was* a padding or shuffling, as of great wet paws on a solid surface. Something *was* approaching. Into his nostrils, from the cracks in that nightmare plank door, poured a noisome animal stench like and yet unlike that of the mammal cages at the zoölogical gardens in Regent's Park.[19]

He did not know now whether Rogers was talking or not. Everything real had faded away, and he was a statue obsessed with dreams and hallucinations so unnatural that they became almost objective and remote from him. He thought he heard a sniffing or snorting from the unknown gulf beyond the door, and when a sudden baying, trumpeting noise assailed his ears he could not feel sure that it came from the tightly bound maniac whose image swam uncertainly in his shaken vision. The photograph of that accursed, unseen wax thing persisted in floating through his consciousness. Such a thing had no right to exist. Had it not driven him mad?

Even as he reflected, a fresh evidence of madness beset him. Something, he thought, was fumbling with the latch of the heavy padlocked door. It was patting and pawing and pushing at the planks. There was a thudding on the stout wood, which grew louder and louder. The stench was horrible. And now the assault on that door from the inside was a malign, determined pounding like the strokes of a battering-ram. There was an ominous cracking—a splintering—a welling foetor—a falling plank—*a black paw ending in a crab-like claw. . . .*

"Help! Help! God help me! . . . Aaaaaaa! . . ."

With intense effort Jones is today able to recall a sudden bursting of his fear-paralysis into the liberation of frenzied automatic flight. What he evidently did must have paralleled curiously the wild, plunging flights of maddest nightmares; for he seems to have leaped across the disordered crypt at almost a single bound, yanked open the outside door, which closed and locked itself after him with a clatter, sprung up the worn stone steps three at a time, and raced frantically and aimlessly out of that dank cobblestoned court and through the squalid streets of Southwark.

Here the memory ends. Jones does not know how he got home, and there is no evidence of his having hired a cab. Probably he raced all the way by blind instinct—over Waterloo Bridge, along the Strand and Charing Cross, and up Haymarket and Regent Street to his own neighbourhood. He still had on the queer mélange of museum costumes when he grew conscious enough to call the doctor.

A week later the nerve specialists allowed him to leave his bed and walk in the open air.

But he had not told the specialists much. Over his whole experience hung a pall of madness and nightmare, and he felt that silence was the only course. When he was up, he scanned intently all the papers which had accumulated since that hideous night, but found no reference to anything queer at the museum. How much, after all, had been reality? Where did reality end and morbid dream begin? Had his mind gone wholly to pieces in that dark exhibition chamber, and had the whole fight with Rogers been a phantasm of fever? It would help to put him on his feet if he could settle some of these maddening points. He *must* have seen that damnable photograph of the wax image called "It", for no brain but Rogers' could ever have conceived such a blasphemy.

It was a fortnight before he dared to enter Southwark Street again. He went in the middle of the morning, when there was the greatest amount of sane, wholesome activity around the ancient, crumbling shops and warehouses. The museum's sign was still there, and as he approached he saw that the place was open. The gateman nodded in a pleasant recognition as he summoned up the courage to enter, and in the vaulted chamber below an attendant touched his cap cheerfully. Perhaps everything had been a dream. Would he dare to knock at the door of the workroom and look for Rogers?

Then Orabona advanced to greet him. His dark, sleek face was a trifle sardonic, but Jones felt that he was not unfriendly. He spoke with a trace of accent.

"Good morning, Mr. Jones. It is some time since we have seen you here. Did you wish Mr. Rogers? I'm sorry, but he is away. He had word of business in America, and had to go. Yes, it was very sudden. I am in charge now— here, and at the house. I try to maintain Mr. Rogers' high standard—till he is back."

The foreigner smiled—perhaps from affability alone. Jones scarcely knew how to reply, but managed to mumble out a few inquiries about the day after his last visit. Orabona seemed greatly amused by the questions, and took considerable care in framing his replies.

"Oh, yes, Mr. Jones—the twenty-eighth of last month. I remember it for many reasons. In the morning—before Mr. Rogers got here, you understand—I found the workroom in quite a mess. There was a great deal of—cleaning up—to do. There had been—late work, you see. Important new specimen given its secondary baking process. I took complete charge when I came.

"It was a hard specimen to prepare—but of course Mr. Rogers has taught me a great deal. He is, as you know, a very great artist. When he came he helped me complete the specimen—helped very materially, I assure you—but he left soon without even greeting the men. As I tell you, he was called away suddenly. There were important chemical reactions involved. They made loud noises—in fact, some teamsters in the court outside fancy they heard several pistol shots—very amusing idea!

"As for the new specimen—that matter is very unfortunate. It is a great masterpiece—designed and made, you understand, by Mr. Rogers. He will see about it when he gets back."

Again Orabona smiled.

"The police, you know. We put it on display a week ago, and there were two or three faintings. One poor fellow had an epileptic fit in front of it. You see, it is a trifle—stronger—than the rest. Larger, for one thing. Of course, it was in the adult alcove. The next day a couple of men from Scotland Yard looked it over and said it was too morbid to be shewn. Said we'd have to remove it. It was a tremendous shame—such a masterpiece of art—but I didn't feel justified in appealing to the courts in Mr. Rogers' absence. He would not like so much publicity with the police now—but when he gets back—when he gets back—"

For some reason or other Jones felt a mounting tide of uneasiness and repulsion. But Orabona was continuing.

"You are a connoisseur, Mr. Jones. I am sure I violate no law in offering you a private view. It may be—subject, of course, to Mr. Rogers' wishes—that we shall destroy the specimen some day—but that would be a crime."

Jones had a powerful impulse to refuse the sight and flee precipitately, but Orabona was leading him forward by the arm with an artist's enthusiasm. The adult alcove, crowded with nameless horrors, held no visitors. In the farther corner a large niche had been curtained off, and to this the smiling assistant advanced.

"You must know, Mr. Jones, that the title of this specimen is 'The Sacrifice to Rhan-Tegoth.'"

Jones started violently, but Orabona appeared not to notice.

"The shapeless, colossal god is a feature in certain obscure legends which Mr. Rogers has studied. All nonsense, of course, as you've so often assured Mr. Rogers. It is supposed to have come from outer space, and to have lived in the Arctic three million years ago. It treated its sacrifices rather peculiarly and horribly, as you shall see. Mr. Rogers had made it fiendishly life-like—even to the face of the victim."

Now trembling violently, Jones clung to the brass railing in front of the curtained niche. He almost reached out to stop Orabona when he saw the curtain beginning to swing aside, but some conflicting impulse held him back.

The foreigner smiled triumphantly.

"Behold!"

Jones reeled in spite of his grip on the railing.

"God!—great God!"

Fully ten feet high despite a shambling, crouching attitude expressive of infinite cosmic malignancy, a monstrosity of unbelievable horror was shewn starting forward from a Cyclopean ivory throne covered with grotesque carvings. In the central pair of its six legs it bore a crushed, flattened, distorted, bloodless thing, riddled with a million punctures, and in places seared as with some pungent acid. Only the mangled head of the victim, lolling upside down at one side, revealed that it represented something once human.

The monster itself needed no title for one who had seen a certain hellish photograph. That damnable print had been all too faithful; yet it could not carry the full horror which lay in the gigantic actuality. The globular torso—the bubble-like suggestion of a head—the three fishy eyes—the foot-long proboscis—the bulging gills—the monstrous capillation of asp-like suckers—the six sinuous limbs with their black paws and crab-like claws—God! the familiarity of that black paw ending in a crab-like claw! . . .

Orabona's smile was utterly damnable. Jones choked, and stared at the hideous exhibit with a mounting fascination which perplexed and disturbed him. What half-revealed horror was holding and forcing him to look longer and search out details? This had driven Rogers mad . . . . Rogers, supreme artist . . . said they weren't artificial. . . .

Then he localised the thing that held him. It was the crushed waxen victim's lolling head, and something that it implied. This head was not entirely devoid of a face, and that face was familiar. It was like the mad face of poor Rogers.

Jones peered closer, hardly knowing why he was driven to do so. Wasn't it natural for a mad egotist to mould his own features into his masterpiece? Was there anything more that subconscious vision had seized on and suppressed in sheer terror?

The wax of the mangled face had been handled with boundless dexterity. Those punctures—how perfectly they reproduced the myriad wounds somehow inflicted on that poor dog! But there was something more. On the left cheek one could trace an irregularity which seemed outside the general scheme—as if the sculptor had sought to cover up a defect of his first modelling. The more Jones looked at it, the more mysteriously it horrified him—and then, suddenly, he remembered a circumstance which brought his horror to a head. That night of hideousness—the tussle— the bound madman—*and the long, deep scratch down the left cheek of the actual living Rogers. . . .*

Jones, releasing his desperate clutch on the railing, sank in a total faint.

Orabona continued to smile.

Out of the Aeon

With Hazel Heald

(Ms. found among the effects of the late Richard H. Johnson, Ph.D., curator of the Cabot Museum of Archaeology, Boston, Mass.)

It is not likely that anyone in Boston—or any alert reader elsewhere—will ever forget the strange affair of the Cabot Museum. The newspaper publicity given to that hellish mummy, the antique and terrible rumours vaguely linked with it, the morbid wave of interest and cult activities during 1932, and the frightful fate of the two intruders on December 1st of that year, all combined to form one of those classic mysteries which go down for generations as folklore and become the nuclei of whole cycles of horrific speculation.

Everyone seems to realise, too, that something very vital and unutterably hideous was suppressed in the public accounts of the culminant horrors. Those first disquieting hints as to the *condition* of one of the two bodies were dismissed and ignored too abruptly—nor were the singular *modifications* in the mummy given the following-up which their news value would normally prompt. It also struck people as queer that the mummy was never restored to its case. In these days of expert taxidermy the excuse that its disintegrating condition made exhibition impracticable seemed a peculiarly lame one.

As curator of the museum I am in a position to reveal all the suppressed facts, but this I shall not do during my lifetime. There are things about the world and universe which it is better for the majority not to know, and I have not departed from the opinion in which all of us—museum staff, physicians, reporters, and police—concurred at the period of the horror itself. At the same time it seems proper that a matter of such overwhelming scientific and historic importance should not remain wholly unrecorded—hence this account which I have prepared for the benefit of serious students. I shall place it among various papers to be examined after my death, leaving its fate to the discretion of my executors. Certain threats and unusual events during the past weeks have led me to believe that my life—as well as that of other museum officials—is in some peril through the enmity of several widespread secret cults of Asiatics, Polynesians, and heterogeneous mystical devotees; hence it is possible that the work of the executors may not be long postponed. [Executor's note: Dr. Johnson died suddenly and rather mysteriously of heart-failure on April 22, 1933. Wentworth Moore, taxidermist of the museum, disappeared around the middle of the preceding month. On February 18 of the same year Dr. William Minot, who superintended a dissection connected with the case, was stabbed in the back, dying the following day.]

The real beginning of the horror, I suppose, was in 1879—long before my term as curator—when the museum acquired that ghastly, inexplicable mummy from the Orient Shipping Company. Its very discovery was monstrous and menacing, for it came from a crypt of unknown origin and fabulous antiquity on a bit of land suddenly upheaved from the Pacific's floor.

On May 11, 1878, Capt. Charles Weatherbee of the freighter *Eridanus,* bound from Wellington, New Zealand, to Valparaiso, Chile, had sighted a new island unmarked on any chart and evidently of volcanic origin. It projected quite boldly out of the sea in the form of a truncated cone. A landing-party under Capt. Weatherbee noted evidences of long submersion on the rugged slopes which they climbed, while at the summit there were signs of recent destruction, as by an earthquake. Among the scattered rubble were massive stones of manifestly artificial shaping, and a little examination disclosed the presence of some of that prehistoric Cyclopean masonry found on certain Pacific islands and forming a perpetual archaeological puzzle.

Finally the sailors entered a massive stone crypt— judged to have been part of a much larger edifice, and to have originally lain far underground—in one corner of which the frightful mummy crouched. After a short period of virtual panic, caused partly by certain carvings on the walls, the men were induced to move the mummy to the ship, though it was only with fear and loathing that they touched it. Close to the body, as if once thrust into its clothes, was a cylinder of an unknown metal containing a roll of thin, bluish-white membrane of equally unknown nature, inscribed with peculiar characters in a greyish, indeterminable pigment. In the centre of the vast stone floor was a suggestion of a trap-door, but the party lacked apparatus sufficiently powerful to move it.

The Cabot Museum, then newly established, saw the meagre reports of the discovery and at once took steps to acquire the mummy and the cylinder. Curator Pickman[1] made a personal trip to Valparaiso and outfitted a schooner to search for the crypt where the thing had been found, though meeting with failure in this matter. At the recorded position of the island nothing but the sea's unbroken expanse could be discerned, and the seekers realised that the same seismic forces which had suddenly thrust the island up had carried it down again to the watery darkness where it had brooded for untold aeons. The secret of that immovable trap-door would never be solved. The mummy and the cylinder, however, remained—and the former was placed on exhibition early in November, 1879, in the museum's hall of mummies.

The Cabot Museum of Archaeology, which specialises in such remnants of ancient and unknown civilisations as do not fall within the domain of art, is a small and scarcely famous institution, though one of high standing in scientific circles. It stands in the heart of Boston's exclusive Beacon Hill district—in Mt. Vernon Street, near Joy—housed in a former private mansion with an added wing in the rear, and was a source of pride to its austere neighbours until the recent terrible events brought it an undesirable notoriety.

The hall of mummies on the western side of the original mansion (which was designed by Bulfinch[2] and erected in 1819), on the second floor, is justly esteemed by historians and anthropologists as harbouring the greatest collection of its kind in America. Here may be found typical examples of Egyptian embalming from the earliest Sakkarah specimens to the last Coptic attempts of the eighth century;[3] mummies of other cultures, including the prehistoric Indian specimens recently found in the Aleutian Islands; agonised Pompeian figures moulded in plaster from tragic hollows in the ruin-choking ashes; naturally mummified bodies from mines and other excavations in all parts of the earth—some surprised by their terrible entombment in the grotesque postures caused by their last, tearing death-throes—everything, in short, which any collection of the sort could well be expected to contain. In 1879, of course, it was much less ample than it is now; yet even then it was remarkable. But that shocking thing from the primal Cyclopean crypt on an ephemeral sea-spawned island was always its chief attraction and most impenetrable mystery.

The mummy was that of a medium-sized man of unknown race, and was cast in a peculiar crouching posture. The face, half shielded by claw-like hands, had its under jaw thrust far forward, while the shrivelled features bore an expression of fright so hideous that few spectators could view them unmoved. The eyes were closed, with lids clamped down tightly over eyeballs apparently bulging and prominent. Bits of hair and beard remained, and the colour of the whole was a sort of dull neutral grey. In texture the thing was half leathery and half stony, forming an insoluble enigma to those experts who sought to ascertain how it was embalmed. In places bits of its substance were eaten away by time and decay. Rags of some peculiar fabric, with suggestions of unknown designs, still clung to the object.

Just what made it so infinitely horrible and repulsive one could hardly say. For one thing, there was a subtle, indefinable sense of limitless antiquity and utter alienage which affected one like a view from the brink of a monstrous abyss of unplumbed blackness—but mostly it was the expression of crazed fear on the puckered, prognathous, half-shielded face. Such a symbol of infinite, inhuman, cosmic fright could not help communicating the emotion to the beholder amidst a disquieting cloud of mystery and vain conjecture.

Among the discriminating few who frequented the

Cabot Museum this relic of an elder, forgotten world soon acquired an unholy fame, though the institution's seclusion and quiet policy prevented it from becoming a popular sensation of the "Cardiff Giant" sort.[4] In the last century the art of vulgar ballyhoo had not invaded the field of scholarship to the extent it has now succeeded in doing. Naturally, savants of various kinds tried their best to classify the frightful object, though always without success. Theories of a bygone Pacific civilisation, of which the Easter Island images and the megalithic masonry of Ponape and Nan-Matol[5] are conceivable vestiges, were freely circulated among students, and learned journals carried varied and often conflicting speculations on a possible former continent whose peaks survive as the myriad islands of Melanesia and Polynesia. The diversity in dates assigned to the hypothetical vanished culture—or continent—was at once bewildering and amusing; yet some surprisingly relevant allusions were found in certain myths of Tahiti and other islands.

Meanwhile the strange cylinder and its baffling scroll of unknown hieroglyphs, carefully preserved in the museum library, received their due share of attention. No question could exist as to their association with the mummy; hence all realised that in the unravelling of their mystery the mystery of the shrivelled horror would in all probability be unravelled as well. The cylinder, about four inches long by seven-eighths of an inch in diameter, was of a queerly iridescent metal utterly defying chemical analysis and seemingly impervious to all reagents. It was tightly fitted with a cap of the same substance, and bore engraved figurings of an evidently decorative and possibly symbolic nature— conventional designs which seemed to follow a peculiarly alien, paradoxical, and doubtfully describable system of geometry.

Not less mysterious was the scroll it contained—a neat roll of some thin, bluish-white, unanalysable membrane, coiled round a slim rod of metal like that of the cylinder, and unwinding to a length of some two feet. The large, bold hieroglyphs, extending in a narrow line down the centre of the scroll and penned or painted with a grey pigment defying analysis, resembled nothing known to linguists and palaeographers, and could not be deciphered despite the transmission of photographic copies to every living expert in the given field.

It is true that a few scholars, unusually versed in the literature of occultism and magic, found vague resemblances between some of the hieroglyphs and certain primal symbols described or cited in two or three very ancient, obscure, and esoteric texts such as the *Book of Eibon,* reputed to descend from forgotten Hyperborea; the Pnakotic fragments, alleged to be pre-human; and the monstrous and forbidden *Necronomicon* of the mad Arab Abdul Alhazred. None of these resemblances, however, was beyond dispute; and because of the prevailing low estimation of occult studies, no effort was made to circulate copies of the hieroglyphs among mystical specialists. Had such circulation occurred at this early date, the later history of the case might have been very different; indeed, a glance at the hieroglyphs by any reader of von Junzt's horrible *Nameless Cults* would have established a linkage of unmistakable significance. At this period, however, the readers of that monstrous blasphemy were exceedingly few; copies having been incredibly scarce in the interval between the suppression of the original Düsseldorf edition (1839) and of the Bridewell translation (1845) and the publication of the expurgated reprint by the Golden Goblin Press in 1909.[6] Practically speaking, no occultist or student of the primal past's esoteric lore had his attention called to the strange scroll until the recent outburst of sensational journalism which precipitated the horrible climax.

II

Thus matters glided along for a half-century following the installation of the frightful mummy at the museum. The gruesome object had a local celebrity among cultivated Bostonians, but no more than that; while the very existence of the cylinder and scroll—after a decade of futile research—was virtually forgotten. So quiet and conservative was the Cabot Museum that no reporter or feature writer ever thought of invading its uneventful precincts for rabble-tickling material.

The invasion of ballyhoo commenced in the spring of 1931, when a purchase of somewhat spectacular nature—that of the strange objects and inexplicably preserved bodies found in crypts beneath the almost vanished and evilly famous ruins of Château Faussesflammes, in Averoigne, France[7]—brought the museum prominently into the news columns. True to its "hustling" policy, the *Boston Pillar* sent a Sunday feature writer to cover the incident and pad it with an exaggerated general account of the institution itself; and this young man—Stuart Reynolds by name—hit upon the nameless mummy as a potential sensation far surpassing the recent acquisitions nominally forming his chief assignment. A smattering of theosophical lore, and a fondness for the speculations of such writers as Colonel Churchward and Lewis Spence[8] concerning lost continents and primal forgotten civilisations, made Reynolds especially alert toward any aeonian relic like the unknown mummy.

At the museum the reporter made himself a nuisance

through constant and not always intelligent questionings and endless demands for the movement of encased objects to permit photographs from unusual angles. In the basement library room he pored endlessly over the strange metal cylinder and its membraneous scroll, photographing them from every angle and securing pictures of every bit of the weird hieroglyphed text. He likewise asked to see all books with any bearing whatever on the subject of primal cultures and sunken continents—sitting for three hours taking notes, and leaving only in order to hasten to Cambridge for a sight (if permission were granted) of the abhorred and forbidden *Necronomicon* at the Widener Library.[9]

On April 5th the article appeared in the Sunday *Pillar,* smothered in photographs of mummy, cylinder, and hieroglyphed scroll, and couched in the peculiarly simpering, infantile style which the *Pillar* affects for the benefit of its vast and mentally immature clientele. Full of inaccuracies, exaggerations, and sensationalism, it was precisely the sort of thing to stir the brainless and fickle interest of the herd—and as a result the once quiet museum began to be swarmed with chattering and vacuously staring throngs such as its stately corridors had never known before.

There were scholarly and intelligent visitors, too, despite the puerility of the article—the pictures had spoken for themselves—and many persons of mature attainments sometimes see the *Pillar* by accident. I recall one very strange character who appeared during November—a dark, turbaned, and bushily bearded man with a laboured, unnatural voice, curiously expressionless face, clumsy hands covered with absurd white mittens, who gave a squalid West End address and called himself "Swami Chandraputra".[10] This fellow was unbelievably erudite in occult lore and seemed profoundly and solemnly moved by the resemblance of the hieroglyphs on the scroll to certain signs and symbols of a forgotten elder world about which he professed vast intuitive knowledge.

By June, the fame of the mummy and scroll had leaked far beyond Boston, and the museum had inquiries and requests for photographs from occultists and students of arcana all over the world. This was not altogether pleasing to our staff, since we are a scientific institution without sympathy for fantastic dreamers; yet we answered all questions with civility. One result of these catechisms was a highly learned article in *The Occult Review* by the famous New Orleans mystic Etienne-Laurent de Marigny,[11] in which was asserted the complete identity of some of the odd geometrical designs on the iridescent cylinder, and of several of the hieroglyphs on the membraneous scroll, with certain ideographs of horrible significance (transcribed from primal monoliths or from the secret rituals of hidden bands of esoteric students and devotees) reproduced in the hellish and suppressed *Black Book* or *Nameless Cults* of von Junzt.

De Marigny recalled the frightful death of von Junzt in 1840, a year after the publication of his terrible volume at Düsseldorf, and commented on his blood-curdling and partly suspected sources of information. Above all, he emphasised the enormous relevance of the tales with which von Junzt linked most of the monstrous ideographs he had reproduced. That these tales, in which a cylinder and scroll were expressly mentioned, held a remarkable suggestion of relationship to the things at the museum, no one could deny; yet they were of such breath-taking extravagance—involving such unbelievable sweeps of time and such fantastic anomalies of a forgotten elder world—that one could much more easily admire than believe them.

Admire them the public certainly did, for copying in the press was universal. Illustrated articles sprang up everywhere, telling or purporting to tell the legends in the *Black Book,* expatiating on the horror of the mummy, comparing the cylinder's designs and the scroll's hieroglyphs with the figures reproduced by von Junzt, and indulging in the wildest, most sensational, and most irrational theories and speculations. Attendance at the museum was trebled, and the widespread nature of the interest was attested by the plethora of mail on the subject—most of it inane and superfluous—received at the museum. Apparently the mummy and its origin formed—for imaginative people—a close rival to the depression as chief topic of 1931 and 1932. For my own part, the principal effect of the furore was to make me read von Junzt's monstrous volume in the Golden Goblin edition—a perusal which left me dizzy and nauseated, yet thankful that I had not seen the utter infamy of the unexpurgated text.

III

The archaic whispers reflected in the *Black Book,* and linked with designs and symbols so closely akin to what the mysterious scroll and cylinder bore, were indeed of a character to hold one spellbound and not a little awestruck. Leaping an incredible gulf of time—behind all the civilisations, races, and lands we know—they clustered round a vanished nation and a vanished continent of the misty, fabulous dawn-years . . . that to which legend has given the name of Mu, and which old tablets in the primal Naacal tongue speak of as flourishing 200,000 years ago,[12] when Europe harboured only hybrid entities, and lost Hyperborea knew the nameless worship of black amorphous

Tsathoggua.

There was mention of a kingdom or province called K'naa in a very ancient land where the first human people had found monstrous ruins left by those who had dwelt there before—vague waves of unknown entities which had filtered down from the stars and lived out their aeons on a forgotten, nascent world. K'naa was a sacred place, since from its midst the bleak basalt cliffs of Mount Yaddith-Gho[13] soared starkly into the sky, topped by a gigantic fortress of Cyclopean stone, infinitely older than mankind and built by the alien spawn of the dark planet Yuggoth, which had colonised the earth before the birth of terrestrial life.

The spawn of Yuggoth had perished aeons before, but had left behind them one monstrous and terrible living thing which could never die—their hellish god or patron daemon Ghatanothoa, which lowered and brooded eternally though unseen in the crypts beneath that fortress on Yaddith-Gho. No human creature had ever climbed Yaddith-Gho or seen that blasphemous fortress except as a distant and geometrically abnormal outline against the sky; yet most agreed that Ghatanothoa was still there, wallowing and burrowing in unsuspected abysses beneath the megalithic walls. There were always those who believed that sacrifices must be made to Ghatanothoa, lest it crawl out of its hidden abysses and waddle horribly through the world of men as it had once waddled through the primal world of the Yuggoth-spawn.

People said that if no victims were offered, Ghatanothoa would ooze up to the light of day and lumber down the basalt cliffs of Yaddith-Gho bringing doom to all it might encounter. For no living thing could behold Ghatanothoa, or even a perfect graven image of Ghatanothoa, however small, without suffering a change more horrible than death itself. Sight of the god, or its image, as all the legends of the Yuggoth-spawn agreed, meant paralysis and petrifaction of a singularly shocking sort, in which the victim was turned to stone and leather on the outside, while the brain within remained perpetually alive—horribly fixed and prisoned through the ages, and maddeningly conscious of the passage of interminable epochs of helpless inaction till chance and time might complete the decay of the petrified shell and leave it exposed to die. Most brains, of course, would go mad long before this aeon-deferred release could arrive. No human eyes, it was said, had ever glimpsed Ghatanothoa, though the danger was as great now as it had been for the Yuggoth-spawn.

And so there was a cult in K'naa which worshipped Ghatanothoa and each year sacrificed to it twelve young warriors and twelve young maidens. These victims were offered up on flaming altars in the marble temple near the mountain's base, for none dared climb Yaddith-Gho's basalt cliffs or draw near to the Cyclopean pre-human stronghold on its crest. Vast was the power of the priests of Ghatanothoa, since upon them alone depended the preservation of K'naa and of all the land of Mu from the petrifying emergence of Ghatanothoa out of its unknown burrows.

There were in the land a hundred priests of the Dark God, under Imash-Mo the High-Priest, who walked before King Thabon at the Nath-feast, and stood proudly whilst the King knelt at the Dhoric shrine. Each priest had a marble house, a chest of gold, two hundred slaves, and a hundred concubines, besides immunity from civil law and the power of life and death over all in K'naa save the priests of the King. Yet in spite of these defenders there was ever a fear in the land lest Ghatanothoa slither up from the depths and lurch viciously down the mountain to bring horror and petrification to mankind. In the latter years the priests forbade men even to guess or imagine what its frightful aspect might be.

It was in the Year of the Red Moon (estimated as B. C. 173,148 by von Junzt) that a human being first dared to breathe defiance against Ghatanothoa and its nameless menace. This bold heretic was T'yog, High-Priest of Shub-Niggurath and guardian of the copper temple of the Goat with a Thousand Young. T'yog had thought long on the powers of the various gods, and had had strange dreams and revelations touching the life of this and earlier worlds. In the end he felt sure that the gods friendly to man could be arrayed against the hostile gods, and believed that Shub-Niggurath, Nug, and Yeb, as well as Yig the Serpent-god,[14] were ready to take sides with man against the tyranny and presumption of Ghatanothoa.

Inspired by the Mother Goddess, T'yog wrote down a strange formula in the hieratic Naacal of his order, which he believed would keep the possessor immune from the Dark God's petrifying power. With this protection, he reflected, it might be possible for a bold man to climb the dreaded basalt cliffs and—first of all human beings—enter the Cyclopean fortress beneath which Ghatanothoa reputedly brooded. Face to face with the god, and with the power of Shub-Niggurath and her sons on his side, T'yog believed that he might be able to bring it to terms and at last deliver mankind from its brooding menace. With humanity freed through his efforts, there would be no limits to the honours he might claim. All the honours of the priests of Ghatanothoa would perforce be transferred to him; and even kingship or godhood might conceivably be within his reach.

So T'yog wrote his protective formula on a scroll of

pthagon membrane (according to von Junzt, the inner skin of the extinct yakith-lizard) and enclosed it in a carven cylinder of *lagh* metal—the metal brought by the Elder Ones from Yuggoth,[15] and found in no mine of earth. This charm, carried in his robe, would make him proof against the menace of Ghatanothoa—it would even restore the Dark God's petrified victims if that monstrous entity should ever emerge and begin its devastations. Thus he proposed to go up the shunned and man-untrodden mountain, invade the alien-angled citadel of Cyclopean stone, and confront the shocking devil-entity in its lair. Of what would follow, he could not even guess; but the hope of being mankind's saviour lent strength to his will.

He had, however, reckoned without the jealousy and self-interest of Ghatanothoa's pampered priests. No sooner did they hear of his plan than—fearful for their prestige and privilege in case the Daemon-God should be dethroned—they set up a frantic clamour against the so-called sacrilege, crying that no man might prevail against Ghatanothoa, and that any effort to seek it out would merely provoke it to a hellish onslaught against mankind which no spell or priestcraft could hope to avert. With those cries they hoped to turn the public mind against T'yog; yet such was the people's yearning for freedom from Ghatanothoa, and such their confidence in the skill and zeal of T'yog, that all the protestations came to naught. Even the King, usually a puppet of the priests, refused to forbid T'yog's daring pilgrimage.

It was then that the priests of Ghatanothoa did by stealth what they could not do openly. One night Imash-Mo, the High-Priest, stole to T'yog in his temple chamber and took from his sleeping form the metal cylinder; silently drawing out the potent scroll and putting in its place another scroll of great similitude, yet varied enough to have no power against any god or daemon. When the cylinder was slipped back into the sleeper's cloak Imash-Mo was content, for he knew T'yog was little likely to study that cylinder's contents again. Thinking himself protected by the true scroll, the heretic would march up the forbidden mountain and into the Evil Presence—and Ghatanothoa, unchecked by any magic, would take care of the rest.

It would no longer be needful for Ghatanothoa's priests to preach against the defiance. Let T'yog go his way and meet his doom. And secretly, the priests would always cherish the stolen scroll—the true and potent charm—handing it down from one High-Priest to another for use in any dim future when it might be needful to contravene the Devil-God's will. So the rest of the night Imash-Mo slept in great peace, with the true scroll in a new cylinder fashioned for its harbourage.

It was dawn on the Day of the Sky-Flames (nomenclature undefined by von Junzt) that T'yog, amidst the prayers and chanting of the people and with King Thabon's blessing on his head, started up the dreaded mountain with a staff of tlath-wood in his right hand. Within his robe was the cylinder holding what he thought to be the true charm—for he had indeed failed to find out the imposture. Nor did he see any irony in the prayers which Imash-Mo and the other priests of Ghatanothoa intoned for his safety and success.

All that morning the people stood and watched as T'yog's dwindling form struggled up the shunned basalt slope hitherto alien to men's footsteps, and many stayed watching long after he had vanished where a perilous ledge led round to the mountain's hidden side. That night a few sensitive dreamers thought they heard a faint tremor con-

vulsing the hated peak; though most ridiculed them for
the statement. Next day vast crowds watched the mountain
and prayed, and wondered how soon T'yog would return.
And so the next day, and the next. For weeks they hoped
and waited, and then they wept. Nor did anyone ever see
T'yog, who would have saved mankind from fears, again.

Thereafter men shuddered at T'yog's presumption,
and tried not to think of the punishment his impiety had
met. And the priests of Ghatanothoa smiled to those who
might resent the god's will or challenge its right to the sacrifices. In later years the ruse of Imash-Mo became known
to the people; yet the knowledge availed not to change the
general feeling that Ghatanothoa were better left alone.
None ever dared to defy it again. And so the ages rolled
on, and King succeeded King, and High-Priest succeeded
High-Priest, and nations rose and decayed, and lands rose
above the sea and returned into the sea. And with many
millennia decay fell upon K'naa—till at last on a hideous
day of storm and thunder, terrific rumbling, and mountain-
high waves, all the land of Mu sank into the sea forever.

Yet down the later aeons thin streams of ancient secrets trickled. In distant lands there met together grey-faced
fugitives who had survived the sea-fiend's rage, and strange
skies drank the smoke of altars reared to vanished gods and
daemons. Though none knew to what bottomless deep
the sacred peak and Cyclopean fortress of dreaded Ghatanothoa had sunk, there were still those who mumbled its
name and offered to it nameless sacrifices lest it bubble up
through leagues of ocean and shamble among men spreading horror and petrifaction.

Around the scattered priests grew the rudiments of a
dark and secret cult—secret because the people of the new
lands had other gods and devils, and thought only evil of

elder and alien ones—and within that cult many hideous things were done, and many strange objects cherished. It was whispered that a certain line of elusive priests still harboured the true charm against Ghatanothoa which Imash-Mo stole from the sleeping T'yog; though none remained who could read or understand the cryptic syllables, or who could even guess in what part of the world the lost K'naa, the dreaded peak of Yaddith-Gho, and the titan fortress of the Devil-God had lain.

Though it flourished chiefly in those Pacific regions around which Mu itself had once stretched, there were rumours of the hidden and detested cult of Ghatanothoa in ill-fated Atlantis, and on the abhorred plateau of Leng. Von Junzt implied its presence in the fabled subterrene kingdom of K'n-yan, and gave clear evidence that it had penetrated Egypt, Chaldaea, Persia, China, the forgotten Semite empires of Africa, and Mexico and Peru in the New World. That it had a strong connexion with the witchcraft movement in Europe, against which the bulls of popes were vainly directed, he more than strongly hinted. The West, however, was never favourable to its growth; and public indignation—aroused by glimpses of hideous rites and nameless sacrifices—wholly stamped out many of its branches. In the end it became a hunted, doubly furtive underground affair—yet never could its nucleus be quite exterminated. It always survived somehow, chiefly in the Far East and on the Pacific Islands, where its teachings became merged into the esoteric lore of the Polynesian *Areoi*.[16]

Von Junzt gave subtle and disquieting hints of actual contact with the cult; so that as I read I shuddered at what was rumoured about his death. He spoke of the growth of certain ideas regarding the appearance of the Devil-God— a creature which no human being (unless it were the too-daring T'yog, who had never returned) had ever seen—and contrasted this habit of speculation with the taboo prevailing in ancient Mu against any attempt to imagine what the horror looked like. There was a peculiar fearfulness about the devotees' awed and fascinated whispers on this subject—whispers heavy with morbid curiosity concerning the precise nature of what T'yog might have confronted in that frightful pre-human edifice on the dreaded and now-sunken mountains before the end (if it was an end) finally came—and I felt oddly disturbed by the German scholar's oblique and insidious references to this topic.

Scarcely less disturbing were von Junzt's conjectures on the whereabouts of the stolen scroll of cantrips against Ghatanothoa, and on the ultimate uses to which this scroll might be put. Despite all my assurance that the whole matter was purely mythical, I could not help shivering at the notion of a latter-day emergence of the monstrous god, and at the picture of an humanity turned suddenly to a race of abnormal statues, each encasing a living brain doomed to inert and helpless consciousness for untold aeons of futurity. The old Düsseldorf savant had a poisonous way of suggesting more than he stated, and I could understand why his damnable book was suppressed in so many countries as blasphemous, dangerous, and unclean.

I writhed with repulsion, yet the thing exerted an unholy fascination; and I could not lay it down till I had finished it. The alleged reproductions of designs and ideographs from Mu were marvellously and startlingly like the markings on the strange cylinder and the characters on the scroll, and the whole account teemed with details having vague, irritating suggestions of resemblance to things connected with the hideous mummy. The cylinder and scroll—the Pacific setting—the persistent notion of old Capt.

Weatherbee that the Cyclopean crypt where the mummy was found had once lain under a vast building . . . somehow I was vaguely glad that the volcanic island had sunk before that massive suggestion of a trap-door could be opened.

IV

What I read in the *Black Book* formed a fiendishly apt preparation for the news items and closer events which began to force themselves upon me in the spring of 1932. I can scarcely recall just when the increasingly frequent reports of police action against the odd and fantastical religious cults in the Orient and elsewhere commenced to impress me; but by May or June I realised that there was, all over the world, a surprising and unwonted burst of activity on the part of bizarre, furtive, and esoteric mystical organisations ordinarily quiescent and seldom heard from.

It is not likely that I would have connected these reports with either the hints of von Junzt or the popular furore over the mummy and cylinder in the museum, but for certain significant syllables and persistent resemblances—sensationally dwelt upon by the press—in the rites and speeches of the various secret celebrants brought to public attention. As it was, I could not help remarking with disquiet the frequent recurrence of a name—in various corrupt forms—which seemed to constitute a focal point of all the cult worship, and which was obviously regarded with a singular mixture of reverence and terror. Some of the forms quoted were G'tanta, Tanotah, Than-Tha, Gatan, and Ktan-Tah—and it did not require the suggestions of my now numerous occultist correspondents to make me see in these variants a hideous and suggestive kinship to the monstrous name rendered by von Junzt as Ghatanothoa.

There were other disquieting features, too. Again and again the reports cited vague, awestruck references to a "true scroll"—something on which tremendous consequences seemed to hinge, and which was mentioned as being in the custody of a certain "Nagob", whoever and whatever he might be. Likewise, there was an insistent repetition of a name which sounded like Tog, Tiok, Yog, Zob, or Yob, and which my more and more excited consciousness involuntarily linked with the name of the hapless heretic T'yog as given in the *Black Book*. This name was usually uttered in connexion with such cryptical phrases as "It is none other than he", "He had looked upon its face", "He knows all, though he can neither see nor feel", "He has brought the memory down through the aeons", "The true scroll will release him", "Nagob has the true scroll", "He can tell where to find it".

Something very queer was undoubtedly in the air, and I did not wonder when my occultist correspondents, as well as the sensational Sunday papers, began to connect the new abnormal stirrings with the legends of Mu on the one hand, and with the frightful mummy's recent exploitation on the other hand. The widespread articles in the first wave of press publicity, with their insistent linkage of the mummy, cylinder, and scroll with the tale in the *Black Book,* and their crazily fantastic speculations about the whole matter, might very well have roused the latent fanaticism in hundreds of those furtive groups of exotic devotees with which our complex world abounds. Nor did the papers cease adding fuel to the flames—for the stories on the cult-stirrings were even wilder than the earlier series of yarns.

As the summer drew on, attendants noticed a curious new element among the throngs of visitors which—after a lull following the first burst of publicity—were again drawn to the museum by the second furore. More and more frequently there were persons of strange and exotic aspect—swarthy Asiatics, long-haired nondescripts, and bearded brown men who seemed unused to European clothes—who would invariably inquire for the hall of mummies and would subsequently be found staring at the hideous Pacific specimen in a veritable ecstasy of fascination. Some quiet, sinister undercurrent in this flood of eccentric foreigners seemed to impress all the guards, and I myself was far from undisturbed. I could not help thinking of the prevailing cult-stirrings among just such exotics as these—and the connexion of those stirrings with myths all too close to the frightful mummy and its cylinder scroll.

At times I was half tempted to withdraw the mummy from exhibition—especially when an attendant told me that he had several times glimpsed strangers making odd obeisances before it, and had overheard sing-song mutterings which sounded like chants or rituals addressed to it at hours when the visiting throngs were somewhat thinned. One of the guards acquired a queer nervous hallucination about the petrified horror in the lone glass case, alleging that he could see from day to day certain vague, subtle, and infinitely slight changes in the frantic flexion of the bony claws, and in the fear-crazed expression of the leathery face. He could not get rid of the loathsome idea that those horrible, bulging eyes were about to pop suddenly open.

It was early in September, when the curious crowds had lessened and the hall of mummies was sometimes vacant, that the attempt to get at the mummy by cutting the glass of its case was made. The culprit, a swarthy Polynesian, was spied in time by a guard, and was overpowered before any damage occurred. Upon investigation the fellow turned out to be an Hawaiian notorious for his activity in certain underground religious cults, and having a considerable police record in connexion with abnormal and inhuman rites and sacrifices. Some of the papers found in his room were highly puzzling and disturbing, including many sheets covered with hieroglyphs closely resembling those on the scroll at the museum and in the *Black Book* of von Junzt; but regarding these things he could not be prevailed upon to speak.

Scarcely a week after this incident, another attempt to get at the mummy—this time by tampering with the lock of his case—resulted in a second arrest. The offender, a Cingalese, had as long and unsavoury a record of loathsome cult activities as the Hawaiian had possessed, and displayed a kindred unwillingness to talk to the police. What made this case doubly and darkly interesting was that a guard had noticed this man several times before, and had heard him addressing to the mummy a peculiar chant containing unmistakable repetitions of the word "T'yog". As a result of this affair I doubled the guards in the hall of mummies, and ordered them never to leave the now notorious specimen out of sight, even for a moment.

As may well be imagined, the press made much of these two incidents, reviewing its talk of primal and fabulous Mu, and claiming boldly that the hideous mummy was none other than the daring heretic T'yog, petrified by something he had seen in the pre-human citadel he had invaded, and preserved intact through 175,000 years of our planet's turbulent history. That the strange devotees represented cults descended from Mu, and that they were worshipping the mummy—or perhaps even seeking to awaken it to life by spells and incantations—was emphasised and reiterated in the most sensational fashion.

Writers exploited the insistence of the old legends

that the *brain* of Ghatanothoa's petrified victims remained conscious and unaffected—a point which served as a basis for the wildest and most improbable speculations. The mention of a "true scroll" also received due attention—it being the prevailing popular theory that T'yog's stolen charm against Ghatanothoa was somewhere in existence, and that cult-members were trying to bring it into contact with T'yog himself for some purpose of their own. One result of this exploitation was that a third wave of gaping visitors began flooding the museum and staring at the hellish mummy which served as a nucleus for the whole strange and disturbing affair.

It was among this wave of spectators—many of whom made repeated visits—that talk of the mummy's vaguely changing aspect first began to be widespread. I suppose—despite the disturbing notion of the nervous guard some months before—that the museum's personnel was too well used to the constant sight of odd shapes to pay close attention to details; in any case, it was the excited whispers of visitors which at length aroused the guards to the subtle mutation which was apparently in progress. Almost simultaneously the press got hold of it—with blatant results which can well be imagined.

Naturally, I gave the matter my most careful observation, and by the middle of October decided that a definite disintegration of the mummy was under way. Through some chemical or physical influence in the air, the half-stony, half-leathery fibres seemed to be gradually relaxing, causing distinct variations in the angles of the limbs and in certain details of the fear-twisted facial expression. After a half-century of perfect preservation this was a highly disconcerting development, and I had the museum's taxidermist, Dr. Moore, go carefully over the gruesome object several times. He reported a general relaxation and softening, and gave the thing two or three astringent sprayings, but did not dare to attempt anything drastic lest there be a sudden crumbling and accelerated decay.

The effect of all this upon the gaping crowds was curious. Heretofore each new sensation sprung by the press had brought fresh waves of staring and whispering visitors, but now—though the papers blathered endlessly about the mummy's changes—the public seemed to have acquired a definite sense of fear which outranked even its morbid curiosity. People seemed to feel that a sinister aura hovered over the museum, and from a high peak the attendance fell to a level distinctly below normal. This lessened attendance gave added prominence to the stream of freakish foreigners who continued to infest the place, and whose numbers seemed in no way diminished.

On November 18th a Peruvian of Indian blood suffered a strange hysterical or epileptic seizure in front of the mummy, afterward shrieking from his hospital cot, "It tried to open its eyes!—T'yog tried to open his eyes and stare at me!" I was by this time on the point of removing the object from exhibition, but permitted myself to be overruled at a meeting of our very conservative directors. However, I could see that the museum was beginning to acquire an unholy reputation in its austere and quiet neighbourhood. After this incident I gave instructions that no one be allowed to pause before the monstrous Pacific relic for more than a few minutes at a time.

It was on November 24th, after the museum's five o'clock closing, that one of the guards noticed a minute opening of the mummy's eyes. The phenomenon was very slight—nothing but a thin crescent of cornea being visible in either eye—but it was none the less of the highest interest. Dr. Moore, having been summoned hastily, was about to study the exposed bits of eyeball with a magnifier when his handling of the mummy caused the leathery lids to fall tightly shut again. All gentle efforts to open them failed, and the taxidermist did not dare to apply drastic measures. When he notified me of all this by telephone I felt a sense of mounting dread hard to reconcile with the apparently simple event concerned. For a moment I could share the popular impression that some evil, amorphous blight from unplumbed deeps of time and space hung murkily and menacingly over the museum.

Two nights later a sullen Filipino was trying to secrete himself in the museum at closing time. Arrested and taken to the station, he refused even to give his name, and was detained as a suspicious person. Meanwhile the strict surveillance of the mummy seemed to discourage the odd hordes of foreigners from haunting it. At least, the number of exotic visitors distinctly fell off after the enforcement of the "move along" order.

It was during the early morning hours of Thursday, December 1st, that a terrible climax developed. At about one o'clock horrible screams of mortal fright and agony were heard issuing from the museum, and a series of frantic telephone calls from neighbours brought to the scene quickly and simultaneously a squad of police and several museum officials, including myself. Some of the policemen surrounded the building while others, with the officials, cautiously entered. In the main corridor we found the night watchman strangled to death—a bit of East Indian hemp still knotted around his neck—and realised that despite all precautions some darkly evil intruder or intruders had gained access to the place. Now, however, a tomb-like silence enfolded everything and we almost feared to advance upstairs to the fateful wing where we knew the core of the trouble must lurk. We felt a bit more steadied after flooding the building with light from the central switches in the corridor, and finally crept reluctantly up the curving staircase and through a lofty archway to the hall of mummies.

V

It is from this point onward that reports of the hideous case have been censored—for we have all agreed that no good can be accomplished by a public knowledge of those terrestrial conditions implied by the further developments. I have said that we flooded the whole building with light before our ascent. Now beneath the beams that beat down on the glistening cases and their gruesome contents, we saw outspread a mute horror whose baffling details testified to happenings utterly beyond our comprehension. There were two intruders—who we afterward agreed must have hidden in the building before closing time—but they would never be executed for the watchman's murder. They had already paid the penalty.

One was a Burmese and the other a Fiji-lslander—both known to the police for their share in frightful and repulsive cult activities. They were dead, and the more we examined them the more utterly monstrous and unnamable we felt their manner of death to be. On both faces was a more wholly frantic and inhuman look of fright than even the oldest policeman had ever seen before; yet in the state of the two bodies there were vast and significant differences.

The Burmese lay collapsed close to the nameless mummy's case, from which a square of glass had been neatly cut.

212

In his right hand was a scroll of bluish membrane which I at once saw was covered with greyish hieroglyphs—almost a duplicate of the scroll in the strange cylinder in the library downstairs, though later study brought out subtle differences. There was no mark of violence on the body, and in view of the desperate, agonised expression on the twisted face we could only conclude that the man died of sheer fright.

It was the closely adjacent Fijian, though, that gave us the profoundest shock. One of the policemen was the first to feel of him, and the cry of fright he emitted added another shudder to that neighbourhood's night of terror. We ought to have known from the lethal greyness of the once-black, fear-twisted face, and of the bony hands—one of which still clutched an electric torch—that something was hideously wrong; yet every one of us was unprepared for what that officer's hesitant touch disclosed. Even now I can think of it only with a paroxysm of dread and repulsion. To be brief—the hapless invader, who less than an hour before had been a sturdy living Melanesian bent on unknown evils, was now a rigid, ash-grey figure of stony, leathery petrification, in every respect identical with the crouching, aeon-old blasphemy in the violated glass case.

Yet that was not the worst. Crowning all other horrors, and indeed seizing our shocked attention before we turned to the bodies on the floor, was the state of the frightful mummy. No longer could its changes be called vague and subtle, for it had now made radical shifts of posture. It had sagged and slumped with a curious loss of rigidity; its bony claws had sunk until they no longer even partly covered its leathery, fear-crazed face; and—God help us!—*its hellish bulging eyes had popped wide open, and seemed to be staring directly at the two intruders who had died of fright or worse.*

That ghastly, dead-fish stare was hideously mesmerising, and it haunted us all the time we were examining the bodies of the invaders. Its effect on our nerves was damnably queer, for we somehow felt a curious rigidity creeping over us and hampering our simplest motions—a rigidity which later vanished very oddly when we passed the hieroglyphed scroll around for inspection. Every now and then I felt my gaze drawn irresistibly toward those horrible bulging eyes in the case, and when I returned to study them after viewing the bodies I thought I detected something very singular about the glassy surface of the dark and marvellously well-preserved pupils. The more I looked, the more fascinated I became; and at last I went down to the office—despite that strange stiffness in my limbs—and brought up a strong multiple magnifying glass. With this I commenced a very close and careful survey of the fishy pupils, while the others crowded expectantly around.

I had always been rather sceptical of the theory that scenes and objects become photographed on the retina of the eye in cases of death or coma; yet no sooner did I look through the lens than I realised the presence of some sort of image other than the room's reflection in the glassy, bulging optics of this nameless spawn of the aeons. Certainly, there was a dimly outlined scene on the age-old retinal surface, and I could not doubt that it formed the last thing on which those eyes had looked in life—countless millennia ago. It seemed to be steadily fading, and I fumbled with the magnifier in order to shift another lens into place. Yet it must have been accurate and clear-cut, even if infinitesimally small, when—in response to some evil spell or act connected with their visit—it had confronted those intruders who were frightened to death. With the extra lens I could make out many details formerly invisible, and the awed group around me hung on the flood of words with which I tried to tell what I saw.

For here, in the year 1932, a man in the city of Boston was looking on something which belonged to an unknown and utterly alien world—a world that vanished from existence and normal memory aeons ago. There was a vast room—a chamber of Cyclopean masonry—and I seemed to be viewing it from one of its corners. On the walls were carvings so hideous that even in this imperfect image their stark blasphemousness and bestiality sickened me. I could not believe that the carvers of these things were human, or that they had ever seen human beings when they shaped the frightful outlines which leered at the beholder. In the centre of the chamber was a colossal trap-door of stone, pushed upward to permit the emergence of some object from below. The object should have been clearly visible—indeed, must have been when the eyes first opened before the fear-stricken intruders—though under my lenses it was merely a monstrous blur.

As it happened, I was studying the right eye only when I brought the extra magnification into play. A moment later I wished fervently that my search had ended there. As it was, however, the zeal of discovery and revelation was upon me, and I shifted my powerful lenses to the mummy's left eye in the hope of finding the image less faded on that retina. My hands, trembling with excitement and unnaturally stiff from some obscure influence, were slow in bringing the magnifier into focus, but a moment later I realised that the image was less faded than in the other eye. I saw in a morbid flash of half-distinctness the insufferable thing which was welling up through the prodigious trap-door in that Cyclopean, immemorially archaic crypt of a lost world—and fell fainting with an inarticulate shriek of which I am not even ashamed.

By the time I revived there was no distinct image of anything in either eye of the monstrous mummy. Sergeant Keefe of the police looked with my glass, for I could not bring myself to face that abnormal entity again. And I thanked all the powers of the cosmos that I had not looked earlier than I did. It took all my resolution, and a great deal of solicitation, to make me relate what I had glimpsed in the hideous moment of revelation. Indeed, I could not speak till we had all adjourned to the office below, out of sight of that daemoniac thing which could not be. For I had begun to harbour the most terrible and fantastic notions about the mummy and its glassy, bulging eyes—that it had a kind of hellish consciousness, seeing all that occurred before it and trying vainly to communicate some frightful message from the gulfs of time. That meant madness—but at last I thought I might be better off if I told what I had half seen.

After all, it was not a long thing to tell. Oozing and surging up out of that yawning trap-door in the Cyclopean crypt I had glimpsed such an unbelievable behemothic monstrosity that I could not doubt the power of its original to kill with its mere sight. Even now I cannot begin to suggest it with any words at my command. I might call it gigantic—tentacled—proboscidian—octopus-eyed—semi-amorphous—plastic—partly squamous and partly rugose—ugh! But nothing I could say could even adumbrate the loathsome, unholy, non-human, extra-galactic horror and hatefulness and unutterable evil of that forbidden spawn of black chaos and illimitable night. As I write these words the associated mental image causes me to lean back faint and nauseated. As I told of the sight to the men around me in the office, I had to fight to preserve the consciousness I had regained.

Nor were my hearers much less moved. Not a man spoke above a whisper for a full quarter-hour, and there were awed, half-furtive references to the frightful lore in the *Black Book,* to the recent newspaper tales of cult-stirrings, and to the sinister events in the museum. Ghatanothoa . . . Even its smallest perfect image could petrify—T'yog— the false scroll—he never came back—the true scroll which could fully or partly undo the petrification—did it survive?—the hellish cults—the phrases overheard—"It is none other than he"—"He had looked upon its face"— "He knows all, though he can neither see nor feel"—"He had brought the memory down through the aeons"—"The true scroll will release him"—"Nagob has the true scroll"— "He can tell where to find it." Only the healing greyness of the dawn brought us back to sanity; a sanity which made of that glimpse of mine a closed topic—something not to be explained or thought of again.

We gave out only partial reports to the press, and later on coöperated with the papers in making other suppressions. For example, when the autopsy shewed the brain and several other internal organs of the petrified Fijian to be fresh and unpetrified, though hermetically sealed by the petrification of the exterior flesh—an anomaly about which physicians are still guardedly and bewilderedly debating—we did not wish a furore to be started. We knew too well what the yellow journals, remembering what was said of the intact-brained and still-conscious state of Ghatanothoa's stony-leathery victims, would make of this detail.

As matters stood, they pointed out that the man who had held the hieroglyphed scroll—and who had evidently thrust it at the mummy through the opening in the case— was not petrified, while the man who had *not* held it was. When they demanded that we make certain experiments—

applying the scroll both to the stony-leathery body of the Fijian and to the mummy itself—we indignantly refused to abet such superstitious notions. Of course, the mummy was withdrawn from public view and transferred to the museum laboratory awaiting a really scientific examination before some suitable medical authority. Remembering past events, we kept it under a strict guard; but even so, an attempt was made to enter the museum at 2:25 a.m. on December 5th. Prompt working of the burglar alarm frustrated the design, though unfortunately the criminal or criminals escaped.

That no hint of anything further ever reached the public, I am profoundly thankful. I wish devoutly that there were nothing more to tell. There will, of course, be leaks, and if anything happens to me I do not know what my executors will do with this manuscript;[17] but at least the case will not be painfully fresh in the multitude's memory when the revelation comes. Besides, no one will believe the facts when they are finally told. That is the curious thing about the multitude. When their yellow press makes hints, they are ready to swallow anything; but when a stupendous and abnormal revelation is actually made, they laugh it aside as a lie. For the sake of general sanity it is probably better so.

I have said that a scientific examination of the frightful mummy was planned. This took place on December 8th, exactly a week after the hideous culmination of events, and was conducted by the eminent Dr. William Minot, in conjunction with Wentworth Moore, Sc.D., taxidermist of the museum. Dr. Minot had witnessed the autopsy of the oddly petrified Fijian the week before. There were also present Messrs. Lawrence Cabot and Dudley Saltonstall[18] of the museum's trustees, Drs. Mason, Wells, and Carver of the museum staff, two representatives of the press, and myself. During the week the condition of the hideous speci-men had not visibly changed, though some relaxation of its fibres caused the position of the glassy, open eyes to shift slightly from time to time. All of the staff dreaded to look at the thing—for its suggestion of quiet, conscious watch-ing had become intolerable—and it was only with an effort that I could bring myself to attend the examination.

Dr. Minot arrived shortly after 1:00 p.m., and within a few minutes began his survey of the mummy. Consider-able disintegration took place under his hands, and in view of this—and of what we told him concerning the gradual relaxation of the specimen since the first of October—he decided that a thorough dissection ought to be made be-fore the substance was further impaired. The proper instru-ments being present in the laboratory equipment, he began at once; exclaiming aloud at the odd, fibrous nature of the grey, mummified substance.

But his exclamation was still louder when he made the first deep incision, for out of that cut there slowly trickled a thick crimson stream whose nature—despite the infinite ages dividing this hellish mummy's lifetime from the pres-ent—was utterly unmistakable. A few more deft strokes revealed various organs in astonishing degrees of non-pet-rified preservation—all, indeed, being intact except where injuries to the petrified exterior had brought about malfor-mation or destruction. The resemblance of this condition to that found in the fright-killed Fiji-lslander was so strong that the eminent physician gasped in bewilderment. The perfection of those ghastly bulging eyes was uncanny, and their exact state with respect to petrification was very dif-ficult to determine.

At 3:30 p.m. the brain-case was opened—and ten minutes later our stunned group took an oath of secrecy which only such guarded documents as this manuscript will ever modify. Even the two reporters were glad to confirm the silence. *For the opening had revealed a pulsing, living brain.*

The Horror in the Burying-Ground

With Hazel Heald

I.

When the state highway to Rutland is closed, travellers are forced to take the Stillwater road past Swamp Hollow.[1] The scenery is superb in places, yet somehow the route has been unpopular for years. There is something depressing about it, especially near Stillwater itself. Motorists feel subtly uncomfortable about the tightly shuttered farmhouse on the knoll just north of the village, and about the white-bearded half-wit who haunts the old burying-ground on the south, apparently talking to the occupants of some of the graves.

Not much is left of Stillwater, now. The soil is played out, and most of the people have drifted to the towns across the distant river or to the city beyond the distant hills. The steeple of the old white church has fallen down, and half of the twenty-odd straggling houses are empty and in various stages of decay. Normal life is found only around Peck's[2] general store and filling-station, and it is here that the curious stop now and then to ask about the shuttered house and the idiot who mutters to the dead.

Most of the questioners come away with a touch of distaste and disquiet. They find the shabby loungers oddly unpleasant and full of unnamed hints in speaking of the long-past events brought up. There is a menacing, portentous quality in the tones which they use to describe very ordinary events—a seemingly unjustified tendency to assume a furtive, suggestive, confidential air, and to fall into awesome whispers at certain points—which insidiously disturbs the listener. Old Yankees often talk like that; but in this case the melancholy aspect of the half-mouldering village, and the dismal nature of the story unfolded, give these gloomy, secretive mannerisms an added significance. One feels profoundly the quintessential horror that lurks behind the isolated Puritan and his strange repressions—feels it, and longs to escape precipitately into clearer air.

The loungers whisper impressively that the shuttered house is that of old Miss Sprague[3]—Sophie Sprague, whose brother Tom was buried on the seventeenth of June, back in '86. Sophie was never the same after that funeral—that and the other thing which happened the same day—and in the end she took to staying in all the time. Won't even be seen now, but leaves notes under the back-door mat and has her things brought from the store by Ned Peck's boy. Afraid of something—the old Swamp Hollow burying-ground most of all. Never could be dragged near there since her brother—and the other one—were laid away. Not much wonder, though, seeing the way crazy Johnny Dow rants. He hangs around the burying-ground all day and sometimes at night, and claims he talks with Tom—and the other. Then he marches by Sophie's house and shouts things at her—that's why she began to keep the shutters closed. He says things are coming from somewhere to get her sometime. Ought to be stopped, but one can't be too hard on poor Johnny. Besides, Steve Barbour always had his opinions.

Johnny does his talking to two of the graves. One of them is Tom Sprague's. The other, at the opposite end of the graveyard, is that of Henry Thorndike, who was buried on the same day. Henry was the village undertaker—the only one in miles—and never liked around Stillwater. A city fellow from Rutland—been to college and full of book learning. Read queer things nobody else ever heard of, and mixed chemicals for no good purpose. Always trying to invent something new—some new-fangled embalming-fluid or some foolish kind of medicine. Some folks said he had tried to be a doctor but failed in his studies and took to the next best profession. Of course, there wasn't much undertaking to do in a place like Stillwater, but Henry farmed on the side.

Mean, morbid disposition—and a secret drinker if you could judge by the empty bottles in his rubbish heap. No wonder Tom Sprague hated him and blackballed him from the Masonic lodge, and warned him off when he tried to make up to Sophie. The way he experimented on animals was against Nature and Scripture. Who could forget the state that collie dog was found in, or what happened to old Mrs. Akeley's cat?[4] Then there was the matter of Deacon Leavitt's calf, when Tom had led a band of the village boys to demand an accounting. The curious thing was that the calf came alive after all in the end, though Tom had found it as stiff as a poker. Some said the joke was on Tom, but Thorndike probably thought otherwise, since he had gone down under his enemy's fist before the mistake was discovered.

Tom, of course, was half drunk at the time. He was a

vicious brute at best, and kept his poor sister half cowed with threats. That's probably why she is such a fear-racked creature still. There were only the two of them, and Tom would never let her leave because that meant splitting the property. Most of the fellows were too afraid of him to shine up to Sophie—he stood six feet one in his stockings—but Henry Thorndike was a sly cuss who had ways of doing things behind folks' backs. He wasn't much to look at, but Sophie never discouraged him any. Mean and ugly as he was, she'd have been glad if anybody could have freed her from her brother. She may not have stopped to wonder how she could get clear of him after he got her clear of Tom.

Well, that was the way things stood in June of '86. Up to this point, the whispers of the loungers at Peck's store are not so unbearably portentous; but as they continue, the element of secretiveness and malign tension grows. Tom Sprague, it appears, used to go to Rutland on periodic sprees, his absences being Henry Thorndike's great opportunities. He was always in bad shape when he got back, and old Dr. Pratt, deaf and half blind though he was, used to warn him about his heart, and about the danger of delirium tremens. Folks could always tell by the shouting and cursing when he was home again.

It was on the ninth of June—on a Wednesday, the day after young Joshua Goodenough[5] finished building his new-fangled silo—that Tom started out on his last and longest spree. He came back the next Tuesday morning and folks at the store saw him lashing his bay stallion the way he did when whiskey had a hold of him. Then there came shouts and shrieks and oaths from the Sprague house, and the first thing anybody knew Sophie was running over to old Dr. Pratt's at top speed.

The doctor found Thorndike at Sprague's when he got

there, and Tom was on the bed in his room, with eyes staring and foam around his mouth. Old Pratt fumbled around and gave the usual tests, then shook his head solemnly and told Sophie she had suffered a great bereavement—that her nearest and dearest had passed through the pearly gates to a better land, just as everybody knew he would if he didn't let up on his drinking.

Sophie kind of sniffled, the loungers whisper, but didn't seem to take on much. Thorndike didn't do anything but smile—perhaps at the ironic fact that he, always an enemy, was now the only person who could be of any use to Thomas Sprague. He shouted something in old Dr. Pratt's half-good ear about the need of having the funeral early on account of Tom's condition. Drunks like that were always doubtful subjects, and any extra delay—with merely rural facilities—would entail consequences, visual and otherwise, hardly acceptable to the deceased's loving mourners. The doctor had muttered that Tom's alcoholic career ought to have embalmed him pretty well in advance, but Thorndike assured him to the contrary, at the same time boasting of his own skill, and of the superior methods he had devised through his experiments.

It is here that the whispers of the loungers grow acutely disturbing. Up to this point the story is usually told by Ezra Davenport, or Luther Fry,[6] if Ezra is laid up with chilblains, as he is apt to be in winter; but from there on old Calvin Wheeler takes up the thread, and his voice has a damnably insidious way of suggesting hidden horror. If Johnny Dow happens to be passing by there is always a pause, for Stillwater does not like to have Johnny talk too much with strangers.

Calvin edges close to the traveller and sometimes seizes a coat-lapel with his gnarled, mottled hand while he half shuts his watery blue eyes.

"Well, sir," he whispers, "Henry he went home an' got his undertaker's fixin's—crazy Johnny Dow lugged most of 'em, for he was always doin' chores for Henry—an' says as Doc Pratt an' crazy Johnny should help lay out the body. Doc always did say as how he thought Henry talked too much—a-boastin' what a fine workman he was, an' how lucky it was that Stillwater had a reg'lar undertaker instead of buryin' folks jest as they was, like they do over to Whitby.

"'Suppose,' says he, 'some fellow was to be took with some of them paralysin' cramps like you read about. How'd a body like it when they lowered him down and begun shovelin' the dirt back? How'd he like it when he was chokin' down there under the new headstone, scratchin' an' tearin' if he chanced to get back the power, but all the time knowin' it wasn't no use? No, sir, I tell you it's a blessin' Stillwater's got a smart doctor as knows when a man's dead and when he ain't, and a trained undertaker who can fix a corpse so he'll stay put without no trouble.'

"That was the way Henry went on talkin', most like he was talkin' to poor Tom's remains; and old Doc Pratt he didn't like what he was able to catch of it, even though Henry did call him a smart doctor. Crazy Johnny kept watchin' of the corpse, and it didn't make it none too pleasant the way he'd slobber about things like, 'He ain't cold, Doc,' or 'I see his eyelids move,' or 'There's a hole in his arm jest like the ones I git when Henry gives me a syringe full of what makes me feel good.' Thorndike shut him up on that, though we all knowed he'd been givin' poor Johnny drugs. It's a wonder the poor fellow ever got clear of the habit.

"But the worst thing, accordin' to the doctor, was the way the body jerked up when Henry begun to shoot it full of embalmin'-fluid. He'd been boastin' about what a fine new formula he'd got practicin' on cats and dogs, when all of a sudden Tom's corpse began to double up like it was alive and fixin' to wrassle. Land of Goshen, but Doc says he was scared stiff, though he knowed the way corpses act when the muscles begin to stiffen. Well, sir, the long and short of it is, that the corpse sat up an' grabbed a holt of Thorndike's syringe so that it got stuck in Henry hisself, an' give him as neat a dose of his own embalmin'-fluid as you'd wish to see. That got Henry pretty scared, though he yanked the point out and managed to get the body down again and shot full of the fluid. He kept measurin' more of the stuff out as though he wanted to be sure there was enough, and kept reassurin' himself as not much had got into him, but crazy Johnny begun singin' out, 'That's what you give Lige Hopkins's dog when it got all dead an' stiff an' then waked up agin. Now you're a-going to get dead an' stiff like Tom Sprague be! Remember it don't set to work till after a long spell if you don't get much.'

"Sophie, she was downstairs with some of the neighbours—my wife Matildy, she that's dead an' gone this thirty year, was one of them. They were all tryin' to find out whether Thorndike was over when Tom came home, and whether findin' him there was what set poor Tom off. I may as well say as some folks thought it mighty funny that Sophie didn't carry on more, nor mind the way Thorndike had smiled. Not as anybody was hintin' that Henry helped Tom off with some of his queer cooked-up fluids and syringes, or that Sophie would keep still if she thought so—but you know how folks will guess behind a body's back. We all knowed the nigh crazy way Thorndike had hated Tom—not without reason, at that—and Emily Barbour says to my Matildy as how Henry was lucky to have ol' Doc Pratt right on the spot with a death certificate as didn't leave no doubt for nobody."

When old Calvin gets to this point he usually begins to mumble indistinguishably in his straggling, dirty white beard. Most listeners try to edge away from him, and he seldom appears to heed the gesture. It is generally Fred Peck, who was a very small boy at the time of the events, who continues the tale.

Thomas Sprague's funeral was held on Thursday, June 17th, only two days after his death. Such haste was thought almost indecent in remote and inaccessible Stillwater, where long distances had to be covered by those who came, but Thorndike had insisted that the peculiar condition of the deceased demanded it. The undertaker had seemed rather nervous since preparing the body, and could be seen frequently feeling his pulse. Old Dr. Pratt thought he must be worrying about the accidental dose of embalming-fluid. Naturally, the story of the "laying out" had spread, so that a double zest animated the mourners who assembled to glut their curiosity and morbid interest.

Thorndike, though he was obviously upset, seemed intent on doing his professional duty in magnificent style. Sophie and others who saw the body were most startled by its utter lifelikeness, and the mortuary virtuoso made doubly sure of his job by repeating certain injections at stated intervals. He almost wrung a sort of reluctant admiration from the townsfolk and visitors, though he tended to spoil that impression by his boastful and tasteless talk. Whenever he administered to his silent charge he would repeat that eternal rambling about the good luck of having a first-class undertaker. What—he would say as if directly addressing the body—if Tom had had one of those careless fellows who bury their subjects alive? The way he harped on the horrors of premature burial was truly barbarous and sickening.

Services were held in the stuffy best room—opened

for the first time since Mrs. Sprague died. The tuneless little parlour organ groaned disconsolately, and the coffin, supported on trestles near the hall door, was covered with sickly-smelling flowers. It was obvious that a record-breaking crowd was assembling from far and near, and Sophie endeavoured to look properly grief-stricken for their benefit. At unguarded moments she seemed both puzzled and uneasy, dividing her scrutiny between the feverish-looking undertaker and the life-like body of her brother. A slow disgust at Thorndike seemed to be brewing within her, and neighbours whispered freely that she would soon send him about his business now that Tom was out of the way—that is, if she could, for such a slick customer was sometimes hard to deal with. But with her money and remaining looks she might be able to get another fellow, and he'd probably take care of Henry well enough.

As the organ wheezed into *Beautiful Isle of Somewhere*[7] the Methodist church choir added their lugubrious voices to the gruesome cacophony, and everyone looked piously at Deacon Leavitt—everyone, that is, except crazy Johnny Dow, who kept his eyes glued to the still form beneath the glass of the coffin. He was muttering softly to himself.

Stephen Barbour—from the next farm—was the only one who noticed Johnny. He shivered as he saw that the idiot was talking directly to the corpse, and even making foolish signs with his fingers as if to taunt the sleeper beneath the plate glass. Tom, he reflected, had kicked poor Johnny around on more than one occasion, though probably not without provocation. Something about this whole event was getting on Stephen's nerves. There was a suppressed tension and brooding abnormality in the air for which he could not account. Johnny ought not to have been allowed in the house—and it was curious what an effort Thorndike seemed to be making not to look at the body. Every now and then the undertaker would feel his pulse with an odd air.

The Reverend Silas Atwood[8] droned on in a plaintive monotone about the deceased—about the striking of Death's sword in the midst of this little family, breaking the earthly tie between this loving brother and sister. Several of the neighbours looked furtively at one another from beneath lowered eyelids, while Sophie actually began to sob nervously. Thorndike moved to her side and tried to reassure her, but she seemed to shrink curiously away from him. His motions were distinctly uneasy, and he seemed to feel acutely the abnormal tension permeating the air. Finally, conscious of his duty as master of ceremonies, he stepped forward and announced in a sepulchral voice that the body might be viewed for the last time.

Slowly the friends and neighbours filed past the bier, from which Thorndike roughly dragged crazy Johnny away. Tom seemed to be resting peacefully. That devil had been handsome in his day. A few genuine sobs—and many feigned ones—were heard, though most of the crowd were content to stare curiously and whisper afterward. Steve Barbour lingered long and attentively over the still face, and moved away shaking his head. His wife, Emily, following after him, whispered that Henry Thorndike had better not boast so much about his work, for Tom's eyes had come open. They had been shut when the services began, for she had been up and looked. But they certainly looked natural—not the way one would expect after two days.

When Fred Peck gets this far he usually pauses as if he did not like to continue. The listener, too, tends to feel that something unpleasant is ahead. But Peck reassures his audience with the statement that what happened isn't as bad as folks like to hint. Even Steve never put into words what he may have thought, and crazy Johnny, of course, can't be counted at all.

It was Luella Morse[9]—the nervous old maid who sang in the choir—who seems to have touched things off. She was filing past the coffin like the rest, but stopped to peer a little closer than anyone else except the Barbours had peered. And then, without warning, she gave a shrill scream and fell in a dead faint.

Naturally, the room was at once a chaos of confusion. Old Dr. Pratt elbowed his way to Luella and called for some water to throw in her face, and others surged up to look at her and at the coffin. Johnny Dow began chanting to himself, "He knows, he knows, he kin hear all we're a-sayin' and see all we're a-doin', and they'll bury him that way"—but no one stopped to decipher his mumbling except Steve Barbour.

In a very few moments Luella began to come out of her faint, and could not tell exactly what had startled her. All she could whisper was, "The way he looked—the way he looked." But to other eyes the body seemed exactly the same. It was a gruesome sight, though, with those open eyes and that high colouring.

And then the bewildered crowd noticed something which put both Luella and the body out of their minds for a moment. It was Thorndike—on whom the sudden excitement and jostling crowd seemed to be having a curiously bad effect. He had evidently been knocked down in the general bustle, and was on the floor trying to drag himself to a sitting posture. The expression on his face was terrifying in the extreme, and his eyes were beginning to take on a glazed, fishy expression. He could scarcely speak aloud, but the husky rattle of his throat held an ineffable desperation which was obvious to all.

"Get me home, quick, and let me be. That fluid I got in my arm by mistake . . . heart action . . . this damned excitement . . . too much . . . wait . . . wait . . . don't think I'm dead if I seem to . . . only the fluid—just get me home and wait . . . I'll come to later, don't know how long . . . all the time I'll be conscious and know what's going on . . . don't be deceived. . . ."

As his words trailed off into nothingness old Dr. Pratt reached him and felt his pulse—watching a long time and finally shaking his head. "No use doing anything—he's gone. Heart no good—and that fluid he got in his arm must have been bad stuff. I don't know what it is."

A kind of numbness seemed to fall on all the company. New death in the chamber of death! Only Steve Barbour thought to bring up Thorndike's last choking words. Was he surely dead, when he himself had said he might falsely seem so? Wouldn't it be better to wait a while and see what would happen? And for that matter, what harm would it do if Doc Pratt were to give Tom Sprague another looking over before burial?

Crazy Johnny was moaning, and had flung himself on Thorndike's body like a faithful dog. "Don't ye bury him, don't ye bury him! He ain't dead no more nor Lige Hopkins's dog nor Deacon Leavitt's calf was when he shot 'em full. He's got some stuff he puts into ye to make ye seem like dead when ye ain't! Ye seem like dead but ye know everything what's a-goin' on, and the next day ye come to as good as ever. Don't ye bury him—he'll come to under the earth an' he can't scratch up! He's a good man, an' not like Tom Sprague. Hope to Gawd Tom scratches an' chokes for hours an' hours. . . ."

But no one save Barbour was paying any attention

H. P. LOVECRAFT

to poor Johnny. Indeed, what Steve himself had said had
evidently fallen on deaf ears. Uncertainty was everywhere.
Old Doc Pratt was applying final tests and mumbling about
death certificate blanks, and unctuous Elder Atwood was
suggesting that something be done about a double interment. With Thorndike dead there was no undertaker this
side of Rutland, and it would mean a terrible expense if one
were to be brought from there, and if Thorndike were not
embalmed in this hot June weather—well, one couldn't
tell. And there were no relatives or friends to be critical unless Sophie chose to be—but Sophie was on the other side
of the room, staring silently, fixedly, and almost morbidly
into her brother's coffin.

Deacon Leavitt tried to restore a semblance of de-
corum, and had poor Thorndike carried across the hall
to the sitting-room, meanwhile sending Zenas Wells and
Walter Perkins over to the undertaker's house for a coffin
of the right size. The key was in Henry's trousers pocket.
Johnny continued to whine and paw at the body, and Elder
Atwood busied himself with inquiring about Thorndike's
denomination—for Henry had not attended local services.
When it was decided that his folks in Rutland—all dead
now—had been Baptists, the Reverend Silas decided that
Deacon Leavitt had better offer the brief prayer.

It was a gala day for the funeral-fanciers of Stillwater
and vicinity. Even Luella had recovered enough to stay.
Gossip, murmured and whispered, buzzed busily while a
few composing touches were given to Thorndike's cooling,
stiffening form. Johnny had been cuffed out of the house,
as most agreed he should have been in the first place, but
his distant howls were now and then wafted gruesomely in.

When the body was encoffined and laid out beside
that of Thomas Sprague, the silent, almost frightening-

233

looking Sophie gazed intently at it as she had gazed at her brother's. She had not uttered a word for a dangerously long time, and the mixed expression on her face was past all describing or interpreting. As the others withdrew to leave her alone with the dead she managed to find a sort of mechanical speech, but no one could make out the words, and she seemed to be talking first to one body and then the other.

And now, with what would seem to an outsider the acme of gruesome unconscious comedy, the whole funeral mummery of the afternoon was listlessly repeated. Again the organ wheezed, again the choir screeched and scraped, again a droning incantation arose, and again the morbidly curious spectators filed past a macabre object—this time a dual array of mortuary repose. Some of the more sensitive people shivered at the whole proceeding, and again Stephen Barbour felt an underlying note of eldritch horror and daemoniac abnormality. God, how life-like both of those corpses were . . . and how in earnest poor Thorndike had been about not wanting to be judged dead . . . and how he hated Tom Sprague . . . but what could one do in the face of common sense—a dead man was a dead man, and there was old Doc Pratt with his years of experience . . . if nobody else bothered, why should one bother oneself? . . . Whatever Tom had got he had probably deserved . . . and if Henry had done anything to him, the score was even now . . . well, Sophie was free at last. . . .

As the peering procession moved at last toward the hall and the outer door, Sophie was alone with the dead once more. Elder Atwood was out in the road talking to the hearse-driver from Lee's livery stable, and Deacon Leavitt was arranging for a double quota of pall-bearers. Luckily the hearse would hold two coffins. No hurry—Ed Plum-

mer and Ethan Stone were going ahead with shovels to dig
the second grave. There would be three livery hacks and any
number of private rigs in the cavalcade—no use trying to
keep the crowd away from the graves.

Then came that frantic scream from the parlour where
Sophie and the bodies were. Its suddenness almost paralysed the crowd and brought back the same sensation which
had surged up when Luella had screamed and fainted. Steve
Barbour and Deacon Leavitt started to go in, but before
they could enter the house Sophie was bursting forth, sob-
bing and gasping about "That face at the window! . . . that
face at the window! . . ."

At the same time a wild-eyed figure rounded the corner of the house, removing all mystery from Sophie's dramatic cry. It was, very obviously, the face's owner—poor
crazy Johnny, who began to leap up and down, pointing
at Sophie and shrieking, "She knows! She knows! I seen
it in her face when she looked at 'em and talked to 'em!
She knows, and she's a-lettin' 'em go down in the earth to
scratch an' claw for air. . . . But they'll talk to her so's she kin
hear 'em . . . they'll talk to her, an' appear to her . . . and some
day they'll come back an' git her!"

Zenas Wells dragged the shrieking half-wit to a woodshed behind the house and bolted him in as best he could.
His screams and poundings could be heard at a distance,
but nobody paid him any further attention. The procession
was made up, and with Sophie in the first hack it slowly
covered the short distance past the village to the Swamp
Hollow burying-ground.

Elder Atwood made appropriate remarks as Thomas
Sprague was laid to rest, and by the time he was through,
Ed and Ethan had finished Thorndike's grave on the other
side of the cemetery—to which the crowd presently shift-

ed. Deacon Leavitt then spoke ornamentally, and the lowering process was repeated. People had begun to drift off in knots, and the clatter of receding buggies and carry-alls was quite universal, when the shovels began to fly again. As the earth thudded down on the coffin-lids, Thorndike's first, Steve Barbour noticed the queer expressions flitting over Sophie Sprague's face. He couldn't keep track of them all, but behind the rest there seemed to lurk a sort of wry, perverse, half-suppressed look of vague triumph. He shook his head.

Zenas had run back and let crazy Johnny out of the woodshed before Sophie got home, and the poor fellow at once made frantically for the graveyard. He arrived before the shovelmen were through, and while many of the curious mourners were still lingering about. What he shouted into Tom Sprague's partly filled grave, and how he clawed at the loose earth of Thorndike's freshly finished mound across the cemetery, surviving spectators still shudder to recall. Jotham Blake, the constable, had to take him back to the town farm by force, and his screams waked dreadful echoes.

This is where Fred Peck usually leaves off the story. What more, he asks, is there to tell? It was a gloomy tragedy, and one can scarcely wonder that Sophie grew queer after that. That is all one hears if the hour is so late that old Calvin Wheeler has tottered home, but when he is still around he breaks in again with that damnably suggestive and insidious whisper. Sometimes those who hear him dread to pass either the shuttered house or the graveyard afterward, especially after dark.

"Heh, heh . . . Fred was only a little shaver then, and don't remember no more than half of what was goin' on! You want to know why Sophie keeps her house shuttered, and why crazy Johnny still keeps a-talkin' to the dead and a-shoutin' at Sophie's windows? Well, sir, I don't know's I know all there is to know, but I hear what I hear."

Here the old man ejects his cud of tobacco and leans forward to buttonhole the listener.

"It was that same night, mind ye—toward mornin', and just eight hours after them burials—when we heard the first scream from Sophie's house. Woke us all up—Steve and Emily Barbour and me and Matildy goes over hot-foo-tin', all in night gear, and finds Sophie all dressed and dead fainted on the settin'-room floor. Lucky she hadn't locked the door. When we got her to she was shakin' like a leaf, and wouldn't let on by so much as a word what was ailin' her. Matildy and Emily done what they could to quiet her down, but Steve whispered things to me as didn't make me none too easy. Come about an hour when we allowed we'd be goin' home soon, that Sophie she begun to tip her head on one side like she was a-listenin' to somethin'. Then on a sudden she screamed again, and keeled over in another faint.

"Well, sir, I'm tellin' what I'm tellin', and won't do no guessin' like Steve Barbour would a done if he dared. He always was the greatest hand for hintin' things . . . died ten years ago of pneumony. . . .

"What we heard so faint-like was just poor crazy Johnny, of course. 'Taint more than a mile to the buryin'-ground, and he must a got out of the window where they'd locked him up at the town farm—even if Constable Blake says he didn't get out that night. From that day to this he hangs around them graves a-talkin' to the both of them—cussin' and kickin' at Tom's mound, and puttin' posies and things on Henry's. And when he ain't a-doin' that he's hangin' around Sophie's shuttered windows howlin' about

MEDUSA'S COIL

what's a-comin' soon to git her.

"She wouldn't never go near the buryin'-ground, and now she won't come out of the house at all nor see nobody. Got to sayin' there was a curse on Stillwater—and I'm dinged if she ain't half right, the way things is a-goin' to pieces these days. There certainly was somethin' queer about Sophie right along. Once when Sally Hopkins was a-callin' on her—in '97 or '98, I think it was—there was an awful rattlin' at her winders—and Johnny was safe locked up at the time—at least, so Constable Dodge swore up and down. But I ain't takin' no stock in their stories about noises every seventeenth of June, or about faint shinin' figures a-tryin' Sophie's door and winders every black mornin' about two o'clock.

"You see, it was about two o'clock in the mornin' that Sophie heard the sounds and keeled over twice that first night after the buryin'. Steve and me, and Matildy and Emily, heard the second lot, faint as it was, just like I told you. And I'm a-tellin' you again as how it must a been crazy Johnny over to the buryin'-ground, let Jotham Blake claim what he will. There ain't no tellin' the sound of a man's voice so far off, and with our heads full of nonsense it ain't no wonder we thought there was two voices—and voices that hadn't ought to be speakin' at all.

"Steve, he claimed to have heard more than I did. I verily believe he took some stock in ghosts. Matildy and Emily was so scared they didn't remember what they heard. And curious enough, nobody else in town—if anybody was awake at the ungodly hour—never said nothin' about hearin' no sounds at all.

"Whatever it was, was so faint it might have been the wind if there hadn't been words. I made out a few, but don't want to say as I'd back up all Steve claimed to have caught. .

238

"'She-devil' . . . 'all the time' . . . 'Henry' . . . and 'alive' was plain . . . and so was 'you know' . . . 'said you'd stand by' . . . 'get rid of him' and 'bury me' . . . in a kind of changed voice. . . . Then there was that awful 'comin' again some day'—in a death-like squawk . . . but you can't tell me John-ny couldn't have made those sounds. . . .

"Hey, you! What's takin' you off in such a hurry? Mebbe there's more I could tell you if I had a mind. . . ."

The Slaying of the Monster

With R. H. Barlow

Great was the clamour in Laen; for smoke had been spied in the Hills of the Dragon. That surely meant the Stirrings of the Monster—the Monster who spat lava and shook the earth as he writhed in its depths. And when the men of Laen spoke together they swore to slay the Monster and keep his fiery breath from searing their minaret-studded city and toppling their alabaster domes.

So it was that by torch-light gathered fully a hundred of the little people, prepared to battle the Evil One in his hidden fast-hold. With the coming of night they began marching in ragged columns into the foot-hills beneath the fulgent lunar rays. Ahead a burning cloud shone clearly through the purple dusk, a guide to their goal.

For the sake of truth it is to be recorded that their spirits sank low long ere they sighted the foe, and as the moon grew dim and the coming of the dawn was heralded by gaudy clouds they wished themselves more than ever at home, dragon or no dragon. But as the sun rose they cheered up slightly, and shifting their spears, resolutely trudged the remaining distance.

Clouds of sulphurous smoke hung pall-like over the world, darkening even the new-risen sun, and always replenished by sullen puffs from the mouth of the Monster. Little tongues of hungry flame made the Laenians move swiftly over the hot stones. "But *where* is the dragon??" whispered one—fearfully and hoping it would not accept the query as an invitation. In vain they looked—there was nothing solid enough to slay.

So shouldering their weapons, they wearily returned home and there set up a stone tablet graven to this effect— "BEING TROUBLED BY A FIERCE MONSTER THE BRAVE CITIZENS OF LAEN DID SET UPON IT AND SLAY IT IN ITS FEARFUL LAIR SAVING THE LAND FROM A DREADFUL DOOM."

These words were hard to read when we dug that stone from its deep, ancient layers of encrusting lava.

The Hoard of the Wizard-Beast

With R. H. Barlow

There had happened in the teeming and many-towered city of Zeth one of those incidents which are prone to take place in all capitals of all worlds. Nor, simply because Zeth lies on a planet of strange beasts and stranger vegetation, did this incident differ greatly from what might have occurred in London or Paris or any of the great governing towns we know. Through the cleverly concealed dishonesty of an aged but shrewd official, the treasury was exhausted. No shining *phrulder,* as of old, lay stacked about the strong-room; and over empty coffers the sardonic spider wove webs of mocking design. When, at last, the *giphath* Yalden entered that obscure vault and discovered the thefts, there were left only some phlegmatic rats which peered sharply at him as at an alien intruder.

There had been no accountings since Kishan the old keeper had died many moon-turns before, and great was Yalden's dismay to find this emptiness instead of the expected wealth. The indifference of the small creatures in the cracks between the flagstones could not spread itself to him. This was a very grave matter, and would have to be met in a very prompt and serious way. Clearly, there was nothing to do but consult Oorn, and Oorn was a highly portentous being.

Oorn, though a creature of extremely doubtful nature, was the virtual ruler of Zeth. It obviously belonged somewhere in the outer abyss, but had blundered into Zeth one night and suffered capture by the *shamith* priests. The coincidence of Its excessively bizarre aspect and Its innate gift of mimicry had impressed the sacred brothers as offering vast possibilities, hence in the end they had set It up as a god and an oracle, organising a new brotherhood to serve It—and incidentally to suggest the edicts it should utter and the replies It should give. Like the Delphi and Dodona of a later world, Oorn grew famous as a giver of judgments and solver of riddles; nor did Its essence differ from them save that It lay infinitely earlier in Time, and upon an elder world where all things might happen. And now Yalden, being not above the credulousness of his day and planet, had set out for the close-guarded and richly-fitted hall wherein Oorn brooded and mimicked the promptings of the priests.

When Yalden came within sight of the Hall, with its tower of blue tile, he became properly religious, and entered the building acceptably, in a humble manner which greatly impeded progress. According to custom, the guardians of the deity acknowledged his obeisance and pecuniary offering, and retired behind heavy curtains to ignite the thuribles. After everything was in readiness, Yalden murmured a conventional prayer and bowed low before a curious empty dais studded with exotic jewels. For a moment—as the ritual prescribed—he stayed in this abased position, and when he arose the dais was no longer empty. Unconcernedly munching something the priests had given It was a large pudgy creature very hard to describe, and covered with short grey fur. Whence It had come in so brief a time only the priests might tell, but the suppliant knew that It was Oorn.

Hesitantly Yalden stated his unfortunate mission and asked advice; weaving into his discourse the type of flattery which seemed to him most discreet. Then, with anxiety, he awaited the oracle's response. Having tidily finished Its food, Oorn raised three small reddish eyes to Yalden and uttered certain words in a tone of vast decisiveness: *"Gumay ere hfotuol leheht teg."* After this It vanished suddenly in a cloud of pink smoke which seemed to issue from behind the curtain where the acolytes were. The acolytes then came forth from their hiding-place and spoke to Yalden, saying: "Since you have pleased the deity with your concise statement of a very deplorable state of affairs, we are honored by interpreting its directions. The aphorism you heard signifies no less than the equally mystic phrase 'Go thou unto thy destination' or more properly speaking, you are to slay the monster-wizard Anathas, and replenish the treasury with its fabled hoard."

With this Yalden was dismissed from the temple. It may not be said in veracity that he was fearless, for in truth, he was openly afraid of the monster Anathas, as were all the inhabitants of Ullathia and the surrounding land. Even those who doubted its actuality would not have chosen to reside in the immediate neighbourhood of the Cave of Three Winds wherein it was said to dwell.

But the prospect was not without romantic appeal, and Yalden was young and consequently unwise. He knew, among other things, that there was always the hope of rescuing some feminine victim of the monster's famed and surprising erotic taste. Of the true aspect of Anathas none could be certain; tales of a widely opposite nature being commonly circulated. Many vowed it had been seen from afar in the form of a giant black shadow peculiarly repugnant to human taste, while others alleged it was a mound of gelatinous substance that oozed hatefully in the manner of putrescent flesh. Still others claimed they had seen it as a monstrous insect with astonishing supernumerary appurtenances. But in one thing all coincided; namely, that it was advisable to have as little traffic as possible with Anathas.

With due supplications to his gods and to their messenger Oorn, Yalden set out for the Cave of Three Winds. In his bosom were mixed an ingrained, patriotic sense of duty, and a thrill of adventurous expectancy regarding the unknown mysteries he faced. He had not neglected such preparations as a sensible man might make, and a wizard of old repute had furnished him with certain singular accessories. He had, for example, a charm which prevented his thirsting or hungering, and wholly did away with his need for provisions. There was likewise a glistening cape to counteract the evil emanations of a mineral that lay scattered over the rocky ground along his course. Other warnings and safeguards dealt with certain gaudy land-crustaceans, and with the deathly-sweet mists which arise at certain points until dispersed by heliotropism.

Thus shielded, Yalden fared without incident until he came to the place of the White Worm. Here of necessity he delayed to make preparations for finding the rest of his way. With patient diligence he captured the small colorless maggot, and surrounded it with a curious mark made with green paint. As was prophesied, the Lord of Worms, whose name was Sarall, made promise of certain things in return for its freedom. Then Yalden released it, and it crawled away after directing him on the course he was to follow.

The sere and fruitless land through which he now travelled was totally uninhabited. Not even the hardier of the beasts were to be seen beyond the edge of that final plateau which separated him from his goal. Far off, in a purplish haze, rose the mountains amidst which dwelt Anathas. It lived not solitary, despite the lonely region around, for strange pets resided with it—some the fabled elder monsters, and others unique beings created by its own fearful craft.

At the heart of its cave, legend said, Anathas had concealed an enormous hoard of jewels, gold, and other things of fabulous value. Why so potent a wonder-worker should care for such gauds, or revel in the counting of money, was by no means clear; but many things attested the truth of these tastes. Great numbers of persons of stronger will and wit than Yalden had died in remarkable manners while seeking the hoard of the wizard-beast, and their bones were laid in a strange pattern before the mouth of the cave, as a warning to others.

When, after countless vicissitudes, Yalden came at last into sight of the Cave of Winds amid the glistening boulders, he knew indeed that report had not lied concerning the isolation of Anathas' lair. The cavern-mouth was well-concealed, and over everything an ominous quiet lowered. There was no trace of habitation, save of course the ossuary ornamentation in the front yard. With his hand on the sword that had been sanctified by a priest of Oorn, Yalden tremblingly advanced. When he had attained the very opening of the lair, he hesitated no longer, for it was evident that the monster was away.

Deeming this the best of all times to prosecute his

business, Yalden plunged at once within the cave. The interior was very cramped and exceedingly dirty, but the roof glittered with an innumerable array of small, varicoloured lights, the source of which was not to be perceived. In the rear yawned another opening, either natural or artificial; and to this black, low-arched burrow Yalden hastened, crawling within it on hands and knees. Before long a faint blue radiance glowed at the farther end, and presently the searcher emerged into an ampler space. Straightening up, he beheld a most singular change in his surroundings. This second cavern was tall and domed as if it had been shapen by supernatural powers, and a soft blue and silver light infused the gloom. Anathas, thought Yalden, lived indeed in comfort; for this room was finer than anything in the Palace of Zeth, or even in the Temple of Oorn, upon which had been lavished unthinkable wealth and beauty. Yalden stood agape, but not for long, since he desired most of all to seek the object of his quest and depart before Anathas should return from wherever it might be. For Yalden did not wish to encounter the monster-sorcerer of which so many tales were told. Leaving therefore this second cave by a narrow cleft which he saw, the seeker followed a devious and unlit way far down through the solid rock of the plateau. This, he felt, would take him to that third and ultimate cavern where his business lay. As he progressed, he glimpsed ahead of him a curious glow; and at last, without warning, the walls receded to reveal a vast open space paved solidly with blazing coals above which flapped and shrieked an obscene flock of wyvern-headed birds. Over the fiery surface green monstrous salamanders slithered, eyeing the intruder with malignant speculation. And on the far side rose the stairs of a metal dais, encrusted with jewels, and piled high with precious objects; the hoard of the wizard-beast.

At sight of this unattainable wealth, Yalden's fervour well-nigh overcame him; and chaffing at his futility, he searched the sea of flame for some way of crossing. This, he soon perceived, was not readily to be found; for in all that glowing crypt there was only a slight crescent of flooring near the entrance which a mortal man might hope to walk on. Desperation, however, possessed him; so that at last he resolved to risk all and try the fiery pavement. Better to die in the quest than to return empty-handed. With teeth set, he started toward the sea of flame, heedless of what might follow.

As it was, surprise seared him almost as vehemently as he had expected the flames to do—for with his advance, the glowing floor divided to form a narrow lane of safe cool earth leading straight to the golden throne. Half dazed, and heedless of whatever might underlie such curiously favouring magic, Yalden drew his sword and strode boldly betwixt the walls of flame that rose from the rifted pavement. The heat hurt him not at all, and the wyvern-creatures drew back, hissing, and did not molest him.

The hoard now glistened close at hand, and Yalden thought of how he would return to Zeth, laden with fabulous spoils and worshipped by throngs as a hero. In his joy he forgot to wonder at Anathas' lax care of its treasures; nor did the very friendly behaviour of the fiery pavement seem in any way remarkable. Even the huge arched opening behind the dais, so oddly invisible from across the cavern, failed to disturb him seriously. Only when he had mounted the broad stair of the dais and stood ankle-deep amid the bizarre golden reliques of other ages and other worlds, and the lovely, luminous gems from unknown mines and of unknown natures and meanings, did Yalden begin to realise that anything was wrong.

But now he perceived that the miraculous passage through the flaming floor was closing again, leaving him marooned on the dais with the glittering treasure he had sought. And when it had fully closed, and his eyes had circled round vainly for some way of escape, he was hardly reassured by the shapeless jelly-like shadow which loomed colossal and stinking in the great archway behind the dais. He was not permitted to faint, but was forced to observe that this shadow was infinitely more hideous than anything hinted in any popular legend, and that its seven iridescent eyes were regarding him with placid amusement.

Then Anathas the wizard-beast rolled fully out of the archway, mighty in necromantic horror, and jested with the small frightened conqueror before allowing that horde of slavering and peculiarly hungry green salamanders to complete their slow, anticipatory ascent of the dais.

The Tree on the Hill

With Duane W. Rimel

I

Southeast of Hampden, near the tortuous Salmon River gorge,[1] is a range of steep, rocky hills which have defied all efforts of sturdy homesteaders. The canyons are too deep and the slopes too precipitous to encourage anything save seasonal livestock grazing. The last time I visited Hampden the region—known as Hell's Acres—was part of the Blue Mountain Forest Reserve.[2] There are no roads linking this inaccessible locality with the outside world, and the hillfolk will tell you that it is indeed a spot transplanted from his Satanic Majesty's front yard. There is a local superstition that the area is haunted—but by what or by whom no one seems to know. Natives will not venture within its mysterious depths, for they believe the stories handed down to them by the Nez Perce Indians,[3] who have shunned the region for untold generations, because, according to them, it is a playground of certain giant devils from the Outside. These suggestive tales made me very curious.

My first excursion—and my last, thank God!—into those hills occurred while Constantine Theunis and I were living in Hampden the summer of 1938. He was writing a treatise on Egyptian mythology, and I found myself alone much of the time, despite the fact that we shared a modest cabin on Beacon Street, within sight of the infamous Pirate House, built by Exer Jones over sixty years ago.

The morning of June 23rd found me walking in those oddly shaped hills, which had, since seven o'clock, seemed very ordinary indeed. I must have been about seven miles south of Hampden before I noticed anything unusual. I was climbing a grassy ridge overlooking a particularly deep canyon, when I came upon an area totally devoid of the usual bunch-grass and greaseweed. It extended southward, over numerous hills and valleys. At first I thought the spot had been burned over the previous fall, but upon examining the turf, I found no signs of a blaze. The nearby slopes and ravines looked terribly scarred and seared, as if some gigantic torch had blasted them, wiping away all vegetation. And yet there was no evidence of fire. . . .

I moved on over rich, black soil in which no grass flourished. As I headed for the approximate center of this desolate area, I began to notice a strange silence. There were no larks, no rabbits, and even the insects seemed to have deserted the place. I gained the summit of a lofty knoll and tried to guess at the size of that bleak, inexplicable region. Then I saw the lone tree.

It stood on a hill somewhat higher than its companions, and attracted the eye because it was so utterly unexpected. I had seen no trees for miles: thorn and hackberry bushes clustered the shallower ravines, but there had been no mature trees. Strange to find one standing on the crest of the hill.

I crossed two steep canyons before I came to it; and a surprise awaited me. It was not a pine tree, nor a fir tree, nor a hackberry tree. I had never, in all my life, seen one to compare with it—and I never have to this day, for which I am eternally thankful!

More than anything it resembled an oak. It had a huge, twisted trunk, fully a yard in diameter, and the large limbs began spreading outward scarcely seven feet from the ground. The leaves were round, and curiously alike in size and design. It might have been a tree painted on a canvas, but I will swear that it was real. I shall always know that it *was* real, despite what Theunis said later.

I recall that I glanced at the sun and judged the time to be about ten o'clock a.m., although I did not look at my watch. The day was becoming warm, and I sat for a while in the welcome shade of the huge tree. Then I regarded the rank grass that flourished beneath it—another singular phenomenon when I remembered the bleak terrain through which I had passed. A wild maze of hills, ravines, and bluffs hemmed me in on all sides, although the rise on which I sat was rather higher than any other within miles. I looked far to the east—and I jumped to my feet, startled and amazed. Shimmering through a blue haze of distance were the Bitterroot Mountains![4] There is no other range of snow-capped peaks within three hundred miles of Hampden; and I knew—at this altitude—that I shouldn't be seeing them at all. For several minutes I gazed at the marvel; then I became drowsy. I lay in the rank grass, beneath the tree. I unstrapped my camera, took off my hat, and relaxed, staring skyward through the green leaves. I closed my eyes.

Then a curious phenomenon began to assail me—a vague, cloudy sort of vision—glimpsing or day-dreaming seemingly without relevance to anything familiar. I thought I saw a great temple by a sea of ooze, where three suns gleamed in a pale red sky. The vast tomb, or temple, was an anomalous color—a nameless blue-violet shade. Large beasts flew in the cloudy sky, and I seemed to hear the pounding of their scaly wings. I went nearer the stone temple, and a huge doorway loomed in front of me. Within that portal were swirling shadows that seemed to dart and leer and try to snatch me inside that awful darkness. I thought I saw three flaming eyes in the shifting void of a doorway, and I screamed with mortal fear. In that noisome depth, I knew, lurked utter destruction—a living hell even worse than death. I screamed again. The vision faded.

I saw the round leaves and the sane earthly sky. I struggled to rise. I was trembling; cold perspiration beaded my brow. I had a mad impulse to flee; run insanely from that sinister tree on the hill—but I checked the absurd intuition and sat down, trying to collect my senses. Never had I dreamed anything so realistic; so horrifying. What had caused the vision? I had been reading several of Theunis' tomes on ancient Egypt. . . . I mopped my forehead, and decided that it was time for lunch. But I did not feel like eating.

Then I had an inspiration. I would take a few snapshots of the tree, for Theunis. They might shock him out of his habitual air of unconcern. Perhaps I would tell him about the dream. . . . Opening my camera, I took half a dozen shots of the tree, and every aspect of the landscape as seen from the tree. Also, I included one of the gleaming, snow-crested peaks. I might want to return, and these photos would help. . . .

Folding the camera, I returned to my cushion of soft grass. Had that spot beneath the tree a certain alien enchantment? I know that I was reluctant to leave it. . . .

I gazed upward at the curious round leaves. I closed my eyes. A breeze stirred the branches, and their whispered music lulled me into tranquil oblivion. And suddenly I saw again the pale red sky and the three suns. The land of three shadows! Again the great temple came into view. I seemed to be floating on the air—a disembodied spirit exploring the wonders of a mad, multi-dimensional world! The temple's oddly angled cornices frightened me, and I knew that this place was one that no man on earth had ever seen in his wildest dreams.

Again the vast doorway yawned before me; and I was sucked within that black, writhing cloud. I seemed to be staring at space unlimited. I saw a void beyond my vocabulary to describe; a dark, bottomless gulf teeming with nameless shapes and entities—things of madness and delirium, as tenuous as a mist from Shamballah.[5]

My soul shrank. I was terribly afraid. I screamed and screamed, and felt that I would soon go mad. Then in my dream I ran and ran in a fever of utter terror, but I did not know what I was running from. . . . I left that hideous temple and that hellish void, yet I knew I must, barring some miracle, return. . . .

At last my eyes flew open. I was not beneath the tree. I was sprawled on a rocky slope, my clothing torn and disordered. My hands were bleeding. I stood up, pain stabbing through me. I recognized the spot—the ridge where I had first seen the blasted area! I must have walked miles—unconscious! The tree was not in sight, and I was glad. . . . Even the knees of my trousers were torn, as if I had crawled part of the way. . . .

I glanced at the sun. Late afternoon! *Where* had I been? I snatched out my watch. It had stopped at 10:34. . . .

II

"So you have the snapshots?" Theunis drawled. I met his gray eyes across the breakfast table. Three days had slipped by since my return from Hell's Acres. I had told him about the dream beneath the tree, and he had laughed.

"Yes," I replied. "They came last night. Haven't had a chance to open them yet. Give 'em a good, careful study—if they aren't all failures. Perhaps you'll change your mind."

Theunis smiled; sipped his coffee. I gave him the unopened envelope and he quickly broke the seal and withdrew the pictures. He glanced at the first one, and the smile faded from his leonine face. He crushed out his cigarette.

"My God, man! Look at this!"

I seized the glossy rectangle. It was the first picture of the tree, taken at a distance of fifty feet or so. The cause of Theunis' excitement escaped me. There it was, standing boldly on the hill, while below it grew the jungle of grass where I had lain. In the distance were my snow-capped mountains!

"There you are," I cried. "The proof of my story—"

"Look at it!" Theunis snapped. "The shadows—there are three for every rock, bush, and tree!"

He was right. . . . Below the tree, spread in fanlike incongruity, lay three overlapping shadows. Suddenly I realized that the picture held an abnormal and inconsistent element. The leaves on the thing were too lush for the work of sane nature, while the trunk was bulged and knotted in the most abhorrent shapes. Theunis dropped the picture on the table.

"There is something wrong," I muttered. "The tree I saw didn't look as repulsive as that—"

"Are you sure?" Theunis grated. "The fact is, you may have seen many things not recorded on this film."

"It shows more than I saw!"

"That's the point. There is something damnably out of place in this landscape; something I can't understand. The tree seems to suggest a thought—beyond my grasp. . . . It is too misty; too uncertain; too unreal to be natural!" He rapped nervous fingers on the table. He snatched the remaining films and shuffled through them, rapidly.

I reached for the snapshot he had dropped, and sensed a touch of bizarre uncertainty and strangeness as my eyes absorbed its every detail. The flowers and weeds pointed at varying angles, while some of the grass grew in the most bewildering fashion. The tree seemed too veiled and clouded to be readily distinguished, but I noted the huge limbs and the half-bent flower stems that were ready to fall over, yet did not fall. And the many, overlapping shadows. . . . They were, altogether, very disquieting shadows—too long or short when compared to the stems they fell below to give one a feeling of comfortable normality. The landscape hadn't shocked me the day of my visit. . . . There was a dark familiarity and mocking suggestion in it; something tangible, yet distant as the stars beyond the galaxy.

Theunis came back to earth. "Did you mention *three* suns in your dreaming orgy?"

I nodded, frankly puzzled. Then it dawned on me. My fingers trembled slightly as I stared at the picture again. My dream! Of course—

"The others are just like it," Theunis said. "That same uncertainness; that *suggestion*. I should be able to catch the mood of the thing; see it in its real light, but it is too . . . Perhaps later I shall find out, if I look at it long enough."

We sat in silence for some time. A thought came to

me, suddenly, prompted by a strange, inexplicable longing to visit the tree again. "Let's make an excursion. I think I can take you there in half a day."

"You'd better stay away," replied Theunis, thoughtfully. "I doubt if you could find the place again if you wanted to."

"Nonsense," I replied. "Surely, with these photos to guide us—"

"Did you see any familiar landmarks in them?"

His observation was uncanny. After looking through the remaining snaps carefully, I had to admit that there were none.

Theunis muttered under his breath and drew viciously on his cigarette. "A perfectly normal—or nearly so—picture of a spot apparently dropped from nowhere. Seeing mountains at this low altitude is preposterous ... but wait!"

He sprang from the chair as a hunted animal and raced from the room. I could hear him moving about in our makeshift library, cursing volubly. Before long he reappeared with an old, leather-bound volume. Theunis opened it reverently, and peered over the odd characters.

"What do you call that?" I inquired.

"This is an early English translation of the *Chronicle of Nath,* written by Rudolf Yergler, a German mystic and alchemist who borrowed some of his lore from Hermes Trismegistus, the ancient Egyptian sorcerer.[6] There is a passage here that might interest you—might make you understand why this business is even further from the natural than you suspect. Listen."

"So in the year of the Black Goat there came unto Nath a shadow that should not be on Earth, and that had no form known to the eyes of Earth. And it fed on the souls of men; they that it gnawed being lured and blinded with dreams till the horror and the endless night lay upon them. Nor did they see that which gnawed them; for the shadow took false shapes that men know or dream of, and only freedom seemed waiting in the Land of the Three Suns. But it was told by priests of the Old Book that he who could see the shadow's true shape, and live after the seeing, might shun its doom and send it back to the starless gulf of its spawning. This none could do save through the Gem; wherefore did Ka-Nefer[7] the High-Priest keep that gem sacred in the temple. And when it was lost with Phrenes, he who braved the horror and was never seen more, there was weeping in Nath. Yet did the Shadow depart sated at last, nor shall it hunger again till the cycles roll back to the year of the Black Goat."

Theunis paused while I stared, bewildered. Finally he spoke. "Now, Single, I suppose you can guess how all this links up. There is no need of going deep into the primal lore behind this business, but I may as well tell you that according to the old legends this is the so-called 'Year of the Black Goat'—when certain horrors from the fathomless Outside are supposed to visit the earth and do infinite harm. We don't know how they'll be manifest, but there's reason to think that strange mirages and hallucinations will be mixed up in the matter. I don't like the thing you've run up against—the story or the pictures. It may be pretty bad, and I warn you to look out. But first I must try to do what old Yergler says—to see if I can glimpse the matter as it is. Fortunately the old Gem he mentions has been rediscovered—I know where I can get at it. We must use it on the photographs and see what we see.

"It's more or less like a lens or prism, though one can't take photographs with it. Someone of peculiar sensitiveness might look through and sketch what he sees. There's a bit of danger, and the looker may have his consciousness shaken a trifle; for the real shape of the shadow isn't pleasant and doesn't belong on this earth. But it would be a lot more dangerous not to do anything about it. Meanwhile, if you value your life and sanity, keep away from that hill— and from the thing you think is a tree on it."

I was more bewildered than ever. "How can there be organized beings from the Outside in our midst?" I cried. "How do we know that such things exist?"

"You reason in terms of this tiny earth," Theunis said. "Surely you don't think that the world is a rule for measuring the universe. There are entities we never dream of floating under our very noses. Modern science is thrusting back the borderland of the unknown and proving that the mystics were not so far off the track—"

Suddenly I knew that I did not want to look at the picture again; I wanted to destroy it. I wanted to run from it. Theunis was suggesting something beyond. . . . A trembling, cosmic fear gripped me and drew me away from the hideous picture, for I was afraid I would recognize some object in it. . . .

I glanced at my friend. He was poring over the ancient book, a strange expression on his face. He sat up straight. "Let's call the thing off for today. I'm tired of this endless guessing and wondering. I must get the loan of the gem from the museum where it is, and do what is to be done."

"As you say," I replied. "Will you have to go to Croydon?"

He nodded.

"Then we'll both go home," I said decisively.

III

I need not chronicle the events of the fortnight that followed. With me they formed a constant and enervating struggle between a mad longing to return to the cryptic tree of dreams and freedom, and a frenzied dread of that selfsame thing and all connected with it. That I did not return is perhaps less a matter of my own will than a matter of pure chance. Meanwhile I knew that Theunis was desperately active in some investigation of the strangest nature—something which included a mysterious motor trip and a return under circumstances of the greatest secrecy. By hints over the telephone I was made to understand that he had somewhere borrowed the obscure and primal object mentioned in the ancient volume as "The Gem," and that he was busy devising a means of applying it to the photographs I had left with him. He spoke fragmentarily of "refraction," "polarization," and "unknown angles of space and time," and indicated that he was building a kind of box or camera obscura for the study of the curious snapshots with the gem's aid.

It was on the sixteenth day that I received the startling message from the hospital in Croydon. Theunis was there, and wanted to see me at once. He had suffered some odd sort of seizure; being found prone and unconscious by friends who found their way into his house after hearing certain cries of mortal agony and fear. Though still weak and helpless, he had now regained his senses and seemed frantic to tell me something and have me perform certain important duties. This much the hospital informed me over the wire; and within half an hour I was at my friend's bedside, marveling at the inroads which worry and tension had made on his features in so brief a time. His first act was to move away the nurses in order to speak in utter confidence.

"Single—I saw it!" His voice was strained and husky. "You must destroy them all—those pictures. I sent it back by seeing it, but the pictures had better go. That tree will never be seen on the hill again—at least, I hope not—till thousands of eons bring back the Year of the Black Goat. You are safe now—mankind is safe." He paused, breathing heavily, and continued.

"Take the Gem out of the apparatus and put it in the safe—you know the combination. It must go back where it came from, for there's a time when it may be needed to save the world. They won't let me leave here yet, but I can rest if I know it's safe. Don't look through the box as it is— it would fix you as it's fixed me. And burn those damned photographs . . . the one in the box and the others. . . ." But Theunis was exhausted now, and the nurses advanced and motioned me away as he leaned back and closed his eyes.

In another half-hour I was at his house and looking curiously at the long black box on the library table beside the overturned chair. Scattered papers blew about in a breeze from the open window, and close to the box I recognized with a queer sensation the envelope of pictures I had taken. It required only a moment for me to examine the box and detach at one end my earliest picture of the tree, and at the other end a strange bit of amber-colored crystal, cut in devious angles impossible to classify. The touch of the glass fragment seemed curiously warm and electric, and I could scarcely bear to put it out of sight in Theunis' wall safe. The snapshot I handled with a disconcerting mixture of emotions. Even after I had replaced it in the envelope with the rest I had a morbid longing to save it and gloat over it and rush out and up the hill toward its original. Peculiar line-arrangements sprang out of its details to assault and puzzle my memory . . . pictures behind pictures . . . secrets lurking in half-familiar shapes. . . . But a saner contrary instinct, operating at the same time, gave me the vigor and avidity of unplaceable fear as I hastily kindled a fire in the grate and watched the problematic envelope burn to ashes. Somehow I felt that the earth had been purged of a horror on whose brink I had trembled, and which was none the less monstrous because I did not know what it was.

Of the source of Theunis' terrific shock I could form no coherent guess, nor did I dare to think too closely about it. It is notable that I did not at any time have the least impulse to look through the box before removing the gem and photograph. What was shown in the picture by the antique crystal's lens or prism-like power was not, I felt curiously certain, anything that a normal brain ought to be called upon to face. Whatever it was, I had myself been close to it—had been completely under the spell of its allurement—as it brooded on that remote hill in the form of a tree and an unfamiliar landscape. And I did not wish to know what I had so narrowly escaped.

Would that my ignorance might have remained complete! I could sleep better at night. As it was, my eye was arrested before I left the room by the pile of scattered papers rustling on the table beside the black box. All but one were blank, but that one bore a crude drawing in pencil. Suddenly recalling what Theunis had once said about sketching the horror revealed by the gem, I strove to turn away; but sheer curiosity defeated my sane design. Looking again almost furtively, I observed the nervous haste of the strokes, and the unfinished edge left by the sketcher's terrified seizure. Then, in a burst of perverse boldness, I looked squarely at the dark and forbidden design—and fell in a faint.

I shall never describe fully what I saw. After a time

I regained my senses, thrust the sheet into the dying fire, and staggered out through the quiet streets to my home. I thanked God that I had not looked through the crystal at the photograph, and prayed fervently that I might forget the drawing's terrible hint of what Theunis had beheld. Since then I have never been quite the same. Even the fairest scenes have seemed to hold some vague, ambiguous hint of the nameless blasphemies which may underlie them and form their masquerading essence. And yet the sketch was so slight—so little indicative of all that Theunis, to judge from his guarded accounts later on, must have discerned!

Only a few basic elements of the landscape were in the thing. For the most part a cloudy, exotic-looking vapor dominated the view. Every object that might have been familiar was seen to be part of something vague and unknown and altogether un-terrestrial—something infinitely vaster than any human eye could grasp, and infinitely alien, monstrous, and hideous as guessed from the fragment within range.

Where I had, in the landscape itself, seen the twisted, half-sentient tree, there was here visible only a gnarled, terrible hand or talon with fingers or feelers shockingly distended and evidently groping toward something on the ground or in the spectator's direction. And squarely below the writhing, bloated digits I thought I saw an outline in the grass where a man had lain. But the sketch was hasty, and I could not be sure.

The Battle That Ended the Century

With R. H. Barlow

(MS. Found in a Time Machine)

n the eve of the year 2001 a vast crowd of interested spectators were present amidst the romantic ruins of Cohen's Garage,[1] on the former site of New York, to witness a fistic encounter between two renowned champions of the strange-story firmament—Two-Gun Bob, the Terror of the Plains,[2] and Knockout Bernie, the Wild Wolf of West Shokan.[3] [The Wolf was fresh from his correspondence course in physical training, sold to him by Mr. Arthur Leeds.[4]] Before the battle the auguries were determined by the venerated Thibetan Lama Bill Lum Li,[5] who evoked the primal serpent-god of Valusia[6] and found unmistakable signs of victory for both sides. Cream-puffs were inattentively vended by Wladislaw Brenryk[7]—the partakers being treated by the official surgeons, Drs. D. H. Killer[8] and M. Gin Brewery.[9]

The gong was sounded at 39 o'clock, after which the air grew red with the gore of battle, lavishly flung about by the mighty Texas slaughterer. Very shortly the first actual damage occurred—the loosening of several teeth in both participants. One, bouncing out from the Wolf's mouth after a casual tap from Two-Gun, described a parabola toward Yucatán; being retrieved in a hasty expedition by Messrs. A. Hijacked Barrell and G. A. Scotland.[10] This incident was used by the eminent sociologist and ex-poet Frank Chimesleep Short, Jr., as the basis of a ballad of proletarian propaganda with three intentionally defective lines.[11] Meanwhile a potentate from a neighbouring kingdom, the Effjay of Akkamin (also known to himself as an amateur critic), expressed his frenzied disgust at the technique of the combatants, at the same time peddling photographs of the fighters (with himself in the foreground) at five cents each.[12]

In round two the Shokan Soaker's sturdy right crashed through the Texan's ribs and became entangled in sundry viscera; thereby enabling Two-Gun to get in several telling blows on his opponent's unprotected chin. Bob was greatly annoyed by the effeminate squeamishness shewn by several onlookers as muscles, glands, gore, and bits of flesh were spattered over the ringside. During this round the eminent magazine-cover anatomist Mrs. M. Blunderage portrayed the battlers as a pair of spirited nudes behind a thin veil of conveniently curling tobacco-smoke,[13] while the late Mr. C. Half-Cent[14] provided a sketch of three Chinamen clad in silk hats and galoshes—this being his own original conception of the affray. Among the amateur sketches made was one by Mr. Goofy Hooey, which later gained fame in the annual Cubist exhibit as "Abstraction of an Eradicated Pudding".[15]

In the third round the fight grew really rough; several ears and other appurtenances being wholly or partially detached from the frontier battler by the Shokan Shocker. Somewhat irritated, Two-Gun countered with some exceptionally sharp blows; severing many fragments from his aggressor, who continued to fight with all his remaining members. At this stage the audience gave signs of much nervous excitement—instances of trampling and goring being frequent. The more enthusiastic members were placed in the custody of Mr. Harry Brobst of the Butler Hospital for Mental Diseases.[16]

The entire affair was reported by Mr. W. Lablache Talcum,[17] his copy being revised by Horse Power Hateart.[18] Throughout the event notes were taken by M. Le Comte d'Erlette for a 200-volume novel-cycle in the Proustian manner, to be entitled *Morning in September,*[19] with illustrations by Mrs. Blunderage. Mr. J. Caesar Warts[20] frequently interviewed both battlers and all the more important spectators; obtaining as souvenirs (after a spirited struggle with the Effjay) an autographed quarter-rib of Two-Gun's, in an excellent state of preservation, and three finger-nails from the Wild Wolf. Lighting effects were supplied by the Electrical Testing Laboratories under the supervision of H. Kanebrake.[21] The fourth round was prolonged eight hours at the request of the official artist, Mr. H. Wanderer, who wished to put certain shadings of fantasy into his representation of the Wolf's depleted physiognomy, which included several supernumerary details supplied by the imagination.[22]

The climax came in round five, when the Texas Tearer's left passed entirely through Battling Bernie's face and brought both sluggers to the mat. This was adjudged a finish by the referee—Robertieff Essovitch Karovsky, the Muscovite Ambassador—who, in view of the Shokan Shocker's gory state, declared the latter to be essentially liquidated according to the Marxian ideology.[23] The Wild Wolf entered an official protest, which was promptly overruled on the ground that all the points necessary to technical death were theoretically present.

The gonfalons sounded a fanfare of triumph for the victor, while the technically vanquished was committed to the care of the official mortician, Mr. Teaberry Quince.[24] During the ceremonies the theoretical corpse strolled away for a bite of bologna, but a tasteful cenotaph was supplied to furnish a focus for the rites. The funeral procession was headed by a gaily bedecked hearse driven by Malik Taus, the Peacock Sultan, who sat on the box in West Point uniform and turban,[25] and steered an expert course over several formidable hedges and stone walls. About half way to the cemetery the cortège was rejoined by the corpse, who sat beside Sultan Malik on the box and finished his bologna sandwich—his ample girth having made it impossible to enter the hastily selected cenotaph. An appropriate dirge was rendered by Maestro Sing Lee Bawledout on the piccolo;[26] Messrs. De Silva, Brown, and Henderson's celebrated aria, "Never Swat a Fly", from the old cantata *Just Imagine,* being chosen for the occasion.[27] The only detail omitted from the funeral was the interment, which was interrupted by the disconcerting news that the official gate-taker—the celebrated financier and publisher Ivar K. Rodent, Esq.—had absconded with the entire proceeds.[28] [This omission was regretted chiefly by the Rev. D. Vest Wind, who was thereby forced to leave unspoken a long and moving sermon revised expressly for the celebration from a former discourse delivered at the burial of a favourite horse.][29]

Mr. Talcum's report of the event, illustrated by the well-known artist Klarkash-Ton (who esoterically depicted the fighters as boneless fungi),[30] was printed—after repeated rejections by the discriminating editor of the *Windy City Grab-Bag*[31]—as a broadside by W. Peter Chef[32] [, with typographical supervision by Vrest Orton].[33] This, through the efforts of Otis Adelbert Kline,[34] was finally placed on sale in the bookshop of Smearum & Weep, three and a half copies finally being disposed of through the alluring catalogue description supplied by Samuelus Philanthropus, Esq.[35]

In response to this wide demand, the text was finally reprinted by Mr. De Merit in the polychromatic pages of Wurst's *Weakly Americana* under the title "Has Science Been Outmoded? Or, The Millers in the Garage".[36] No copies, however, remain in circulation; since all which were not snapped up by fanatical bibliophiles were seized by the police in connexion with the libel suit of the Wild Wolf, who was, after several appeals ending with the World Court, adjudged not only officially alive but the clear winner of the combat.

"Till A' the Seas"

With R. H. Barlow

I

Upon an eroded cliff-top rested the man, gazing far across the valley. Lying thus, he could see a great distance, but in all the sere expanse there was no visible motion. Nothing stirred the dusty plain, the disintegrated sand of long-dry river-beds, where once coursed the gushing streams of Earth's youth. There was little greenery in this ultimate world, this final stage of mankind's prolonged presence upon the planet. For unnumbered aeons the drought and sandstorms had ravaged all the lands. The trees and bushes had given way to small, twisted shrubs that persisted long through their sturdiness; but these, in turn, perished before the onslaught of coarse grasses and stringy, tough vegetation of strange evolution.

The ever-present heat, as Earth drew nearer to the sun, withered and killed with pitiless rays. It had not come at once; long aeons had gone before any could feel the change. And all through those first ages man's adaptable form had followed the slow mutation and modelled itself to fit the more and more torrid air. Then the day had come when men could bear their hot cities but ill, and a gradual recession began, slow yet deliberate. Those towns and settlements closest to the equator had been first, of course, but later there were others. Man, softened and exhausted, could cope no longer with the ruthlessly mounting heat. It seared him as he was, and evolution was too slow to mould new resistances in him.

Yet not at first were the great cities of the equator left to the spider and the scorpion. In the early years there were many who stayed on, devising curious shields and armours against the heat and the deadly dryness. These fearless souls, screening certain buildings against the encroaching sun, made miniature worlds of refuge wherein no protective armour was needed. They contrived marvellously ingenious things, so that for a while men persisted in the rusting towers, hoping thereby to cling to old lands till the searing should be over. For many would not believe what the astronomers said, and looked for a coming of the mild olden world again. But one day the men of Dath, from the new city of Niyara, made signals to Yuanario,[1] their immemorially ancient capital, and gained no answer from the few who remained therein. And when explorers reached that millennial city of bridge-linked towers they found only silence. There was not even the horror of corruption, for the scavenger lizards had been swift.

Only then did the people fully realize that these cities were lost to them; know that they must forever abandon them to nature. The other colonists in the hot lands fled from their brave posts, and total silence reigned within the high basalt walls of a thousand empty towns. Of the dense throngs and multitudinous activities of the past, nothing finally remained. There now loomed against the rainless deserts only the blistered towers of vacant houses, factories, and structures of every sort, reflecting the sun's dazzling radiance and parching in the more and more intolerable heat.

Many lands, however, had still escaped the scorching blight, so that the refugees were soon absorbed in the life of a newer world. During strangely prosperous centuries the hoary deserted cities of the equator grew half-forgotten and entwined with fantastic fables. Few thought of those spectral, rotting towers . . . those huddles of shabby walls and cactus-choked streets, darkly silent and abandoned. . . .

Wars came, sinful and prolonged, but the times of peace were greater. Yet always the swollen sun increased its radiance as Earth drew closer to its fiery parent. It was as if the planet meant to return to that source whence it was snatched, aeons ago, through the accidents of cosmic growth.

After a time the blight crept outward from the central belt. Southern Yarat burned as a tenantless desert—and then the north. In Perath and Baling,[2] those ancient cities where brooding centuries dwelt, there moved only the scaly shapes of the serpent and the salamander, and at last Loton[3] echoed only to the fitful falling of tottering spires and crumbling domes.

Steady, universal, and inexorable was the great eviction of man from the realms he had always known. No land within the widening stricken belt was spared; no people left unrouted. It was an epic, a titan tragedy whose plot was unrevealed to the actors—this wholesale desertion of the cities of men. It took not years or even centuries, but millennia of ruthless change. And still it kept on—sullen, inevitable, savagely devastating.

Agriculture was at a standstill, the world fast became too arid for crops. This was remedied by artificial substitutes, soon universally used. And as the old places that had known the great things of mortals were left, the loot salvaged by the fugitives grew smaller and smaller. Things of the greatest value and importance were left in dead museums—lost amid the centuries—and in the end the heritage of the immemorial past was abandoned. A degeneracy both physical and cultural set in with the insidious heat. For man had so long dwelt in comfort and security that this exodus from past scenes was difficult. Nor were these events received phlegmatically; their very slowness was terrifying. Degradation and debauchery were soon common; government was disorganized, and the civilizations aimlessly slid back toward barbarism.

When, forty-nine centuries after the blight from the equatorial belt, the whole western hemisphere was left unpeopled, chaos was complete. There was no trace of order or decency in the last scenes of this titanic, wildly impressive migration. Madness and frenzy stalked through them, and fanatics screamed of an Armageddon close at hand.

Mankind was now a pitiful remnant of the elder races, a fugitive not only from the prevailing conditions, but from his own degeneracy. Into the northland and the antarctic went those who could; the rest lingered for years in an incredible saturnalia, vaguely doubting the forthcoming disasters. In the city of Borligo[4] a wholesale execution of the new prophets took place, after months of unfulfilled expectations. They thought the flight to the northland unnecessary, and looked no longer for the threatened ending.

How they perished must have been terrible indeed—those vain, foolish creatures who thought to defy the universe. But the blackened, scorched towns are mute. . . .

272

These events, however, must not be chronicled—for there are larger things to consider than this complex and unhastening downfall of a lost civilization. During a long period morale was at lowest ebb among the courageous few who settled upon the alien arctic and antarctic shores, now mild as were those of southern Yarat in the long-dead past. But here there was respite. The soil was fertile, and forgotten pastoral arts were called into use anew. There was, for a long time, a contented little epitome of the lost lands; though here were no vast throngs or great buildings. Only a sparse remnant of humanity survived the aeons of change and peopled those scattered villages of the later world.

How many millennia this continued is not known. The sun was slow in invading this last retreat; and as the eras passed there developed a sound, sturdy race, bearing no memories or legends of the old, lost lands. Little navigation was practiced by this new people, and the flying machine was wholly forgotten. Their devices were of the simplest type, and their culture was simple and primitive. Yet they were contented, and accepted the warm climate as something natural and accustomed.

But unknown to these simple peasant-folk, still further rigours of nature were slowly preparing themselves. As the generations passed, the waters of the vast and unplumbed ocean wasted slowly away; enriching the air and the desiccated soil, but sinking lower and lower each century. The splashing surf still glistened bright, and the swirling eddies were still there, but a doom of dryness hung over the whole watery expanse. However, the shrinkage could not have been detected save by instruments more delicate than any then known to the race. Even had the people realized the ocean's contraction, it is not likely that any vast alarm or great disturbance would have resulted, for the losses were so slight, and the seas so great. . . . Only a few inches during many centuries—but in many centuries; increasing—

* * *

So at last the oceans went, and water became a rarity on a globe of sun-baked drought. Man had slowly spread over all the arctic and antarctic lands; the equatorial cities, and many of later habitation, were forgotten even to legend.

And now again the peace was disturbed, for water was scarce, and found only in deep caverns. There was little enough, even of this; and men died of thirst wandering in far places. Yet so slow were these deadly changes, that each new generation of man was loath to believe what it heard from its parents. None would admit that the heat had been less or the water more plentiful in the old days, or take warning that days of bitterer burning and drought were to come. Thus it was even at the end, when only a few hundred human creatures panted for breath beneath the cruel sun; a piteous huddled handful out of all the unnumbered millions who had once dwelt on the doomed planet.

And the hundreds became small, till man was to be reckoned only in tens. These tens clung to the shrinking dampness of the caves, and knew at last that the end was near. So slight was their range that none had ever seen the tiny, fabled spots of ice left close to the planet's poles—if such indeed remained. Even had they existed and been known to man, none could have reached them across the trackless and formidable deserts. And so the last pathetic few dwindled. . . .

It cannot be described, this awesome chain of events that depopulated the whole Earth; the range is too tremendous for any to picture or encompass. Of the people of Earth's fortunate ages, billions of years before, only a few prophets and madmen could have conceived that which was to come—could have grasped visions of the still, dead lands, and long-empty sea-beds. The rest would have doubted . . . doubted alike the shadow of change upon the planet and the shadow of doom upon the race. For man has always thought himself the immortal master of natural things. . . .

II

When he had eased the dying pangs of the old woman, Ull wandered in a fearful daze out into the dazzling sands. She had been a fearsome thing, shrivelled and so dry; like withered leaves. Her face had been the colour of the sickly yellow grasses that rustled in the hot wind, and she was loathsomely old.

But she had been a companion; someone to stammer out vague fears to, to talk to about this incredible thing; a comrade to share one's hopes for succour from those silent other colonies beyond the mountains. He could not believe none lived elsewhere, for Ull was young, and not certain as are the old.

For many years he had known none but the old woman—her name was Mladdna. She had come that day in his eleventh year, when all the hunters went to seek food, and did not return. Ull had no mother that he could remember, and there were few women in the tiny group. When the men vanished, those three women, the young one and the two old, had screamed fearfully, and moaned long. Then the young one had gone mad, and killed herself with a sharp stick. The old ones buried her in a shallow hole dug with their nails, so Ull had been alone when this still older

Mladdna came.

She walked with the aid of a knotty pole, a priceless relique of the old forests, hard and shiny with years of use. She did not say whence she came, but stumbled into the cabin while the young suicide was being buried. There she waited till the two returned, and they accepted her incuriously.

That was the way it had been for many weeks, until the two fell sick, and Mladdna could not cure them. Strange that those younger two should have been stricken, while she, infirm and ancient, lived on. Mladdna had cared for them many days, and at length they died, so that Ull was left with only the stranger. He screamed all the night, so she became at length out of patience, and threatened to die too. Then, hearkening, he became quiet at once; for he was not desirous of complete solitude. After that he lived with Mladdna and they gathered roots to eat.

Mladdna's rotten teeth were ill suited to the food they gathered, but they contrived to chop it up till she could manage it. This weary routine of seeking and eating was Ull's childhood.

Now he was strong, and firm, in his nineteenth year, and the old woman was dead. There was naught to stay for, so he determined at once to seek out those fabled huts beyond the mountains, and live with the people there. There was nothing to take on the journey. Ull closed the door of his cabin—why, he could not have told, for no animals had been there for many years—and left the dead woman within. Half-dazed, and fearful at his own audacity, he walked long hours in the dry grasses, and at length reached the first of the foothills. The afternoon came, and he climbed until he was weary, and lay down on the grasses. Sprawled there, he thought of many things. He wondered at the strange life, passionately anxious to seek out the lost colony beyond the mountains; but at last he slept.

When he awoke there was starlight on his face, and he felt refreshed. Now that the sun was gone for a time, he travelled more quickly, eating little, and determining to hasten before the lack of water became difficult to bear. He had brought none; for the last people, dwelling in one place and never having occasion to bear their precious water away, made no vessels of any kind. Ull hoped to reach his goal within a day, and thus escape thirst; so he hurried on beneath the bright stars, running at times in the warm air, and at other times lapsing into a dogtrot.

So he continued until the sun arose, yet still he was within the small hills, with three great peaks looming ahead. In their shade he rested again. Then he climbed all the morning, and at mid-day surmounted the first peak, where he lay for a time, surveying the space before the next range.

Upon an eroded cliff-top rested the man, gazing far across the valley. Lying thus he could see a great distance, but in all the sere expanse there was no visible motion....

The second night came, and found Ull amid the rough peaks, the valley and the place where he had rested far behind. He was nearly out of the second range now, and hurrying still. Thirst had come upon him that day, and he regretted his folly. Yet he could not have stayed there with the corpse, alone in the grasslands. He sought to convince himself thus, and hastened ever on, tiredly straining.

And now there were only a few steps before the cliff wall would part and allow a view of the land beyond. Ull stumbled wearily down the stony way, tumbling and bruising himself even more. It was nearly before him, this land where men were rumoured to have dwelt; this land of which he had heard tales in his youth. The way was long, but the goal was great. A boulder of giant circumference cut off his view; upon this he scrambled anxiously. Now at last he could behold by the sinking orb his long-sought destination, and his thirst and aching muscles were forgotten as he saw joyfully that a small huddle of buildings clung to the base of the farther cliff.

Ull rested not; but, spurred on by what he saw, ran and staggered and crawled the half mile remaining. He fancied that he could detect forms among the rude cabins. The sun was nearly gone; the hateful, devastating sun that had slain humanity. He could not be sure of details, but soon the cabins were near.

They were very old, for clay blocks lasted long in the still dryness of the dying world. Little, indeed, changed but the living things—the grasses and these last men.

Before him an open door swung upon rude pegs. In the fading light Ull entered, weary unto death, seeking painfully the expected faces.

Then he fell upon the floor and wept, for at the table was propped a dry and ancient skeleton.

* * *

He rose at last, crazed by thirst, aching unbearably, and suffering the greatest disappointment any mortal could know. He was, then, the last living thing upon the globe. His the heritage of the Earth . . . all the lands, and all to him equally useless. He staggered up, not looking at the dim white form in the reflected moonlight, and went through the door. About the empty village he wandered, searching for water and sadly inspecting this long-empty place so spectrally preserved by the changeless air. Here

278

there was a dwelling, there a rude place where things had been made—clay vessels holding only dust, and nowhere any liquid to quench his burning thirst.

Then, in the centre of the little town, Ull saw a well-curb. He knew what it was, for he had heard tales of such things from Mladdna. With pitiful joy, he reeled forward and leaned upon the edge. There, at last, was the end of his search. Water—slimy, stagnant, and shallow, but water—before his sight.

Ull cried out in the voice of a tortured animal, groping for the chain and bucket. His hand slipped on the slimy edge; and he fell upon his chest across the brink. For a moment he lay there—then soundlessly his body was precipitated down the black shaft.

There was a slight splash in the murky shallowness as he struck some long-sunken stone, dislodged aeons ago from the massive coping. The disturbed water subsided into quietness.

And now at last the Earth was dead. The final, pitiful survivor had perished. All the teeming billions; the slow aeons; the empires and civilizations of mankind were summed up in this poor twisted form—and how titanically meaningless it all had been! Now indeed had come an end and climax to all the efforts of humanity—how monstrous and incredible a climax in the eyes of those poor complacent fools of the prosperous days! Not ever again would the planet know the thunderous tramping of human millions—or even the crawling of lizards and the buzz of insects, for they, too, had gone. Now was come the reign of sapless branches and endless fields of tough grasses. Earth, like its cold, imperturbable moon, was given over to silence and blackness forever.

The stars whirred on; the whole careless plan would

continue for infinities unknown. This trivial end of a negligible episode mattered not to distant nebulae or to suns new-born, flourishing, and dying. The race of man, too puny and momentary to have a real function or purpose, was as if it had never existed. To such a conclusion the aeons of its farcically toilsome evolution had led.

But when the deadly sun's first rays darted across the valley, a light found its way to the weary face of a broken figure that lay in the slime.

Collapsing Cosmoses

With R. H. Barlow

am Bor glued each of his six eyes to the lenses of the cosmoscope. His nasal tentacles were orange with fear, and his antennae buzzed hoarsely as he dictated his report to the operator behind him. "It has come!" he cried. "That blur in the ether can be nothing less than a fleet from outside the space-time continuum we know. Nothing like this has ever appeared before. It must be an enemy. Give the alarm to the Inter-Cosmic Chamber of Commerce. There's no time to lose—at this rate they'll be upon us in less than six centuries. Hak Ni must have a chance to get the fleet in action at once."

[I glanced up from the *Windy City Grab-Bag*,[1] which had beguiled my inactive peace-time days in the Super-Galactic Patrol. The handsome young vegetable, with whom I shared my bowl of caterpillar custard since earliest infancy, and with whom I had been thrown out of every joint in the intra-dimensional city of Kastor-Ya,] had really a worried look upon his lavender face. After he had given the alarm we jumped on our ether-bikes and hastened across to the outer planet on which the Chamber held its sessions.

[Within the Great Council Chamber, which measured twenty-eight square feet (with quite a high ceiling), were gathered delegates from all the thirty-seven galaxies of our immediate universe. Oll Stof, President of the Chamber and representative of the Milliner's Soviet, raised his eyeless snout with dignity] and prepared to address the assembled multitude. He was a highly developed protozoan organism from Nov-Kas, and spoke by emitting alternate waves of heat and cold.

["Gentlemen," he radiated, "a terrible peril has come upon us which I feel I must bring to your attention."

Everybody applauded riotously, as a wave of excitement rippled through the variegated audience; those who were handless slithering their tentacles together.

He continued: "Hak Ni, crawl upon the dais!"

There was a thunderous silence, during which a faint prompting was heard] from the dizzy summit of the platform. [Hak Ni, the yellow-furred and valorous commander of our ranks through numerous installments, ascended to the towering peak inches above the floor.

"My friends—" he began, with an eloquent scraping of his posterior limbs, "these treasured walls and pillars shall not mourn on my account. . . ." At this point, one of his numerous relatives cheered. "Well do I remember when . . ."

Oll Stof interrupted him.] "You have anticipated my thoughts and orders. Go forth and win for dear old Inter-Cosmic."

[Two paragraphs later found us soaring out past innumerable stars toward where a faint blur half a million light-years long marked the presence of the hated enemy, whom we had not seen. What monsters of malformed grotesqueness seethed out there among the moons of infinity, we really didn't know, but there was a malign menace in the glow that steadily increased until it spanned the entire heavens. Very soon we made out separate objects in the blur. Before all my horror-stricken vision-areas there spread an endless array of scissors-shaped space-ships of totally unfamiliar form.

Then from the direction of the enemy there came a terrifying sound, which I soon recognised as a hail and a challenge. An answering thrill crept through me as I met with uplifted antennae this threat of battle with a monstrous intrusion upon our fair system from unknown outside abysses.]

At the sound, [which was something like that of a rusty sewing-machine, only more horrible,] Hak Ni too raised his snout in defiance, radiating a masterful order to the captains of the fleet. Instantly the huge space-ships swung into battle formation, with only a hundred or two of them many light-years out of line.

The Challenge from Beyond

With C. L. Moore, A. Merritt, Robert E. Howard,
and Frank Belknap Long

[C]. L. Moore:] George Campbell opened
sleep-fogged eyes upon darkness and lay gazing out of the
tent flap upon the pale August night for some minutes
before he roused enough even to wonder what had wak-
ened him. There was in the keen, clear air of these Canadian woods a soporific as potent as any drug. Campbell lay
quiet for a moment, sinking slowly back into the delicious
borderlands of sleep, conscious of an exquisite weariness,
an unaccustomed sense of muscles well used, and relaxed
now into perfect ease. These were vacation's most delightful moments, after all—rest, after toil, in the clear, sweet
forest night.

Luxuriously, as his mind sank backward into oblivion, he assured himself once more that three long months
of freedom lay before him—freedom from cities and monotony, freedom from pedagogy and the University and
students with no rudiments of interest in the geology he
earned his daily bread by dinning into their obdurate ears.
Freedom from—

Abruptly the delightful somnolence crashed about

him. Somewhere outside the sound of tin shrieking across tin slashed into his peace. George Campbell sat up jerkily and reached for his flashlight. Then he laughed and put it down again, straining his eyes through the midnight gloom outside where among the tumbling cans of his supplies a dark anonymous little night beast was prowling. He stretched out a long arm and groped about among the rocks at the tent door for a missile. His fingers closed on a large stone, and he drew back his hand to throw.

But he never threw it. It was such a queer thing he had come upon in the dark. Square, crystal smooth, obviously artificial, with dull rounded corners. The strangeness of its rock surfaces to his fingers was so remarkable that he reached again for his flashlight and turned its rays upon the thing he held.

All sleepiness left him as he saw what it was he had picked up in his idle groping. It was clear as rock crystal, this queer, smooth cube. Quartz, unquestionably, but not in its usual hexagonal crystallized form. Somehow—he could not guess the method—it had been wrought into a perfect cube, about four inches in measurement over each worn face. For it was incredibly worn. The hard, hard crystal was rounded now until its corners were almost gone and the thing was beginning to assume the outlines of a sphere. Ages and ages of wearing, years almost beyond counting, must have passed over this strange clear thing.

But the most curious thing of all was that shape he could make out dimly in the heart of the crystal. For imbedded in its center lay a little disc of a pale and nameless substance with characters incised deep upon its quartz-enclosed surface. Wedge-shaped characters, faintly reminiscent of cuneiform writing.

George Campbell wrinkled his brows and bent closer

above the little enigma in his hands, puzzling helplessly. How could such a thing as this have imbedded in pure rock crystal? Remotely a memory floated through his mind of ancient legends that called quartz crystals ice which had frozen too hard to melt again. Ice—and wedge-shaped cuneiforms—yes, didn't that sort of writing originate among the Sumerians who came down from the north in history's remotest beginnings to settle in the primitive Mesopotamian valley? Then hard sense regained control and he laughed. Quartz, of course, was formed in the earliest of earth's geological periods, when there was nothing anywhere but heat and heaving rock. Ice had not come for tens of millions of years after this thing must have been formed.

And yet—that writing. Man-made, surely, although its characters were unfamiliar save in their faint hinting at cuneiform shapes. Or could there, in a Paleozoic world, have been things with a written language who might have graven these cryptic wedges upon the quartz-enveloped disc he held? Or—might a thing like this have fallen meteor-like out of space into the unformed rock of a still molten world? Could it—

Then he caught himself up sharply and felt his ears going hot at the luridness of his own imagination. The silence and the solitude and the queer thing in his hands were conspiring to play tricks with his common sense. He shrugged and laid the crystal down at the edge of his pallet, switching off the light. Perhaps morning and a clear head would bring him an answer to the questions that seemed so insoluble now.

But sleep did not come easily. For one thing, it seemed to him as he flashed off the light, that the little cube had shone for a moment as if with sustained light before it faded into the surrounding dark. Or perhaps he was wrong.

Perhaps it had been only his dazzled eyes that seemed to see the light forsake it reluctantly, glowing in the enigmatic deeps of the thing with queer persistence.

He lay there unquietly for a long while, turning the unanswered questions over and over in his mind. There was something about this crystal cube out of the unmeasured past, perhaps from the dawn of all history, that constituted a challenge that would not let him sleep.

[A. Merritt:] He lay there, it seemed to him, for hours. It had been the lingering light, the luminescence that seemed so reluctant to die, which held his mind. It was as though something in the heart of the cube had awakened, stirred drowsily, become suddenly alert . . . and intent upon him.

Sheer fantasy, this. He stirred impatiently and flashed his light upon his watch. Close to one o'clock; three hours more before the dawn. The beam fell and was focused upon the warm crystal cube. He held it there closely, for minutes. He snapped it out, then watched.

There was no doubt about it now. As his eyes accustomed themselves to the darkness, he saw that the strange crystal was glimmering with tiny fugitive lights deep within it like threads of sapphire lightnings. They were at its center and they seemed to him to come from the pale disc with its disturbing markings. And the disc itself was becoming larger . . . the markings shifting shapes . . . the cube was growing . . . was it illusion brought about by the tiny lightnings. . . .

He heard a sound. It was the very ghost of a sound, like the ghosts of harp strings being plucked with ghostly fingers. He bent closer. It came from the cube. . . .

There was squeaking in the underbrush, a flurry of bodies and an agonized wailing like a child in death throes and swiftly stilled. Some small tragedy of the wilderness,

killer and prey. He stepped over to where it had been enact-
ed, but could see nothing. He again snapped off the flash
and looked toward his tent. Upon the ground was a pale
blue glimmering. It was the cube. He stooped to pick it up;
then obeying some obscure warning, drew back his hand.

And again, he saw, its glow was dying. The tiny sapphire lightnings flashing fitfully, withdrawing to the disc
from which they had come. There was no sound from it.

He sat, watching the luminescence glow and fade,
glow and fade, but steadily becoming dimmer. It came to
him that two elements were necessary to produce the phenomenon. The electric ray itself, and his own fixed attention. His mind must travel along the ray, fix itself upon the
cube's heart, if its beat were to wax, until . . . what?

He felt a chill of spirit, as though from contact with
some alien thing. It was alien, he knew it; not of this earth.
Not of earth's life. He conquered his shrinking, picked up
the cube and took it into the tent. It was neither warm nor
cold; except for its weight he would not have known he
held it. He put it upon the table, keeping the torch turned
from it; then stepped to the flap of the tent and closed it.

He went back to the table, drew up the camp chair,
and turned the flash directly upon the cube, focusing it so
far as he could upon its heart. He sent all his will, all his
concentration, along it; focusing will and sight upon the
disc as he had the light.

As though at command, the sapphire lightnings
burned forth. They burst from the disc into the body of
the crystal cube, then beat back, bathing the disc and the
markings. Again these began to change, shifting, moving,
advancing, and retreating in the blue gleaming. They were
no longer cuneiform. They were things . . . objects.

He heard the murmuring music, the plucked harp

strings. Louder grew the sound and louder, and now all the body of the cube vibrated to their rhythm. The crystal walls were melting, growing misty as though formed of the mist of diamonds. And the disc itself was growing . . . the shapes shifting, dividing and multiplying as though some door had been opened and into it companies of phantasms were pouring. While brighter, more bright grew the pulsing light.

He felt swift panic, tried to withdraw sight and will, dropped the flash. The cube had no need now of the ray . . . and he could not withdraw . . . could not withdraw? Why, he himself was being sucked into that disc which was now a globe within which unnameable shapes danced to a music that bathed the globe with steady radiance.

There was no tent. There was only a vast curtain of sparkling mist behind which shone the globe. . . .

He felt himself drawn through that mist, sucked through it as if by a mighty wind, straight for the globe.

[H. P. Lovecraft:] As the mist-blurred light of the sapphire suns grew more and more intense, the outlines of the globe ahead wavered and dissolved to a churning chaos. Its pallor and its motion and its music all blended themselves with the engulfing mist—bleaching it to a pale steel-colour and setting it undulantly in motion. And the sapphire suns, too, melted imperceptibly into the greying infinity of shapeless pulsation.

Meanwhile the sense of forward, outward motion grew intolerably, incredibly, cosmically swift. Every standard of speed known to earth seemed dwarfed, and Campbell knew that any such flight in physical reality would mean instant death to a human being. Even as it was—in this strange, hellish hypnosis or nightmare—the quasi-visual impression of meteor-like hurtling almost paralysed his mind. Though there were no real points of reference in the grey, pulsing void, he felt that he was approaching and passing the speed of light itself. Finally his consciousness did go under—and merciful blackness swallowed everything.

It was very suddenly, and amidst the most impenetrable darkness, that thoughts and ideas again came to George Campbell. Of how many moments—or years—or eternities—had elapsed since his flight through the grey void, he could form no estimate. He knew only that he seemed to be at rest and without pain. Indeed, the absence of all physical sensation was the salient quality of his condition. It made even the blackness seem less solidly black—suggesting as it did that he was rather a disembodied intelligence in a state beyond physical senses, than a corporeal being with senses deprived of their accustomed objects of perception. He could think sharply and quickly—almost preternaturally so—yet could form no idea whatsoever of his situation.

Half by instinct, he realised that he was not in his own tent. True, he might have awaked there from a nightmare to a world equally black; yet he knew this was not so. There was no camp cot beneath him—he had no hands to feel the blankets and canvas surface and flashlight that ought to be around him—there was no sensation of cold in the air—no flap through which he could glimpse the pale night outside . . . something was wrong, dreadfully wrong.

He cast his mind backward and thought of the fluorescent cube which had hypnotised him—of that, and all which had followed. He had known that his mind was going, yet had been unable to draw back. At the last moment there had been a shocking, panic fear—a subconscious fear beyond even that caused by the sensation of daemonic flight. It had come from some vague flash or remote recollection—just what, he could not at once tell. Some cell-group in the back of his head had seemed to find a cloud-ily familiar quality in the cube—and that familiarity was fraught with dim terror. Now he tried to remember what the familiarity and the terror were.

Little by little it came to him. Once—long ago, in connection with his geological life-work—he had read of something like that cube. It had to do with those debat-able and disquieting clay fragments called the Eltdown Shards,[1] dug up from pre-carboniferous strata in southern England thirty years before. Their shape and markings were so queer that a few scholars hinted at artificiality, and made wild conjectures about them and their origin. They came, clearly, from a time when no human beings could exist on the globe—but their contours and figurings were damna-bly puzzling. That was how they got their name.

It was not, however, in the writings of any sober sci-entist that Campbell had seen that reference to a crystal, disc-holding globe. The source was far less reputable, and infinitely more vivid. About 1912 a deeply learned Sus-sex clergyman of occultist leanings—the Reverend Arthur Brooke Winters-Hall—had professed to identify the mark-ings on the Eltdown Shards with some of the so-called "pre-human hieroglyphs" persistently cherished and esoterically handed down in certain mystical circles, and had published at his own expense what purported to be a "translation" of the primal and baffling "inscriptions"—a "translation" still quoted frequently and seriously by occult writers. In this "translation"—a surprisingly long brochure in view of the limited number of "shards" existing—had occurred the narrative, supposedly of pre-human authorship, containing the now frightening reference.

As the story went, there dwelt on a world—and eventually on countless other worlds—of outer space a mighty order of worm-like beings whose attainments and whose control of nature surpassed anything within the range of terrestrial imagination. They had mastered the art of interstellar travel early in their career, and had peopled every habitable planet in their own galaxy—killing off the races they found.

Beyond the limits of their own galaxy—which was not ours—they could not navigate in person; but in their quest for knowledge of all space and time they discovered a means of spanning certain transgalactic gulfs with their minds. They devised peculiar objects—strangely energized cubes of a curious crystal containing hypnotic talismen and enclosed in space-resisting spherical envelopes of an unknown substance—which could be forcibly expelled beyond the limits of their universe, and which would respond to the attraction of cool solid matter only.

These, of which a few would necessarily land on various inhabited worlds in outside universes, formed the ether-bridges needed for mental communication. Atmospheric friction burned away the protecting envelope, leaving the cube exposed and subject to discovery by the intelligent minds of the world where it fell. By its very nature, the cube would attract and rivet attention. This, when coupled with the action of light, was sufficient to set its special properties working.

The mind that noticed the cube would be drawn into it by the power of the disc, and would be sent on a thread of obscure energy to the place whence the disc had come—the remote world of the worm-like space-explorers across stupendous galactic abysses. Received in one of the machines to which each cube was attuned, the captured mind would remain suspended without body or senses until examined by one of the dominant race. Then it would, by an obscure process of interchange, be pumped of all its contents. The investigator's mind would now occupy the strange machine while the captive mind occupied the interrogator's worm-like body. Then, in another interchange, the interrogator's mind would leap across boundless space to the captive's vacant and unconscious body on the trans-galactic world—animating the alien tenement as best it might, and exploring the alien world in the guise of one of its denizens.

When done with exploration, the adventurer would use the cube and its disc in accomplishing his return—and sometimes the captured mind would be restored safely to its own remote world. Not always, however, was the dominant race so kind. Sometimes, when a potentially important race capable of space travel was found, the worm-like folk would employ the cube to capture and annihilate minds by the thousands, and would extirpate the race for diplomatic reasons—using the exploring minds as agents of destruction.

In other cases sections of the worm-folk would permanently occupy a trans-galactic planet—destroying the captured minds and wiping out the remaining inhabitants preparatory to settling down in unfamiliar bodies. Never, however, could the parent civilization be quite duplicated in such a case; since the new planet would not contain all the materials necessary for the worm-race's arts. The cubes, for example, could be made only on the home planet.

Only a few of the numberless cubes sent forth ever found a landing and response on an inhabited world—since there was no such thing as *aiming* them at goals beyond sight or knowledge. Only three, ran the story, had ever landed on peopled worlds in our own particular universe. One of these had struck a planet near the galactic rim two thousand billion years ago, while another had lodged three billion years ago on a world near the centre of the galaxy. The third—and the only one ever known to have invaded the solar system—had reached our own earth 150,000,000 years ago.

It was with this latter that Dr. Winters-Hall's "translation" chiefly dealt. When the cube struck the earth, he wrote, the ruling terrestrial species was a huge, cone-shaped race surpassing all others before or since in mentality and achievements.[2] This race was so advanced that it had actually sent minds abroad in both space *and time* to explore the cosmos, hence recognised something of what had happened when the cube fell from the sky and certain individuals had suffered mental change after gazing at it.

Realising that the changed individuals represented invading minds, the race's leaders had them destroyed—even at the cost of leaving the displaced minds exiled in alien space. They had had experience with even stranger transitions. When, through a mental exploration of space and time, they formed a rough idea of what the cube was, they carefully hid the thing from light and sight, and guarded it as a menace. They did not wish to destroy a thing so rich in later experimental possibilities. Now and then some rash, unscrupulous adventurer would furtively gain access to it and sample its perilous powers despite the consequences—but all such cases were discovered, and safely and drastically dealt with.

Of this evil meddling the only bad result was that the worm-like outside race learned from the new exiles what had happened to their explorers on earth, and conceived a violent hatred of the planet and all its life-forms. They would have depopulated it if they could, and indeed sent additional cubes into space in the wild hope of striking it

by accident in unguarded places—but that accident never
came to pass.

The cone-shaped terrestrial beings kept the one existing cube in a special shrine as a relique and basis for experiments, till after aeons it was lost amidst the chaos of war and
the destruction of the great polar city where it was guarded.
When, fifty million years ago, the beings sent their minds
ahead into the infinite future to avoid a nameless peril of inner earth, the whereabouts of the sinister cube from space
were unknown.

This much, according to the learned occultist, the
Eltdown Shards had said. What now made the account so
obscurely frightful to Campbell was the minute accuracy
with which the alien cube had been described. Every detail tallied—dimensions, consistency, hieroglyphed central
disc, hypnotic effects. As he thought the matter over and
over amidst the darkness of his strange situation, he began
to wonder whether his whole experience with the crystal
cube—indeed, its very existence—were not a nightmare
brought on by some freakish subconscious memory of this
old bit of extravagant, charlatanic reading. If so, though,
the nightmare must still be in force; since his present apparently bodiless state had nothing of normality in it.

Of the time consumed by this puzzled memory and
reflection, Campbell could form no estimate. Everything
about his state was so unreal that ordinary dimensions and
measurements became meaningless. It seemed an eternity,
but perhaps it was not really long before the sudden interruption came. What happened was as strange and inexplicable as the blackness it succeeded. There was a sensation—of the mind rather than of the body—and all at
once Campbell felt his thoughts swept or sucked beyond
his control in tumultuous and chaotic fashion.

Memories arose irresponsibly and irrelevantly. All that he knew—all his personal background, traditions, experiences, scholarship, dreams, ideas, and inspirations—welled up abruptly and simultaneously, with a dizzying speed and abundance which soon made him unable to keep track of any separate concept. The parade of all his mental contents became an avalanche, a cascade, a vortex. It was as horrible and vertiginous as his hypnotic flight through space when the crystal cube pulled him. Finally it sapped his consciousness and brought on fresh oblivion.

Another measureless blank—and then a slow trickle of sensation. This time it was physical, not mental. Sapphire light, and a low rumble of distant sound. There were tactile impressions—he could realise that he was lying at full length on something, though there was a baffling strangeness about the feel of his posture. He could not reconcile the pressure of the supporting surface with his own outlines—or with the outlines of the human form at all. He tried to move his arms, but found no definite response to the attempt. Instead, there were little, ineffectual nervous twitches all over the area which seemed to mark his body.

He tried to open his eyes more widely, but found himself unable to control their mechanism. The sapphire light came in a diffused, nebulous manner, and could nowhere be voluntarily focussed into definiteness. Gradually, though, visual images began to trickle in curiously and indecisively. The limits and qualities of vision were not those which he was used to, but he could roughly correlate the sensation with what he had known as sight. As this sensation gained some degree of stability, Campbell realised that he must still be in the throes of nightmare.

He seemed to be in a room of considerable extent—of medium height, but with a large proportionate area. On every side—and he could apparently see all four sides at once—were high, narrowish slits which seemed to serve as combined doors and windows. There were singular low tables or pedestals, but no furniture of normal nature and proportions. Through the slits streamed floods of sapphire light, and beyond them could be mistily seen the sides and roofs of fantastic buildings like clustered cubes. On the walls—in the vertical panels between the slits—were strange markings of an oddly disquieting character. It was some time before Campbell understood why they disturbed him so—then he saw that they were, in repeated instances, precisely like some of the hieroglyphs on the crystal cube's disc.

The actual nightmare element, though, was something more than this. It began with the living thing which presently entered through one of the slits, advancing deliberately toward him and bearing a metal box of bizarre proportions and glassy, mirror-like surfaces. For this thing was nothing human—nothing of earth—nothing even of man's myths and dreams. It was a gigantic, pale-grey worm or centipede, as large around as a man and twice as long, with a disc-like, apparently eyeless, cilia-fringed head bearing a purple central orifice. It glided on its rear pairs of legs, with its fore part raised vertically—the legs, or at least two pairs of them, serving as arms. Along its spinal ridge was a curious purple comb, and a fan-shaped tail of some grey membrane ended its grotesque bulk. There was a ring of flexible red spikes around its neck, and from the twistings of these came clicking, twanging sounds in measured, deliberate rhythms.

Here, indeed, was outré nightmare at its height—capricious fantasy at its apex. But even this vision of delirium was not what caused George Campbell to lapse a third time into unconsciousness. It took one more thing—one final, unbearable touch—to do that. As the nameless worm advanced with its glistening box, the reclining man caught in the mirror-like surface a glimpse of what should have been his own body. Yet—horribly verifying his disordered and unfamiliar sensations—it was not his own body at all that he saw reflected in the burnished metal. It was, instead, the loathsome, pale-grey bulk of one of the great centipedes.

[Robert E. Howard:] From that final lap of senselessness, he emerged with a full understanding of his situation. His mind was imprisoned in the body of a frightful native of an alien planet, while, somewhere on the other side of the universe, his own body was housing the monster's personality.

He fought down an unreasoning horror. Judged from a cosmic standpoint, why should his metamorphosis horrify him? Life and consciousness were the only realities in the universe. *Form* was unimportant. His present body was hideous only according to terrestrial standards. Fear and revulsion were drowned in the excitement of titanic adventure.

What was his former body but a cloak, eventually to be cast off at death anyway? He had no sentimental illusions about the life from which he had been exiled. What had it ever given him save toil, poverty, continual frustration and repression? If this life before him offered no more, at least it offered no less. Intuition told him it offered more—much more.

With the honesty possible only when life is stripped to its naked fundamentals, he realized that he remembered with pleasure only the physical delights of his former life. But he had long ago exhausted all the physical possibilities contained in that earthly body. Earth held no new thrills.

But in the possession of this new, alien body he felt promises of strange, exotic joys.

A lawless exultation rose in him. He was a man without a world, free of all conventions or inhibitions of Earth, or of this strange planet, free of every artificial restraint in the universe. He was a god! With grim amusement he thought of his body moving in earth's business and society, with all the while an alien monster staring out of the windows that were George Campbell's eyes on people who would flee if they knew.

Let him walk the earth slaying and destroying as he would. Earth and its races no longer had any meaning to George Campbell. There he had been one of a billion nonentities, fixed in place by a mountainous accumulation of conventions, laws and manners, doomed to live and die in his sordid niche. But in one blind bound he had soared above the commonplace. This was not death, but re-birth— the birth of a full-grown mentality, with a new-found freedom that made little of physical captivity on Yekub.

He started. Yekub! It was the name of this planet, but how had he known? Then he knew, as he knew the name of him whose body he occupied—Tothe. Memory, deep grooved in Tothe's brain, was stirring in him—shadows of the knowledge Tothe had. Carved deep in the physical tissues of the brain, they spoke dimly as implanted instincts to George Campbell; and his human consciousness seized them and translated them to show him the way not only to safety and freedom, but to the power his soul, stripped to its primitive impulses, craved. Not as a slave would he dwell on Yekub, but as a king! Just as of old barbarians had sat on the throne of lordly empires.

For the first time he turned his attention to his surroundings. He still lay on the couch-like thing in the midst of that fantastic room, and the centipede man stood before him, holding the polished metal object, and clashing its neck-spikes. Thus it spoke to him, Campbell knew, and what it said he dimly understood, through the implanted thought processes of Tothe, just as he knew the creature was Yukth, supreme lord of science.

But Campbell gave no heed, for he had made his desperate plan, a plan so alien to the ways of Yekub that it was beyond Yukth's comprehension and caught him wholly unprepared. Yukth, like Campbell, saw the sharp-pointed metal shard on a nearby table, but to Yukth it was only a scientific implement. He did not even know it could be used as a weapon. Campbell's earthly mind supplied the knowledge and the action that followed, driving Tothe's body into movements no man of Yekub had ever made before.

Campbell snatched the pointed shard and struck, ripping savagely upward. Yukth reared and toppled, his entrails spilling on the floor. In an instant Campbell was streaking for a door. His speed was amazing, exhilarating, first fulfillment of the promise of novel physical sensations.

As he ran, guided wholly by the instinctive knowledge implanted in Tothe's physical reflexes, it was as if he were borne by a separate consciousness in his legs. Tothe's body was bearing him along a route it had traversed ten thousand times when animated by Tothe's mind.

Down a winding corridor he raced, up a twisted stair, through a carved door, and the same instincts that had brought him there told him he had found what he sought. He was in a circular room with a domed roof from which shone a livid blue light. A strange structure rose in the middle of the rainbow-hued floor, tier on tier, each of a separate, vivid color. The ultimate tier was a purple cone, from the apex of which a blue smoky mist drifted upward to a sphere that poised in mid-air—a sphere that shone like translucent ivory.

This, the deep-grooved memories of Tothe told Campbell, was the god of Yekub, though why the people of Yekub feared and worshipped it had been forgotten a million years. A worm-priest stood between him and the altar which no hand of flesh had ever touched. That it could be touched was a blasphemy that had never occurred to a man of Yekub. The worm-priest stood in frozen horror until Campbell's shard ripped the life out of him.

On his centipede-legs Campbell clambered the tiered altar, heedless of its sudden quiverings, heedless of the change that was taking place in the floating sphere, heedless of the smoke that now billowed out in blue clouds. He was drunk with the feel of power. He feared the superstitions of Yekub no more than he feared those of earth. With that globe in his hands he would be king of Yekub. The worm men would dare deny him nothing, when he held their god as hostage. He reached a hand for the ball—no longer ivory-hued, but red as blood. . . .

[Frank Belknap Long:] Out of the tent into the pale August night walked the body of George Campbell. It moved with a slow, wavering gait between the bodies of enormous trees, over a forest path strewed with sweet scented pine needles. The air was crisp and cold. The sky was an inverted bowl of frosted silver flecked with stardust, and far to the north the Aurora Borealis splashed streamers of fire.

The head of the walking man lolled hideously from side to side. From the corners of his lax mouth drooled thick threads of amber froth, which fluttered in the night breeze. He walked upright at first, as a man would walk, but gradually as the tent receded, his posture altered. His torso began almost imperceptibly to slant, and his limbs to shorten.

In a far-off world of outer space the centipede creature that was George Campbell clasped to its bosom a god whose lineaments were red as blood, and ran with insect-like quiverings across a rainbow-hued hall and out through massive portals into the bright glow of alien suns.

Weaving between the trees of earth in an attitude that suggested the awkward loping of a werebeast, the body of George Campbell was fulfilling a mindless destiny. Long, claw-tipped fingers dragged leaves from a carpet of odorous pine needles as it moved toward a wide expanse of gleaming water.

In the far-off, extra-galactic world of the worm people, George Campbell moved between cyclopean blocks of black masonry down long, fern-planted avenues holding aloft the round red god.

There was a harsh animal cry in the underbrush near the gleaming lake on earth where the mind of a worm creature dwelt in a body swayed by instinct. Human teeth sank into soft animal fur, tore at black animal flesh. A little silver fox sank its fangs in frantic retaliation into a furry human wrist, and thrashed about in terror as its blood spurted. Slowly the body of George Campbell arose, its mouth splashed with fresh blood. With upper limbs swaying oddly it moved towards the waters of the lake.

As the variform creature that was George Campbell crawled between the black blocks of stone thousands of worm-shapes prostrated themselves in the scintillating dust before it. A godlike power seemed to emanate from its weaving body as it moved with a slow, undulant motion toward a throne of spiritual empire transcending all the sovereignties of earth.

A trapper stumbling wearily through the dense woods of earth near the tent where the worm-creature dwelt in the body of George Campbell came to the gleaming waters of the lake and discerned something dark floating there. He had been lost in the woods all night, and weariness enveloped him like a leaden cloak in the pale morning light.

But the shape was a challenge that he could not ignore. Moving to the edge of the water he knelt in the soft mud and reached out toward the floating bulk. Slowly he pulled it to the shore.

Far off in outer space the worm-creature holding the glowing red god ascended a throne that gleamed like the constellation Cassiopeia under an alien vault of hyper-suns. The great deity that he held aloft energized his worm tenement, burning away in the white fire of a supermundane spirituality all animal dross.

On earth the trapper gazed with unutterable horror into the blackened and hairy face of the drowned man. It was a bestial face, repulsively anthropoid in contour, and from its twisted, distorted mouth black ichor poured.

"He who sought your body in the abysses of Time will occupy an unresponsive tenement," said the red god. "No spawn of Yekub can control the body of a human.

"On all earth, living creatures rend one another, and feast with unutterable cruelty on their kith and kin. No worm-mind can control a bestial man-body when it yearns to raven. Only man-minds instinctively conditioned through the course of ten thousand generations can keep the human instincts in thrall. Your body will destroy itself on earth, seeking the blood of its animal kin, seeking the cool water where it can wallow at its ease. Seeking eventually destruction, for the death-instinct is more powerful in it than the instincts of life and it will destroy itself in seeking to return to the slime from which it sprang."

Thus spoke the round red god of Yekub in a far-off segment of the space-time continuum to George Campbell as the latter, with all human desire purged away, sat on a throne and ruled an empire of worms more wisely, kindly, and benevolently than any man of earth had ever ruled an empire of men.

The Disinterment

With Duane W. Rimel

awoke abruptly from a horrible dream and stared wildly about. Then, seeing the high, arched ceiling and the narrow stained windows of my friend's room, a flood of uneasy revelation coursed over me; and I knew that all of Andrews' hopes had been realized. I lay supine in a large bed, the posts of which reared upward in dizzy perspective; while on vast shelves about the chamber were the familiar books and antiques I was accustomed to seeing in that secluded corner of the crumbling and ancient mansion which had formed our joint home for many years. On a table by the wall stood a huge candelabrum of early workmanship and design, and the usual light window-curtains had been replaced by hangings of somber black, which took on a faint, ghostly luster in the dying light.

I recalled forcibly the events preceding my confinement and seclusion in this veritable medieval fortress. They were not pleasant, and I shuddered anew when I remembered the couch that had held me before my tenancy of the present one—the couch that everyone supposed would be my last. Memory burned afresh regarding those hideous circumstances which had compelled me to choose between a true death and a hypothetical one—with a later re-animation by therapeutic methods known only to my comrade, Marshall Andrews. The whole thing had begun when I returned from the Orient a year before and discovered, to my utter horror, that I had contracted leprosy while abroad. I had known that I was taking grave chances in caring for my stricken brother in the Philippines, but no hint of my own affliction appeared until I returned to my native land. Andrews himself had made the discovery, and kept it from me as long as possible; but our close acquaintance soon disclosed the awful truth.

At once I was quartered in our ancient abode atop the crags overlooking crumbling Hampden, from whose musty halls and quaint, arched doorways I was never permitted to go forth. It was a terrible existence, with the yellow shadow hanging constantly over me; yet my friend never faltered in his faith, taking care not to contract the dread scourge, but meanwhile making life as pleasant and comfortable as possible. His widespread though somewhat sinister fame as a surgeon prevented any authority from discovering my plight and shipping me away.

It was after nearly a year of this seclusion—late in August—that Andrews decided on a trip to the West Indies—to study "native" medical methods, he said. I was left in care of venerable Simes, the household factotum.[1] So far no outward signs of the disease had developed, and I enjoyed a tolerable though almost completely private existence during my colleague's absence. It was during this time that I read many of the tomes Andrews had acquired in the course of his twenty years as a surgeon, and learned why his reputation, though locally of the highest, was just a bit shady. For the volumes included any number of fanciful subjects hardly related to modern medical knowledge: treatises and unauthoritative articles on monstrous experiments in surgery; accounts of the bizarre effects of glandular transplantation and rejuvenation in animals and men alike; brochures on attempted brain transference, and a host of other fanatical speculations not countenanced by orthodox physicians. It appeared, too, that Andrews was an authority on obscure medicaments; some of the few books I waded through revealing that he had spent much time in chemistry and in the search for new drugs which might be used as aids in surgery. Looking back at those studies now, I find them hellishly suggestive when associated with his later experiments.

Andrews was gone longer than I expected, returning early in November, almost four months later; and when he did arrive, I was quite anxious to see him, since my condition was at last on the brink of becoming noticeable. I had reached a point where I must seek absolute privacy to keep from being discovered. But my anxiety was slight as compared with his exuberance over a certain new plan he had hatched while in the Indies—a plan to be carried out with the aid of a curious drug he had learned of from a native "doctor" in Haiti. When he explained that his idea concerned me, I became somewhat alarmed; though in my position there could be little to make my plight worse. I had, indeed, considered more than once the oblivion that would come with a revolver or a plunge from the roof to the jagged rocks below.

On the day after his arrival, in the seclusion of the dimly lit study, he outlined the whole grisly scheme. He had found in Haiti a drug, the formula for which he would develop later, which induced a state of profound sleep in anyone taking it; a trance so deep that death was closely counterfeited—with all muscular reflexes, even the respiration and heart-beat, completely stilled for the time being. Andrews had, he said, seen it demonstrated on natives many times. Some of them remained somnolent for days at a time, wholly immobile and as much like death as death itself. This suspended animation, he explained further, would even pass the closest examination of any medical man. He himself, according to all known laws, would have to report as dead a man under the influence of such a drug. He stated, too, that the subject's body assumed the precise appearance of a corpse—even a slight *rigor mortis* developing in prolonged cases.

For some time his purpose did not seem wholly clear, but when the full import of his words became apparent I felt weak and nauseated. Yet in another way I was relieved; for the thing meant at least a partial escape from my curse, an escape from the banishment and shame of an ordinary death of the dread leprosy. Briefly, his plan was to administer a strong dose of the drug to me and call the local authorities, who would immediately pronounce me dead, and see that I was buried within a very short while. He felt assured that with their careless examination they would fail to notice my leprosy symptoms, which in truth had hardly appeared. Only a trifle over fifteen months had passed since I had caught the disease, whereas the corruption takes seven years to run its entire course.

Later, he said, would come resurrection. After my interment in the family graveyard—beside my centuried dwelling and barely a quarter-mile from his own ancient pile—the appropriate steps would be taken. Finally, when my estate was settled and my decease widely known, he would secretly open the tomb and bring me to his own abode again, still alive and none the worse for my adventure. It seemed a ghastly and daring plan, but to me it offered the only hope for even a partial freedom; so I accepted his proposition, but not without a myriad of misgivings. What if the effect of the drug should wear off while I was in my tomb? What if the coroner should discover the awful ruse, and fail to inter me? These were some of the hideous doubts which assailed me before the experiment. Though death would have been a release from my curse, I feared it even worse than the yellow scourge; feared it even when I could see its black wings constantly hovering over me.

Fortunately I was spared the horror of viewing my own funeral and burial rites. They must, however, have gone just as Andrews had planned, even to the subsequent disinterment; for after the initial dose of the poison from Haiti I lapsed into a semi-paralytic state and from that to a profound, night-black sleep. The drug had been administered in my room, and Andrews had told me before giving it that he would recommend to the coroner a verdict of heart failure due to nerve strain. Of course, there was no embalming—Andrews saw to that—and the whole procedure, leading up to my secret transportation from the graveyard to his crumbling manor, covered a period of three days. Having been buried late in the afternoon of the third day, my body was secured by Andrews that very night. He had replaced the fresh sod just as it had been when the workmen left. Old Simes, sworn to secrecy, had helped Andrews in his ghoulish task.

Later I had lain for over a week in my old familiar bed. Owing to some unexpected effect of the drug, my whole body was completely paralyzed, so that I could move my head only slightly. All my senses, however, were fully alert, and by another week's time I was able to take nourishment in good quantities. Andrews explained that my body would gradually regain its former sensibilities; though owing to the presence of the leprosy it might take considerable time. He seemed greatly interested in analyzing my daily symptoms, and always asked if there was any feeling present in my body.

Many days passed before I was able to control any part of my anatomy, and much longer before the paralysis crept from my enfeebled limbs so that I could feel the ordinary bodily reactions. Lying and staring at my numb hulk was like having it injected with a perpetual anesthetic. There was a total alienation I could not understand, considering that my head and neck were quite alive and in good health.

Andrews explained that he had revived my upper half first and could not account for the complete bodily paralysis; though my condition seemed to trouble him little considering the damnably intent interest he centered upon my reactions and stimuli from the very beginning. Many times during lulls in our conversation I would catch a strange gleam in his eyes as he viewed me on the couch—a glint of victorious exultation which, queerly enough, he never voiced aloud; though he seemed to be quite glad that I had run the gauntlet of death and had come through alive. Still, there was that horror I was to meet in less than six years, which added to my desolation and melancholy during the tedious days in which I awaited the return of normal bodily functions. But I would be up and about, he assured me, before very long, enjoying an existence few men had ever experienced. The words did not, however, impress me with their true and ghastly meaning until many days later.

During that awful siege in bed Andrews and I became somewhat estranged. He no longer treated me so much like a friend as like an implement in his skilled and greedy fingers. I found him possessed of unexpected traits—little examples of baseness and cruelty, apparent even to the hard-ened Simes, which disturbed me in a most unusual manner. Often he would display extraordinary cruelty to live speci-mens in his laboratory, for he was constantly carrying on various hidden projects in glandular and muscular trans-plantation on guinea-pigs and rabbits. He had also been employing his newly discovered sleeping-potion in curious experiments with suspended animation. But of these things he told me very little; though old Simes often let slip chance comments which shed some light on the proceedings. I was not certain how much the old servant knew, but he had surely learned considerable, being a constant companion to both Andrews and myself.

With the passage of time, a slow but consistent feeling began creeping into my disabled body; and at the reviving symptoms Andrews took a fanatical interest in my case. He still seemed more coldly analytical than sympathetic to-ward me, taking my pulse and heart-beat with more than usual zeal. Occasionally, in his fevered examinations, I saw his hands tremble slightly—an uncommon sight with so skilled a surgeon—but he seemed oblivious of my scrutiny. I was never allowed even a momentary glimpse of my full body, but with the feeble return of the sense of touch, I was aware of a bulk and heaviness which at first seemed awk-ward and unfamiliar.

Gradually I regained the use of my hands and arms; and with the passing of the paralysis came a new and ter-rible sensation of physical estrangement. My limbs had dif-ficulty in following the commands of my mind, and every movement was jerky and uncertain. So clumsy were my hands, that I had to become accustomed to them all over again. This must, I thought, be due to my disease and the advance of the contagion in my system. Being unaware of how the early symptoms affected the victim (my brother's being a more advanced case), I had no means of judging; and since Andrews shunned the subject, I deemed it better to remain silent.

One day I asked Andrews—I no longer considered him a friend—if I might try rising and sitting up in bed. At first he objected strenuously, but later, after cautioning me to keep the blankets well up around my chin so that I would not be chilled, he permitted it. This seemed strange, in view of the comfortable temperature. Now that late autumn was slowly turning into winter, the room was always well heated. A growing chilliness at night, and occasional glimpses of a leaden sky through the window, had told me of the changing season; for no calendar was ever in sight upon the dingy walls. With the gentle help of Simes I was eased to a sitting position, Andrews coldly watching from the door to the laboratory. At my success a slow smile spread across his leering features, and he turned to disappear from the darkened doorway. His mood did nothing to improve my condition. Old Simes, usually so regular and consistent, was now often late in his duties, sometimes leaving me alone for hours at a time.

The terrible sense of alienation was heightened by my new position. It seemed that the legs and arms inside my gown were hardly able to follow the summoning of my mind, and it became mentally exhausting to continue movement for any length of time. My fingers, woefully clumsy, were wholly unfamiliar to my inner sense of touch, and I wondered vaguely if I were to be accursed the rest of my days with an awkwardness induced by my dread malady.

It was on the evening following my half-recovery that the dreams began. I was tormented not only at night but during the day as well. I would awaken, screaming horribly, from some frightful nightmare I dared not think about outside the realm of sleep. These dreams consisted mainly of ghoulish things; graveyards at night, stalking corpses, and lost souls amid a chaos of blinding light and shadow. The terrible *reality* of the visions disturbed me most of all: it seemed that some *inside* influence was inducing the grisly vistas of moonlit tombstones and endless catacombs of the restless dead. I could not place their source; and at the end of a week I was quite frantic with abominable thoughts which seemed to obtrude themselves upon my unwelcome consciousness.

By that time a slow plan was forming whereby I might escape the living hell into which I had been propelled. Andrews cared less and less about me, seeming intent only on my progress and growth and recovery of normal muscular reactions. I was becoming every day more convinced of the nefarious doings going on in that laboratory across the threshold—the animal cries were shocking, and rasped hideously on my overwrought nerves. And I was gradually beginning to think that Andrews had not saved me from deportation solely for my own benefit, but for some accursed reason of his own. Simes's attention was slowly becoming slighter and slighter, and I was convinced that the aged servitor had a hand in the deviltry somewhere. Andrews no longer eyed me as a friend, but as an object of experimentation; nor did I like the way he fingered his scalpel when he stood in the narrow doorway and stared at me with crafty alertness. I had never before seen such a transformation come over any man. His ordinarily handsome features were now lined and whisker-grown, and his eyes gleamed as if some imp of Satan were staring from them. His cold, calculating gaze made me shudder horribly, and gave me a fresh determination to free myself from his bondage as soon as possible.

I had lost track of time during my dream-orgy, and had no way of knowing how fast the days were passing. The curtains were often drawn in the daytime, the room being lit by waxen cylinders in the large candelabrum. It was a nightmare of living horror and unreality; though through it all I was gradually becoming stronger. I always gave careful responses to Andrews' inquiries concerning my returning physical control, concealing the fact that a new life was vibrating through me with every passing day—an altogether strange sort of strength, but one which I was counting on to serve me in the coming crisis.

Finally, one chilly evening when the candles had been extinguished, and a pale shaft of moonlight fell through the dark curtains upon my bed, I determined to rise and carry out my plan of action. There had been no movement from either of my captors for several hours, and I was confident that both were asleep in adjoining bedchambers. Shifting my cumbersome weight carefully, I rose to a sitting position and crawled cautiously out of bed, down upon the floor. A vertigo gripped me momentarily, and a wave of weakness flooded my entire being. But finally strength returned, and by clutching at a bed-post I was able to stand upon my feet for the first time in many months. Gradually a new strength coursed through me, and I donned the dark robe which I had seen hanging on a nearby chair. It was quite long, but served as a cloak over my nightdress. Again came that feeling of awful unfamiliarity which I had experienced in bed; that sense of alienation, and of difficulty in making my limbs perform as they should. But there was need for haste before my feeble strength might give out. As a last precaution in dressing, I slipped some old shoes over my feet; but though I could have sworn they were my own, they seemed abnormally loose, so that I decided they must belong to the aged Simes.

Seeing no other heavy objects in the room, I seized from the table the huge candelabrum, upon which the moon shone with a pallid glow, and proceeded very quietly toward the laboratory door.

My first steps came jerkily and with much difficulty, and in the semi-darkness I was unable to make my way very rapidly. When I reached the threshold, a glance within revealed my former friend seated in a large overstuffed chair; while beside him was a smoking-stand upon which were assorted bottles and a glass. He reclined half-way in the moonlight through the large window, and his greasy features were creased in a drunken smirk. An opened book lay in his lap—one of the hideous tomes from his private library.

For a long moment I gloated over the prospect before me, and then, stepping forward suddenly, I brought the heavy weapon down upon his unprotected head. The dull crunch was followed by a spurt of blood, and the fiend crumpled to the floor, his head laid half open. I felt no contrition at taking the man's life in such a manner. In the hideous, half-visible specimens of his surgical wizardry scattered about the room in various stages of completion and preservation, I felt there was enough evidence to blast his soul without my aid. Andrews had gone too far in his practices to continue living, and as one of his monstrous specimens—of that I was now hideously certain—it was my duty to exterminate him.

Simes, I realized, would be no such easy matter; indeed, only unusual good fortune had caused me to find Andrews unconscious. When I finally reeled up to the servant's bedchamber door, faint from exhaustion, I knew it would take all my remaining strength to complete the ordeal.

The old man's room was in utmost darkness, being on the north side of the structure, but he must have seen me silhouetted in the doorway as I came in. He screamed hoarsely, and I aimed the candelabrum at him from the threshold. It struck something soft, making a sloughing sound in the darkness; but the screaming continued. From that time on events became hazy and jumbled together, but I remember grappling with the man and choking the life from him little by little. He gibbered a host of awful things before I could lay hands on him—cried and begged for mercy from my clutching fingers. I hardly realized my own strength in that mad moment which left Andrews' associate in a condition like his own.

Retreating from the darkened chamber, I stumbled for the stairway door, sagged through it, and somehow reached the landing below. No lamps were burning, and my only light was a filtering of moonbeams coming from the narrow windows in the hall. But I made my jerky way over the cold, damp slabs of stone, reeling from the terrible weakness of my exertion, and reached the front door after ages of fumbling and crawling about in the darkness.

Vague memories and haunting shadows came to taunt me in that ancient hallway; shadows once friendly and understandable, but now grown alien and unrecognizable, so that I stumbled down the worn steps in a frenzy of something more than fear. For a moment I stood in the shadow of the giant stone manor, viewing the moonlit trail down which I must go to reach the home of my forefathers, only a quarter of a mile distant. But the way seemed long, and for a while I despaired of ever traversing the whole of it.

At last I grasped a piece of dead wood as a cane and set out down the winding road. Ahead, seemingly only a few rods away in the moonlight, stood the venerable mansion where my ancestors had lived and died. Its turrets rose spectrally in the shimmering radiance, and the black shadow cast on the beetling hillside appeared to shift and waver, as if belonging to a castle of unreal substance. There stood the monument of half a century; a haven for all my family old and young, which I had deserted many years ago to live with the fanatical Andrews. It stood empty on that fateful night, and I hope that it may always remain so.

In some manner I reached the aged place; though I do not remember the last half of the journey at all. It was enough to be near the family cemetery, among whose moss-covered and crumbling stones I would seek the oblivion I had desired. As I approached the moonlit spot the old familiarity—so absent during my abnormal existence—returned to plague me in a wholly unexpected way. I drew close to my own tombstone, and the feeling of homecoming grew stronger; with it came a fresh flood of that awful sense of alienation and disembodiment which I knew so well. I was satisfied that the end was drawing near; nor did I stop to analyze emotions till a little later, when the full horror of my position burst upon me.

Intuitively I knew my own tombstone; for the grass had scarcely begun to grow between the pieces of sod. With feverish haste I began clawing at the mound, and scraping the wet earth from the hole left by the removal of the grass and roots. How long I worked in the nitrous soil before my fingers struck the coffin-lid, I can never say; but sweat was pouring from me and my nails were but useless, bleeding hooks.

At last I threw out the last bit of loose earth, and with trembling fingers tugged on the heavy lid. It gave a trifle; and I was prepared to lift it completely open when a fetid and nauseous odor assailed my nostrils. I started erect, horrified. Had some idiot placed my tombstone on the wrong grave, causing me to unearth another body? For surely there could be no mistaking that awful stench. Gradually a hideous uncertainty came over me and I scrambled from the hole. One look at the newly made headpiece was enough. This was indeed my own grave . . . but what fool had buried within it another corpse?

All at once a bit of the unspeakable truth propelled itself upon my brain. The odor, in spite of its putrescence, seemed somehow familiar—horribly *familiar*. . . . Yet I could not credit my senses with such an idea. Reeling and cursing, I fell into the black cavity once more, and by the aid of a hastily lit match, lifted the long lid completely open. Then the light went out, as if extinguished by a malignant hand, and I clawed my way out of that accursed pit, screaming in a frenzy of fear and loathing.

When I regained consciousness I was lying before the door of my own ancient manor, where I must have crawled after that hideous rendezvous in the family cemetery. I realized that dawn was close at hand, and rose feebly, opening the aged portal before me and entering the place which had known no footsteps for over a decade. A fever was ravaging my weakened body, so that I was hardly able to stand, but I made my way slowly through the musty, dimly lit chambers and staggered into my own study—the study I had deserted so many years before.

When the sun has risen, I shall go to the ancient well beneath the old willow tree by the cemetery and cast my deformed *self* into it. No other man shall ever view this blasphemy which has survived life longer than it should have. I do not know what people will say when they see my disordered grave, but this will not trouble me if I can find oblivion from that which I beheld amidst the crumbling, moss-crusted stones of the hideous place.

I know now why Andrews was so secretive in his actions; so damnably gloating in his attitude toward me after my artificial death. He had meant me for a specimen all the time—a specimen of his greatest feat of surgery, his masterpiece of unclean witchery . . . an example of perverted artistry for him alone to see. Where Andrews obtained that *other* with which I lay accursed in his moldering mansion I shall probably never know; but I am afraid that it was brought from Haiti along with his fiendish medicine. At least these long hairy arms and horrible short legs are alien to me . . . alien to all natural and sane laws of mankind. The thought that I shall be tortured with that *other* during the rest of my brief existence is another hell.

Now I can but wish for that which once was mine; that which every man blessed of God ought to have at death; that which I saw in that awful moment in the ancient burial ground when I raised the lid on the coffin—my own shrunken, decayed, and headless body.

The Diary of Alonzo Typer

With William Lumley

EDITOR'S NOTE: Alonzo Hasbrouck Typer of Kingston, N.Y.,[1] was last seen and recognised on April 17, 1908, around noon, at the Hotel Richmond in Batavia.[2] He was the only survivor of an ancient Ulster County family, and was fifty-three years old at the time of his disappearance.

Mr. Typer was educated privately and at Columbia and Heidelberg Universities. All his life was spent as a student; the field of his researches including many obscure and generally feared borderlands of human knowledge. His papers on vampirism, ghouls, and poltergeist phenomena were privately printed after rejection by many publishers. He resigned from the Society for Psychical Research in 1902[3] after a series of peculiarly bitter controversies.

At various times Mr. Typer travelled extensively, sometimes dropping out of sight for long periods. He is known to have visited obscure spots in Nepal, India, Thibet, and Indo-China, and passed most of the year 1899 on mysterious Easter Island. The extensive search for Mr. Typer after his disappearance yielded no results, and his estate was divided among distant cousins in New York City.

The diary herewith presented was allegedly found in the ruins of a large country house near Attica, N.Y.,[4] which had borne a curiously sinister reputation for generations before its collapse. The edifice was very old, antedating the general white settlement of the region, and had formed the home of a strange and secretive family named van der Heyl, which had migrated from Albany in 1746 under a curious cloud of witchcraft suspicion. The structure probably dated from about 1760.

Of the history of the van der Heyls very little is known. They remained entirely aloof from their normal neighbours, employed negro servants brought directly from Africa and speaking little English, and educated their children privately and at European colleges. Those of them who went out into the world were soon lost to sight, though not before gaining evil repute for association with Black Mass groups and cults of even darker significance.

Around the dreaded house a straggling village arose, populated by Indians and later by renegades from the surrounding country, which bore the dubious name of Chorazin.[5] Of the singular hereditary strains which afterward appeared in the mixed Chorazin villagers, several monographs have been written by ethnologists. Just behind the village, and in sight of the van der Heyl house, is a steep hill crowned with a peculiar ring of ancient standing stones which the Iroquois always regarded with fear and loathing. The origin and nature of the stones, whose date, according to archaeological and climatological evidence, must be fabulously early, is a problem still unsolved.

From about 1795 onward, the legends of the incoming pioneers and later population have much to say about strange cries and chants proceeding at certain seasons from

Chorazin and from the great house and hill of standing stones; though there is reason to suppose that the noises ceased about 1872, when the entire van der Heyl household—servants and all—suddenly and simultaneously disappeared.

Thenceforward the house was deserted; for other disastrous events—including three unexplained deaths, five disappearances, and four cases of sudden insanity—occurred when later owners and interested visitors attempted to stay in it. The house, village, and extensive rural areas on all sides reverted to the state and were auctioned off in the absence of discoverable van der Heyl heirs. Since about 1890 the owners (successively the late Charles A. Shields and his son Oscar S. Shields, of Buffalo) have left the entire property in a state of absolute neglect, and have warned all inquirers not to visit the region.

Of those known to have approached the house during the last forty years, most were occult students, police officers, newspaper men, and odd characters from abroad. Among the latter was a mysterious Eurasian, probably from Cochin-China,[6] whose later appearance with blank mind and bizarre mutilations excited wide press notice in 1903.

Mr. Typer's diary—a book about 6 x 3½ inches in size, with tough paper and an oddly durable binding of thin sheet metal—was discovered in the possession of one of the decadent Chorazin villagers on Nov. 16, 1935, by a state policeman sent to investigate the rumoured collapse of the deserted van der Heyl mansion. The house had indeed fallen, obviously from sheer age and decrepitude, in the severe gale of Nov. 12. Disintegration was peculiarly complete, and no thorough search of the ruins could be made for several weeks. John Eagle, the swarthy, simian-faced, Indian-like villager who had the diary, said that he found the book quite near the surface of the debris, in what must have been an upper front room.

Very little of the contents of the house could be identified, though an enormous and astonishingly solid brick vault in the cellar (whose ancient iron door had to be blasted open because of the strangely figured and perversely tenacious lock) remained intact and presented several puzzling features. For one thing, the walls were covered with still undeciphered hieroglyphs roughly incised in the brickwork. Another peculiarity was a huge circular aperture in the rear of the vault, blocked by a cave-in evidently caused by the collapse of the house.

But strangest of all was the apparently *recent* deposit of some foetid, slimy, pitch-black substance on the flagstoned floor, extending in a yard-broad, irregular line with one end at the blocked circular aperture. Those who first opened the vault declared that the place smelled like the snake-house at a zoo.

The diary, which was apparently designed solely to cover an investigation of the dreaded van der Heyl house by the vanished Mr. Typer, has been proved by handwriting experts to be genuine. The script shews signs of increasing nervous strain as it progresses toward the end, in places becoming almost illegible. Chorazin villagers—whose stupidity and taciturnity baffle all students of the region and its secrets—admit no recollection of Mr. Typer as distinguished from other rash visitors to the dreaded house.

The text of the diary is here given verbatim and without comment. How to interpret it, and what, other than the writer's madness, to infer from it, the reader must decide for himself. Only the future can tell what its value may be in solving a generation-old mystery. It may be remarked that genealogists confirm Mr. Typer's belated memory in the matter of *Adriaen Sleght*.

THE DIARY

April 17, 1908

Arrived here about 6 p.m. Had to walk all the way from Attica in the teeth of an oncoming storm, for no one would rent me a horse or rig, and I can't run an automobile. This place is even worse than I had expected, and I dread what is coming, even though I long at the same time to learn the secret. All too soon will come the night— the old Walpurgis Sabbat horror—and after that time in Wales I know what to look for. Whatever comes, I shall not flinch. Prodded by some unfathomable urge, I have given my whole life to the quest of unholy mysteries. I came here for nothing else, and will not quarrel with fate.

It was very dark when I got here, though the sun had by no means set. The storm-clouds were the densest I had ever seen, and I could not have found my way but for the lightning flashes. The village is a hateful little backwater, and its few inhabitants no better than idiots. One of them saluted me in a queer way, as if he knew me. I could see very little of the landscape—just a small, swampy valley of strange brown weed-stalks and dead fungi surrounded by scraggly, evilly twisted trees with bare boughs. But behind the village is a dismal-looking hill on whose summit is a circle of great stones with another stone at the centre. That, without question, is the vile primordial thing V———— told me about at the N————estbat.

The great house lies in the midst of a park all overgrown with curious-looking briers. I could scarcely break through, and when I did the vast age and decrepitude of the building almost stopped me from entering. The place looked filthy and diseased, and I wondered how so leprous a bulk could hang together. It is wooden; and though its original lines are hidden by a bewildering tangle of wings added at various dates, I think it was first built in the square colonial fashion of New England. Probably that was easier to build than a Dutch stone house—and then, too, I recall that Dirck van der Heyl's wife was from Salem, a daughter of the unmentionable Abaddon Corey. There was a small pillared porch, and I got under it just as the storm burst. It was a fiendish tempest—black as midnight, with rain in sheets, thunder and lightning like the day of general dissolution, and a wind that actually clawed at me. The door was unlocked, so I took out my electric torch and went inside. Dust was inches thick on floor and furniture, and the place smelled like a mould-caked tomb. There was a hall reaching all the way through, and a curving staircase on the right. I ploughed a way upstairs and selected this front room to camp out in. The whole place seems fully furnished, though most of the furniture is breaking down. This is written at eight o'clock, after a cold meal from my travelling-case. After this the village people will bring me supplies—though they won't agree to come any closer than the ruins of the park gate until (as they say) later. I wish I could get rid of an unpleasant feeling of familiarity with this place.

Later

I am conscious of several presences in this house. One in particular is decidedly hostile toward me—a malevolent will which is seeking to break down my own and overcome me. I must not countenance this for an instant, but must use all my forces to resist it. It is appallingly evil, and definitely non-human. I think it must be allied to powers outside earth—powers in the spaces behind time and beyond the universe. It towers like a colossus, bearing out what is said in the Aklo writings.[7] There is such a feeling of vast size connected with it that I wonder these chambers can contain its bulk—and yet it has no visible bulk. Its age must be unutterably vast—shockingly, indescribably so.

April 18

Slept very little last night. At 3 a.m. a strange, creeping wind began to pervade the whole region—ever rising until the house rocked as if in a typhoon. As I went down the staircase to see to the rattling front door the darkness took half-visible forms in my imagination. Just below the landing I was pushed violently from behind—by the wind, I suppose, though I could have sworn I saw the dissolving outlines of a gigantic black paw as I turned quickly about. I did not lose my footing, but safely finished the descent and shot the heavy bolt of the dangerously shaking door.

I had not meant to explore the house till dawn; yet now, unable to sleep again and fired with mixed terror and curiosity, I felt reluctant to postpone my search. With my powerful torch I ploughed through the dust to the great south parlour, where I knew the portraits would be. There they were, just as V——— had said, and as I seemed to know from some obscurer source as well. Some were so blackened, mouldy, and dust-clouded that I could make little or nothing of them, but from those I could trace I recognised that they were indeed of the hateful line of the van der Heyls. Some of the paintings seemed to suggest faces I had known; but just *what* faces, I could not recall.

The outlines of that frightful hybrid Joris—spawned in 1773 by old Dirck's youngest daughter—were clearest of all, and I could trace the green eyes and the serpent look in his face. Every time I shut off the flashlight that face would seem to glow in the dark until I half fancied it shone with a faint, greenish light of its own. The more I looked, the more evil it seemed, and I turned away to avoid hallucinations of changing expression.

But that to which I turned was even worse. The long, dour face, small, closely set eyes, and swine-like features identified it at once, even though the artist had striven to make the snout look as human as possible. This was what V—— had whispered about. As I stared in horror, I thought the eyes took on a reddish glow—and for a moment the background seemed replaced by an alien and seemingly irrelevant scene—a lone, bleak moor beneath a dirty yellow sky, whereon grew a wretched-looking blackthorn bush. Fearing for my sanity, I rushed from that accursed gallery to the dust-cleared corner upstairs where I have my "camp".

Later

Decided to explore some of the labyrinthine wings of the house by daylight. I cannot get lost, for my footprints are distinct in the ankle-deep dust—and I can trace other identifying marks when necessary. It is curious how easily I learn the intricate windings of the corridors. Followed a long, outflung northerly "ell" to its extremity, and came to a locked door, which I forced. Beyond was a very small room quite crowded with furniture, and with the panelling badly worm-eaten. On the outer wall I spied a black space behind the rotting woodwork, and discovered a narrow secret passage leading downward to unknown black depths. It was a steeply inclined chute or tunnel without steps or handholds, and I wondered what its use could have been.

Above the fireplace was a mouldy painting, which I found on close inspection to be that of a young woman in the dress of the late eighteenth century. The face is of classic beauty, yet with the most fiendishly evil expression which I have ever known the human countenance to bear. Not merely callousness, greed, and cruelty, but some quality hideous beyond human comprehension seems to sit upon those finely carved features. And as I looked it seemed to me that the artist—or the slow processes of mould and decay—had imparted to that pallid complexion a sickly greenish cast, and the least suggestion of an almost imperceptibly scaly texture. Later I ascended to the attic, where I found several chests of strange books—many of utterly alien aspect in letters and in physical form alike. One contained variants of the Aklo formulae which I had never known to exist. I have not yet examined the books on the dusty shelves downstairs.

April 19

There are certainly unseen presences here, even though the dust as yet bears no footprints but my own. Cut a path through the briers yesterday to the park gate where my supplies are left, but this morning I found it closed. Very odd, since the bushes are hardly stirring with spring sap. Again I had that feeling of something at hand so colossal that the chambers can scarcely contain it. This time I feel more than one of the presences is of such a size, and I know now that the third Aklo ritual—which I found in that book in the attic yesterday—would make such beings solid and visible. Whether I shall dare to try this materialisation remains to be seen. The perils are great.

Last night I began to glimpse evanescent shadow-faces and forms in the dim corners of the halls and chambers—faces and forms so hideous and loathsome that I dare not describe them. They seem allied in substance to that titanic paw which tried to push me down the stairs night before last—and must of course be phantoms of my disturbed imagination. What I am seeking would not be quite like these things. I have seen the paw again—sometimes alone and sometimes with its mate—but I have resolved to ignore all such phenomena.

Early this afternoon I explored the cellar for the first time—descending by a ladder found in a storeroom, since the wooden steps had rotted away. The whole place is a mass of nitrous encrustations, with amorphous mounds marking the spots where various objects have disintegrated. At the farther end is a narrow passage which seems to extend under the northerly "ell" where I found the little locked room, and at the end of this is a heavy brick wall with a locked iron door. Apparently belonging to a vault of some sort, this wall and door bear evidences of eighteenth-century workmanship and must be contemporary with the oldest additions to the house—clearly pre-Revolutionary. On the lock—which is obviously older than the rest of the ironwork—are engraved certain symbols which I cannot decipher.

V—— had not told me about this vault. It fills me with a greater disquiet than anything else I have seen, for every time I approach it I have an almost irresistible impulse to *listen* for something. Hitherto no untoward *sounds* have marked my stay in this malign place. As I left the cellar I wished devoutly that the steps were still there—for my progress up the ladder seemed maddeningly slow. I do not want to go down there again—and yet some evil genius urges me to try it *at night* if I would learn what is to be learned.

April 20
I have sounded the depths of horror—only to be made

aware of still lower depths. Last night the temptation was too strong, and in the black small hours I descended once more into that nitrous, hellish cellar with my flashlight— tiptoeing among the amorphous heaps to that terrible brick wall and locked door. I made no sound, and refrained from whispering any of the incantations I knew, but I listened— listened with mad intentness.

At last I heard the sounds from beyond those barred plates of sheet iron—the menacing padding and mutter- ing, as of gigantic night-things within. Then, too, there was a damnable slithering, as of a vast serpent or sea-beast drag- ging its monstrous folds over a paved floor. Nearly para- lysed with fright, I glanced at the huge rusty lock, and at the alien, cryptic hieroglyphs graven upon it. They were signs I could not recognise, and something in their vaguely Mon- goloid technique hinted at a blasphemous and indescrib- able antiquity. At times I fancied I could see them glowing with a greenish light.

I turned to flee, but found that vision of the titan paws before me—the great talons seeming to swell and become more tangible as I gazed. Out of the cellar's evil blackness they stretched, with shadowy hints of scaly wrists beyond them, and with a waxing, malignant will guiding their horrible gropings. Then I heard from behind me—within that abominable vault—a fresh burst of muffled reverbera- tions which seemed to echo from far horizons like distant thunder. Impelled by this greater fear, I advanced toward the shadowy paws with my flashlight and saw them vanish before the full force of the electric beam. Then up the lad- der I raced, torch between my teeth, nor did I rest till I had regained my upstairs "camp".

What is to be my ultimate end, I dare not imagine. I came as a seeker, but now I know that something is seeking me. I could not leave if I wished. This morning I tried to go to the gate for my supplies, but found the briers twisted tightly in my path. It was the same in every direction—behind and on all sides of the house. In places the brown, barbed vines had uncurled to astonishing heights—forming a steel-like hedge against my egress. The villagers are connected with all this. When I went indoors I found my supplies in the great front hall, though without any clue to how they came there. I am sorry now that I swept the dust away. I shall scatter some more and see what prints are left.

This afternoon I read some of the books in the great shadowy library at the rear of the ground floor, and formed certain suspicions which I cannot bear to mention. I had never seen the text of Pnakotic Manuscripts[8] or of the Eltdown Shards before, and would not have come here had I known what they contain. I believe it is too late now—for the awful Sabbat is only ten days away. It is for that night of horror that *they* are saving me.

April 21

I have been studying the portraits again. Some have names attached, and I noticed one—of an evil-faced woman, painted some two centuries ago—which puzzled me. It bore the name of Trintje van der Heyl Sleght, and I have a distinct impression that I once met the name of Sleght before, in some significant connexion. It was not horrible then, though it becomes so now. I must rack my brain for the clue.

The *eyes* of these pictures haunt me. Is it possible that some of them are emerging more distinctly from their shrouds of dust and decay and mould? The serpent-faced and swine-faced warlocks stare horribly at me from their blackened frames, and a score of other hybrid faces are beginning to peer out of shadowy backgrounds. There is a hideous look of family resemblance in them all—and that which is human is more horrible than that which is non-human. I wish they reminded me less of other faces—faces I have known in the past. They were an accursed line, and Cornelis of Leyden was the worst of them. It was *he* who broke down the barrier after his father had found that other key. I am sure that V——— knows only a fragment of the horrible truth, so that I am indeed unprepared and defenceless. What of the line before old Claes? What he did in 1591 could never have been done without generations of evil heritage, or some link with the outside. And what of the branches this monstrous line has sent forth? Are they scattered over the world, all awaiting their common heritage of horror? I must recall the place where I once so particularly noticed the name of Sleght.

I wish I could be sure that these pictures stay always in their frames. For several hours now I have been seeing momentary presences like the earlier paws and shadow-faces and forms, but closely duplicating some of the ancient portraits. Somehow I can never glimpse a presence and the portrait it resembles at the same time—the light is always wrong for one or the other, or else the presence and the portrait are in different rooms.

Perhaps, as I have hoped, the presences are mere figments of imagination; but I cannot be sure now. Some are female, and of the same hellish beauty as the picture in the little locked room. Some are like no portrait I have seen, yet make me feel that their painted features lurk unrecognised beneath the mould and soot of canvases I cannot decipher. A few, I desperately fear, have approached materialisation in solid or semi-solid form—and some have a dreadful and unexplained familiarity.

There is one woman who in fell loveliness excels all the rest. Her poisonous charms are like a honeyed flower growing on the brink of hell. When I look at her closely she vanishes, only to reappear later. Her face has a greenish cast, and now and then I fancy I can spy a suspicion of the squamose in its smooth texture. Who is she? Is she that being who must have dwelt in the little locked room a century and more ago?

My supplies were again left in the front hall—that, clearly, is to be the custom. I had sprinkled dust about to catch footprints, but this morning the whole hall was swept clean by some unknown agency.

April 22

This has been a day of horrible discovery. I explored the cobwebbed attic again, and found a carved, crumbling chest—plainly from Holland—full of blasphemous books and papers far older than any hitherto encountered here. There was a Greek *Necronomicon,* a Norman-French *Livre d'Eibon,* and a first edition of old Ludvig Prinn's *De Vermis Mysteriis.*[9] But the old bound manuscript was the worst. It was in low Latin, and full of the strange, crabbed handwriting of Claes van der Heyl—being evidently the diary or notebook kept by him between 1560 and 1580. When I unfastened the blackened silver clasp and opened the yellowed leaves a coloured drawing fluttered out—the likeness of a monstrous creature resembling nothing so much as a squid, beaked and tentacled, with great yellow eyes, and with certain abominable approximations to the human form in its contours.

I had never before seen so utterly loathsome and nightmarish a form. On the paws, feet, and head-tentacles were curious claws—reminding me of the colossal shadow-shapes which have groped so horribly in my path—while the entity as a whole sat upon a great throne-like pedestal inscribed with unknown hieroglyphs of vaguely Chinese cast. About both writing and image there hung an air of sinister evil so profound and pervasive that I could not think it the product of any one world or age. Rather must that monstrous shape be a focus for all the evil in unbounded space, throughout the aeons past and to come— and those eldritch symbols be vile sentient eikons endowed with a morbid life of their own and ready to wrest themselves from the parchment for the reader's destruction. To the meaning of that monster and of those hieroglyphs I had no clue, but I knew that both had been traced with a hellish precision and for no namable purpose. As I studied the leering characters, their kinship to the symbols on that ominous lock in the cellar became more and more manifest. I left the picture in the attic, for never could sleep come to me with such a thing nearby.

All the afternoon and evening I read in the manuscript book of old Claes van der Heyl, and what I read will cloud and make horrible whatever period of life lies ahead of me. The genesis of the world, and of previous worlds, unfolded itself before my eyes. I learned of the city Shamballah, built by the Lemurians fifty million years ago, yet inviolate still behind its walls of psychic force in the eastern desert. I learned of the Book of Dzyan,[10] whose first six chapters antedate the earth, and which was old when the lords of Venus came through space in their ships to civilise our planet. And I saw recorded in writing for the first time that name which others had spoken to me in whispers, and which I had known in a closer and more horrible way—the shunned and dreaded name of *Yian-Ho*.[11]

In several places I was held up by passages requiring

a key. Eventually, from various allusions, I gathered that old Claes had not dared to embody all his knowledge in one book, but had left certain points for another. Neither volume can be wholly intelligible without its fellow; hence I have resolved to find the second one if it lies anywhere within this accursed house. Though plainly a prisoner, I have not lost my lifelong zeal for the unknown; and am determined to probe the cosmos as deeply as possible before doom comes.

April 23

Searched all the morning for the second diary, and found it about noon in a desk in the little locked room. Like the first, it is in Claes van der Heyl's barbarous Latin; and it seems to consist of disjointed notes referring to various sections of the other. Glancing through the leaves, I spied at once the abhorred name of Yian-Ho—of Yian-Ho, that lost and hidden city wherein brood aeon-old secrets, and of which dim memories older than the body lurk behind the minds of all men. It was repeated many times, and the text around it was strown with crudely drawn hieroglyphs plainly akin to those on the pedestal in that hellish drawing I had seen. Here, clearly, lay the key to that monstrous tentacled shape and its forbidden message. With this knowledge I ascended the creaking stairs to the attic of cobwebs and horror.

When I tried to open the attic door it stuck as never before. Several times it resisted every effort to open it, and when at last it gave way I had a distinct feeling that some colossal, unseen shape had suddenly released it—a shape that soared away on non-material but audibly beating wings. When I found the horrible drawing I felt that it was not precisely where I had left it. Applying the key in the other book, I soon saw that the latter was no instant guide to the secret. It was only a clue—a clue to a secret too black to be left lightly guarded. It would take hours—perhaps days—to extract the awful message.

Shall I live long enough to learn the secret? The shadowy black arms and paws haunt my vision more and more now, and seem even more titanic than at first. Nor am I ever long free from those vague, unhuman presences whose nebulous bulk seems too vast for the chambers to contain. And now and then the grotesque, evanescent faces and forms, and the mocking portrait-shapes, troop before me in bewildering confusion.

Truly, there are terrible primal arcana of earth which had better be left unknown and unevoked; dread secrets which have nothing to do with man, and which man may learn only in exchange for peace and sanity; cryptic truths which make the knower evermore an alien among his kind, and cause him to walk alone on earth. Likewise are there dread survivals of things older and more potent than man; things that have blasphemously straggled down through the aeons to ages never meant for them; monstrous entities that have lain sleeping endlessly in incredible crypts and remote caverns, outside the laws of reason and causation, and ready to be waked by such blasphemers as shall know their dark forbidden signs and furtive passwords.

April 24

Studied the picture and the key all day in the attic. At sunset I heard strange sounds, of a sort not encountered before and seeming to come from far away. Listening, I realised that they must flow from that queer abrupt hill with the circle of standing stones, which lies behind the village and some distance north of the house. I had heard that there was a path from the house leading up that hill to the primal cromlech, and had suspected that at certain seasons the van der Heyls had much occasion to use it; but the whole matter had hitherto lain latent in my consciousness. The present sounds consisted of a shrill piping intermingled with a peculiar and hideous sort of hissing or whistling—a bizarre, alien kind of music, like nothing which the annals of earth describe. It was very faint, and soon faded, but the matter has set me thinking. It is toward the hill that the long, northerly "ell" with the secret chute, and the locked brick vault under it, extend. Can there be any connexion which has so far eluded me?

April 25

I have made a peculiar and disturbing discovery about the nature of my imprisonment. Drawn toward the hill by a sinister fascination, I found the briers giving way before me, *but in that direction only.* There is a ruined gate, and beneath the bushes the traces of the old path no doubt exist. The briers extend part way up and all around the hill, though the summit with the standing stones bears only a curious growth of moss and stunted grass. I climbed the hill and spent several hours there, noticing a strange wind which seems always to sweep around the forbidding monoliths and which sometimes seems to whisper in an oddly articulate though darkly cryptic fashion.

These stones, both in colour and in texture, resemble nothing I have seen elsewhere. They are neither brown nor grey, but rather of a dirty yellow merging into an evil green and having a suggestion of chameleon-like variability. Their texture is queerly like that of a scaled serpent, and is inexplicably nauseous to the touch—being as cold and clammy as the skin of a toad or other reptile. Near the central menhir is a singular stone-rimmed hollow which I cannot explain, but which may possibly form the entrance to a long-choked well or tunnel. When I sought to descend the hill at points away from the house I found the briers intercepting me as before, though the path toward the house was easily retraceable.

April 26

Up on the hill again this evening, and found that windy whispering much more distinct. The almost angry humming came close to actual speech—of a vague sibilant sort—and reminded me of the strange piping chant I had heard from afar. After sunset there came a curious flash of premature summer lightning on the northern horizon, followed almost at once by a queer detonation high in the fading sky. Something about this phenomenon disturbed me greatly, and I could not escape the impression that the noise ended in a kind of unhuman hissing speech which trailed off into guttural cosmic laughter. Is my mind tottering at last, or has my unwarranted curiosity evoked unheard-of horrors from the twilight spaces? The Sabbat is close at hand now. What will be the end?

April 27

At last my dreams are to be realised! Whether or not my life or spirit or body will be claimed, I shall enter the gateway! Progress in deciphering those crucial hieroglyphs in the picture has been slow, but this afternoon I hit upon the final clue. By evening I knew their meaning—and that meaning can apply in only one way to the things I have encountered in this house.

There is beneath this house—sepulchred I know not where—an ancient forgotten One who will shew me the

338

gateway I would enter, and give me the lost signs and words I shall need. How long It has lain buried here—forgotten save by those who reared the stones on the hill, and by those who later sought out this place and built this house—I cannot conjecture. It was in search of this Thing, beyond question, that Hendrik van der Heyl came to New-Netherland in 1638. Men of this earth know It not, save in the secret whispers of the fear-shaken few who have found or inherited the key. No human eye has even yet glimpsed It—unless, perhaps, the vanished wizards of this house delved farther than has been guessed.

With knowledge of the symbols came likewise a mastery of the Seven Lost Signs of Terror—and a tacit recognition of the hideous and unutterable Words of Fear. All that remains for me to accomplish is the Chant which will transfigure that Forgotten One who is Guardian of the Ancient Gateway. I marvel much at the Chant. It is composed of strange and repellent gutturals and disturbing sibilants resembling no language I have ever encountered—even in the blackest chapters of the *Livre d'Eibon*. When I visited the hill at sunset I tried to read it aloud, but evoked in response only a vague, sinister rumbling on the far horizon, and a thin cloud of elemental dust that writhed and whirled like some evil living thing. Perhaps I do not pronounce the alien syllables correctly, or perhaps it is only on the Sabbat—that hellish Sabbat for which the Powers in this house are without question holding me—that the great Transfiguration can occur.

Had an odd spell of fright this morning. I thought for a moment that I recalled where I had seen that baffling name of Sleght before, and the prospect of realisation filled me with unutterable horror.

April 28

Today dark ominous clouds have hovered intermittently over the circle on the hill. I have noticed such clouds several times before, but their contours and arrangements now hold a fresh significance. They are snake-like and fantastic, and curiously like the evil shadow-shapes I have seen in the house. They float in a circle around the primal cromlech—revolving repeatedly as though endowed with a sinister life and purpose. I could swear, too, that they give forth an angry murmuring. After some fifteen minutes they sail slowly away, ever to the eastward, like the units of a straggling battalion. Are they indeed those dread Ones whom Solomon knew of old—those giant black beings whose number is legion and whose tread doth shake the earth?

I have been rehearsing the Chant that will transfigure the Nameless Thing, yet strange fears assail me even when I utter the syllables under my breath. Piecing all evidence together, I have now discovered that the only way to It is through the locked cellar vault. That vault was built with a hellish purpose, and must cover the hidden burrow leading to the Immemorial Lair. What guardians live endlessly within, flourishing from century to century on an unknown nourishment, only the mad may conjecture. The warlocks of this house, who called them out of inner earth, have known them only too well, as the shocking portraits and memories of the place reveal.

What troubles me most is the limited nature of the Chant. It evokes the Nameless One, yet provides no method for the control of That Which is evoked. There are, of course, the general signs and gestures, but whether they will prove effective toward such an One remains to be seen. Still, the rewards are great enough to justify any danger— and I could not retreat if I would, since an unknown force plainly urges me on.

I have discovered one more obstacle. Since the locked cellar vault must be traversed, the key to that place must be found. The lock is infinitely too strong for forcing. That the key is somewhere hereabouts cannot be doubted, but the time before the Sabbat is very short. I must search diligently and thoroughly. It will take courage to unlock that iron door, for what prisoned horrors may not lurk within?

Later

I have been shunning the cellar for the past day or two, but late this afternoon I again descended to those forbidding precincts. At first all was silent, but within five minutes the menacing padding and muttering began once more beyond the iron door. This time it was loud and more terrifying than on any previous occasion, and I likewise recognised the slithering that bespoke some monstrous sea-beast—now swifter and nervously intensified, as if the thing were striving to force its way through the portal to where I stood.

As the pacing grew louder, more restless, and more sinister, there began to pound through it those hellish and unidentifiable reverberations which I had heard on my second visit to the cellar—those muffled reverberations which seemed to echo from far horizons like distant thunder. Now, however, their volume was magnified an hundredfold, and their timbre freighted with new and terrifying implications. I can compare the sound to nothing more aptly than to the roar of some dread monster of the vanished saurian age, when primal horrors roamed the earth, and Valusia's serpent-men[12] laid the foundation-stones of evil magic. To such a roar—but swelled to deafening heights reached by no known organic throat—was this shocking sound akin.

Dare I unlock the door and face the onslaught of what lies beyond?

April 29

The key to the vault is found. I came upon it this noon in the little locked room—buried beneath rubbish in a drawer of the ancient desk, as if some belated effort to conceal it had been made. It was wrapped in a crumbling newspaper dated Oct. 31, 1872; but there was an inner wrapping of dried skin—evidently the hide of some unknown reptile—which bore a Low Latin message in the same crabbed writing as that of the notebooks I found. As I had thought, the lock and key were vastly older than the vault. Old Claes van der Heyl had them ready for something he or his descendants meant to do—and how much older than he they were I could not estimate. Deciphering the Latin message, I trembled in a fresh access of clutching terror and nameless awe.

"The secrets of the monstrous primal Ones," ran the crabbed text, "whose cryptic words relate the hidden things that were before man; the things no one of earth should learn, lest peace be forever forfeited; shall by me never suffer revelation. To Yian-Ho, that lost and forbidden city of countless aeons whose place may not be told, I have been in the veritable flesh of this body, as none other among the living has been. Therein have I found, and thence have I borne away, that knowledge which I would gladly lose, though I may not. I have learnt to bridge a gap that should not be bridged, and must call out of the earth That Which should not be waked or called. And what is sent to follow me will not sleep till I or those after me have found and done what is to be found and done.

"That which I have awaked and borne away with me,

342

I may not part with again. So is it written in the Book of Hidden Things.[13] That which I have willed to be has twined its dreadful shape around me, and—if I live not to do the bidding—around those children born and unborn who shall come after me, until the bidding be done. Strange may be their joinings, and awful the aid they may summon till the end be reached. Into lands unknown and dim must the seeking go, and a house must be built for the outer Guardians.

"This is the key to that lock which was given me in the dreadful, aeon-old, and forbidden city of Yian-Ho; the lock which I or mine must place upon the vestibule of That Which is to be found. And may the Lords of Yaddith[14] succour me—or him—who must set that lock in place or turn the key thereof."

Such was the message—a message which, once I had read it, I seemed to have known before. Now, as I write these words, the key is before me. I gaze on it with mixed dread and longing, and cannot find words to describe its aspect. It is of the same unknown, subtly greenish frosted metal as the lock; a metal best compared to brass tarnished with verdigris. Its design is alien and fantastic, and the coffin-shaped end of the ponderous bulk leaves no doubt of the lock it was meant to fit. The handle roughly forms a strange, non-human image, whose exact outlines and identity cannot now be traced. Upon holding it for any length of time I seem to feel an alien, anomalous *life* in the cold metal—a quickening or pulsing too feeble for ordinary recognition. Below the eidolon is graven a faint, aeon-worn legend in those blasphemous, Chinese-like hieroglyphs I have come to know so well. I can make out only the beginning—the words "my vengeance lurks"—before the text fades to indistinctness. There is some fatality in this timely finding of the key—*for tomorrow night comes the hellish Sabbat.* But strangely enough, amidst all this hideous expectancy, that question of the Sleght name bothers me more and more. Why should I dread to find it linked with the van der Heyls?

Walpurgis-Eve—April 30

The time has come. I waked last night to see the sky glowing with a lurid greenish radiance—that same morbid green which I have seen in the eyes and skin of certain portraits here, on the shocking lock and key, on the monstrous menhirs of the hill, and in a thousand other recesses of my consciousness. There were strident whispers in the air—sibilant whistlings like those of the wind around that dreadful cromlech. Something spoke to me out of the frore aether of space, and it said, "The hour falls." It is an omen, and I laugh at my own fears. Have I not the dread words and the Seven Lost Signs of Terror—the power coercive of any Dweller in the cosmos or in the unknown darkened spaces? I will no longer hesitate.

The heavens are very dark, as if a terrific storm were coming on—a storm even greater than that of the night when I reached here, nearly a fortnight ago. From the village—less than a mile away—I hear a queer and unwonted babbling. It is as I thought—these poor degraded idiots are within the secret, and keep the awful Sabbat on the hill. Here in the house the shadows gather densely. In the darkness the key before me almost glows with a greenish light of its own. I have not yet been to the cellar. It is better that I wait, lest the sound of that muttering and padding—those slitherings and muffled reverberations—unnerve me before I can unlock the fateful door.

Of what I shall encounter, and what I must do, I have

only the most *general* idea. Shall I find my task in the vault itself, or must I burrow deeper into the nighted heart of our planet? There are things I do not yet understand—or at least, prefer not to understand—despite a dreadful, increasing, and inexplicable sense of bygone familiarity with this fearsome house. That chute, for instance, leading down from the little locked room. But I think I know why the wing with the vault extends toward the hill.

6 p.m.

Looking out the north windows, I can see a group of villagers on the hill. They seem unaware of the lowering sky, and are digging near the great central menhir. It occurs to me that they are working on that stone-rimmed hollow place which looks like a long-choked tunnel entrance. What is to come? How much of the olden Sabbat rites have these people retained? That key glows horribly—it is not imagination. Dare I use it as it must be used? Another matter has greatly disturbed me. Glancing nervously through a book in the library I came upon an ampler form of the name that has teased my memory so sorely: Trintje, wife of Adriaen Sleght. The *Adriaen* leads me to the very brink of recollection.

Midnight

Horror is unleashed, but I must not weaken. The storm has broken with pandaemoniac fury, and lightning has struck the hill three times, yet the hybrid, malformed villagers are gathering within the cromlech. I can see them in the almost constant flashes. The great standing stones loom up shockingly, and have a dull green luminosity that reveals them even when the lightning is not there. The peals of thunder are deafening, and every one seems to be horribly *answered* from some indeterminate direction. As I write, the creatures on the hill have begun to chant and howl and scream in a degraded, half-simian version of the ancient ritual. Rain pours down like a flood, yet they leap and emit sounds in a kind of diabolic ecstasy.

"*Iä! Shub-Niggurath! The Goat with a Thousand Young!*"

But the worst thing is within the house. Even at this height, I have begun to hear sounds from the cellar. *It is the padding and muttering and slithering and muffled reverberations within the vault. . . .*

Memories come and go. That name of Adriaen Sleght pounds oddly at my consciousness. Dirck van der Heyl's son-in-law—his child old Dirck's granddaughter and Abaddon Corey's great-granddaughter. . . .

Later

Merciful God! *At last I know where I saw that name.* I know, and am transfixed with horror. All is lost. . . .

The key has begun to feel warm as my left hand nervously clutches it. At times that vague quickening or pulsing is so distinct that I can almost feel the living metal move. It came from Yian-Ho for a terrible purpose, and to me—who all too late know the thin stream of van der Heyl blood that trickles down through the Sleghts into my own lineage—has descended the hideous task of fulfilling that purpose. . . .

My courage and curiosity wane. I know the horror that lies beyond that iron door. What if Claes van der Heyl was my ancestor—need I expiate his nameless sin? *I will not—I swear I will not!* . . .

[*Writing here grows indistinct*]

Too late—cannot help self—black paws materialise— am dragged away toward the cellar. . . .

In the Wall of Eryx

With Kenneth Sterling

Before I try to rest I will set down these notes in preparation for the report I must make. What I have found is so singular, and so contrary to all past experience and expectations, that it deserves a very careful description.

I reached the main landing on Venus March 18, terrestrial time; VI, 9 of the planet's calendar. Being put in the main group under Miller, I received my equipment—watch tuned to Venus's slightly quicker rotation—and went through the usual mask drill. After two days I was pronounced fit for duty.

Leaving the Crystal Company's post at Terra Nova[1] around dawn, VI, 12, I followed the southerly route which Anderson had mapped out from the air. The going was bad, for these jungles are always half impassable after a rain. It must be the moisture that gives the tangled vines and creepers that leathery toughness; a toughness so great that a knife has to work ten minutes on some of them. By noon it was dryer—the vegetation getting soft and rubbery so that the knife went through it easily—but even then I could not make much speed. These Carter oxygen masks are too heavy—just carrying one half wears an ordinary man out. A Dubois mask with sponge-reservoir instead of tubes would give just as good air at half the weight.

The crystal-detector seemed to function well, pointing steadily in a direction verifying Anderson's report. It is curious how that principle of affinity works—without any of the fakery of the old "divining rods" back home. There must be a great deposit of crystals within a thousand miles, though I suppose those damnable man-lizards always watch and guard it. Possibly they think we are just as foolish for coming to Venus to hunt the stuff as we think they are for grovelling in the mud whenever they see a piece of it, or for keeping that great mass on a pedestal in their temple. I wish they'd get a new religion, for they have no use for the crystals except to pray to. Barring theology, they would let us take all we want—and even if they learned to tap them for power there'd be more than enough for their planet and the earth besides. I for one am tired of passing up the main deposits and merely seeking separate crystals out of jungle river-beds. Sometime I'll urge the wiping out of these scaly beggars by a good stiff army from home. About twenty ships could bring enough troops across to turn the trick. One can't call the damned things men for all their "cities" and towers. They haven't any skill except building—and using swords and poison darts—and I don't believe their so-called "cities" mean much more than ant-hills or beaver-dams. I doubt if they even have a real language—all the talk about psychological communication through those tentacles down their chests strikes me as bunk. What misleads people is their upright posture; just an accidental physical resemblance to terrestrial man.

I'd like to go through a Venus jungle for once without having to watch out for skulking groups of them or

dodge their cursed darts. They may have been all right before we began to take the crystals, but they're certainly a
bad enough nuisance now—with their dart-shooting and
their cutting of our water pipes. More and more I come to
believe that they have a special sense like our crystal-detec-
tors. No one ever knew them to bother a man—apart from
long-distance sniping—who didn't have crystals on him.

Around 1 p.m. a dart nearly took my helmet off, and
I thought for a second one of my oxygen tubes was punctured. The sly devils hadn't made a sound, but three of them
were closing in on me. I got them all by sweeping in a circle
with my flame pistol, for even though their colour blended
with the jungle, I could spot the moving creepers. One of
them was fully eight feet tall, with a snout like a tapir's. The
other two were average seven-footers. All that makes them
hold their own is sheer numbers—even a single regiment
of flame throwers could raise hell with them. It is curious,
though, how they've come to be dominant on the planet.
Not another living thing higher than the wriggling akmans
and skorahs, or the flying tukahs[2] of the other continent—
unless of course those holes in the Dionaean Plateau[3] hide
something.

About two o'clock my detector veered westward, indi-
cating isolated crystals ahead on the right. This checked up
with Anderson, and I turned my course accordingly. It was
harder going—not only because the ground was rising, but
because the animal life and carnivorous plants were thicker.
I was always slashing ugrats and stepping on skorahs, and
my leather suit was all speckled from the bursting darohs[4]
which struck it from all sides. The sunlight was all the
worse because of the mist, and did not seem to dry up the
mud in the least. Every time I stepped my feet sank down
five or six inches, and there was a sucking sort of *blup* ev-

ery time I pulled them out. I wish somebody would invent a safe kind of suiting other than leather for this climate. Cloth of course would rot; but some thin metallic tissue that couldn't tear—like the surface of this revolving decay-proof record scroll—ought to be feasible some time.

I ate about 3:30—if slipping these wretched food tablets through my mask can be called eating. Soon after that I noticed a decided change in the landscape—the bright, poisonous-looking flowers shifting in colour and getting wraith-like. The outlines of everything shimmered rhythmically, and bright points of light appeared and danced in the same slow, steady tempo. After that the temperature seemed to fluctuate in unison with a peculiar rhythmic drumming.

The whole universe seemed to be throbbing in deep, regular pulsations that filled every corner of space and flowed through my body and mind alike. I lost all sense of equilibrium and staggered dizzily, nor did it change things in the least when I shut my eyes and covered my ears with my hands. However, my mind was still clear, and in a very few minutes I realised what had happened.

I had encountered at last one of those curious *mirage-plants* about which so many of our men told stories. Anderson had warned me of them, and described their appearance very closely—the shaggy stalk, the spiky leaves, and the mottled blossoms whose gaseous, dream-breeding exhalations penetrate every existing make of mask.

Recalling what happened to Bailey three years ago, I fell into a momentary panic, and began to dash and stagger about in the crazy, chaotic world which the plant's exhalations had woven around me. Then good sense came back, and I realised all I need do was retreat from the dangerous blossoms; heading away from the source of the pulsations, and cutting a path blindly—regardless of what might seem to swirl around me—until safely out of the plant's effective radius.

Although everything was spinning perilously, I tried to start in the right direction and hack my way ahead. My route must have been far from straight, for it seemed hours before I was free of the mirage-plant's pervasive influence. Gradually the dancing lights began to disappear, and the shimmering spectral scenery began to assume the aspect of solidity. When I did get wholly clear I looked at my watch and was astonished to find that the time was only 4:20. Though eternities had seemed to pass, the whole experience could have consumed little more than a half-hour.

Every delay, however, was irksome, and I had lost ground in my retreat from the plant. I now pushed ahead in the uphill direction indicated by the crystal-detector, bending every energy toward making better time. The jungle was still thick, though there was less animal life. Once a carnivorous blossom engulfed my right foot and held it so tightly that I had to hack it free with my knife; reducing the flower to strips before it let go.

In less than an hour I saw that the jungle growths were thinning out, and by five o'clock—after passing through a belt of tree-ferns with very little underbrush—I emerged on a broad mossy plateau. My progress now became rapid, and I saw by the wavering of my detector-needle that I was getting relatively close to the crystal I sought. This was odd, for most of the scattered, egg-like spheroids occurred in jungle streams of a sort not likely to be found on this tree-less upland.

The terrain sloped upward, ending in a definite crest. I reached the top about 5:30, and saw ahead of me a very extensive plain with forests in the distance. This, without question, was the plateau mapped by Matsugawa from the air fifty years ago, and called on our maps "Eryx" or the "Erycinian Highland". But what made my heart leap was a smaller detail, whose position could not have been far from the plain's exact centre. It was a single point of light, blazing through the mist and seeming to draw a piercing, concentrated luminescence from the yellowish, vapour-dulled sunbeams. This, without doubt, was the crystal I sought— a thing possibly no larger than a hen's egg, yet containing enough power to keep a city warm for a year. I could hardly wonder, as I glimpsed the distant glow, that those miserable man-lizards worship such crystals. And yet they have not the least notion of the powers they contain.

Breaking into a rapid run, I tried to reach the unexpected prize as soon as possible; and was annoyed when the firm moss gave place to a thin, singularly detestable mud studded with occasional patches of weeds and creepers. But I splashed on heedlessly—scarcely thinking to look around for any of the skulking man-lizards. In this open space I was not very likely to be waylaid. As I advanced, the light ahead seemed to grow in size and brilliancy, and I began to notice some peculiarity in its situation. Clearly, this was a crystal of the very finest quality, and my elation grew with every spattering step.

It is now that I must begin to be careful in making my report, since what I shall henceforward have to say involves unprecedented—though fortunately verifiable—matters. I was racing ahead with mounting eagerness, and had come within a hundred yards or so of the crystal—whose position on a sort of raised place in the omnipresent slime seemed very odd—when a sudden, overpowering force struck my chest and the knuckles of my clenched fists and knocked me over backward into the mud. The splash of my fall was terrific, nor did the softness of the ground and the presence of some slimy weeds and creepers save my head from a bewildering jarring. For a moment I lay supine, too utterly startled to think. Then I half-mechanically stumbled to my feet and began to scrape the worst of the mud and scum from my leather suit.

Of what I had encountered I could not form the faintest idea. I had seen nothing which could have caused the shock, and I saw nothing now. Had I, after all, merely slipped in the mud? My sore knuckles and aching chest forbade me to think so. Or was this whole incident an illusion brought on by some hidden mirage-plant? It hardly seemed probable, since I had none of the usual symptoms, and since there was no place near by where so vivid and typical a growth could lurk unseen. Had I been on the earth, I would have suspected a barrier of N-force laid down by some government to mark a forbidden zone, but in this humanless region such a notion would have been absurd.

Finally pulling myself together, I decided to investigate in a cautious way. Holding my knife as far as possible ahead of me, so that it might be first to feel the strange force, I started once more for the shining crystal—preparing to advance step by step with the greatest deliberation. At the third step I was brought up short by the impact of the knife-point on an apparently solid surface—a solid surface where my eyes saw nothing.

After a moment's recoil I gained boldness. Extending my gloved left hand, I verified the presence of invisible solid matter—or a tactile illusion of solid matter—ahead of me. Upon moving my hand I found that the barrier was of substantial extent, and of an almost glassy smoothness, with no evidence of the joining of separate blocks. Nerving myself for further experiments, I removed a glove and tested the thing with my bare hand. It was indeed hard and glassy, and of a curious coldness as contrasted with the air around. I strained my eyesight to the utmost in an effort to glimpse some trace of the obstructing substance, but could discern nothing whatsoever. There was not even any evidence of refractive power as judged by the aspect of the landscape ahead. Absence of reflective power was proved by the lack of a glowing image of the sun at any point.

Burning curiosity began to displace all other feelings, and I enlarged my investigations as best I could. Exploring with my hands, I found that the barrier extended from the ground to some level higher than I could reach, and that it stretched off indefinitely on both sides. It was, then, a *wall* of some kind—though all guesses as to its materials and its purpose were beyond me. Again I thought of the mirage-plant and the dreams it induced, but a moment's reasoning put this out of my head.

Knocking sharply on the barrier with the hilt of my knife, and kicking at it with my heavy boots, I tried to interpret the sounds thus made. There was something suggestive of cement or concrete in these reverberations, though my hands had found the surface more glassy or metallic in feel. Certainly, I was confronting something strange beyond all previous experience.

The next logical move was to get some idea of the wall's dimensions. The height problem would be hard if not insoluble, but the length and shape problem could perhaps be sooner dealt with. Stretching out my arms and pressing close to the barrier, I began to edge gradually to the left— keeping very careful track of the way I faced. After several steps I concluded that the wall was not straight, but that I was following part of some vast circle or ellipse. And then my attention was distracted by something wholly different—something connected with the still-distant crystal which had formed the object of my quest.

I have said that even from a greater distance the shining object's position seemed indefinably queer—on a slight mound rising from the slime. Now—at about a hundred yards—I could see plainly despite the engulfing mist just what that mound was. It was the body of a man in one of the Crystal Company's leather suits, lying on his back, and with his oxygen mask half buried in the mud a few inches away. In his right hand, crushed convulsively against his chest, was the crystal which had led me here—a spheroid of incredible size, so large that the dead fingers could scarcely close over it. Even at the given distance I could see that the body was a recent one. There was little visible decay, and I reflected that in this climate such a thing meant death not more than a day before. Soon the hateful farnoth-flies[5] would begin to cluster about the corpse. I wondered who the man was. Surely no one I had seen on this trip. It must have been one of the old-timers absent on a long roving commission, who had come to this especial region independently of Anderson's survey. There he lay, past all trouble, and with the rays of the great crystal streaming out from between his stiffened fingers.

For fully five minutes I stood there staring in bewilderment and apprehension. A curious dread assailed me, and I had an unreasonable impulse to run away. It could not have been done by those slinking man-lizards, for he still held the crystal he had found. Was there any connexion with the invisible wall? Where had he found the crystal? Anderson's instrument had indicated one in this quarter well before this man could have perished. I now began to regard the unseen barrier as something sinister, and recoiled from it with a shudder. Yet I knew I must probe the mystery all the more quickly and thoroughly because of this recent tragedy.

Suddenly—wrenching my mind back to the problem I faced—I thought of a possible means of testing the wall's height, or at least of finding whether or not it extended indefinitely upward. Seizing a handful of mud, I let it drain until it gained some coherence and then flung it high in the air toward the utterly transparent barrier. At a height of perhaps fourteen feet it struck the invisible surface with a resounding splash, disintegrating at once and oozing downward in disappearing streams with surprising rapidity. Plainly, the wall was a lofty one. A second handful, hurled at an even sharper angle, hit the surface about eighteen feet from the ground and disappeared as quickly as the first.

I now summoned up all my strength and prepared to throw a third handful as high as I possibly could. Letting the mud drain, and squeezing it to maximum dryness, I flung it up so steeply that I feared it might not reach the obstructing surface at all. It did, however, and this time it crossed the barrier and fell in the mud beyond with a violent spattering. At last I had a rough idea of the height of the wall, for the crossing had evidently occurred some twenty or twenty-one feet aloft.

With a nineteen- or twenty-foot vertical wall of glassy flatness, ascent was clearly impossible. I must, then, continue to circle the barrier in the hope of finding a gate, an ending, or some sort of interruption. Did the obstacle form a complete round or other closed figure, or was it merely an arc or semicircle? Acting on my decision, I resumed my slow leftward circling, moving my hands up and down over the unseen surface on the chance of finding some window or other small aperture. Before starting, I tried to mark my position by kicking a hole in the mud, but found the slime too thin to hold any impression. I did, though, gauge the place approximately by noting a tall cycad in the distant forest which seemed just on a line with the gleaming crystal a hundred yards away. If no gate or break existed I could now tell when I had completely circumnavigated the wall.

I had not progressed far before I decided that the curvature indicated a circular enclosure of about a hundred yards' diameter—provided the outline was regular. This would mean that the dead man lay near the wall at a point almost opposite the region where I had started. Was he just inside or just outside the enclosure? This I would soon ascertain.

As I slowly rounded the barrier without finding any gate, window, or other break, I decided that the body was lying within. On closer view, the features of the dead man seemed vaguely disturbing. I found something alarming in his expression, and in the way the glassy eyes stared. By the time I was very near I believed I recognised him as Dwight, a veteran whom I had never known, but who was pointed out to me at the post last year. The crystal he clutched was certainly a prize—the largest single specimen I had ever seen.

I was so near the body that I could—but for the barrier—have touched it, when my exploring left hand encountered a corner in the unseen surface. In a second I had learned that there was an opening about three feet wide, extending from the ground to a height greater than I could reach. There was no door, nor any evidence of hinge-marks bespeaking a former door. Without a moment's hesitation I stepped through and advanced two paces to the prostrate body—which lay at right angles to the hallway I had entered, in what seemed to be an intersecting, doorless corridor. It gave me a fresh curiosity to find that the interior of this vast enclosure was divided by partitions.

Bending to examine the corpse, I discovered that it bore no wounds. This scarcely surprised me, since the continued presence of the crystal argued against the pseudo-reptilian natives. Looking about for some possible cause of death, my eyes lit upon the oxygen mask lying close to the body's feet. Here, indeed, was something significant. Without this device no human being could breathe the air of Venus for more than thirty seconds, and Dwight—if it were he—had obviously lost his. Probably it had been carelessly buckled, so that the weight of the tubes worked the straps loose—a thing which could not happen with a Dubois sponge-reservoir mask. The half-minute of grace had been too short to allow the man to stoop and recover his protection—or else the cyanogen content of the atmosphere was abnormally high at the time. Probably he had been busy admiring the crystal—wherever he may have found it. He had, apparently, just taken it from the pouch in his suit, for the flap was unbuttoned.

I now proceeded to extricate the huge crystal from the dead prospector's fingers—a task which the body's stiffness made very difficult. The spheroid was larger than a man's fist, and glowed as if alive in the reddish rays of the westering sun. As I touched the gleaming surface I shuddered involuntarily—as if by taking this precious object I had transferred to myself the doom which had overtaken its earlier bearer. However, my qualms soon passed, and I carefully buttoned the crystal into the pouch of my leather suit. Superstition has never been one of my failings.

Placing the man's helmet over his dead, staring face, I straightened up and stepped back through the unseen doorway to the entrance hall of the great enclosure. All my curiosity about the strange edifice now returned, and I racked my brain with speculations regarding its material, origin, and purpose. That the hands of men had reared it I could not for a moment believe. Our ships first reached Venus only 72 years ago, and the only human beings on the planet have been those at Terra Nova. Nor does human knowledge include any perfectly transparent, non-refractive solid such as the substance of this building. Prehistoric human invasions of Venus can be pretty well ruled out, so that one must turn to the idea of native construction. Did a forgotten race of highly evolved beings precede the man-lizards as masters of Venus? Despite their elaborately built cities, it seemed hard to credit the pseudo-reptiles with anything of this kind. There must have been another race aeons ago, of which this is perhaps the last relique. Or will other ruins of kindred origin be found by future expeditions? The *purpose* of such a structure passes all conjecture—but its strange and seemingly non-practical material suggests a religious use.

Realising my inability to solve these problems, I decided that all I could do was to explore the invisible structure itself. That various rooms and corridors extended over the seemingly unbroken plain of mud I felt convinced; and I believed that a knowledge of their plan might lead to something significant. So, feeling my way back through the doorway and edging past the body, I began to advance along the corridor toward those interior regions whence the dead man had presumably come. Later on I would investigate the hallway I had left.

Groping like a blind man despite the misty sunlight, I moved slowly onward. Soon the corridor turned sharply and began to spiral in toward the centre in ever-diminishing curves. Now and then my touch would reveal a doorless intersecting passage, and I several times encountered junctions with two, three, or four diverging avenues. In these latter cases I always followed the inmost route, which seemed to form a continuation of the one I had been traversing. There would be plenty of time to examine the branches after I had reached and returned from the main regions. I can scarcely describe the strangeness of the experience—threading the unseen ways of an invisible structure reared by forgotten hands on an alien planet!

At last, still stumbling and groping, I felt the corridor end in a sizeable open space. Fumbling about, I found I was in a circular chamber about ten feet across; and from the position of the dead man against certain distant forest landmarks I judged that this chamber lay at or near the centre of the edifice. Out of it opened five corridors besides the one through which I had entered, but I kept the latter in mind by sighting very carefully past the body to a particular tree on the horizon as I stood just within the entrance.

There was nothing in this room to distinguish it—merely the floor of thin mud which was everywhere present. Wondering whether this part of the building had any roof, I repeated my experiment with an upward-flung handful of mud, and found at once that no covering existed. If there had ever been one, it must have fallen long ago, for not a trace of debris or scattered blocks ever halted my feet. As I reflected, it struck me as distinctly odd that this apparently primordial structure should be so devoid of tumbling masonry, gaps in the walls, and other common attributes of dilapidation.

What was it? What had it ever been? Of what was it made? Why was there no evidence of separate blocks in the glassy, bafflingly homogeneous walls? Why were there no traces of doors, either interior or exterior? I knew only that I was in a round, roofless, doorless edifice of some hard, smooth, perfectly transparent, non-refractive, and non-reflective material, a hundred yards in diameter, with many corridors, and with a small circular room at the centre. More than this I could never learn from a direct investigation.

I now observed that the sun was sinking very low in the west—a golden-ruddy disc floating in a pool of scarlet and orange above the mist-clouded trees of the horizon. Plainly, I would have to hurry if I expected to choose a sleeping-spot on dry ground before dark. I had long before decided to camp for the night on the firm, mossy rim of the plateau near the crest whence I had first spied the shining crystal, trusting to my usual luck to save me from an attack by the man-lizards. It has always been my contention that we ought to travel in parties of two or more, so that some-one can be on guard during sleeping hours, but the really small number of night attacks makes the Company careless about such things. Those scaly wretches seem to have difficulty in seeing at night, even with curious glow-torches.

Having picked out again the hallway through which I had come, I started to return to the structure's entrance. Additional exploration could wait for another day. Groping a course as best I could through the spiral corridor—with only general sense, memory, and a vague recognition of some of the ill-defined weed patches on the plain as guides—I soon found myself once more in close proximity to the corpse. There were now one or two farnoth-flies swooping over the helmet-covered face, and I knew that decay was setting in. With a futile instinctive loathing I raised my hand to brush away this vanguard of the scavengers—when a strange and astonishing thing became manifest. An invisible wall, checking the sweep of my arm, told me that—notwithstanding my careful retracing of the

361

way—I had not indeed returned to the corridor in which the body lay. Instead, I was in a parallel hallway, having no doubt taken some wrong turn or fork among the intricate passages behind.

Hoping to find a doorway to the exit hall ahead, I continued my advance, but presently came to a blank wall. I would, then, have to return to the central chamber and steer my course anew. Exactly where I had made my mistake I could not tell. I glanced at the ground to see if by any miracle guiding footprints had remained, but at once realised that the thin mud held impressions only for a very few moments. There was little difficulty in finding my way to the centre again, and once there I carefully reflected on the proper outward course. I had kept too far to the right before. This time I must take a more leftward fork somewhere—just where, I could decide as I went.

As I groped ahead a second time I felt quite confident of my correctness, and diverged to the left at a junction I was sure I remembered. The spiralling continued, and I was careful not to stray into any intersecting passages. Soon, however, I saw to my disgust that I was passing the body at a considerable distance; this passage evidently reached the outer wall at a point much beyond it. In the hope that another exit might exist in the half of the wall I had not yet explored, I pressed forward for several paces, but eventually came once more to a solid barrier. Clearly, the plan of the building was even more complicated than I had thought.

I now debated whether to return to the centre again or whether to try some of the lateral corridors extending toward the body. If I chose this second alternative, I would run the risk of breaking my mental pattern of where I was; hence I had better not attempt it unless I could think of some way of leaving a visible trail behind me. Just how to leave a trail would be quite a problem, and I ransacked my mind for a solution. There seemed to be nothing about my person which could leave a mark on anything, nor any material which I could scatter—or minutely subdivide and scatter.

My pen had no effect on the invisible wall, and I could not lay a trail of my precious food tablets. Even had I been willing to spare the latter, there would not have been even nearly enough—besides which the small pellets would have instantly sunk from sight in the thin mud. I searched my pockets for an old-fashioned notebook—often used unofficially on Venus despite the quick rotting-rate of paper in the planet's atmosphere—whose pages I could tear up and scatter, but could find none. It was obviously impossible to tear the tough, thin metal of this revolving decay-proof record scroll, nor did my clothing offer any possibilities. In Venus's peculiar atmosphere I could not safely spare my stout leather suit, and underwear had been eliminated because of the climate.

I tried to smear mud on the smooth, invisible walls after squeezing it as dry as possible, but found that it slipped from sight as quickly as did the height-testing handfuls I had previously thrown. Finally I drew out my knife and attempted to scratch a line on the glassy, phantom surface—something I could recognise with my hand, even though I would not have the advantage of seeing it from afar. It was useless, however, for the blade made not the slightest impression on the baffling, unknown material.

Frustrated in all attempts to blaze a trail, I again sought the round central chamber through memory. It seemed easier to get back to this room than to steer a definite, predetermined course away from it, and I had little difficulty in finding it anew. This time I listed on my record scroll every turn I made—drawing a crude hypothetical diagram of my route, and marking all diverging corridors. It was, of course, maddeningly slow work when everything had to be determined by touch, and the possibilities of error were infinite; but I believed it would pay in the long run.

The long twilight of Venus was thick when I reached the central room, but I still had hopes of gaining the outside before dark. Comparing my fresh diagram with previous recollections, I believed I had located my original mistake, so once more set out confidently along the invisible hallways. I veered further to the left than during my previous attempts, and tried to keep track of my turnings on the record scroll in case I was still mistaken. In the gathering dusk I could see the dim line of the corpse, now the centre of a loathsome cloud of farnoth-flies. Before long, no doubt, the mud-dwelling sificlighs[6] would be oozing in from the plain to complete the ghastly work. Approaching the body with some reluctance, I was preparing to step past it when a sudden collision with a wall told me I was again astray.

I now realised plainly that I was lost. The complications of this building were too much for offhand solution, and I would probably have to do some careful checking before I could hope to emerge. Still, I was eager to get to dry ground before total darkness set in; hence I returned once more to the centre and began a rather aimless series of trials and errors—making notes by the light of my electric lamp. When I used this device I noticed with interest that it produced no reflection—not even the faintest glistening—in the transparent walls around me. I was, however, prepared for this; since the sun had at no time formed a gleaming image in the strange material.

I was still groping about when the dusk became total. A heavy mist obscured most of the stars and planets, but the earth was plainly visible as a glowing, bluish-green point in the southeast. It was just past opposition, and would have been a glorious sight in a telescope. I could even make out the moon beside it whenever the vapours momentarily thinned. It was now impossible to see the corpse—my only landmark—so I blundered back to the central chamber after a few false turns. After all, I would have to give up hope of sleeping on dry ground. Nothing could be done till daylight, and I might as well make the best of it here. Lying down in the mud would not be pleasant, but in my leather suit it could be done. On former expeditions I had slept under even worse conditions, and now sheer exhaustion would help to conquer repugnance.

So here I am, squatting in the slime of the central room and making these notes on my record scroll by the light of the electric lamp. There is something almost humorous in my strange, unprecedented plight. Lost in a building without doors—a building which I cannot see! I shall doubtless get out early in the morning, and ought to be back at Terra Nova with the crystal by late afternoon. It certainly is a beauty—with surprising lustre even in the feeble light of this lamp. I have just had it out examining it. Despite my fatigue, sleep is slow in coming, so I find myself writing at great length. I must stop now. Not much danger of being bothered by those cursed natives in this place. The thing I like least is the corpse—but fortunately my oxygen mask saves me from the worst effects. I am using the chlorate cubes very sparingly. Will take a couple of food tablets now and turn in. More later.

Later—Afternoon, VI, 13

There has been more trouble than I expected. I am

still in the building, and will have to work quickly and wisely if I expect to rest on dry ground tonight. It took me a long time to get to sleep, and I did not wake till almost noon today. As it was, I would have slept longer but for the glare of the sun through the haze. The corpse was a rather bad sight—wriggling with sificlighs, and with a cloud of farnoth-flies around it. Something had pushed the helmet away from the face, and it was better not to look at it. I was doubly glad of my oxygen mask when I thought of the situation.

At length I shook and brushed myself dry, took a couple of food tablets, and put a new potassium chlorate cube in the electrolyser of the mask. I am using these cubes slowly, but wish I had a larger supply. I felt much better after my sleep, and expected to get out of the building very shortly.

Consulting the notes and sketches I had jotted down, I was impressed by the complexity of the hallways, and by the possibility that I had made a fundamental error. Of the six openings leading out of the central space, I had chosen a certain one as that by which I had entered—using a sighting-arrangement as a guide. When I stood just within the opening, the corpse fifty yards away was exactly in line with a particular lepidodendron in the far-off forest. Now it occurred to me that this sighting might not have been of sufficient accuracy—the distance of the corpse making its difference of direction in relation to the horizon comparatively slight when viewed from the openings next to that of my first ingress. Moreover, the tree did not differ as distinctly as it might from other lepidodendra on the horizon.

Putting the matter to a test, I found to my chagrin that I could not be sure which of three openings was the right one. Had I traversed a different set of windings at each attempted exit? This time I would be sure. It struck me that despite the impossibility of trailblazing there was one marker I could leave. Though I could not spare my suit, I could—because of my thick head of hair—spare my helmet; and this was large and light enough to remain visible above the thin mud. Accordingly I removed the roughly hemispherical device and laid it at the entrance of one of the corridors—the right-hand one of the three I must try.

I would follow this corridor on the assumption that it was correct; repeating what I seemed to recall as the proper turns, and constantly consulting and making notes. If I did not get out, I would systematically exhaust all possible variations; and if these failed, I would proceed to cover the avenues extending from the next opening in the same way—continuing to the third opening if necessary. Sooner or later I could not avoid hitting the right path to the exit, but I must use patience. Even at worst, I could scarcely fail to reach the open plain in time for a dry night's sleep.

Immediate results were rather discouraging, though they helped me eliminate the right-hand opening in little more than an hour. Only a succession of blind alleys, each ending at a great distance from the corpse, seemed to branch from this hallway; and I saw very soon that it had not figured at all in the previous afternoon's wanderings. As before, however, I always found it relatively easy to grope back to the central chamber.

About 1 p.m. I shifted my helmet marker to the next opening and began to explore the hallways beyond it. At first I thought I recognised the turnings, but soon found myself in a wholly unfamiliar set of corridors. I could not get near the corpse, and this time seemed cut off from the central chamber as well, even though I thought I had recorded every move I made. There seemed to be tricky twists and crossings too subtle for me to capture in my crude diagrams, and I began to develop a kind of mixed anger and discouragement. While patience would of course win in the end, I saw that my searching would have to be minute, tireless, and long-continued.

Two o'clock found me still wandering vainly through strange corridors—constantly feeling my way, looking alternately at my helmet and at the corpse, and jotting data on my scroll with decreasing confidence. I cursed the stupidity and idle curiosity which had drawn me into this tangle of unseen walls—reflecting that if I had let the thing alone and headed back as soon as I had taken the crystal from the body, I would even now be safe at Terra Nova.

Suddenly it occurred to me that I might be able to tunnel under the invisible walls with my knife, and thus effect a short cut to the outside—or to some outward-leading corridor. I had no means of knowing how deep the building's foundations were, but the omnipresent mud argued the absence of any floor save the earth. Facing the distant and increasingly horrible corpse, I began a course of feverish digging with the broad, sharp blade.

There was about six inches of semi-liquid mud, below which the density of the soil increased sharply. This lower soil seemed to be of a different colour—a greyish clay rather like the formations near Venus's north pole. As I continued downward close to the unseen barrier I saw that the ground was getting harder and harder. Watery mud rushed into the excavation as fast as I removed the clay, but I reached through it and kept on working. If I could bore any kind of a passage beneath the wall, the mud would not stop my wriggling out.

About three feet down, however, the hardness of the soil halted my digging seriously. Its tenacity was beyond anything I had encountered before, even on this planet, and was linked with an anomalous heaviness. My knife had to split and chip the tightly packed clay, and the fragments I brought up were like solid stones or bits of metal. Finally even this splitting and chipping became impossible, and I had to cease my work with no lower edge of wall in reach.

The hour-long attempt was a wasteful as well as futile one, for it used up great stores of my energy and forced me both to take an extra food tablet, and to put an additional chlorate cube in the oxygen mask. It has also brought a pause in the day's gropings, for I am still much too exhausted to walk. After cleaning my hands and arms of the worst of the mud I sat down to write these notes—leaning against an invisible wall and facing away from the corpse.

That body is simply a writhing mass of vermin now—the odour has begun to draw some of the slimy akmans from the far-off jungle. I notice that many of the efjeh-weeds on the plain are reaching out necrophagous feelers toward the thing; but I doubt if any are long enough to reach it. I wish some really carnivorous organisms like the skorahs would appear, for then they might scent me and wriggle a course through the building toward me. Things like that have an odd sense of direction. I could watch them as they came, and jot down their approximate route if they failed to form a continuous line. Even that would be a great help. When I met any the pistol would make short work of them.

But I can hardly hope for as much as that. Now that these notes are made I shall rest a while longer, and later will do some more groping. As soon as I get back to the central chamber—which ought to be fairly easy—I shall try the extreme left-hand opening. Perhaps I can get outside by dusk after all.

Night—VI, 13

New trouble. My escape will be tremendously difficult, for there are elements I had not suspected. Another night here in the mud, and a fight on my hands tomorrow. I cut my rest short and was up and groping again by four o'clock. After about fifteen minutes I reached the central chamber and moved my helmet to mark the last of the three possible doorways. Starting through this opening, I seemed to find the going more familiar, but was brought up short in less than five minutes by a sight that jolted me more than I can describe.

It was a group of four or five of those detestable manlizards emerging from the forest far off across the plain. I could not see them distinctly at that distance, but thought they paused and turned toward the trees to gesticulate, after which they were joined by fully a dozen more. The augmented party now began to advance directly toward the invisible building, and as they approached I studied them carefully. I had never before had a close view of the things outside the steamy shadows of the jungle.

The resemblance to reptiles was perceptible, though I knew it was only an apparent one, since these beings have no point of contact with terrestrial life. When they drew nearer they seemed less truly reptilian—only the flat head and the green, slimy, frog-like skin carrying out the idea. They walked erect on their odd, thick stumps, and their suction-discs made curious noises in the mud. These were average specimens, about seven feet in height, and with four long, ropy pectoral tentacles. The motions of those tentacles—if the theories of Fogg, Ekberg, and Janat are right, which I formerly doubted but am now more ready to believe—indicated that the things were in animated conversation.

I drew my flame pistol and was ready for a hard fight. The odds were bad, but the weapon gave me a certain advantage. If the things knew this building they would come through it after me, and in this way would form a key to getting out, just as carnivorous skorahs might have done. That they would attack me seemed certain; for even though they could not see the crystal in my pouch, they could divine its presence through that special sense of theirs.

Yet, surprisingly enough, they did not attack me. Instead they scattered and formed a vast circle around me—at a distance which indicated that they were pressing close to the unseen wall. Standing there in a ring, the beings stared silently and inquisitively at me, waving their tentacles and sometimes nodding their heads and gesturing with their upper limbs. After a while I saw others issue from the forest, and these advanced and joined the curious crowd. Those near the corpse looked briefly at it but made no move to disturb it. It was a horrible sight, yet the man-lizards seemed quite unconcerned. Now and then one of them would brush away the farnoth-flies with its limbs or tentacles, or crush a wriggling sificligh or akman, or an out-reaching efjeh-weed, with the suction-discs on its stumps.

Staring back at these grotesque and unexpected intruders, and wondering uneasily why they did not attack me at once, I lost for the time being the will power and nervous energy to continue my search for a way out. Instead I leaned limply against the invisible wall of the passage where I stood, letting my wonder merge gradually into a chain of the wildest speculations. A hundred mysteries which had previously baffled me seemed all at once to take on a new and sinister significance, and I trembled with an acute fear unlike anything I had experienced before.

I believed I knew why these repulsive beings were hovering expectantly around me. I believed, too, that I had the secret of the transparent structure at last. The alluring crystal which I had seized, the body of the man who had seized it before me—all these things began to acquire a dark and threatening meaning.

It was no common series of mischances which had made me lose my way in this roofless, unseen tangle of corridors. Far from it. Beyond doubt, the place was a genuine maze—a labyrinth deliberately built by these hellish beings whose craft and mentality I had so badly underestimated. Might I not have suspected this before, knowing of their uncanny architectural skill? The purpose was all too plain. It was a trap—a trap set to catch human beings, and with the crystal spheroid as bait. These reptilian things, in their war on the takers of crystals, had turned to strategy and were using our own cupidity against us.

Dwight—if this rotting corpse were indeed he—was a victim. He must have been trapped some time ago, and had failed to find his way out. Lack of water had doubtless maddened him, and perhaps he had run out of chlorate cubes as well. Probably his mask had not slipped accidentally after all. Suicide was a likelier thing. Rather than face a lingering death he had solved the issue by removing the mask deliberately and letting the lethal atmosphere do its work at once. The horrible irony of his fate lay in his position—only a few feet from the saving exit he had failed to find. One minute more of searching and he would have been safe.

And now I was trapped as he had been. Trapped, and with this circling herd of curious starers to mock at my predicament. The thought was maddening, and as it sank in I was seized with a sudden flash of panic which set me running aimlessly through the unseen hallways. For several moments I was essentially a maniac—stumbling, tripping, bruising myself on the invisible walls, and finally collapsing in the mud as a panting, lacerated heap of mindless, bleeding flesh.

The fall sobered me a bit, so that when I slowly struggled to my feet I could notice things and exercise my reason. The circling watchers were swaying their tentacles in an odd, irregular way suggestive of sly, alien laughter, and I shook my fist savagely at them as I rose. My gesture seemed to increase their hideous mirth—a few of them clumsily imitating it with their greenish upper limbs. Shamed into sense, I tried to collect my faculties and take stock of the situation.

After all, I was not as badly off as Dwight had been. Unlike him, I knew what the situation was—and forewarned is forearmed. I had proof that the exit was attainable in the end, and would not repeat his tragic act of impatient despair. The body—or skeleton, as it would soon be—was constantly before me as a guide to the sought-for aperture, and dogged patience would certainly take me to it if I worked long and intelligently enough.

I had, however, the disadvantage of being surrounded by these reptilian devils. Now that I realised the nature of the trap—whose invisible material argued a science and technology beyond anything on earth—I could no longer discount the mentality and resources of my enemies. Even with my flame pistol I would have a bad time getting away—though boldness and quickness would doubtless see me through in the long run.

But first I must reach the exterior—unless I could lure or provoke some of the creatures to advance toward me. As I prepared my pistol for action and counted over my generous supply of ammunition it occurred to me to try the effect of its blasts on the invisible walls. Had I overlooked a feasible means of escape? There was no clue to the chemical composition of the transparent barrier, and conceivably it might be something which a tongue of fire could cut like cheese. Choosing a section facing the corpse, I carefully discharged the pistol at close range and felt with my knife where the blast had been aimed. Nothing was changed. I had seen the flame spread when it struck the surface, and now I realised that my hope had been vain. Only a long, tedious search for the exit would ever bring me to the outside.

So, swallowing another food tablet and putting another cube in the electrolyser of my mask, I recommenced the long quest; retracing my steps to the central chamber and starting out anew. I constantly consulted my notes and sketches, and made fresh ones—taking one false turn after another, but staggering on in desperation till the afternoon light grew very dim. As I persisted in my quest I looked from time to time at the silent circle of mocking starers, and noticed a gradual replacement in their ranks. Every now and then a few would return to the forest, while others would arrive to take their places. The more I thought of their tactics the less I liked them, for they gave me a hint of the creatures' possible motives. At any time these devils could have advanced and fought me, but they seemed to prefer watching my struggles to escape. I could not but infer that they enjoyed the spectacle—and this made me shrink with double force from the prospect of falling into their hands.

With the dark I ceased my searching, and sat down in the mud to rest. Now I am writing in the light of my lamp, and will soon try to get some sleep. I hope tomorrow will see me out; for my canteen is low, and lacol tablets are a poor substitute for water. I would hardly dare to try the moisture in this slime, for none of the water in the mud-regions is potable except when distilled. That is why we run such long pipe lines to the yellow clay regions—or depend on rain-water when those devils find and cut our pipes. I have none too many chlorate cubes either, and must try to cut down my oxygen consumption as much as I can. My tunnelling attempt of the early afternoon, and my later panic flight, burned up a perilous amount of air. Tomorrow I will reduce physical exertion to the barest minimum until I meet the reptiles and have to deal with them. I must have a good cube supply for the journey back to Terra Nova. My enemies are still on hand; I can see a circle of their feeble glow-torches around me. There is a horror about those lights which will keep me awake.

Night—VI, 14

Another full day of searching and still no way out! I am beginning to be worried about the water problem, for my canteen went dry at noon. In the afternoon there was a burst of rain, and I went back to the central chamber for the helmet which I had left as a marker—using this as a bowl, and getting about two cupfuls of water. I drank most of it, but have put the slight remainder in my canteen. Lacol tablets make little headway against real thirst, and I hope there will be more rain in the night. I am leaving my helmet bottom up to catch any that falls. Food tablets are none too plentiful, but not dangerously low. I shall halve my rations from now on. The chlorate cubes are my real worry, for even without violent exercise the day's endless tramping burned a dangerous number. I feel weak from my forced economies in oxygen, and from my constantly mounting thirst. When I reduce my food I suppose I shall feel still weaker.

There is something damnable—something uncanny—about this labyrinth. I could swear that I had eliminated certain turns through charting, and yet each new trial belies some assumption I had thought established. Never before did I realise how lost we are without visual landmarks. A blind man might do better—but for most of us *sight* is the king of the senses. The effect of all these fruitless wanderings is one of profound discouragement. I can understand how poor Dwight must have felt. His corpse is now just a skeleton, and the sificlighs and akmans and far-noth-flies are gone. The efjeh-weeds are nipping the leather clothing to pieces, for they were longer and faster-growing than I had expected. And all the while those relays of tentacled starers stand gloatingly around the barrier laughing at me and enjoying my misery. Another day and I shall go mad if I do not drop dead from exhaustion.

However, there is nothing to do but persevere. Dwight would have got out if he had kept on a minute longer. It is just possible that somebody from Terra Nova will come looking for me before long, although this is only my third day out. My muscles ache horribly, and I can't seem to rest at all lying down in this loathsome mud. Last night, despite my terrific fatigue, I slept only fitfully, and tonight I fear will be no better. I live in an endless nightmare—poised between waking and sleeping, yet neither truly awake nor truly asleep. My hand shakes, I can write no more for the time being. That circle of feeble glow-torches is hideous.

Late Afternoon—VI, 15

Substantial progress! Looks good. Very weak, and did not sleep much till daylight. Then I dozed till noon, though without being at all rested. No rain, and thirst leaves me very weak. Ate an extra food tablet to keep me going, but without water it didn't help much. I dared to try a little of the slime water just once, but it made me violently sick and left me even thirstier than before. Must save chlorate cubes, so am nearly suffocating for lack of oxygen. Can't walk much of the time, but manage to crawl in the mud. About 2 p.m. I thought I recognised some passages, and got substantially nearer to the corpse—or skeleton—than I had been since the first day's trials. I was sidetracked once in a blind alley, but recovered the main trail with the aid of my chart and notes. The trouble with these jottings is that there are so many of them. They must cover three feet of the record scroll, and I have to stop for long periods to untangle them. My head is weak from thirst, suffocation, and exhaustion, and I cannot understand all I have set down. Those damnable green things keep staring and laughing with their tentacles, and sometimes they gesticulate in a way that makes me think they share some terrible joke just beyond my perception.

It was three o'clock when I really struck my stride. There was a doorway which, according to my notes, I had not traversed before; and when I tried it I found I could crawl circuitously toward the weed-twined skeleton. The route was a sort of spiral, much like that by which I had first reached the central chamber. Whenever I came to a lateral doorway or junction I would keep to the course which seemed best to repeat that original journey. As I circled nearer and nearer to my gruesome landmark, the watchers outside intensified their cryptic gesticulations and sardonic silent laughter. Evidently they saw something grimly amusing in my progress—perceiving no doubt how helpless I would be in any encounter with them. I was content to leave them to their mirth; for although I realised my extreme weakness, I counted on the flame pistol and its numerous extra magazines to get me through the vile reptilian phalanx.

Hope now soared high, but I did not attempt to rise to my feet. Better to crawl now, and save my strength for the coming encounter with the man-lizards. My advance was very slow, and the danger of straying into some blind alley very great, but none the less I seemed to curve steadily toward my osseous goal. The prospect gave me new strength, and for the nonce I ceased to worry about my pain, my thirst, and my scant supply of cubes. The creatures were now all massing around the entrance—gesturing, leaping, and laughing with their tentacles. Soon, I reflected, I would have to face the entire horde—and perhaps such reinforcements as they would receive from the forest.

I am now only a few yards from the skeleton, and am pausing to make this entry before emerging and breaking through the noxious band of entities. I feel confident that with my last ounce of strength I can put them to flight despite their numbers, for the range of this pistol is tremendous. Then a camp on the dry moss at the plateau's edge, and in the morning a weary trip through the jungle to Terra Nova. I shall be glad to see living men and the buildings of human beings again. The teeth of that skull gleam and grin horribly.

Toward Night—VI, 15

Horror and despair. Baffled again! After making the previous entry I approached still closer to the skeleton, but suddenly encountered an intervening wall. I had been deceived once more, and was apparently back where I had been three days before, on my first futile attempt to leave the labyrinth. Whether I screamed aloud I do not know—perhaps I was too weak to utter a sound. I merely lay dazed in the mud for a long period, while the greenish things outside leaped and laughed and gestured.

After a time I became more fully conscious. My thirst and weakness and suffocation were fast gaining on me, and with my last bit of strength I put a new cube in the electrolyser—recklessly, and without regard for the needs of my journey to Terra Nova. The fresh oxygen revived me slightly, and enabled me to look about more alertly.

It seemed as if I were slightly more distant from poor Dwight than I had been at that first disappointment, and I dully wondered if I could be in some other corridor a trifle more remote. With this faint shadow of hope I laboriously dragged myself forward—but after a few feet encountered a dead end as I had on the former occasion.

This, then, was the end. Three days had taken me nowhere, and my strength was gone. I would soon go mad from thirst, and I could no longer count on cubes enough to get me back. I feebly wondered why the nightmare things had gathered so thickly around the entrance as they mocked me. Probably this was part of the mockery—to make me think I was approaching an egress which they knew did not exist.

I shall not last long, though I am resolved not to hasten matters as Dwight did. His grinning skull has just turned toward me, shifted by the groping of one of the efjeh-weeds that are devouring his leather suit. The ghoulish stare of those empty eye-sockets is worse than the staring of those lizard horrors. It lends a hideous meaning to that dead, white-toothed grin.

I shall lie very still in the mud and save all the strength I can. This record—which I hope may reach and warn those who come after me—will soon be done. After I stop writing I shall rest a long while. Then, when it is too dark for those frightful creatures to see, I shall muster up my last reserves of strength and try to toss the record scroll over the wall and the intervening corridor to the plain outside. I shall take care to send it toward the left, where it will not hit the leaping band of mocking beleaguerers. Perhaps it will be lost forever in the thin mud—but perhaps it will land in some widespread clump of weeds and ultimately reach the hands of men.

If it does survive to be read, I hope it may do more than merely warn men of this trap. I hope it may teach our race to let those shining crystals stay where they are. They belong to Venus alone. Our planet does not truly need them, and I believe we have violated some obscure and mysterious law—some law buried deep in the arcana of the cosmos—in our attempts to take them. Who can tell what dark, potent, and widespread forces spur on these reptilian things who guard their treasure so strangely? Dwight and I have paid, as others have paid and will pay. But it may be that these scattered deaths are only the prelude of greater horrors to come. Let us leave to Venus that which belongs only to Venus.

* * *

I am very near death now, and fear I may not be able to throw the scroll when dusk comes. If I cannot, I suppose the man-lizards will seize it, for they will probably realise what it is. They will not wish anyone to be warned of the labyrinth—and they will not know that my message holds a plea in their own behalf. As the end approaches I feel more kindly toward the things. In the scale of cosmic entity who can say which species stands higher, or more nearly approaches a space-wide organic norm—theirs or mine?

* * *

I have just taken the great crystal out of my pouch to look at in my last moments. It shines fiercely and menacingly in the red rays of the dying day. The leaping horde have noticed it, and their gestures have changed in a way I cannot understand. I wonder why they keep clustered around the entrance instead of concentrating at a still closer point in the transparent wall.

* * *

I am growing numb and cannot write much more. Things whirl around me, yet I do not lose consciousness. Can I throw this over the wall? That crystal glows so, yet the twilight is deepening.

* * *

Dark. Very weak. They are still laughing and leaping around the doorway, and have started those hellish glow-torches.

* * *

Are they going away? I dreamed I heard a sound . . . light in the sky. . . .

REPORT OF WESLEY P. MILLER, SUPT. GROUP A, VENUS CRYSTAL CO.

(Terra Nova on Venus—VI, 16)

Our Operative A-49, Kenton J. Stanfield of 5317 Marshall Street, Richmond, Va., left Terra Nova early on VI, 12 for a short-term trip indicated by detector. Due back 13th or 14th. Did not appear by evening of 15th, so Scouting Plane FR-58 with five men under my command set out at 8 p.m. to follow route with detector. Needle shewed no change from earlier readings.

Followed needle to Erycinian Highland, played strong searchlights all the way. Triple-range flame-guns and D-radiation-cylinders could have dispersed any ordinary hostile force of natives, or any dangerous aggregation of carnivorous skorahs.

When over the open plain on Eryx we saw a group of moving lights which we knew were native glow-torches. As we approached, they scattered into the forest. Probably 75 to 100 in all. Detector indicated crystal on spot where they had been. Sailing low over this spot, our lights picked out objects on the ground. Skeleton tangled in efjeh-weeds, and complete body ten feet from it. Brought plane down near bodies, and corner of wing crashed on unseen obstruction.

Approaching bodies on foot, we came up short against a smooth, invisible barrier which puzzled us enormously. Feeling along it near the skeleton, we struck an opening, beyond which was a space with another opening leading to the skeleton. The latter, though robbed of clothing by weeds, had one of the company's numbered metal helmets beside it. It was Operative B-9, Frederick N. Dwight of

Koenig's division,[7] who had been out of Terra Nova for two months on a long commission.

Between this skeleton and the complete body there seemed to be another wall, but we could easily identify the second man as Stanfield. He had a record scroll in his left hand and a pen in his right, and seemed to have been writing when he died. No crystal was visible, but the detector indicated a huge specimen near Stanfield's body.

We had great difficulty in getting at Stanfield, but finally succeeded. The body was still warm, and a great crystal lay beside it, covered by the shallow mud. We at once studied the record scroll in the left hand, and prepared to take certain steps based on its data. The contents of the scroll forms the long narrative prefixed to this report; a narrative whose main descriptions we have verified, and which we append as an explanation of what was found. The later parts of this account shew mental decay, but there is no reason to doubt the bulk of it. Stanfield obviously died of a combination of thirst, suffocation, cardiac strain, and psychological depression. His mask was in place, and freely generating oxygen despite an alarmingly low cube supply.

Our plane being damaged, we sent a wireless and called out Anderson with Repair Plane FG-7, a crew of wreckers, and a set of blasting materials. By morning FR-58 was fixed, and went back under Anderson carrying the two bodies and the crystal. We shall bury Dwight and Stanfield in the company graveyard, and ship the crystal to Chicago on the next earth-bound liner. Later, we shall adopt Stanfield's suggestion—the sound one in the saner, earlier part of his report—and bring across enough troops to wipe out the natives altogether. With a clear field, there can be scarcely any limit to the amount of crystal we can secure.

In the afternoon we studied the invisible building or

trap with great care, exploring it with the aid of long guiding cords, and preparing a complete chart for our archives. We were much impressed by the design, and shall keep specimens of the substance for chemical analysis. All such knowledge will be useful when we take over the various cities of the natives. Our type C diamond drills were able to bite into the unseen material, and wreckers are now planting dynamite preparatory to a thorough blasting. Nothing will be left when we are done. The edifice forms a distinct menace to aërial and other possible traffic.

In considering the plan of the labyrinth one is impressed not only with the irony of Dwight's fate, but with that of Stanfield's as well. When trying to reach the second body from the skeleton, we could find no access on the right, but Markheim found a doorway from the first inner space some fifteen feet past Dwight and four or five past Stanfield. Beyond this was a long hall which we did not explore till later, but on the right-hand side of that hall was another doorway leading directly to the body. Stanfield could have reached the outside entrance by walking 22 or 23 feet if he had found the opening which lay directly *behind* him—an opening which he overlooked in his exhaustion and despair.

The Night Ocean

With R. H. Barlow

I went to Ellston Beach not only for the pleasures of sun and ocean, but to rest a weary mind. Since I knew no person in the little town, which thrives on summer vacationists and presents only blank windows during most of the year, there seemed no likelihood that I might be disturbed. This pleased me, for I did not wish to see anything but the expanse of pounding surf and the beach lying before my temporary home.

My long work of the summer was completed when I left the city, and the large mural design produced by it had been entered in the contest. It had taken me the bulk of the year to finish the painting, and when the last brush was cleaned I was no longer reluctant to yield to the claims of health and find rest and seclusion for a time. Indeed, when I had been a week on the beach I recalled only now and then the work whose success had so recently seemed all-important. There was no longer the old concern with a hundred complexities of colour and ornament; no longer the fear and mistrust of my ability to render a mental image actual, and turn by my own skill alone the dim-conceived idea into the careful draught of a design. And yet that which later befell me by the lonely shore may have grown solely from the mental constitution behind such concern and fear and mistrust. For I have always been a seeker, a dreamer, and a ponderer on seeking and dreaming; and who can say that such a nature does not open latent eyes sensitive to unsuspected worlds and orders of being?

Now that I am trying to tell what I saw I am conscious of a thousand maddening limitations. Things seen by the inward sight, like those flashing visions which come as we drift into the blankness of sleep, are more vivid and meaningful to us in that form than when we have sought to weld them with reality. Set a pen to a dream, and the colour drains from it. The ink with which we write seems diluted with something holding too much of reality, and we find that after all we cannot delineate the incredible memory. It is as if our inward selves, released from the bonds of daytime and objectivity, revelled in prisoned emotions which are hastily stifled when we would translate them. In dreams and visions lie the greatest creations of man, for on them rests no yoke of line or hue. Forgotten scenes, and lands more obscure than the golden world of childhood, spring into the sleeping mind to reign until awakening puts them to rout. Amid these may be attained something of the glory and contentment for which we yearn; some adumbration of sharp beauties suspected but not before revealed, which are to us as the Graal to holy spirits of the mediaeval world. To shape these things on the wheel of art, to seek to bring some faded trophy from that intangible realm of shadow and gossamer, requires equal skill and memory. For although dreams are in all of us, few hands may grasp their moth-wings without tearing them.

Such skill this narrative does not have. If I might, I

would reveal to you the hinted events which I perceived dimly, like one who peers into an unlit realm and glimpses forms whose motion is concealed. In my mural design, which then lay with a multitude of others in the building for which they were planned, I had striven equally to catch a trace of this elusive shadow-world, and had perhaps succeeded better than I shall now succeed. My stay in Ellston was to await the judging of that design; and when days of unfamiliar leisure had given me perspective, I discovered that—in spite of those weaknesses which a creator always detects most clearly—I had indeed managed to retain in line and colour some fragments snatched from the endless world of imagining. The difficulties of the process, and the resulting strain on all my powers, had undermined my health and brought me to the beach during this period of waiting. Since I wished to be wholly alone, I rented (to the delight of the incredulous owner) a small house some distance from the village of Ellston—which, because of the waning season, was alive with a moribund bustle of tourists, uniformly uninteresting to me. The house, dark from the sea-wind though it had not been painted, was not even a satellite of the village; but swung below it on the coast like a pendulum beneath a still clock; quite alone upon a hill of weed-grown sand. Like a solitary warm animal it crouched facing the sea, and its inscrutable dirty windows stared upon a lonely realm of earth and sky and enormous sea. It will not do to use too much imagining in a narrative whose facts, could they be augmented and fitted into a mosaic, would be strange enough in themselves; but I thought the little house was lonely when I saw it, and that like myself, it was conscious of its meaningless nature before the great sea.

I took the place in late August, arriving a day before I

was expected, and encountering a van and two workingmen unloading the furniture provided by the owner. I did not know then how long I would stay, and when the truck that brought the goods had left I settled my small luggage and locked the door (feeling very proprietary at having a house after months of a rented room) to go down the weedy hill and on the beach. Since it was quite square and had but one room, the house had required little exploration. Two windows in each side provided a great quantity of light, and somehow a door had been squeezed in as an after-thought on the oceanward wall. The place had been built about ten years previously, but on account of its distance from Ellston village was difficult to rent even during the active summer season. There being no fireplace, it stood empty and alone from October until far into spring. Though actually less than a mile below Ellston, it seemed more remote; since a bend in the coast caused one to see only grassy dunes in the direction of the village.

The first day, half-gone when I was installed, I spent in the enjoyment of the sun and the restless water—things whose quiet majesty made the designing of murals seem distant and tiresome. But this was the natural reaction to a long concern with one set of habits and activities. I was through with my work and my vacation was begun. This fact, while elusive for the moment, showed in everything which surrounded me that afternoon of my arrival; and in the utter change from old scenes. There was an effect of bright sun upon a shifting sea of waves whose mysteriously impelled curves were strewn with what appeared to be rhinestones. Perhaps a water-colour might have caught the solid masses of intolerable light which lay upon the beach where the sea mingled with the sand. Although the ocean bore her own hue, it was dominated wholly and incredibly by the enormous glare. There was no other person near me, and I enjoyed the spectacle without the annoyance of any alien object upon the stage. Each of my senses was touched in a different way, but sometimes it seemed that the roar of the sea was akin to that great brightness, or as if the waves were glaring instead of the sun, each of these being so vigorous and insistent that impressions coming from them were mingled. Curiously, I saw no one bathing near my little square house during that or succeeding afternoons, although the curving shore included a wide beach even more inviting than that at the village, where the surf was dotted with random figures. I supposed that this was because of the distance, and because there had never been other houses below the town. Why this unbuilt stretch existed, I could not imagine, since many dwellings straggled along the northward coast, facing the sea with aimless eyes.

I swam until the afternoon had gone, and later, having rested, walked into the little town. Darkness hid the sea from me as I entered, and I found in the dingy lights of the street tokens of a life which was not even conscious of the great, gloom-shrouded thing lying so close. There were painted women in tinsel adornments, and bored men who were no longer young—a throng of foolish marionettes perched on the lip of the ocean-chasm; unseeing, unwilling to see, what lay above them and about, in the multitudinous grandeur of the stars and the leagues of the night ocean. I walked along that darkened sea as I went back to the bare little house, sending the beams of my flashlight out upon the naked and impenetrable void. In the absence of the moon, this light made a solid bar athwart the walls of the uneasy tide; and I felt an indescribable emotion born of the noise of the waters and the perception of my inconceivable smallness as I cast that tiny beam upon a realm immense in itself, yet only the black border of the earthly deep. That nighted deep, upon which ships were moving alone in the darkness where I could not see them, gave off the murmur of a distant, angry rabble.

When I reached my high residence I knew that I had passed no one during the mile's walk from the village, and yet there somehow lingered the impression that I had been all the while accompanied by the spirit of the lonely sea. It was, I thought, personified in a shape which was not revealed to me, but which moved quietly about beyond my range of comprehension. It was like those actors who wait behind darkened scenery in readiness for the lines which will shortly call them before our eyes to move and speak in the sudden revelation of the footlights. At last I shook off this fancy and sought my key to enter the place, whose bare walls gave a sudden feeling of security.

My cottage was entirely free of the village, as if it had wandered down the coast and was unable to return; and there I heard nothing of the disturbing clamour when I returned each night after supper. I generally stayed but a short while upon the streets of Ellston, though sometimes I went into the place for the sake of the walk it provided. There were all the multitude of curio-shops and falsely regal theater-fronts that clutter vacation towns, but I never went into these; and the place seemed useful only for its restaurants. It was astonishing the number of useless things people found to do.

There was a succession of sun-filled days at first. I rose early, and beheld the grey sky agleam with promise of sunrise; a prophecy fulfilled as I stood witness. Those dawns were cold, and their colours faint in comparison to that uniform radiance of day which gives to every hour the quality of white noon. That great light, so apparent the first day, made each succeeding day a yellow page in the book of time. I noticed that many of the beach-people were displeased by the inordinate sun, whereas I sought it. After grey months of toil the lethargy induced by a physical existence in a region governed by the simple things—the wind and light and water—had a prompt effect upon me; and since I was anxious to continue this healing process, I spent all my time outdoors in the sunlight. This induced a state at once impassive and submissive, and gave me a feeling of security against the ravenous night. As darkness is akin to death, so is light to vitality. Through the heritage of a million years ago, when men were closer to the mother sea, and when the creatures of which we are born lay languid in the shallow, sun-pierced water, we still seek the primal things when we are tired, steeping ourselves within their lulling security like those early half-mammals which had not yet ventured upon the oozy land.

The monotony of the waves gave repose, and I had no other occupation than witnessing a myriad ocean moods. There is a ceaseless change in the waters—colours and shades pass over them like the insubstantial expressions of a well-known face; and these are at once communicated to us by half-recognized senses. When the sea is restless, remembering old ships that have gone over her chasms, there comes up silently in our hearts the longing for a vanished horizon. But when she forgets, we forget also. Though we know her a lifetime, she must always hold an alien air, as if something too vast to have shape were lurking in the universe to which she is a door. The morning ocean, glimmering with a reflected mist of blue-white cloud and expanding diamond foam, has the eyes of one who ponders on strange things, and her intricately woven webs, through which dart a myriad coloured fishes, hold the air of some great idle thing which will arise presently from the hoary immemorial chasms and stride upon the land.

I was content for many days, and glad that I had chosen the lonely house which sat like a small beast upon those rounded cliffs of sand. Among the pleasantly aimless amusements fostered by such a life, I took to following the edge of the tide (where the waves left a damp irregular outline rimmed with evanescent foam) for long distances; and sometimes I found curious bits of shell in the chance litter of the sea. There was an astonishing lot of debris on that inward-curving coast which my bare little house overlooked, and I judged that currents whose courses diverge from the village beach must reach that spot. At any rate, my pockets—when I had any—generally held vast stores of trash; most of which I threw away an hour or two after picking it up, wondering why I had kept it. Once, however, I found a small bone whose nature I could not identify, save that it was certainly nothing out of a fish; and I kept this, along with a large metal bead whose minutely carven design was rather unusual. This latter depicted a fishy thing against a patterned background of seaweed instead of the usual floral or geometrical designs, and was still clearly traceable though worn with years of tossing in the surf. Since I had never seen anything like it, I judged that it represented some fashion, now forgotten, of a previous year at Ellston, where similar fads were common.

I had been there perhaps a week when the weather began a gradual change. Each stage of this progressive darkening was followed by another subtly intensified, so that in the end the entire atmosphere surrounding me had shifted from day to evening. This was more obvious to me in a series of mental impressions than in what I actually witnessed, for the small house was lonely under grey skies, and there was sometimes a beating wind that came out of the ocean bearing moisture. The sun was displaced by long intervals of cloudiness—layers of grey mist beyond whose unknown depth the sun lay cut off. Though it might glare with the old intensity above that enormous veil, it could not penetrate. The beach was a prisoner in a hueless vault for hours at a time, as if something of the night were welling into other hours.

Although the wind was invigorating and the ocean whipped into little churning spirals of activity by the vagrant flapping, I found the water growing chill, so I was not in it as long as I had previously been, and thus fell into the habit of long walks, which—when I was unable to swim—provided the exercise that I was so careful to obtain. These walks covered a greater range of sea-edge than my previous wanderings, and since the beach extended in a stretch of miles beyond the tawdry village, I often found myself wholly isolated upon an endless area of sand as evening drew close. When this occurred, I would stride hastily along the whispering sea-border, following its outline so that I should not wander inland and lose my way. And sometimes, when these walks were late (as they grew increasingly to be) I would come upon the crouching house that looked like a harbinger of the village. Insecure upon the wind-gnawed cliffs, a dark blot upon the morbid hues of the ocean sunset, it was more lonely than by the full light of either orb; and seemed to my imagination like a mute, questioning face turned toward me expectant of some action. That the place was isolated I have said, and this at first pleased me; but in that brief evening hour when the sun left in a gore-splattered decline and darkness lumbered on like an expanding shapeless blot, there was an alien presence about the place: a spirit, a mood, an impression that came from the surging wind, the gigantic sky, and that sea which drooled blackening waves upon a beach grown abruptly strange. At these times I felt an uneasiness which had no very definite cause, although my solitary nature had made me long accustomed to the ancient silence and the ancient voice of nature. These misgivings, to which I could have put no sure name, did not affect me long, yet I think now that all the while a gradual consciousness of the ocean's immense loneliness crept upon me, a loneliness that was made subtly horrible by intimations—which were never more than such—of some animation or sentience preventing me from being wholly alone.

The noisy, yellow streets of the town, with their curiously unreal activity, were very far away, and when I went there for my evening meal (mistrusting a diet entirely of my own ambiguous cooking) I took increasing and quite unreasonable care that I should return to the cottage before the late darkness, although I was often abroad until ten or so.

You will say that such action is unreasonable; that if I had feared the darkness in some childish way, I would have entirely avoided it. You will ask me why I did not leave the place since its loneliness was depressing me. To all this I have no reply, save that whatever unrest I felt, whatever of remote disturbance there was to me in brief aspects of the darkening sun or in the eager salt-brittle wind or in the robe of the dark sea that lay crumpled like an enormous garment so close to me, was something which had an origin half in my own heart, which showed itself only at fleeting moments, and which had no very long effect upon me. In the recurrent days of diamond light, with sportive waves flinging blue peaks at the basking shore, the memory of dark moods seemed rather incredible; yet only an hour or two afterward I might again experience these moods, and descend to a dim region of despair.

Perhaps these inward emotions were only a reflection of the sea's own mood; for although half of what we see is coloured by the interpretation placed upon it by our minds, many of our feelings are shaped quite distinctly by external, physical things. The sea can bind us to her many moods, whispering to us by the subtle token of a shadow or a gleam upon the waves, and hinting in these ways of her mournfulness or rejoicing. Always, she is remembering old things, and these memories, though we may not grasp them, are imparted to us, so that we share her gaiety or remorse. Since I was doing no work, seeing no person that I knew, I was perhaps susceptible to shades of her cryptic meaning which would have been overlooked by another. The ocean ruled my life during the whole of that late summer; demanding it as recompense for the healing she had brought me.

There were drownings at the beach that year, and while I heard of these only casually (such is our indifference to a death which does not concern us, and which we do not witness), I knew that their details were unsavoury. The people who died—some of them swimmers of a skill beyond the average—were sometimes not found until many days had elapsed, and the hideous vengeance of the deep had scourged their rotten bodies. It was as if the sea had dragged them into a chasm-lair and had mulled them about in the darkness until, satisfied that they were no longer of any use, she had floated them horribly ashore. No one seemed to know what had caused these deaths. Their frequency excited alarm, since the undertow at Ellston was not strong, and since there were known to be no sharks at hand. Whether the bodies showed marks of any attacks I did not learn, but the dread of a death which moves among the waves and comes on lone people from a lightless, motionless place is a dread which men know and do not like. They must quickly find a reason for such a death, even if there are no sharks. Since sharks formed only a suspected cause, and one never to my knowledge confirmed, the swimmers who continued during the rest of the season were on guard against treacherous tides rather than against any possible sea-animal.

Autumn, indeed, was not a great distance off, and some people used this as an excuse for leaving the sea, where men were snared by death, and going to the security of inland fields, where one cannot even hear the ocean. So August ended, and I had been at the beach many days.

There had been a threat of storm since the fourth of the new month, and on the sixth, when I set out for a walk in the damp wind, there was a mass of formless cloud, colourless and oppressive, above the ruffled leaden sea. The motion of the wind, directed toward no especial goal but stirring uneasily, provided a sensation of coming animation—a hint of life in the elements which might be the long-expected storm. I had eaten my luncheon at Ellston, and though the heavens seemed the closing lid of a great casket, I ventured far down the beach and away from both the town and my no-longer-to-be-seen house. As the universal grey became spotted with a carrion purple—curiously brilliant despite its sombre hue—I found that I was several miles from any possible shelter. This, however, did not seem very important; for despite the dark skies with their added glow of unknown presage I was in a curious mood of detachment paralleling that glow—a mood which flashed through a body grown suddenly alert and sensitive to the outline of shapes and meanings that were previously dim. Obscurely, a memory came to me; suggested by the likeness of the scene to one I had imagined when a story was read to me in childhood. That tale—of which I had not thought for many years—concerned a woman who was loved by the dark-bearded king of an underwater realm of blurred cliffs where fish-things lived, and who was taken from the golden-haired youth of her troth by a dark being crowned with a priest-like mitre and having the features of a withered ape. What had remained in the corner of my fancy was the image of cliffs beneath the water against the hueless, dusky no-sky of such a realm; and this, though I had forgotten most of the story, was recalled quite unexpectedly by the same pattern of cliff and sky which I then beheld. The sight was similar to what I had imagined in a year now lost save for random, incomplete impressions. Suggestions of this story may have lingered behind certain irritatingly unfinished memories, and in certain values hinted to my senses by scenes whose actual worth was bafflingly small. Frequently, in flashes of momentary perception (the conditions more than the object being significant), we feel that certain isolated scenes and arrangements—a feathery landscape, a woman's dress along the curve of a road in the afternoon, or the solidity of a century-defying tree against the pale morning sky—hold something precious, some golden virtue that we must grasp. And yet when such a scene or arrangement is viewed later, or from another point, we find that it has lost its value and meaning for us. Perhaps this is because the thing we seek does not hold that elusive quality, but only suggests to the mind some very different thing which remains unremembered. The baffled mind, not wholly sensing the cause of its flashing appreciation, seizes on the object exciting it, and is surprised when there is nothing of worth therein. Thus it was when I beheld the purpling clouds. They held the stateliness and mystery of old monastery towers at twilight, but their aspect was also that of the cliffs in the old fairy-tale. Suddenly reminded of this lost image, I half expected to see, in the fine-spun dirty foam and among the waves which were now as if they had been poured of flawed black glass, the horrid figure of that ape-faced creature, wearing a mitre old with verdigris, advancing from its kingdom in some lost gulf to which those waves were sky.

I did not see any such creature from the realm of imagining, but as the chill wind veered, slitting the heavens like a rustling knife, there lay in the gloom of merging cloud and water only a grey object, like a piece of driftwood, tossing obscurely on the foam. This was a considerable distance out, and since it vanished shortly, may have been not wood, but a porpoise coming to the troubled surface.

I soon found that I had stayed too long contemplating the rising storm and linking my early fancies with its grandeur, for an icy rain began spotting down, bringing a more uniform gloom upon a scene already too dark for the hour. Hurrying along the grey sand, I felt the impact of cold drops upon my back, and before many moments my clothing was soaked throughout. At first I had run, put to flight by the colourless drops whose pattern hung in long linking strands from an unseen sky, but after I saw that refuge was too far to reach in anything like a dry state, I slackened my pace, and returned home as if I had walked under clear skies. There was not much reason to hurry, although I did not idle as upon previous occasions. The constraining wet garments were cold upon me; and with the gathering darkness, and the wind that rose endlessly from the ocean, I could not repress a shiver. Yet there was, beside the discomfort of the precipitous rain, an exhilaration latent in the purplish ravelled masses of cloud and the stimulated reactions of my body. In a mood half of exultant pleasure from resisting the rain (which streamed from me now, and filled my shoes and pockets) and half of strange appreciation of those morbid, dominant skies which hovered with dark wings above the shifting eternal sea, I tramped along the grey corridor of Ellston Beach. More rapidly than I had expected the crouching house showed in the oblique, flapping rain, and all the weeds of the sand cliff writhed in accompaniment to the frantic wind, as if they would uproot themselves to join the far-travelling element. Sea and sky had altered not at all, and the scene was that which had accompanied me, save that there was now painted upon it the hunching roof that seemed to bend from the assailing rain. I hurried up the insecure steps, and let myself into a dry room, where, unconsciously surprised that I was free of the nagging wind, I stood for a moment with water rilling from every inch of me.

There are two windows in the front of that house, one on each side, and these face nearly straight upon the ocean; which I saw now half obscured by the combined veils of the rain and of the imminent night. From these windows I looked as I dressed myself in a motley array of dry garments seized from convenient hangers and from a chair too laden to sit upon. I was prisoned on all sides by an unnaturally increased dusk which had filtered down at some undefined hour under cover of the storm. How long I had been on the reaches of wet grey sand, or what the real time was, I could not tell, though a moment's search produced my watch— fortunately left behind and thus avoiding the uniform wetness of my clothing. I half guessed the hour from the dimly seen hands, which were only slightly less indecipherable than the surrounding figures. In another moment my sight penetrated the gloom (greater in the house than beyond the bleared window) and saw that it was 6:45.

There had been no one upon the beach as I came in, and naturally I expected to see no further swimmers that night. Yet when I looked again from the window there appeared surely to be figures blotting the grime of the wet evening. I counted three moving about in some incomprehensible manner, and close to the house another—which may not have been a person, but a wave-ejected log, for the surf was now pounding fiercely. I was startled to no little degree, and wondered for what purpose those hardy persons stayed out in such a storm. And then I thought that perhaps like myself they had been caught unintentionally in the rain and had surrendered to the watery gusts. In another moment, prompted by a certain civilised hospitality which overcame my love of solitude, I stepped to the door and emerged momentarily (at the cost of another wetting, for the rain promptly descended upon me in exultant fury) on the small porch, gesticulating toward the people. But whether they did not see me, or did not understand, they made no returning signal. Dim in the evening, they stood as if half-surprised, or as if they awaited some other action from me. There was in their attitude something of that cryptic blankness, signifying anything or nothing, which the house wore about itself as seen in the morbid sunset. Abruptly there came to me a feeling that a sinister quality lurked about those unmoving figures who chose to stay in the rainy night upon a beach deserted by all people, and I closed the door with a surge of annoyance which sought all too vainly to disguise a deeper emotion of fear; a consuming fright that welled up from the shadows of my consciousness. A moment later, when I had stepped to the window, there seemed to be nothing outside but the portentous night. Vaguely puzzled, and even more vaguely frightened—like one who has seen no alarming thing, but is apprehensive of what may be found in the dark street he is soon compelled to cross—I decided that I had very possibly seen no one, and that the murky air had deceived me.

The aura of isolation about the place was increased that night, though just out of sight on the northward beach a hundred houses rose in the rainy darkness, their light bleared and yellow above streets of polished glass, like goblin-eyes reflected in an oily forest pool. Yet because I could not see them, or even reach them in bad weather— since I had no car nor any way to leave the crouching house except by walking in the figure-haunted darkness—I realized quite suddenly that I was, to all intents, alone with the dreary sea that rose and subsided unseen, unkenned, in the mist. And the voice of the sea had become a hoarse groan, like that of something wounded which shifts about before trying to rise.

Fighting away the prevalent gloom with a soiled lamp—for the darkness crept in at my windows and sat peering obscurely at me from the corners like a patient animal—I prepared my food, since I had no intention of going to the village. The hour seemed incredibly advanced, though it was not yet nine o'clock when I went to bed. Darkness had come early and furtively, and throughout the remainder of my stay lingered evasively over each scene and action which I beheld. Something had settled out of the night—something forever undefined, but stirring a latent sense within me, so that I was like a beast expecting the momentary rustle of an enemy.

There were hours of wind, and sheets of the downpour flapped endlessly on the meagre walls barring it from me. Lulls came in which I heard the mumbling sea, and I could guess that large formless waves jostled one another in the pallid whine of the winds, and flung on the beach

401

a spray bitter with salt. Yet in the very monotony of the restless elements I found a lethargic note, a sound that beguiled me, after a time, into slumber grey and colourless as the night. The sea continued its mad monologue, and the wind her nagging, but these were shut out by the walls of unconsciousness, and for a time the night ocean was banished from a sleeping mind.

Morning brought an enfeebled sun—a sun like that which men will see when the earth is old, if there are any men left: a sun more weary than the shrouded, moribund sky. Faint echo of its old image, Phoebus strove to pierce the ragged, ambiguous clouds as I awoke, at moments sending a wash of pale gold rippling across the northwestern interior of my house, at others waning till it was only a luminous ball, like some incredible plaything forgotten on the celestial lawn. After a while the failing rain—which must have continued throughout the previous night—succeeded in washing away those vestiges of purple cloud which had resembled the ocean-cliffs in an old fairy-tale. Cheated alike of the setting and rising sun, that day merged with the day before, as if the intervening storm had not ushered a long darkness into the world, but had swollen and subsided into one long afternoon. Gaining heart, the furtive sun exerted all his force in dispelling the old mist, streaked now like a dirty window, and cast it from his realm. The shallow blue day advanced as those grimy wisps retreated, and the loneliness which had encircled me welled back into a watchful place of retreat, whence it went no farther, but crouched and waited.

The ancient brightness was now once more upon the sun, and the old glitter on the waves, whose playful blue shapes had flocked upon that coast ere man was born, and would rejoice unseen when he was forgotten in the sepulchre of time. Influenced by these thin assurances, like one who believes the smile of friendship on an enemy's features, I opened my door, and as it swung outward, a black spot upon the inward burst of light, I saw the beach washed clean of any track, as if no foot before mine had disturbed the smooth sand. With the quick lift of spirit that follows a period of uneasy depression, I felt—in a purely yielding fashion and without volition—that my own memory was washed clean of all the mistrust and suspicion and disease-like fear of a lifetime, just as the filth of the water's edge succumbs to a particularly high tide, and is carried out of sight. There was a scent of soaked, brackish grass, like the mouldy pages of a book, commingled with a sweet odour born of the hot sunlight upon inland meadows, and these were borne into me like an exhilarating drink, seeping and tingling through my veins as if they would convey to me something of their own impalpable nature, and float me dizzily in the aimless breeze. And conspiring with these things, the sun continued to shower upon me, like the rain of yesterday, an incessant array of bright spears; as if it also wished to hide that suspected background presence which moved beyond my sight and was betrayed only by a care-less rustle on the borders of my consciousness, or by the aspect of blank figures staring out of an ocean void. That sun, a fierce ball solitary in the whirlpool of infinity, was like a horde of golden moths against my upturned face. A bubbling white grail of fire divine and incomprehensible, it withheld from me a thousand promised mirages where it granted one. For the sun did actually seem to indicate realms, secure and fanciful, where if I but knew the path I might wander in this curious exultation. Such things come of our own natures, for life has never yielded for one moment her secrets; and it is only in our interpretation of their hinted images that we may find ecstasy or dullness, according to a deliberately induced mood. Yet ever and again we must succumb to her deceptions, believing for the moment that we may this time find the withheld joy. And in this way the fresh sweetness of the wind, on a morning following the haunted darkness (whose evil intimations had given me a greater uneasiness than any menace to my body), whispered to me of ancient mysteries only half-linked with earth, and of pleasures that were the sharper because I felt that I might experience only a part of them. The sun and wind and that scent that rose upon them told me of festivals of gods whose senses are a millionfold more poignant than man's, and whose joys are a millionfold more subtle and prolonged. These things, they hinted, could be mine if I gave myself wholly into their bright deceptive power. And the sun, a crouching god with naked celestial flesh, an unknown, too-mighty furnace upon which eye might not look, seemed almost sacred in the glow of my newly sharpened emotions. The ethereal thunderous light it gave was something before which all things must worship astonished. The slinking leopard in his green-chasmed forest must have paused briefly to consider its leaf-scattered rays, and all things nurtured by it must have cherished its bright message on such a day. For when it is absent in the far reaches of eternity, earth will be lost and black against an illimitable void. That morning, in which I shared the fire of life, and whose brief moment of pleasure is secure against the ravenous years, was astir with the beckoning of strange things whose elusive names can never be written.

As I made my way toward the village, wondering how it might look after a long-needed scrubbing by the industrious rain, I saw, tangled in a glimmer of sunlit moisture that was poured over it like a yellow vintage, a small object like

404

a hand, some twenty feet ahead of me, and touched by the repetitious foam. The shock and disgust born in my startled mind when I saw that it was indeed a piece of rotten flesh overcame my new contentment and engendered a shocked suspicion that it might actually be a hand. Certainly, no fish, or part of one, could assume that look, and I thought I saw mushy fingers wed in decay. I stepped close and turned the thing over with my foot, not wishing to touch so foul an object, and it adhered stickily to the leather shoe, as if clutching with the grasp of corruption. The thing, whose shape was nearly lost, held too much resemblance to what I feared it might be; and I pushed it into the willing grasp of a seething wave, which took it from sight with an alacrity not often shown by those ravelled edges of the sea.

Perhaps I should have reported my find, yet its nature was too ambiguous to make action natural. Since it had been partly *eaten* by some ocean-dwelling monstrousness, I did not think it identifiable enough to form evidence of an unknown but possible tragedy. The numerous drownings, of course, came into my mind—as well as other things lacking in wholesomeness, some of which remained only as possibilities. Whatever the storm-dislodged fragment may have been, and whether it were fish or some animal akin to man, I have never spoken of it until now. After all, there was no proof that it had not merely been distorted by rottenness into that shape.

I approached the town, sickened by the presence of such an object amidst the apparent beauty of the clean beach, though it was horribly typical of the indifference of death in a nature which mingles rottenness with beauty, and perhaps loves the former more. In Ellston I heard of no recent drowning or other mishap of the sea, and found no reference to such in the columns of the local paper—the only one I read during my stay.

It is difficult to describe the mental state in which succeeding days found me. Always susceptible to morbid emotions whose dark anguish might be induced by things outside myself, or might spring from the abysses of my own spirit, I was ridden by a feeling which was not fear or despair, or anything akin to these, but was rather a perception of the brief hideousness and underlying filth of life—a feeling partly a reflection of my internal nature and partly a result of broodings induced by that gnawed rotten object which may have been a hand. In those days my mind was a place of shadowed cliffs and dark moving figures, like the ancient unsuspected realm which the fairy-tale recalled to me. I felt, in brief agonies of disillusionment, the gigantic blackness of this overwhelming universe, in which my days and the days of my race were as nothing to the shattered stars; a universe in which each action is vain and even the emotion of grief a wasted thing. The hours I had previously spent in something of regained health, contentment, and physical well-being were given now (as if those days of the previous week were something definitely ended) to an indolence like that of a man who no longer cares to live. I was engulfed by a piteous lethargic fear of some ineluctable doom which would be, I felt, the completed hate of the peering stars and of the black enormous waves that hoped to clasp my bones within them—the vengeance of all the indifferent, horrendous majesty of the night ocean.

Something of the darkness and restlessness of the sea had penetrated my heart, so that I lived in an unreasoning, unperceiving torment, a torment none the less acute because of the subtlety of its origin and the strange, unmotivated quality of its vampiric existence. Before my eyes lay the phantasmagoria of the purpling clouds, the strange silver bauble, the recurrent stagnant foam, the loneliness of that bleak-eyed house, and the mockery of the puppet town. I no longer went to the village, for it seemed only a travesty of life. Like my own soul, it stood upon a dark enveloping sea—a sea grown slowly hateful to me. And among these images, corrupt and festering, dwelt that of an object whose human contours left ever smaller the doubt of what it once had been.

These scribbled words can never tell of the hideous loneliness (something I did not even wish assuaged, so deeply was it embedded in my heart) which had insinuated itself within me, mumbling of terrible and unknown things stealthily circling nearer. It was not a madness: rather was it a too clear and naked perception of the darkness beyond this frail existence, lit by a momentary sun no more secure than ourselves: a realization of futility that few can experience and ever again touch the life about them: a knowledge that turn as I might, battle as I might with all the remaining power of my spirit, I could neither win an inch of ground from the inimical universe, nor hold for even a moment the life entrusted to me. Fearing death as I did life, burdened with a nameless dread yet unwilling to leave the scenes evoking it, I awaited whatever consummating horror was shifting itself in the immense region beyond the walls of consciousness.

Thus autumn found me, and what I had gained from the sea was lost back into it. Autumn on the beaches—a drear time betokened by no scarlet leaf nor any other accustomed sign. A frightening sea which changes not, though man changes. There was only a chilling of the waters, in which I no longer cared to enter—a further darkening of the pall-like sky, as if eternities of snow were waiting to descend upon the ghastly waves. Once that descent began, it would never cease, but would continue beneath the white and the yellow and the crimson sun, and beneath that ultimate small ruby which shall yield only to the futilities of night. The once friendly waters babbled meaningfully at me, and eyed me with a strange regard; yet whether the darkness of the scene were a reflection of my own broodings, or whether the gloom within me were caused by what lay without, I could not have told. Upon the beach and me alike had fallen a shadow, like that of a bird which flies silently overhead—a bird whose watching eyes we do not suspect till the image on the ground repeats the image in the sky, and we look suddenly upward to find that something has been circling above us hitherto unseen.

The day was in late September, and the town had closed the resorts where mad frivolity ruled empty, fear-haunted lives, and where raddled puppets performed their summer antics. The puppets were cast aside, smeared with the painted smiles and frowns they had last assumed, and there were not a hundred people left in the town. Again the gaudy, stucco-fronted buildings lining the shore were permitted to crumble undisturbed in the wind. As the month advanced to the day of which I speak, there grew in me the light of a grey infernal dawn, wherein I felt some dark thaumaturgy would be completed. Since I feared such a thaumaturgy less than a continuance of my horrible suspicions—less than the too-elusive hints of something monstrous lurking behind the great stage—it was with more speculation than actual fear that I waited unendingly for the day of horror which seemed to be nearing. The day, I repeat, was late in September, though whether the 22nd or 23rd I am uncertain. Such details have fled before the recollection of those uncompleted happenings—episodes with which no orderly existence should be plagued, because of the damnable suggestions (and only suggestions) they contain. I knew the time with an intuitive distress of spirit—a recognition too deep for me to explain. Throughout those daylight hours I was expectant of the night; impatient, perhaps, so that the sunlight passed like a half-glimpsed reflection in rippled water—a day of whose events I recall nothing.

It was long since that portentous storm had cast a shadow over the beach, and I had determined, after hesitations caused by nothing tangible, to leave Ellston, since the year was chilling and there was no return of my earlier contentment. When a telegram came for me (lying two days in the Western Union office before I was located, so little was my name known) saying that my design had been accepted—winning above all others in the contest—I set a date for leaving. This news, which earlier in the year would have affected me strongly, I now received with a curious apathy. It seemed as unrelated to the unreality about me, as little pertinent to me, as if it were directed to another person whom I did not know, and whose message had come to me through some accident. None the less, it was that which forced me to complete my plans and leave the cottage by the shore.

There were only four nights of my stay remaining when there occurred the last of those events whose meaning lies in the darkly sinister impression surrounding. Night had settled over Ellston and the coast, and a pile of soiled dishes attested both to my recent meal and to my lack of industry. Darkness came as I sat with a cigarette before the seaward window, and it was a liquid which gradually filled the sky, washing in a floating moon, monstrously elevated. The flat sea bordering upon the gleaming sand, the utter absence of tree or figure or life of any sort, and the regard of that high moon made the vastness of my surroundings abruptly clear. There were only a few stars pricking through as if to accentuate by their smallness the majesty of the lunar orb and of the restless shifting tide.

I had stayed indoors, fearing somehow to go out before the sea on such a night of shapeless portent, but I heard it mumbling secrets of an incredible lore. Borne to me on a wind out of nowhere was the breath of some strange and palpitant life—the embodiment of all I had felt and of all I had suspected—stirring now in the chasms of the sky or beneath the mute waves. In what place this mystery turned from an ancient, horrible slumber I could not tell, but like one who stands by a figure lost in sleep, knowing that it will awake in a moment, I crouched by the windows, holding a nearly burnt-out cigarette, and faced the rising moon.

Gradually there passed into that never-stirring landscape a brilliance intensified by the overhead glimmerings, and I seemed more and more under some compulsion to watch whatever might follow. The shadows were draining from the beach, and I felt that they took with them all which might have been a harbour for my thoughts when the hinted thing should come. Where any of them did remain they were ebon and blank: still lumps of darkness sprawling beneath the cruel brilliant rays. The endless tableau of the lunar orb—dead now, whatever her past was, and cold as the unhuman sepulchres she bears amid the ruin of dusty centuries older than man—and the sea—astir, perhaps, with some unkenned life, some forbidden sentience—confronted me with a horrible vividness. I arose and shut the windo; partly because of an inward prompting, but mostly, I think, as an excuse for transferring momentarily the stream of thought. No sound came to me now as I stood before the closed panes. Minutes or eternities were alike. I was waiting, like my own fearing heart and the motionless scene beyond, for the token of some ineffable life. I had set the lamp upon a box in the western corner of the room, but the moon was brighter, and her bluish rays invaded places where the lamplight was faint. The ancient glow of the round silent orb lay upon the beach as it had lain for aeons, and I waited in a torment of expectancy made doubly acute by the delay in fulfillment, and the uncertainty of what strange completion was to come.

Outside the crouching hut a white illumination suggested vague spectral forms whose unreal, phantasmal motions seemed to taunt my blindness, just as unheard voices mocked my eager listening. For countless moments I was still, as if Time and the tolling of her great bell were hushed into nothingness. And yet there was nothing which I might fear: the moon-chiselled shadows were unnatural in no contour, and veiled nothing from my eyes. The night was silent—I knew that despite my closed window—and all the stars were fixed mournfully in a listening heaven of dark grandeur. No motion from me then, or word now, could reveal my plight, or tell of the fear-racked brain imprisoned in flesh which dared not break the silence, for all the torture it brought. As if expectant of death, and assured that nothing could serve to banish the soul-peril I confronted, I crouched with a forgotten cigarette in my hand. A silent world gleamed beyond the cheap, dirty windows, and in one corner of the room a pair of dirty oars, placed there before my arrival, shared the vigil of my spirit. The lamp burned endlessly, yielding a sick light hued like a corpse's flesh. Glancing at it now and again, for the desperate distraction it gave, I saw that many bubbles unaccountably rose and vanished in the kerosene-filled base. Curiously enough, there was no heat from the wick. And suddenly I became aware that the night as a whole was neither warm nor cold, but strangely neutral—as if all physical forces were suspended, and all the laws of a calm existence disrupted.

Then, with an unheard splash which sent from the silver water to the shore a line of ripples echoed in fear by my heart, a swimming thing emerged beyond the breakers. The figure may have been that of a dog, a human being, or something more strange. It could not have known that I watched—perhaps it did not care—but like a distorted fish it swam across the mirrored stars and dived beneath the surface. After a moment it came up again, and this time, since it was closer, I saw that it was carrying something across its shoulder. I knew, then, that it could be no animal, and that it was a man or something like a man, which came toward the land from a dark ocean. But it swam with a horrible ease.

As I watched, dread-filled and passive, with the fixed stare of one who awaits death in another yet knows he cannot avert it, the swimmer approached the shore—though too far down the southward beach for me to discern its outlines or features. Obscurely loping, with sparks of moonlit foam scattered by its quick gait, it emerged and was lost among the inland dunes.

Now I was possessed by a sudden recurrence of fear, which had died away in the previous moments. There was a tingling coldness all over me—though the room, whose window I dared not open now, was stuffy. I thought it would be very horrible if something were to enter a window which was not closed.

Now that I could no longer see the figure, I felt that it lingered somewhere in the close shadows, or peered hideously at me from whatever window I did not watch. And so I turned my gaze, eagerly and frantically, to each successive pane; dreading that I might indeed behold an intrusive regarding face, yet unable to keep myself from the terrifying inspection. But though I watched for hours, there was no longer anything upon the beach.

So the night passed, and with it began the ebbing of that strangeness—a strangeness which had surged up like an evil brew within a pot, had mounted to the very rim in a breathless moment, had paused uncertainly there, and had subsided, taking with it whatever unknown message it had borne. Like the stars that promise the revelation of terrible and glorious memories, goad us into worship by this deception, and then impart nothing, I had come frighteningly near to the capture of an old secret which ventured close to man's haunts and lurked cautiously just beyond the edge of the known. Yet in the end I had nothing. I was given only a glimpse of the furtive thing; a glimpse made obscure by the veils of ignorance. I cannot even conceive what might have shown itself had I been too close to that swimmer who went shoreward instead of into the ocean. I do not know what might have come if the brew had passed the rim of the pot and poured outward in a swift cascade of revelation. The night ocean withheld whatever it had nurtured. I shall know nothing more.

Even yet I do not know why the ocean holds such a fascination for me. But then, perhaps none of us can solve those things—they exist in defiance of all explanation. There are men, and wise men, who do not like the sea and its lapping surf on yellow shores; and they think us strange who love the mystery of the ancient and unending deep. Yet for me there is a haunting and inscrutable glamour in all the ocean's moods. It is in the melancholy silver foam beneath the moon's waxen corpse; it hovers over the silent and eternal waves that beat on naked shores; it is there when all is lifeless save for unknown shapes that glide through sombre depths. And when I behold the awesome billows surging in endless strength, there comes upon me an ecstasy akin to fear; so that I must abase myself before this mightiness, that I may not hate the clotted waters and their overwhelming beauty.

Vast and lonely is the ocean, and even as all things came from it, so shall they return thereto. In the shrouded depths of time none shall reign upon the earth, nor shall any motion be, save in the eternal waters. And these shall beat on dark shores in thunderous foam, though none shall remain in that dying world to watch the cold light of the enfeebled moon playing on the swirling tides and coarse-grained sand. On the deep's margin shall rest only a stagnant foam, gathering about the shells and bones of perished shapes that dwelt within the waters. Silent, flabby things will toss and roll along the shores, their sluggish life extinct. Then all shall be dark, for at last even the white moon on the waves shall wink out. Nothing shall be left, neither above nor below the sombre waters. And until that last millennium, as after it, the sea will thunder and toss throughout the dismal night.

Appendix

Notes to "Medusa's Coil"

(1.) Son kills wife with hastily seized machete, hacks off hair in savage rage since he deems this the cause of Marsh's attraction & also connects it with her hideous nature & malignly magical affiliations—also, with her newly discovered racial identity. *But the hair* slithers out of the room of its own volition, as if transformed to some monstrous black snake.* At this sight son goes half mad. Follows hair up to studio, & sees it coil itself around the slowly recovering form of Marsh. Hair strangles Marsh—the evil voodoo sorceress having recognised M. as an enemy when she saw the manner in which he had painted her. Son, witnessing this, goes *wholly* mad. Cowers & mutters around room till father enters. Then the shrieking explanation & the struggle. Son either kills himself or is killed by father. (Attempts to kill both father & self because he thinks family blood contaminated by his marriage to negress.) Father left alone with portrait & bodies & *hair.* Buries victims of tragedy in cellar & settles down to live as hermit. Picture affects him strangely—he cannot break away from it. He fears hair will emerge vampirically from Marsh's grave. Sophonisba is sullen—continually wanders into cellar & haunts Marsh's secret grave, though the servants are not supposed to know that anyone has died there. Marsh, son, & wife supposed to have gone away. Later freed hands servants & chauffeur all changed, money wanes, Sophonisba refuses to leave. Finally dies on Marsh's cellar grave, muttering.

let it be emphasised in every possible place that Marsh has seen some specific horror in Marceline which son (up to unveiling of picture) has been unable to see.

Manner of Narration

I. Father finds Marceline's body as described in text. Trail of blood & line of bloody footprints leading upstairs.

II.   In attic studio finds son armed & cowering. Gibbered explanation†—struggle—son's death

III.   Marsh's body—strangled by demoniacally animated coil of very slighty kinky hair. It clings to the body, as if with a kind of morbid affection. Then the portrait—sight of which nearly unhinges old man's mind. He cannot bear to describe it. Picture holds old man by kind of hypnotism. Fear of what buried hair (twined around Marsh's body) will do *if pictured hair is violated.* Must guard picture. Conceals tragedy—explains absences—but place seen to be haunted. Curious forms hover in cellar where bodies are buried. Queer black snake (hair) seen gliding about at times—frightens servants. Tales of the indestructibility of dead hair. A wailing from old Sophonisba's distant cabin.

IV.   Visitor is now shewn the fateful painting. It is badly mildewed, but enough is discernible to send visitor into fit of trembling. Not quite finished. Symbols of horror—voodoo—black mass—Cthulhu-cult—&c. &c.—Hair alive with independent life—woman revealed as vampire, lamia, &c. &c.—& unmistakably (surprise to reader as in original text) a negress.

V.   Aftermath? Portrait, disturbed by visitor,

crumbles—causing panic & flight? Suspicion of pursuing coil of hair? At any rate—conversation lasts till dawn.

*after attacking Denis but being beaten off by his machete
†son tells how he returned & sent servants away

Notes to "The Challenge From Beyond"

On a far orb in a distant galaxy dwell a vastly superior race of semi-material beings who navigate their own galaxy but cannot navigate others. They have extirpated every other form of life which once tenanted their galaxy since in the past a low form once discovered space navigation and menaced this race. They cannot navigate beyond their own galaxy in physical person, but can launch into space certain objects of communication which will enable them to project their minds to any trans-galactic region where these objects may chance to alight. Only a few, of course, ever land anywhere—and when one does land it is useless unless it can be set working by contact with a local living intelligence—which must reach it by gliding along a beam of light. These objects—inscribed discs enclosed in peculiar crystal—are so arranged as to attract and fascinate intelligences wherever they may fall. When a local intelligence responds and correlates on any of these objects, it is sucked in and projected to the world of the beings—taking up its abode (without senses) in a machine—one of a prodigious number along the walls of a vast edifice. Each machine is attuned to one of the sent-forth objects, and glows with violet light whenever a distant intelligence enters the corresponding object where it has landed. The machines are watched by a special official; and when one glows another official—an investigator—gets into telepathic communication with it and learns all it knows. Meanwhile the body of the questioned being remains on its distant orb in a coma before the object its mind has entered. After the investigator has pumped the mind of its contents, he projects his own mind through space (and through the two machines, one at each end) into the inert body of the distant being— thus landing, as it were, on the far planet. He can also carry the object around and ensnare any number of others—the mind of each being exchanged with that of a member of the mighty race. Machine can hold more than one mind— so that one cube on a distant planet can trap any number of beings rapidly. During the stage of complete exchange, the mind of the captured being remains *in the body of the displacer*—not in the wall machine—the process consisting of two transfers: (a) distant being to wall machine, (b) investigator exchanging with wall machine, (c) wall machine exchanging with vacant body of distant being. On several occasions planets were completely overrun and subjugated by this means—the advanced race once voluntarily remaining in its new region and bodies after the killing off of the displaced native stock. Return accomplished in corresponding way. Extirpation accomplished by killing of distant body (quasi-suicide) at moment of return. Bodiless distant mind then returns to machine and is annihilated unless some use for it exists. Race has found by experience that certain beings are pestiferous and destructive, hence mean to kill all they find after exhausting their knowledge for historic records. All, that is, who shew any signs of being able to navigate space and thus overrun universe.

Aeons ago, when cone-shaped Great Race inhabited earth, a cube from the outsiders reached the earth. It drew several minds away, but the race were so advanced that they recognised the alienage of the usurping minds in the affected bodies and destroyed them after torture—sacrificing the exiled minds of their own people. Casting back in time and exchanging minds with other-planetarians, they discovered roughly what was occurring, and kept the cube as a relique safely shut away from the public. Occasional lawless or adventurous souls tried to meddle with it, once or twice succeeding—but always found out. If succeeding, were left in exile while bodies with usurping minds killed. Back on outside world, knowledge of the Great Race gained from these exiled captives—they know that their explorers have been killed, and long for revenge, but have no way of getting it. Naturally they keep the earth bombarded with cubes as best they can calculate, but none ever lands again. Those parts of this business which can be known on earth are handed down in the disquieting and debatable Eltdown Shards.

Orb is one of a cluster of a dozen sapphire suns. Always faces its star, but others perpetually lighten dark side. Atmosphere dense with CO_2 and water vapour—lush vegetation—violent storms. Beings inhabit boxlike houses of concrete clusters—rooms high but doorways low. Every sort of strange fauna and flora present.

The Sorcery of Aphlar

By Duane W. Rimel

The council of twelve seated on the jewelled celestial dais ordered that Aphlar be cast from the gates of Bel-hazen. He sat too much alone, they decreed, and brooded when toil should have been his lot.[1] And in his obscure and hidden delvings he read all too frequently those papyri of Elder aeons which reposed in the Guothic shrine and were to be consulted only for rare and special purposes.

The twilight city of Bel-haz-en had climbed backward in its knowledge. No longer did philosophers sit upon street corners speaking wise words to the populace, for stupid ignorance ruled within the crumbling and immemorially ancient walls. Where once the wisdom of the stars abounded, only feebleness and desolation now lay upon the place; spreading like a monstrous blight and sucking foul nurture from the stupid dwellers. And out of the waters of the Oll that meandered from the mountains of Azlakka to pass by the aged city, there rose often great clouds of pestilence that racked the people sorely, leaving them pale and near to dying. All this their loss of wisdom brought. And now the council had sent their last and greatest wise man from them.

Aphlar wandered to the mountains far above the city and built a cavern for protection from the summer heat and winter chill. There he read his scrolls in silence and told his mighty wisdom to the wind about the crags and to the swallows on the wing. All day he sat and watched below or drew queer drawings on small bits of stone and chanted to them, for he knew that some day men would seek the cave and slay him. The cunning of the twelve did not mislead him. Had not the last exiled wise man's screams rent the night two moon-rounds before when people thought him safely gone? Had not his own eyes seen the priest's sword-slashed form floating by in the poison waters? He knew no lion had killed old Azik, let the council say what they might. Does a lion slash with a sword and leave his prey uneaten?

Through many seasons Aphlar sat upon the mountain, gazing at the muddy Oll as it wound into the misty distance to the land where none ever ventured. He spoke his words of wisdom to the snails that worked in the ground by his feet. They seemed to understand, and waved their slimy feelers before they sank beneath the sand again. On moonlit nights he climbed the hill above his cave and made strange offerings to the moon-God Alo; and when the night-birds heard the sound they drew close and listened to the whispering. And when queer winged things flapped across the darkened sky and loomed up dimly against the moon Aphlar was content. Those which he had addressed had heeded his beckoning. His thoughts were always far away, and his prayers were offered to the pale fancies of dusk.

Then one day past noontide Aphlar rose from his earthen chair and strode down the rock mountainside. His eyes, heeding not the rotten, stone-walled city, held steadfast to the river. When he drew near its muddy brink he paused and looked up the bosom of the stream. A small object floated near the rushes, and this Aphlar rescued with tender and curious care. Then, wrapping the thing in the folds of his robe, he climbed up again to his cave in the hills. All day he sat and gazed upon the object; rummaging now and then in his musty chronicles, and muttering awful syllables as he drew faint figures on a piece of parchment.

That night the gibbous moon rose high, but Aphlar did not climb above his dwelling. Queer night-birds flew past the cavern's mouth, chirped eerily, and fled away into the shadows.

Many days passed before the council sent their messengers of murder; but at last the time was thought ripe, and seven dark-browed men stole away to the hills. Yet when that grim seven ventured within the cave they saw not the wise man Aphlar. Instead, small blades of grass were sprouting in his natural chair of earth. All about lay papyri dim and musty, with faint figures drawn upon them. The seven shuddered and left forthwith when they beheld these things, but as the last man tremblingly withdrew he saw a round and unknown thing lying on the ground. He picked it up, and his fellows drew close in curiosity; but they saw upon it only alien symbols which they could not read, yet which made them shrink and quaver without knowing why. Then he who had found it cast it quickly over the steep precipice beside him, but no sound came from the slope below whereon it should have fallen. And the thrower trembled, fearing many things that are not known but only whispered about. Then, when he told how the sphere he had held was without the weight a thing of stone should have; how it was like to have floated on air as the thistledown floats; he and the six with him slunk as one from the spot and swore it was a place accursed.

But after they had gone a snail crawled slowly from a sandy crevice and slid intently over to where the blades of grass were growing. And when it reached the spot, two slimy feelers stretched forth and bent oddly downward, as if eager to watch forever the winding river.

The Diary of Alonzo Typer

Found after his mysterious disappearance.

By William Lumley

Arrived here yesterday at 6 p.m. There was a dreadful storm coming on, [and I] was unable to get any conveyance to take me to my destination. The place is no better than an old back-water and its few inhabitants little better than idiotic. May 1 after Walpurgis Night, witches sabbaths, and all that, yet I have always been fascinated by unholy mysteries, for what else has brought me to this shunned old house? Well the coming storm so darkened everything, I got but a glimpse of my surroundings as I hurried on to reach my destination before it broke. I could only see by the lightning flashes—it sets in a small swampy valley of strange weeds and fungus surrounded by scraggy ill-looking trees while at its back just beyond this [sits] a dismal looking hill upon whose top stand several great stones seemingly within a circle. The house has a decidedly forbidding aspect, which does not belie the rumors I have heard about it. This was all I could see. I managed to reach the porch just as a terrific downpour of rain fell, accompanied by a bolt of thunder that might well have announced the day of general dissolution to be at hand.

————

I am conscious of several evil presences in this house, one in particular that is decidedly hostile towards me. A presence with a malevolent will that is seeking to break down my own, and overcome me. I must not countenance this for an instant. I must use all my forces to resist it; as I have said, this presence is evil but of a superhuman quality as though allied unto powers not of earth but emanating from some ante-human twilight space unknown. Its presence, too, though unseen, seems colossal—like to tower o'er, and its [?] bulk the chambers might scarce contain, likewise of an unutterable age as to be indescribable.

Last night,—or rather about 3 a.m. this morning, a strange creeping wind seemed to pervade the place and ever rising until the house rocked as within a typhoon. And as I passed down the stairs to the floor below, a huge black claw-like hand emerged from the darkness and endeavored to thrust me down the stairs. I escaped it however, and as I passed the room where the warlocks' portraits hung, suddenly that of the serpentlike one glowed with a luminous fire (green), and the features seemed to take on a more hideous aspect; a cold chill crept o'er me as I gazed upon it, and I noticed the eyes of the wild, swinelike one were lurid with an unmistakable evil glow. Also the background had changed unto a lone bleak moor with a dirty-yellow sky, whereon grew a wretched looking black thorn bush.

————

Today within the little locked room I discovered another painting to the likeness of a woman, or rather a she-thing of some sort for although the face and form is of a fair girl, her pale skin is greenish and scaled, and her beautiful features bear the most fiendish expression I have ever beheld.

————

There are unseen presences here as I have said, some of them so great (seemingly) the rooms might scarce contain them. There is a formula of Evocation in the old conjuring book (I found in the attic) to compel them to materialize, but I greatly fear to do this. There are also faces and forms to be seen at odd times within the dim corners of the halls and chambers, faces and forms so hideous, and loathsome as to defy description, and today when I descended into the locked vault-like cellar beneath, I distinctly heard the menacing padding and mutterings as of gigantic things within;

likewise the slithering as of a great sea-beast dragging its bulk over the stone floor. What can be contained within that locked cellar? I would not open it for worlds. The lock is old and encrusted with rust, and the evil looking hieroglyphics upon it may be graven Elder signs for they seem to be of an indescribable old age, and at times to glow with greenish hue.

––––

The black clutching hands that ofttimes appear in my pathway have assumed more formidable dimensions; they appeared today from out the darkness of the cellar, and seemed to be alive with a far greater malevolent will. Also muffled reverberations emanated from behind the locked vault that seemed to echo upon the far horizon like distant thunder. What is to be my ultimate end within this place? I might not leave here now if I would, for a strange command, or rather power, holds me back.

––––

As I have said, the house is very, very old, and has an undeniable bad reputation. It is built in no particular recognizable style, for so many repairs have been added at different times it would be impossible to discover the original one. There are two portraits in the lower dwelling room of the warlocks who I suppose lived here at different times. One has the most disconcerting countenance I have ever beheld. It is serpent-like with great green eyes. The other has a longish face resembling a thin wild swine; the eyes are set near together and seem when evening falls to glow with a baleful light. They are cheerful companions, these two. I wonder if any murders have been committed here (or suicides)? The atmosphere of the place might well suggest these and worse.

————

There are several female presences that have dimly materialized. They are of the same hellish beauty as the portrait I found in the hall's locked room. There is one whose fell loveliness is above all the rest; her poisonous charms are like a honeyed flower growing on the brink of hell.

I have found in an old trunk in the attic a book on magic and an old diary. These are very old, torn, and mouldy. The book dates back to the sixteenth century and the diary seems fully as old. It is filled with a strange crabbed writing, and a colored drawing fell out of it when I opened it. This is of a hideous creature resembling nothing so much as a squid, beaked and tentacled with great yellow eyes; yet is not such, for the human form is decidedly intermingled in its construction. For instance the head, hands, and feet . . . these are strangely clawed. It is seated upon a pedestal resembling a throne and upon this are symbols and seeming words like I have never seen before. They resemble Chinese but they are surely not such; there is a sinister atmosphere about both the writing and drawing I cannot describe, save that the evil of ages seems to be centered in the unnamable creature depicted in the drawing, and the unknown characters of writing seem to be endowed with an evil life of their own as though sentient, and fain would wrest themselves forth from the parchment and wreak a mischief upon whomsoever gazes upon them. This is a delusion but whoever depicted the strange monster wrought it with a hellish precision, and the letters with an unholy purport.

————

Found today in the little locked room an old note-book evidently the property of one of the warlocks. It is in barbarous Latin and almost indecipherable. It seems to be a collection of hurried notes jotted down at random, the name Yian-Ho appearing many times within it. Yian Ho! that lost and hidden city wherein lurk secrets aeons-old! There seems to be a sort of cryptic key running through the maze of almost unintelligible sentences; perhaps this will enable me to translate the sinister writing aforementioned. Also noticed that the attic door resisted all my efforts to open, when it at last gave way a seemingly colossal unseen shape flew or rather soared away. I could distinctly hear the beating of gigantic wings; also noted that the black [. . .] and hands appear more often now and have grown until they assume gigantic proportions. What I may not grasp is the several un-human presences here whose shadowy bulk is so vast I cannot conceive in what manner the chambers may contain them. There are terrible primal arcana of Earth that are better unknown; there are dread secrets (un-hu-man) that none may know and have peace—more secrets that render whosoever knoweth them an alien unto the tribe he belongs to, that cause him to walk alone on earth, for he who takes pays. Likewise there are dread un-human survivals that have straggled down through the aeons, none know how, monstrous blasphemous entities that have slept or lain in secret crypts and in remote places for unhallowed ages governed (as I have said) by neither logic nor reason as we know it, to be awakened from their age-long sleep by whosoever knoweth the rites, the signs, and words, for they die not but shall be until the ending of all things.

———

Upon this day of St. John's Eve I was conscious at sunset of a distant sound coming apparently from the strange circle of stones upon the hill. It was a shrill [. . .] intermingled with a hideous hissing and haunting sound resembling no earthly music I have ever heard.

———

Today I spent several hours on the hill. There is a strange wind that whirls about the forbidding monoliths, from which emanates at times a faint cryptic utterance or whisper. These monoliths are certainly of no Druidic origin and unlike in both hue and texture any stone I have ever seen. They are neither brown nor gray but rather a dirty yellow blending into an evil green. Yet do they seem to change and ever change whilst their texture resembles that of a scaled serpent, and nauseous to touch, it being cold and clammy as a toad or other reptile.

Noticed today, Lammas day, that the whispers were unmistakably louder, angry, and humming. I could almost distinguish words of a hissing sibilant character resembling those of the unspeakable chant aforementioned and like unto a faint blink of summer lightning for a brief moment. Lit up the distant horizon whereat a sinister detonation as from out the evil cosmos seemingly from miles and miles away, yet 'twas not such for I could distinctly hear an indescribable colossal un-human terrible voice give utterance to dread hissing words which ended in a peal of gutteral laughter! Gods, what has my unwarranted curiosity evoked from out the twilight spaces? What will be the end?

————

At last my dreams are to be realized in this shunned old house. I have come across an ancient forgotten one who will show me the gateway I would enter, the lost signs and words. I wonder how long he, or rather it, has lain buried and forgotten within, one whom ones of earth no longer know, whose name is only whispered by a few who fear to utter it even in secret, or why none have ever glimpsed it in the crypt wherein it has lain?

At last I have learned the meaning of the dread symbols and have mastered the seven lost signs of terror. I have learned likewise in silence the hideous unspeakable words of fear. All that remains for me to accomplish is their chant which will transfigure that forgotten one who is guardian of the ancient gateway. I marvel much at the chant; it is composed of strange repellent gutteral sounds and hissing sibilant syllables resembling no language I have ever heard. I was tempted to read this aloud upon the hill today but my efforts were seemingly futile, for I succeeded in eliciting a strange sinister rumbling echo perhaps from the evil cosmos, along with a cloud of dust—not dust as we know it but a cloud of hideous blinding elemental dust like an evil living thing. Better luck next time.

————

Today dark ominous clouds hovered o'er the circle on the hill. I have noticed them several times before. They are smokelike and seemingly of fantastic forms; one might indeed fancy them to be evil presences, more especially by the manner in which they float in a circle about the monoliths, ever in a circle as though endowed with an evil life of their own. I could swear that an angry murmuring emanated from them. Also they never seem to stay above a quarter of an hour; then they slowly sail away ever eastward in the manner of a straggling battalion. Could they indeed be those dread ones whom Solomon knew of old—seeming like great flocks whose number is legion, whose tread doth shake the earth?

Rehearsed today the chant that will transfigure the nameless thing, yet strange fears assail me when I utter it even under my breath, and the only way to it is through the locked cellar wherein it rests amid the horrors that lurk within, and though this chant is the station [?], there is no formula for controlling what is evoked, save it be the formal signs and gestures. Also where is the key that will unlock the prisoned horrors pent within? I greatly fear for all this, yet an unknown force urges me on. I may not disobey; I must unlock the cellar at any cost.

Late this afternoon I descended to the forbidding precincts. At first all was silent; then the menacing padding began anew, this time louder and more formidable. Also the slithering as of a great sea-beast seemed swifter and intensified, as though it were striving to force its way through into where I stood. While the restless muffled pacing ever grew more restless and more sinister, suddenly began the old reverberations, but louder—increased a hundredfold. I can liken it to nothing save the roar of some dread monster of the last saurian age, when fell primordial reptiles roamed the earth. How may I bear the onslaught of these dreadful ones when I unlock it?

———

Found today in the little locked room the key. It was buried beneath a host of rubbish as though its owner sought to conceal it. It was tightly wrapped within the dried skin of some unknown reptile, and upon the inner side were written in the same crabbed characters as the diary the following words: "I shall never reveal the secrets of those monstrous primal ones whose cryptic characters reveal dread ante-human secrets, secrets of things no one of earth should learn would he know peace [any] more, for I have been to Yian-Ho, that lost and aeon-old city, and have found and borne away one from that dreadful and forbidding place, for frightful things I saw therein and shapes more dread than these. And lo! that which I have awakened and borne away with me I may not part with again, nor may we be separated [any] more as it is written within the *Book of Forbidden Things,* for lo! that which I have willed to live hath turned the dreadful shape about me as it is written, yet if I pass untimely it must abide a while for its time is not yet." I am at a loss to describe this key; like the lock it is of a greenish metal (frosted), resembling brass tarnished with verdigrease and wrought to fit the coffin-shaped opening; like the lock it is ponderous, the handle being a rough attempt at an un-human image of some sort no longer recognizable. It is passing strange that though an inert object of metal, I could distinctly feel it quicken in my hand when held there any length of time. Below the image is graven in the eternal Chinese-like characters "My vengeance lurks"—the rest of the inscription is undecipherable through age. Awakened last night to see the key glow lurid green even as the lock has done, and strange hissing whispers seemed to emanate from it, wherein these words were manifest: "The Hour Falls." It is an omen, and I laugh at my own fears. Have I not the dread words of fear and the seven lost signs of terror? The power that is coercive of any Dweller of the Evil Cosmos or darkened spaces unknown? I will no longer hesitate; there is a terrific storm coming on, even greater than the one I encountered upon my arrival three months ago. The lightning renders the fell circle of stones upon the hill a lurid green, and the menacing padding and muffled reverberations below echo upon the distant horizon louder than the dread thunder with which they are intermingled.

Notes

Abbreviations:

AHT   Arkham House transcripts
A.Ms.   autograph manuscript
AT   *The Ancient Track: Complete Poetical Works* (2001)
CE   *Collected Essays* (2004–06; 5 vols.)
D   *Dagon and Other Macabre Tales* (1986)
DH   *The Dunwich Horror and Others* (1984)
ES   *Essential Solitude: The Letters of H. P. Lovecraft and August Derleth* (2008)
HM   *The Horror in the Museum and Other Revisions* (1970/1989)
JHL   H. P. Lovecraft Papers, John Hay Library, Brown University (Providence, R.I.)
IAP   S. T. Joshi, *I Am Providence* (2010)
LL   S. T. Joshi, *Lovecraft's Library: A Catalogue* (2002)
LR   Peter Cannon, ed., *Lovecraft Remembered* (1998)
MM   *At the Mountains of Madness and Other Novels* (1985)
OED   *Oxford English Dictionary* (1933 ed.)
OFF   *O Fortunate Floridian: H. P. Lovecraft's Letters to R. H. Barlow* (2007)
SL   *Selected Letters* (1965–76; 5 vols.)
T.Ms.   typed manuscript

Introduction

1. HPL to Clark Ashton Smith, 4 April 1932 (*SL* 4.37).
2. HPL to Farnsworth Wright, 6 January 1933 (*SL* 4.127).
3. A. Langley Searles, "Fantasy and Outré Themes in the Short Fiction of Edward Lucas White and Henry S. Whitehead," in *American Supernatural Fiction: From Edith Wharton to the* Weird Tales *Writers,* ed. Douglas Robillard (New York: Garland, 1996), 70–71.
4. HPL to R. H. Barlow, 9 July 1936; *OFF* 351.
5. HPL to R. H. Barlow, 21 October 1935; *OFF* 299.

Medusa's Coil

HPL worked on "Medusa's Coil" for Zealia Bishop in May 1930, while he was in Richmond, Virginia; he finished it in August (HPL to R. H. Barlow, [24 May 1935], *OFF* 276; HPL to Clark Ashton Smith, [6 August 1930]; ms., JHL). A page of notes to the story survives in AHT (see Appendix), which includes both a plot outline and a "Manner of Narration" (a synopsis of events in order of narration); and here it is made clear that the final revelation—"woman revealed as vampire, lamia, &c. &c.—& unmistakably (surprise to reader as in original text) a negress"—is meant to be the culminating horror of the tale. The mention here of an "original text" may suggest that there was a preexisting draft of some kind by Bishop; but if so, it does not survive.

The existing typescript of the tale appears to have been prepared by Frank Belknap Long, then acting as Bishop's agent. Long was evidently unable to read HPL's handwriting in certain sections, so some passages are garbled and words or phrases seem to have been omitted; these omissions are indicated here by a horizontal rule enclosed in brackets.

The tale was rejected by *Weird Tales*. Later in the year HPL discussed with Long the possibility of sending it to *Ghost Stories* (HPL to Frank Belknap Long, [November 1930]; AHT), but if it was sent there, it was also rejected. Like "The Mound," "Medusa's Coil" was heavily altered and rewritten by August Derleth for its magazine appearance, and he continued to reprint the adulterated text in book form up to his death. The corrected text did not see print until 1989.

It might be thought that the story contains an excess of supernaturalism—a problem that afflicts many of HPL's early tales. Also, like "The Last Test," the plot depends on a conflict of characters, a point of literary technique that was not HPL's strong suit. As such, it is one of the more disappointing of HPL's later revisions.

Texts: T.Ms. (JHL); *Weird Tales* 33, no. 1 (January 1939): 26–53 (abridged); in *Marginalia* (1944); in Bishop's *The Curse of Yig* (Arkham House, 1953); in *HM* (1970/1989).

1. The reference is to architecture in the manner of the Venetian architect Andrea Palladio (1508–1580), known for its elegance, symmetry, and reliance on forms evolved in Graeco-Roman antiquity.

2. Confederate States of America, the formal designation of the Southern states that seceded from the Union (1861–65).

3. HPL may be recalling his own childhood: his father, Winfield Scott Lovecraft, died when he was young (in

1898, when HPL was eight), and he was raised largely by his mother, Sarah Susan Phillips Lovecraft (1857–1921), and his grandfather, Whipple Van Buren Phillips (1833–1904).

4. The Spanish-American War began in 1898, so that Denis de Russy was presumably born in 1887.

5. HPL may have been thinking of the novel *Là-Bas* (1891) by Joris-Karl Huysmans (1848–1907), which features a description of a modern-day Black Mass. See further n. 15.

6. Hearn (1850–1904), Irish-born fantaisiste, journalist, and essayist, was not a pictorial artist like Gauguin and Van Gogh, but he had lived in New Orleans from 1877 to 1887, which is presumably the time when Frank Marsh would have known him. During this time, Hearn wrote the weird sketches that were later collected as *Fantastics* (1914).

7. St. Clair Academy is fictitious.

8. Great Zimbabwe refers to a ruined city that was the capital of the Kingdom of Zimbabwe in southern Africa; the city flourished from approximately 1270 to 1550 C.E. Cf. "The Outpost" (1929): "When evening cools the yellow stream, / And shadow stalks the jungle's ways, / Zimbabwe's palace flares ablaze / For the great King who fears to dream" (*AT* 61). HPL admitted that he had heard about Zimbabwe from his friend Edward L. Sechrist, who had visited the region. The Hoggar, or Ahaggar, Mountains are a highland region in the central Sahara. The region was first cited in "The Last Test" (see Vol. 1, p. 146).

9. The reference is to Berenice II (267?–221 B.C.E.), the wife of Ptolemy III Euergetes (r. 246–222 B.C.E.). She was not his sister. On one occasion she dedicated her hair to Aphrodite, and it subsequently disappeared, leading to the myth that it had been transported to the heavens and

become the constellation Coma Berenices ("Berenice's Hair").

10. Tanit was a Phoenician lunar goddess worshipped in Carthage. Isis was the Egyptian god of nature and magic, but her worship spread throughout the Graeco-Roman world beginning no later than the first century B.C.E.

11. The drawings of British artist Aubrey Beardsley (1872–1898) came to typify the sophistication and decadence of the Yellow Nineties. HPL owned a volume of *The Art of Aubrey Beardsley* (1918 or 1925; *LL* #71), containing many of Beardsley's most celebrated illustrations.

12. Lemuria is a continent once thought to have existed in the Indian Ocean; it was hypothesized by the biologist Ernst Haeckel (1834–1919) to account for the presence of lemurs and other animals and plants in southern Africa and the Malay Peninsula. HPL, although philosophically influenced by Haeckel, learned of Lemuria primarily from W. Scott-Elliot's *The Story of Atlantis and the Lost Lemuria* (1925), which is mentioned in "The Call of Cthulhu" (*DH* 128).

13. During HPL's childhood at 454 Angell Street in Providence, one of the family's servants was named Delilah (presumably an African American). See HPL to Lillian D. Clark, 22–23 December 1925 (ms., JHL); cited in *IAP* 1.97.

14. The reference is to three celebrated French writers of the period: Arthur Rimbaud (1854–1891), Decadent poet; Charles Baudelaire (1821–1867), poet, critic, and translator, and author of the poetry collection *Les Fleurs du mal* (1857); and the Comte de Lautréamont (pseudonym of Isidore Lucien Ducasse, 1846–1870), author of the prose work *Les Chants de Maldoror* (1869).

15. HPL refers to several artists who became celebrat-

ed for their weird work: Henry Fuseli (Johann Heinrich Füssli, 1741–1825), British painter of German-Swiss origin whose painting "The Nightmare" (1781) has become iconic; Francisco José Goya y Lucientes (1746–1828), Spanish painter; Sidney Sime (1867–1941), British artist who gained celebrity by illustrating the early works of Lord Dunsany; and Clark Ashton Smith (1893–1961), American fantaisiste who was also a painter and sculptor; he became acquainted with HPL in 1922 and remained one of his closest friends and colleagues until HPL's death.

16. HPL refers to the protagonists of Joris-Karl Huysmans's two most celebrated novels: in *Là-Bas* (1891; usually translated as *Down There*), Durtal seeks to relieve his ennui by engaging in Satanism and other bizarre activities; in *À Rebours* (1884; usually translated as *Against the Grain*), Jean des Esseintes is similarly bored and indulges a variety of aesthetic whims.

17. Evidently a reference to Auteuil, a region of Paris between the Seine River and the Bois du Boulogne, and formerly a gathering place for French writers and artists.

18. Yuggoth had been invented by HPL in the sonnet series *Fungi from Yuggoth* (1929–30), where it was evidently conceived as a planet or some other heavenly body. He later used it in "The Whisperer in Darkness" (1930), identifying it with the newly discovered planet Pluto. R'lyeh is the underwater city where Cthulhu is imprisoned in "The Call of Cthulhu" (1926).

19. HPL first cited Kadath in "The Other Gods" (1921; *D* 127); it was extensively used in *The Dream-Quest of Unknown Kadath* (1926–27).

20. The image is reminiscent of the red stain on the ceiling seen by the narrator of "The Picture in the House" (1920), indicative of the cannibalistic tendencies of the old

man he has encountered: "I thought of the rain and of a leaky roof, but rain is not red" (*DH* 124).

21. Cthulhu is the cosmic entity trapped in the underwater city of R'lyeh as cited in "The Call of Cthulhu" (1926). The term "Elder Ones" is used on several occasions in HPL's stories—see "The Strange High House in the Mist" (*D* 277f.), *The Dream-Quest of Unknown Kadath* (*MM* 311f.), etc.—but it is not clear that these citations all refer to the same entities. Here the reference is similarly unclear.

22. HPL's imaginary grimoire, the *Necronomicon,* was first cited in "The Hound" (1922). HPL was persistently fascinated by the stone statues found on Easter Island; his citation here is the first in any of his tales. Donald Wandrei would later make use of Easter Island in his novel *Dead Titans, Waken!* (written 1931–32; published in revised form as *The Web of Easter Island*).

23. The entity—evidently a kind of fertility goddess and later declared to be the wife of Yog-Sothoth—was first cited in HPL's revision of Adolphe de Castro's "The Last Test" (1927; see Vol. 1, p. 152), and subsequently cited in many of his own tales.

24. This phonetic rendering of Cthulhu points to HPL's preferred pronunciation of the name: "The actual sound—as nearly as human organs could imitate it or human letters record it—may be taken as something like *Khûl'-hloo,* with the first syllable pronounced gutturally and very thickly. The *u* is about like that in *full;* and the first syllable is not unlike *klul* in sound, since the *h* represents the guttural thickness. The second syllable is not very well rendered—the *l* sound being unrepresented" (*SL* 5.11).

25. The N'bangus are a fictitious African tribe first cited in "Facts concerning the Late Arthur Jermyn and His

Family" (1920; *D* 79–81).

26. The word is found in the *OED;* but the proper noun *Aigipan* ("goat-Pan," or goat-footed Pan) is found in the Greek writers Eratosthenes and Plutarch. Cf. "The Horror at Red Hook" (1925): ". . . aegipans chased endlessly after misshapen fauns over rocks twisted like swollen toads" (*D* 260), where the reference appears to be to a certain type of fantastic monster. The adjective *aegipanic* appears in "Under the Pyramids" (1924; Vol. 1, p. 87).

27. In Greek mythology, Hecate is a goddess associated with magic and witchcraft.

The Trap

"The Trap" was written with Henry S. Whitehead (1882–1932), well-known author of horror and adventure tales for the pulps. The two writers evidently worked on the story during HPL's visit to Whitehead in Dunedin, Florida, in late May to mid-June 1931, or perhaps after HPL returned to Providence shortly thereafter. HPL noted in one letter that he "revised & totally recast" the tale (HPL to August Derleth, 23 December 1931; *ES* 1.432), and in another letter said that he "suppl[ied] the central part myself" (HPL to R. H. Barlow, 25 February 1932; *OFF* 24). I believe that the latter three-fourths of the story is HPL's.

Because this was a tale that would appear under Whitehead's name—HPL, in his gentlemanly way, refused a collaborative byline—HPL did not include references (whimsical or otherwise) to his pseudomythology as he had done in the tales ghostwritten for Zealia Bishop or Adolphe de Castro. The story does feature Gerald Canevin, a recurring character in many of Whitehead's tales, especially those set in the Caribbean. Whitehead's and HPL's

styles do not seem to me to meld very well, and the urbane-
ly conversational style of Whitehead's beginning abruptly
gives way to HPL's long paragraphs of dense exposition.
The tale's publication in *Strange Tales* constitutes HPL's
only "appearance" in that short-lived magazine, as its editor, Harry Bates, rejected several of HPL's own tales.

Texts: Strange Tales 2, no. 1 (March 1932): 73–88; in
Whitehead's *West India Lights* (Arkham House, 1946); in
Uncollected Prose and Poetry II (1980); in *HM* (1989 ed.
only).

1. HPL refers to the three leading psychologists of his
age: the Austrian Sigmund Freud (1856–1939), the Swiss
Carl Gustav Jung (1875–1961), and the Austrian Alfred
Adler (1870–1937). The fact that these three figures are
cited here suggests HPL's authorship; see *SL* 3.146: "This
'love' business is pretty well disposed of by the psycho-ana-
lysts—Freud, Jung, Adler . . ."

2. HPL's first reference to non-Euclidean mathematics occurs in "The Call of Cthulhu" (1926): "He [Wilcox]
had said that the *geometry* of the dream-place he saw was
abnormal, non-Euclidean, and loathsomely redolent of
spheres and dimensions apart from ours" (*DH* 151).

3. The magic lantern was an early type of image pro-
jector developed by Christian Huygens in the 1650s. It was
frequently used in magic shows.

4. Bokhara (more properly Bukhara) is the capital
of Bukhara province in Uzbekistan. The term "Bokhara
rug" came to be applied to hand-made rugs fashioned by
Turkmen tribes in central Asia, but these rugs were not in
fact produced in Bukhara; that city was, however, on the
so-called Silk Road—a series of overland routes whereby
goods from China, India, Persia, and elsewhere were trans-

ported to the West. HPL used the phrase "Bokhara rug" again in "Through the Gates of the Silver Key" (1932–33; *MM* 421).

5. HPL appears to be using the term as a synonym for "Satanist."

6. Loki is, in Norse myth, a shapeshifter and a kind of assistant to the gods. He is the father of Fenrir (or the Fenris-wolf), a vicious wolf who kills the god Odin.

7. The Aegis is a shield designed by Hephaestus for Athene (identified by the Romans with the god Minerva). The Norse god Thor habitually carries a hammer, named Mjöllnir.

8. Sandwich glass refers to glass manufactured by the Boston & Sandwich Glass Company in Sandwich, Massachusetts, on Cape Cod. Founded in 1825, the company became renowned for the quality of its glass products, which became collector's items.

The Man of Stone

"The Man of Stone" is the first of five stories written for Hazel Heald (1896–1961), a woman about whom little is known. She was born and apparently spent most of her life in Somerville, Massachusetts, and, as far as is known, published nothing aside from the stories HPL revised or ghostwrote for her. Unlike Zealia Bishop, she wrote no memoir of Lovecraft, so that it is not clear how she came in touch with him and what their professional or personal relations were like. Muriel Eddy (if we can trust her on this point) reports that Heald had joined a writers' club established by the Eddys, and that the latter steered her to Lovecraft when the tenor of her work became evident. Eddy goes on to say that Heald confided to her a vague romantic interest in Lovecraft: she managed to persuade Lovecraft to come to her home in Somerville on one occasion, when she arranged a candlelight dinner with him (*The Gentleman from Angell Street* [1961], in *LR* 61–63).

Heald wrote to August Derleth about the tale: "Lovecraft helped me on this story as much as on the others, and did actually rewrite paragraphs. He would criticize paragraph after paragraph and pencil remarks beside them, and then make me rewrite them until they pleased him" (30 September 1944; quoted in a footnote in the 1970 ed. of *HM,* 27). Probably the entirety of this utterance is false or suspect. Judging from HPL's comments on Heald's stories, it is unlikely that he merely touched up an existing draft or recommended revisions that Heald herself then carried out; instead, most or all of the stories were based on mere synopses and were written by HPL almost entirely on his own. HPL does not mention "The Man of Stone" in any extant correspondence, but he must have worked on it by the summer of 1932 at the latest in order for it to have appeared in the October *Wonder Stories.* The story appears to involve a formula in the *Book of Eibon* for turning any living creature into a stone statue, but it is later said that the formula "depends more on plain chemistry than on the Outer Powers" and that "What it amounts to is a kind of petrification infinitely speeded up"—a pseudo-scientific explanation that evidently was sufficient to pass muster with *Wonder Stories* editor Hugo Gernsback.

Texts: Wonder Stories 4, no. 5 (October 1932): 440–45, 470; in *Marginalia* (1944); in *HM* (1970/1989).

1. Lake Placid is a large lake in the upper reaches of the Adirondack Mountains in northern New York, in Essex County. There is also a village in the area called Lake

Placid (site of the Winter Olympics of 1932 and 1980). It is unclear whether HPL is referring to the lake or the village.

2. The village of Mountain Top is fictitious.

3. "Black Goat" has usually been taken to be an attribute of Shub-Niggurath (as in the frequent incantation, *"Iä! Shub-Niggurath! The Black Goat of the Woods with a Thousand Young!"* ["The Whisperer in Darkness" (1930), *DH* 227]; see also p. 109 below), but in a late letter HPL suggests that the two terms are distinct: "Yog-Sothoth's wife is the hellish cloud-like entity Shub-Niggurath, in whose honour nameless cults hold the rite of the Goat with a Thousand Young" (*SL* 5.303).

4. Wijtgaart is a village in the province of Friesland in the Netherlands. It is not clear whether HPL is referring to an actual witch trial in 1587. There were many witchcraft trials in the Netherlands during this period; see *Witchcraft in the Netherlands,* ed. Marijke Gijswijt-Hofstra and Willem Firjhoff (Rotterdam: Universitaire Pers Rotterdam, 1991).

5. This is, chronologically, HPL's second citation of the *Book of Eibon,* following that in "The Dreams in the Witch House" (*MM* 263). The book was invented by Clark Ashton Smith and first cited in "The Holiness of Azéderac" (written 19 May 1931; *Weird Tales,* November 1933), although the sorcerer Eibon was first cited in "The Door to Saturn" (written 25 July 1930; *Strange Tales,* January 1932).

6. The term Rensselaerswyck (not Rensselaerwyck) refers to a colonial manor in Rensselaer County in east-central New York; HPL probably means to refer to the nearby town of Rensselaer. Esopus is a town several miles south of Rensselaer, near the town of Kingston, in Ulster

County. HPL visited this area—which includes the colonial towns of Hurley and New Paltz—in 1929 and on several later occasions, as his friend Bernard Austin Dwyer lived in Kingston.

7. Yoth was first cited in "The Mound" (see Vol. 1, p. 274), as a "red-litten" region below the underground world of K'n-yan.

8. Sugar Loaf (no hyphen) is a hamlet within the town of Chester in Orange County, in the southern portion of New York.

9. HPL alludes to an ancient Greek axiom, "The mills of the gods grind slowly."

10. Tsathoggua was a toad-god invented by Clark Ashton Smith in the story "The Tale of Satampra Zeiros" (written 16 November 1929). HPL first cited the entity in "The Mound" (see Vol. 1, p. 283).

11. *Lunger* (pronounced LUNG-er) is American slang for someone who has pulmonary tuberculosis.

12. The name was probably chosen for its similarity to *Hoag*—a reference to Jonathan E. Hoag (1831–1927), an amateur poet with whom HPL became acquainted around 1918. Hoag lived in Troy, N.Y., the seat of Rensselaer County.

13. *To piggle* is American slang for the attempt to pry something (such as a label) off a hard surface with a fingernail.

Winged Death

This story was probably written in the summer of 1932. HPL discussed the story in a letter to August Derleth that probably dates to August 1932: "Sorry your new story parallelled [*sic*] an earlier author's work. Something odd befell a client of mine the other day—involving a story-element which I had intended & introduced under the impression that it was strictly original with me. The tale was sent to Handsome Harry [Bates], & he rejected it on the ground that the element in question (the act of an insect dipping itself in ink & writing on a white surface with its own body) formed the crux of another tale which he had accepted. Hell's bells!—& I thought I'd hit on an idea of absolute novelty & uniqueness!" (*ES* 2.497). The story in question has not been identified, but the note about the tale's submission to *Strange Tales* is of some interest. It is plausible that the earlier Heald tales were written with this better-paying market in view. There is no evidence that the other tales were submitted there; they could well have been, assuming that they were written prior to the magazine's folding at the end of the year. HPL submitted "Winged Death" to Farnsworth Wright of *Weird Tales,* but the latter must have delayed in accepting the tale, for it was published only in the March 1934 issue. When it appeared, HPL wrote: "'Winged Death' is nothing to run a temperature over . . . My share in it is something like 90 to 95%" (*SL* 4.403).

Texts: *Weird Tales* 23, no. 3 (March 1934): 299–315; in *Marginalia* (1944); in *HM* (1970/1989).

1. Bloemfontein is the capital of Free State province in central South Africa. The Orange Hotel is presumably fictitious; it is an allusion to the Orange Free State (1854–1902), the independent Boer republic in the region of which Bloemfontein was the capital.

2. Slauenwite, although an American citizen, was serving in a South African regiment because the United States had not yet declared war against Germany and entered World War I on the side of the Allies; it would do

so only in April 1917. Cf. "Herbert West—Reanimator" (1921–22): "In 1915 I was a physician with the rank of First Lieutenant in a Canadian regiment in Flanders, one of many Americans to precede the government itself into the gigantic struggle" (*D* 153).

3. Mombasa is a city in southern Kenya. At this time, Mombasa was part of the protectorate of British East Africa.

4. M'gonga is fictitious.

5. The title is of course fictitious. *Diptera* is the name of a large order of insects that includes flies, mosquitoes, gnats, midges, and others.

6. *Galla* is a derogatory name for the Oromo, an ethnic group in Ethiopia.

7. *Glossina palpalis* and *Glossina marsitans* are two of the three major species of tsetse-flies, dwelling in rivers and the savannah, respectively. The other species is *Glossina fusca,* dwelling in forests.

8. Tryparsamide is an arsenic compound used in treating sleeping sickness. It was developed in 1915 at the Rockefeller Institute.

9. The expression was first cited in the poem "The Outpost" (1929): "The ancient Fishers from Outside— / Were there not tales the high-priest told, / Of how they found the worlds of old, / And took what pelf their fancy spied?" (*AT* 62). The poem is set in Africa.

10. Variant spellings of Tsathoggua and Cthulhu, made to seem as if they were devised by Africans.

11. Mlolo does exist as a proper name in Africa, but Lake Mlolo is fictitious.

12. Nyangwe was a city in the province of Maniema in the Congo, in west-central Africa. It was one of the main centers for the African slave trade. It no longer exists.

13. Gambian sleeping sickness.

14. Ukala is also a proper name and a word meaning "hunting," but the city of Ukala is fictitious.

15. Prussian blue and Turnbull's blue are both a kind of dye or synthetic pigment.

16. The name appears to anticipate that of Nevil Kingston-Brown, a minor character in "The Shadow out of Time" (1934–35) (see *DH* 395). Francis Wayland Thurston is the narrator of "The Call of Cthulhu." Wayland is the name of an old Providence family.

17. The name is reminiscent of HPL's longtime friend James Ferdinand Morton (1870–1941), with whom he had been acquainted since 1922.

18. Both the Ubandes and the N'kini jungle are fictitious.

The Horror in the Museum

"The Horror in the Museum" appears to be a conscious parody of HPL's own myth-cycle. Here we are introduced to a new "god," Rhan-Tegoth, which the curator of a waxworks museum, George Rogers, claims to have found on an expedition to Alaska. The stylistic extravagance of the story points clearly to parody. It could be read as a parody of both "Pickman's Model" and "The Call of Cthulhu."

The story is mentioned in a letter of October 1932: "My latest revisory job comes so near to pure fictional ghost-writing that I am up against all the plot-devising problems of my bygone auctorial days" (HPL to E. Hoffmann Price, 20 October 1932; ms., JHL). HPL goes on to recite the plot of the story in a lurid manner that I hope indicates his awareness of its parodic nature. Elsewhere he writes: "'The Horror in the Museum'—a piece which I 'ghost-wrote' for a client from a synopsis so poor that I well-nigh discarded it—is virtually my own work" (*SL* 4.229). This story seems to have been readily accepted by *Weird Tales,* and it appeared in the same issue as "The Dreams in the Witch House." HPL must have been wryly amused when a letter by Bernard J. Kenton (the pseudonym of Jerry Siegel, later the co-creator of *Superman*) appeared in "The Eyrie" for May 1934 in praise of the work: "Even Lovecraft—as powerful and artistic as he is with macabre suggestiveness—could hardly, I suspect, have surpassed the grotesque scene in which the other-dimensional shambler leaps out upon the hero."

Texts: Weird Tales 22, no. 1 (July 1933): 49–68; in *Terror by Night,* ed. Christine Campbell Thomson (London: Selwyn & Blount, 1934), 111–41; in *The "Not at Night" Omnibus,* ed. Christine Campbell Thomson (London: Selwyn & Blount, 1937), 279–307; in *Beyond the Wall of Sleep* (1943); in *HM* (1970/1989).

1. Madame Tussaud's wax museum was opened in London in 1835 by Madame Tussaud (Anna Maria Grosholtz, 1761–1850).

2. Hawley Harvey Crippen (1862–1910) was an American homeopathic physician who was hanged in England for the murder of his wife, Cora. Henri Désiré Landru (1869–1922) was a French soldier and tradesman who was guillotined at Versailles for the murder of at least ten women and a boy. Madame Demers is unidentified. David Rizzio (1533?–1566) was an Italian courtier who became the private secretary of Mary Queen of Scots. He was murdered at the instigation of Mary's husband, Henry Stuart, Lord Darnley. Lady Jane Grey (1536?–1554) was Queen Regnant of England for 9 days after the death of Edward VI

in 1553. She was executed early the next year.

3. Gilles de Rais (or Retz) (1404–1440) was a French nobleman who was executed for the murder of dozens, perhaps hundreds, of children. Donatien Alphonse François, marquis de Sade (1740–1814) was a French nobleman who became notorious for engaging in violent sexual practices; his actions gave rise to the word sadism. Both Rais (as Retz) and Sade were first mentioned by HPL in "The Rats in the Walls" (1923; *DH* 30).

4. Chaugnar Faugn, the elephant god of Tsang, was invented by Frank Belknap Long (1901–1994) in the short novel *The Horror from the Hills* (*Weird Tales*, January/February and March 1931).

5. Von Junzt and his book (originally titled *Nameless Cults*) was invented by Robert E. Howard (1906–1936) in "The Children of the Night" (*Weird Tales*, April/May 1931). The German title of his book was devised in discussions by August Derleth, Farnsworth Wright, E. Hoffmann Price, and C. C. Senf; it was first cited by HPL in "The Dreams in the Witch House" (1932; *MM* 263).

6. The "Pnakotic manuscripts" were invented by HPL in "Polaris" (1918; *D* 22–23). The Dhol chants were first cited here. Leng was first cited in "Celephaïs" (1920; *D* 87) and featured extensively in *The Dream-Quest of Unknown Kadath*.

7. The Tcho-Tchos were invented by August Derleth and Mark Schorer in the story "The Lair of the Star-Spawn" (*Weird Tales*, August 1932). The authors refer to them as a "weird race of people" who live "near or on the Plateau of Sung," evidently in Burma. HPL cited them again in "The Shadow out of Time" (*DH* 395).

8. Lomar is an ancient polar region invented in "Polaris" (*D* 22–23) and subsequently cited in many later tales.

9. The Noatak River is a river in northwestern Alaska. Fort Morton is fictitious (see n. 17 to "Winged Death").

10. The phrase is taken from Deuteronomy 12:23: "Only be sure that thou eat not the blood: for the blood is the life; and thou mayest not eat the life with the flesh."

11. For Sidney Sime, see n. 14 to "Medusa's Coil." Gustave Doré 1832–1883) was a French artist and illustrator and one of the titans of weird art. His illustrated edition of Coleridge's *Rime of the Ancient Mariner* (1870) helped to inspire HPL's love of the weird (see *IAP* 1.33).

12. Leopold Blaschka (not Blatschka) (1822–1895) and his son Rudolf (1857–1939) were German glass artists who became renowned for the beauty and precision of their glass sculptures of biological entities, especially marine species.

13. Yog-Sothoth was first cited by HPL in *The Case of Charles Dexter Ward* (1927; *MM* 151). He is featured extensively in "The Dunwich Horror" (1928), but HPL provides no physical description of him, except indirectly in the form of his son, the invisible twin brother of Wilbur Whateley. In a later letter HPL states: "Yog doesn't *always* have long, ropy arms, since he assumes a variety of shapes— solid, liquid, and gaseous—at will" (*SL* 5.303).

14. HPL cited the name Gnophkehs as the name of a species of animal in "Polaris" (1918), referring to them as "the hairy, long-armed, cannibal Gnophkehs" (*D* 22). A similar description appears in *The Dream-Quest of Unknown Kadath* (*MM* 310) and "The Mound" (see Vol. 1, p. 284).

15. Noth-Yidik and K'thun are cited only here in HPL's work.

16. Azathoth was first cited in the novel-fragment "Azathoth" (1922), although the entity is not actually men-

tioned in the 500 words of surviving text. He is described in *The Dream-Quest of Unknown Kadath* as a "boundless daemon-sultan . . . whose name no lips dare speak aloud, and who gnaws hungrily in inconceivable, unlighted chambers beyond time amidst the muffled, maddening beating of vile drums and the thin, monotonous whine of accursed flutes" (*MM* 308).

17. These two words—meaning either "Cthulhu waits" or "Cthulhu [is] dreaming"—were first cited in "The Call of Cthulhu" (*DH* 136).

18. For Yuggoth, see n. 17 to "Medusa's Coil."

19. HPL refers to the London Zoo at Regent's Park, established in 1828.

Out of the Aeons

"Out of the Aeons"—which Lovecraft was working on in early August 1933 (*SL* 4.222)—is perhaps the best of the Heald revisions, although it too contains elements of extravagance that border on self-parody. The tale makes extensive use of von Junzt's *Black Book* or *Nameless Cults* of von Junzt, which tells of the god Ghatanothoa, "whom no living thing could behold . . . without suffering a change more horrible than death itself. Sight of the god, or its image . . . meant paralysis and petrification of a singularly shocking sort, in which the victim was turned to stone and leather on the outside, while the brain within remained perpetually alive . . ." This idea is suspiciously like the drug utilized in "The Man of Stone."

It is obvious that Heald's sole contribution to this tale is the core notion of a mummy with a living brain; all the rest—Ghatanothoa, the setting on Mu, and, of course, all the prose of the tale—are HPL's. He admits as much when

he says: "Regarding the scheduled 'Out of the Æons'—
I should say *I did* have a hand in it . . . I *wrote* the damn
thing!" (*SL* 5.130). The story is of interest in uniting the
atmosphere of his early "Dunsanian" tales with that of his
later "Mythos" tales: T'yog's ascent of Yaddith-Gho bears
thematic and stylistic similarities with Barzai the Wise's
scaling of Ngranek in "The Other Gods," and the entire
subnarrative about Mu is narrated in a style analogous to
that of Dunsany's tales and plays of gods and men.

Texts: Weird Tales 25, no. 4 (April 1935): 478–96 (as
by "Hazel Heald"); in *Beyond the Wall of Sleep* (1943); in
HM (1970/1989).

Further Reading: William Fulwiler, "Mu in 'Bothon'
and 'Out of the Eons,'" *Crypt of Cthulhu* no. 11 (Candle-
mas 1983): 20–24. Robert M. Price, "New Clues to Lovecraft's Role in 'Out of the Eons' and 'The Crawling Chaos,'"
Crypt of Cthulhu no. 17 (Hallowmas 1983): 29–31.

1. An obvious allusion to Richard Upton Pickman
in "Pickman's Model" (1926). See also Edward Pickman
Derby, a central character in "The Thing on the Doorstep,"
which HPL wrote just after writing "Out of the Aeons"
(21–24 August 1933).

2. Charles Bulfinch (1763–1844), New England architect who worked in the classical style and designed,
among many other buildings, the domed Massachusetts
State House (1798) as well as many private residences.

3. Sakkarah (more properly Saqqara) is the ancient
burial-ground of Memphis, Egypt, dating to as early as the
First Dynasty (c. 3000 B.C.E.). By "Coptic" HPL here refers to the burial practices of the Copts, Egyptian Chris-
tians who date to at least the second century C.E. With the
Arab conquest of Egypt in 641, the Copts became a perse-

cuted minority.

4. The Cardiff Giant was a hoax perpetrated by George Hull, who in 1869 claimed to have unearthed a ten-foot petrified man near Cardiff, New York. A model of the giant was later displayed by P. T. Barnum. Late in 1869 Hull confessed to the hoax.

5. Ponape (now Pohnpei) is an island in Micronesia. Nan-Matol (now Nan Madol) is a ruined city on Ponape that features megalithic structures dating to the 12th or 13th century C.E. HPL first cited these structures in "The Shadow over Innsmouth" (1931; *DH* 329). He may have derived them from A. Merritt's novelette "The Moon Pool" (1918), which is set in that region.

6. All three of these editions were first cited by Robert E. Howard in "The Black Stone" (*Weird Tales,* November 1931).

7. The château was cited in several tales of Clark Ashton Smith's Averoigne cycle, beginning with "The End of the Story" (*Weird Tales,* May 1930).

8. Colonel James Churchward (1851–1936) was a British occultist who wrote several books about the supposedly submerged Pacific continent of Mu, including *The Lost Continent of Mu* (1926). HPL admitted that he never read Churchward's books but only "fairly indicative reviews of them" (HPL to E. Hoffmann Price, 15 February 1933; ms., JHL). Churchward was first mentioned in the collaborative story "Through the Gates of the Silver Key" (1932–33; *MM* 425). Lewis Spence (1874–1955) was a Scottish journalist and folklorist who wrote several books about Atlantis. HPL owned his *Encyclopedia of Occultism* (1920; *LL* #827).

9. The Harry Elkins Widener Memorial Library (opened in 1915) was then and is now the main library of

Harvard University. In "The Dunwich Horror," HPL stated that a copy of the *Necronomicon* was housed there (*DH* 169).

10. The character was first cited in "Through the Gates of the Silver Key"; it is in fact Randolph Carter in disguise, since he is at this time in the alien body of Zkauba the Wizard.

11. The *Occult Review* was an actual monthly periodical (1905–51) issued in Britain. Etienne-Laurent de Marigny was first cited as a friend of Randolph Carter in "Through the Gates of the Silver Key."

12. The Naacal language was a fabrication of Col. Churchward (see n. 8). HPL cites the language in "Through the Gates of the Silver Key" (*MM* 422f.).

13. Yaddith had first been cited in sonnet XXXII ("Alienation") of *Fungi from Yuggoth:* "He had seen Yaddith, yet retained his mind" (*AT* 77). It was cited frequently in "Through the Gates of the Silver Key" as a distant planet on which Randolph Carter, in the body of Zkauba the Wizard, finds himself (*MM* 447f.).

14. Nug and Yeb were first cited in "The Last Test" (see Vol. 1, p. 152); indeed, they are cited only in that story, "The Mound," and "Out of the Aeons." In a later letter HPL refers to them (perhaps whimsically) as the twin offspring of Yog-Sothoth and Shub-Niggurath (*SL* 4.183, 5.303). Yig was invented for the story "The Curse of Yig" (see Vol. 1, p. 172).

15. For "Elder Ones," see n. 20 to "Medusa's Coil."

16. *Areoi* were a Polynesian secret society, chiefly for religious purposes.

17. Cf. "The Call of Cthulhu" (1926): "Let me pray that, if I do not survive this manuscript, my executors may put caution before audacity and see that it meets no other

eye" (*DH* 154).

18. In other stories, Saltonstall Street is a thorough-fare in Arkham, Mass. See "The Whisperer in Darkness" (*DH* 216), "The Dreams in the Witch House" (*MM* 271), and "The Thing on the Dorstep" (*DH* 278).

The Horror in the Burying-Ground

The date of writing of this story is uncertain; HPL never mentions it in any correspondence I have seen. Probably it was written in 1933 or 1934, as HPL does not seem to have had much contact with Heald after the latter date. Much of the story is narrated in a backwoods patois reminiscent—and perhaps a parody—of that used in "The Dunwich Horror." Other in-jokes—such as the use of the character names from previous stories by HPL or from people he knew—suggest that the story is meant, if not as an actual parody, at least as an instance of graveyard humor.

It is clear from the synopses of all the Heald stories that several of them feature the same fundamental plot element: the idea of a living brain encased in a dead or immobilized body. This encompasses "Out of the Aeons" and "The Horror in the Burying-Ground"; in "The Horror in the Museum" the effect of Rhan-Tegoth's depradations is to leave the victim looking like a wax statue, a fate somewhat similar to that of "The Man of Stone"; while "Winged Death" presents a human brain or personality in an alien form. One wonders how much beyond this nucleus was provided by Heald, if indeed she even supplied this much.

Texts: Weird Tales 29, no. 5 (May 1937): 596–606; in *Something about Cats* (1949); in *HM* (1970/1989).

1. The sentence echoes the first sentence of "The Dun-

wich Horror" (1928): "When a traveller in north central Massachusetts takes the wrong fork at the junction of the Aylesbury pike just beyond Dean's Corners he comes upon a lonely and curious country" (*DH* 155–56).

2. Darius Peck and the Peck Valley Cemetery were cited in "In the Vault" (1925; *DH* 3f.). A Dr. Peck is a minor character in *The Case of Charles Dexter Ward* (*MM* 192, 196).

3. William Sprague IV (1830–1915) was governor of Rhode Island from 1860 to 1863 and subsequently a U.S. Senator (1863–75). His large burial plot is close to that of the Phillips family where HPL is now buried in Swan Point Cemetery.

4. The name is an obvious echo of Henry Wentworth Akeley in "The Whisperer in Darkness."

5. Another obvious echo, this time of Arthur Goodenough (1871–1936), a Vermont poet whom HPL met on several occasions.

6. The Frye family are featured prominently in "The Dunwich Horror" (*DH* 179f.).

7. "Beautiful Isle of Somewhere" (1897) is a hymn (words by Jessie B. Pounds, music by John S. Fearis).

8. A Professor Atwood is cited frequently in *At the Mountains of Madness* (*MM* 5f.). A Seth Atwood is the subject of sonnet XI ("The Well") of *Fungi from Yuggoth*.

9. The name may have been suggested by the ghost story "Luella Miller," by Mary E. Wilkins Freeman, included in her collection *The Wind in the Rose-bush and Other Stories of the Supernatural* (1903).

The Slaying of the Monster

This is the first story HPL revised for R[obert]

H[ayward] Barlow (1918–1951), a young friend with whom he first came into contact in 1931 (he did not at the time realize that Barlow was thirteen years old) and who became HPL's literary executor. In February 1933 HPL evaluated three items sent by Barlow, one of which was "The Slaying of the Monster" (the title, as is plain from the manuscript, was supplied by HPL): "I read your stories with a great deal of interest, & really think that they display a gratifying degree of merit & promise. You have a good idea of what a dramatic situation is, & seem to be distinctly sensitive to the nuances of style. Of course, there are at present many marks of the beginner's work—but these are only to be expected. Emphatically, I think you are headed in the right direction. . . . In 'The Slaying of the Monster' I have taken the liberty of changing many words in order to carry out fully the Dunsanian prose-poetic effect which you are obviously seeking. . . . In changing parts of your text I have sought to give it some of the smoothness or rhythm which this kind of writing demands" (*OFF* 51). The story is slight and was not published in HPL's or Barlow's lifetime. Like several of Barlow's early tales, it betrays the influence of such fantasy writers as Lord Dunsany and Clark Ashton Smith.

Texts: T.Ms. (revised by HPL); in *The Hoard of the Wizard-Beast and One Other* (1994); in Barlow, *Eyes of the God* (2002).

The Hoard of the Wizard-Beast

This story is related to one of the segments of Barlow's story-cycle "Annals of the Jinns," the first nine episodes of which appeared in the *Fantasy Fan* (October 1933–February 1935). One of the segments, "The Sacred Bird" (*Fan-*

tasy Fan, January 1934), is set in the land of Ulathia; this term is spelled "Ullathia" in "The Hoard of the Wizard-Beast," and the story as a whole appears to be a loose sequel to "The Sacred Bird." Barlow has dated the manuscript to September 1933, but HPL first saw it in a letter dating to December. He discusses the story at length:

"Your new tale is highly colourful & interesting, & I have taken the liberty to make a few changes in wording, rhythm, & transitional modulation, which may perhaps bring it a bit closer to the Dunsanian ideal evidently animating it. . . . If there is any defect, it is possibly a certain lack of compactness & unity—that is, the tale is not a closely-knit account of a *single episode,* but is rather a loosely-constructed record with much early space given to a description of the *occasion* for Yalden's journey, while the latter parts involve the *journey itself* in a way essentially dissociated from the *occasion.* An ideal short story would concentrate on a *single thing* like the *journey itself,* disposing of the *journey's reason* in as brief an explanatory paragraph as possible. The kind of vehicle for composite & diffuse narratives of this sort is the novel or picaresque romance. Still—it is to be admitted that Dunsany often creates similarly non-unified sketches of short story length, hence this specimen must not be criticised too severely. I'm letting it alone so far as this point goes. . . . As for your new tale— my changes largely concern certain niceties of language, & certain handlings of emotional stress at important turns of the action. A study of the altered text itself will be more instructive than any comment I can make here. What you need is simply more practice—which the years will readily supply" (*OFF* 90).

Like its predecessor, "The Hoard of the Wizard-Beast" was not published in HPL's or Barlow's lifetime.

Texts: T.Ms. (with HPL's revisions); In *The Hoard of the Wizard-Beast and One Other* (1994); in Barlow, *Eyes of the God* (2002).

The Tree on the Hill

This is the first of two stories that HPL revised for Duane W. Rimel (1915–1996), a young correspondent in Asotin, Washington. (For a possible third story, see Appendix.) In HPL's correspondence with Rimel, the story was mentioned in a letter of March 1934; HPL saw it in May while in Florida with Barlow. He wrote: "I read your 'Tree on the Hill' with great interest, & believe it truly captures the essence of the weird. I like it exceedingly despite a certain cumbrousness & tendency toward anticlimax in the later parts. I've made a few emendations which you may find helpful, & have tried a bit of strengthening toward the end. Hope you'll like what I've done" (HPL to Duane W. Rimel, 13 May 1934; ms., JHL).

Of the three sections of the story, the final one—as well as the citation from a mythical volume, the *Chronicle of Nath* by Rudolf Yergler, in the second section—is certainly by HPL. Some have believed that much of the actual prose of the second section is also HPL's, but this is an open question that must be decided merely from internal evidence, since no manuscript survives. Rimel has made it clear that both the title *Chronicle of Nath* and the extract from it are Lovecraft's invention (see Further Reading).

Texts: Polaris (September 1940): 4–11; *Crypt of Cthulhu* no. 16 (Michaelmas 1983): 5–12; in *HM* (1989 ed. only).

Further Reading: Donald R. Burleson, Peter Cannon, William Fulwiler, S. T. Joshi, Steven J. Mariconda, Will

Murray, Robert M. Price, David E. Schultz, "A Symposium on 'The Tree on the Hill,'" *Crypt of Cthulhu* no. 17 (Hallowmas 1983): 3–21. Duane W. Rimel, "A History of *The Chronicle of Nath*," *Etchings and Odysseys* no. 9 (1986): 80.

1. Hampden is fictitious, but the Salmon River is a major river that runs east-west through central Idaho and then turns south at the town of Salmon, in eastern Idaho.

2. The Blue Mountain Forest is in northeastern Oregon, some distance from the Salmon River.

3. The Nez Perce are a major Native American tribe in the Pacific Northwest. They were among the tribes encountered by the Lewis and Clark expedition of 1805.

4. The Bitterroot Mountains extend along the border of northern Idaho and Montana, somewhat north of the Salmon River.

5. Shamballah is a term out of Tibetan Buddhism, referring to a mythical city where all the inhabitants are equally enlightened. It was cited in *The Book of Dzyan,* a purportedly ancient work that theosophist Helena P. Blavatsky claimed was the basis of her treatise *The Secret Doctrine* (1875); *The Book of Dzyan* was probably written by Blavatsky. E. Hoffmann Price brought this material to HPL's notice in early 1933 (see *SL* 4.155), and HPL had actually cited Shamballah in his draft of the collaborative tale "Through the Gates of the Silver Key" (1932–33), but on Price's suggestion he removed the reference.

6. Hermes Trismegistos ("thrice-great Hermes") is the putative author of a series of occultist and alchemical works written in Greek and Latin from the first to the third centuries C.E. Hermes was first cited in *The Case of Charles Dexter Ward* (*MM* 121), and also in "The Evil Clergyman" (*D* 287).

7. Ka-Nefer is fictitious, but bears a phonetic resemblance to the (fictitious) pharaoh Nephren-Ka, cited in "The Outsisder" (1921; *DH* 52), *The Case of Charles Dexter Ward* (*MM* 197), and "The Haunter of the Dark" (1935; *DH* 106).

The Battle That Ended the Century

This celebrated collaboration was written during HPL's first visit to Barlow in Florida (2 May–21 June 1934). Barlow was clearly the originator of this squib, as typescripts prepared by him survive, one with extensive revisions in pen by HPL. The idea was to make joking mention of as many of the authors' mutual colleagues as possible in the course of the document, which purported to report the heavyweight fight between Two-Gun Bob, the Terror of the Plains (Robert E. Howard) and Knockout Bernie, the Wild Wolf of West Shokan (Bernard Austin Dwyer). More than thirty individuals are mentioned. Barlow had initially cited them by their actual names, but HPL felt that this was not very interesting, so he devised parodic or punning names for them.

The idea was to circulate the whimsy, but in such a way that its authorship would not be immediately evident. The plan appears to have been as follows: Barlow would mimeograph the item (copies exist in two long 8½ × 14" sheets, each with text on one side only) and then have the copies mailed from some other location, so that they could not be traced to either HPL or Barlow. It appears that the 50 duplicated copies were prepared toward the middle of June and were sent to Washington, D.C., where they would be mailed (possibly by Elizabeth Toldridge, a colleague of both HPL's and Barlow's but not associated with the weird fiction circle). This seems to have been done just before HPL himself left DeLand and began heading north, so that the items would already be in the hands of associates by the time Lovecraft reached Washington.

Previous attempts to identify the names have occasionally resulted in errors. The text as presented here also includes within brackets some sentences that were omitted from the final draft.

Texts: T.Mss. (JHL); *The Battle That Ended the Century* ([DeLand, FL: R. H. Barlow, 1934]); *Acolyte* 2, no. 4 (Fall 1944): 9–12; in *Something about Cats* (1949); in *The Battle That Ended the Century/Collapsing Cosmoses* (1992); in *Miscellaneous Writings* (1995); in Barlow, *Eyes of the God* (2002).

1. Kelly's Stables, a night club in New York "where there was some celebrated case of fisticuffs . . . movie folks involved maybe" (T. O. Mabbott to August Derleth, 3 December 1949; ms., Wisconsin Historical Society).

2. Robert E[ervin] Howard (1906–1936) of Cross Plains, Texas. Howard was a regular contributor to *Weird Tales* and other pulp magazines.

3. Bernard Austin Dwyer (1897–1943) of West Shokan, N.Y. He published little if any fiction. The story is sprinkled with references to Dwyer's ample girth.

4. Arthur Leeds (1882–1952) of New York, Kalem Club member, at one time connected with the writing courses of the Home Correspondence School of Springfield, Mass.

5. William Lumley (1880–1960), an occultist correspondent of HPL in Buffalo, N.Y. See headnote to "The Diary of Alonzo Typer" below.

6. The serpent-men of Valusia were cited in "The

Shadow Kingdom" (*Weird Tales,* August 1929), a King Kull story by Robert E. Howard.

7. H[arold] Warner Munn (1903–1981). The name refers to a character in Munn's story "The Werewolf of Ponkert" (*Weird Tales,* July 1925). In a letter to R. H. Barlow, HPL refers to Munn's "cream-puff vending."

8. Dr. David H. Keller (1880–1966), weird fiction writer and a physician, specializing in neuropsychiatry.

9. Miles G. Breuer (1889–1947), science fiction writer for the pulps.

10. A[lpheus] Hyatt Verrill (1871–1954) and George Allen England (1877 – 1936), early science fiction writers.

11. Frank Belknap Long, Jr. (1901–1994), friend of HPL since 1920, Kalem Club member, and weird fiction writer for the pulps. Long was at this time flirting with communism. When HPL and R. H. Barlow printed and published a collection of Long's verse, *The Goblin Tower* (Cassia: Dragon-Fly Press, 1935), HPL mentioned to correspondents that he and Barlow not only organized the contents of the book but also revised the poems somewhat, to Long's indifference.

12. Forest J. Ackerman (1916–2008), science fiction fan, editor, and publisher. HPL lampooned Ackerman with the epithets "slimy efjeh-weeds" and "wriggling akmans" in "In the Walls of Eryx" (see below), written with Kenneth Sterling. A vitriolic debate between Ackerman and various weird tale enthusiasts (including HPL and R. H. Barlow) was published in the *Fantasy Fan* in a column called "The Boiling Point" (September 1933–February 1934). Ackerman was known for selling photographs of himself and various writers in the pulp world, even of writers whose work he denigrated.

13. Margaret Brundage (1900–1976), artist for *Weird*

Tales, referred to as an "anatomist" because of her famous cover art depicting nudes (in scenes not described in the stories) adorned as described here.

14. C. C. Senf (1873–1949), artist for *Weird Tales.* HPL frequently accused Senf of providing illustrations that did not depict scenes from stories (as in Senf's illustration of Chaugnar Faugn in Long's *The Horror from the Hills*).

15. Guy L[incoln] Huey (b. 1912), an illustrator for *Marvel Tales,* another artist whose work did not match the contents of the publication it adorned.

16. Harry K. Brobst (1909–2010), a friend of HPL's, was a nurse at Butler Hospital in Providence where he tended to mental patients.

17. Wilfred Blanch Talman (1904–1986) of New York, Kalem Club member and for a time a reporter for the *New York Times.* HPL revised some of Talman's work.

18. HPL.

19. August W. Derleth (1909–1971) of Sauk City, Wis. Derleth, alluded to as Comte d'Erlette (a name in Derleth's ancestry), author of *Cultes des Goules,* in HPL's fiction, had ambitious plans for a long fictional work about Wisconsin that he called the "Sac Prairie Saga." HPL had read Derleth's numerous revisions to the novel *Evening in Spring* in manuscript.

20. Julius Schwartz (1915–2004). Schwartz edited *Fantasy Magazine.* As an agent, he sold HPL's *At the Mountains of Madness* to *Astounding.*

21. H[erman] C. Koenig (1893–1959). Koenig had given HPL a tour of the Electrical Testing Laboratories, where he worked, and lent him many books.

22. Howard Wandrei (1909–1956), brother of Donald Wandrei. He was known for his intricately detailed pen and ink drawings and paintings. He illustrated his brother's

volume of poetry *Dark Odyssey* (1931).

23. Robert S[pencer] Carr (1909–1994), pulp writer who, like Long, espoused Marxism.

24. Seabury Quinn (1899–1966), prolific pulp writer. Besides writing for *Weird Tales,* Quinn was a lawyer and editor of the mortician's journal, *Casket and Sunnyside.*

25. E[dgar] Hoffmann Price (1898–1988). HPL referred to Price, a West Point graduate, as "The Peacock Sultan" because of Price's affinity for peacocks and because of his interest in the Middle East.

26. F. Lee Baldwin (1913–1987), weird fiction fan and correspondent of HPL. He had an extensive interest in music.

27. George Gard ("Buddy") DeSylva (1895–1950), Lew Brown (1893–1958), and Ray Henderson (1896–1970), a song-writing team.

28. Hugo Gernsback (1884–1967), editor of *Amazing Stories* and *Wonder Stories*. As with Ackerman, HPL lampooned Gernsback in "In the Wall of Eryx" by referring to "ugrats" (i.e., Hugo the Rat) and, more obliquely, by referring to "scificlighs" (i.e., Science Fiction League, founded by Gernsback). Gernsback was notorious for late payment for stories he published.

29. This sentence was omitted from the published story. "D. Vest Wind" may refer to David Van Bush (1882–1959), a perennial revision client of HPL who specialized in pop psychology and also wrote poetry.

30. Clark Ashton Smith (1893–1961), prolific writer of weird, fantasy, and science fiction stories for the pulps. He was addressed by HPL as Klarkash-Ton in correspondence, and also mentioned as such in "The Whisperer in Darkness" (*DH* 254). HPL delighted in Smith's paintings of unearthly, fungoid vegetation.

31. *Weird Tales* (its offices were in Chicago, the Windy City). HPL alludes to the frequency with which his own tales, as well as tales by his colleagues, would be initially rejected by the editor, Farnsworth Wright, before being accepted.

32. W. Paul Cook (1880–1948), legendary amateur editor and publisher. Cook published Donald Wandrei's *Ecstasy and Other Poems* (1928) and printed (but did not bind or distribute) HPL's *The Shunned House* (1928).

33. This phrase was also omitted in the published version. The reference is to Vrest Orton (1897–1986), late member of the Kalem Club and director of the Stephen Daye Press in Vermont.

34. Otis Adelbert Kline (1891–1946), literary agent and author. HPL and Barlow evidently neglected to render his name parodically; HPL later took note of the omission, remarking to correspondents that the name should have been rendered as Oatmeal Addlepate Crime (HPL to Duane W. Rimel, 10 August 1934; ms., JHL).

35. Dauber and Pine, the New York City bookstore where Sam Loveman (1887–1976), Kalem Club member, was employed.

36. The allusions are as follows: A[braham] Merritt (1884–1943), leading fantasy writer for the pulps; Hearst's *American Weekly* (where Merritt worked); Henshaw Ward's "Science Has Not Gone Mystical," *Atlantic Monthly* 152, no. 2 (August 1933): 186–94; and Merritt's *The Dwellers in the Mirage* (1932).

"Till A' the Seas"

This story exists in a typescript by Barlow that HPL has radically overhauled. The two authors worked on the revision on New Year's night of 1935 in New York, staying up till 3 A.M. HPL has made no significant structural changes, merely making a number of cosmetic changes in style and diction; but he has written the bulk of the concluding section, especially the cosmic reflections when the last man on earth finally meets his ironic death. HPL took issue with Barlow's contention that human beings would be the last living creatures on the earth; in a note at the bottom of the last page of the ms., he has written: "Actually, insects & other life-forms will undoubtedly oulast man & his fellow-mammals." The title is taken from Robert Burns's famous poem "A Red, Red Rose" (1794): "And I will luve thee still, my dear, / Till a' the seas gang dry" (ll. 7–8). In the *Crypt of Cthulhu* appearance, the words, phrases, and sentences added by HPL are indicated in brackets.

Texts: T.Ms. (JHL); *Californian* 3, no. 1 (Summer 1935): 3–7; in *HM* (1970/1989); *Crypt of Cthulhu* no. 17 (Hallowmas 1983): 33–39 (as "Lovecraft's Contribution to '"Till A' the Seas"'"; ed. S. T. Joshi); in Barlow, *Eyes of the God* (2002).

1. The names of these cities, as with those that follow, appear to be perversions of known cities—as if, with the immense passage of time, their names have become distorted. Dath is unidentified; Niyara evokes New York; Yuanario, as the "capital," is presumably Washington, D.C.

2. Yarat is unidentified; Perath and Baling are Paris and Berlin.

3. London.

4. Unidentified.

Collapsing Cosmoses

This fragmentary sketch was written when HPL was

visiting R. H. Barlow at his home in DeLand, Florida (9 June–18 August 1935). The idea was for each author to write every other paragraph or so, although on occasion HPL only wrote a few words before yielding the pen back to his younger colleague, so that considerably more than half the piece is Barlow's, as are a fair number of the better jokes. As a satire on the space-opera brand of science fiction popularised by Edmond Hamilton, E. E. "Doc" Smith, and others, "Collapsing Cosmoses" is undeniably effective; the fact that it is unfinished makes little difference, for the absurdity of the plot would have precluded any neat resolution in any event. In the present text, Barlow's passages are presented in brackets.

Texts: T.Ms. (JHL); *Leaves* 2 (1938): 100–101; in *Uncollected Prose and Poetry II* (1980); in *The Battle That Ended the Century/Collapsing Cosmoses* (1992); in *Miscellaneous Writings* (1995); in Barlow, *Eyes of the God* (2002).

1. See n. 31 to "The Battle That Ended the Century."

The Challenge from Beyond

"The Challenge from Beyond" was the brainchild of Julius Schwartz, who wanted two round-robin stories of the same title, one weird and one science fiction, for the third anniversary issue of *Fantasy Magazine* (September 1935). He initially signed up C. L. Moore, Frank Belknap Long, A. Merritt, HPL, and a fifth undecided writer for the weird version, and Stanley G. Weinbaum, Donald Wandrei, E. E. "Doc" Smith, Harl Vincent, and Murray Leinster for the science fiction version. It was an impressive accomplishment to have harnessed all these writers—especially the resolutely professional A. Merritt—for such a venture, in which each author would write a section building upon what his or her predecessor had done; but the weird version did not go quite according to plan. Moore initiated the story with a rather lackluster account of a man named George Campbell who, while camping alone in the Canadian wilderness, comes upon a curious quartzlike cube for whose exact nature and purpose he cannot account. Long then wrote what Lovecraft called "a rather clever development" (*SL* 5.200); but this left Merritt in the position of actually developing the story. Merritt balked, saying that Long had somehow deviated from the subject-matter suggested by the title, and refused to participate unless Long's section were dropped and Merritt allowed to write one of his own. Schwartz, not wanting to lose such a big name (Long, not having such an impressive reputation, was apparently considered expendable), weakly went along with the plan. Merritt's own version is pretty inane and fails to move the story along in any meaningful way: Campbell is merely impressed with the bizarrerie of the object and, while peering into it, finds his mind sucked into the core of the object. HPL, next on the list, realized that he would have to take the story in hand and actually make it go somewhere.

Notes to HPL's segment survive (see Appendix) and make interesting reading—if only for the drawings of the alien entities he introduces into the tale (not reproduced here; they can be found in *CE*) and for the clear borrowings he has made from the plot of "The Shadow out of Time" (1934–35), a story he had written some months earlier and which was then unpublished. HPL's segment of "The Challenge from Beyond" is nothing more than an adaptation of the central conception of that story—mind-exchange. Here the exchange is effected by the cubes, which draw the mind of anyone who looks into it and fling it back to the transgalactic world of the centipede creatures, where it is somehow housed in a machine; by the reverse method one of the centipedes casts his mind into the body of the mind so captured. Campbell manages to figure out what has happened to him because he has, handily enough, read "those debatable and disquieting clay fragments called the Eltdown Shards" which tell the whole story of this centipede race and their explorations of space via the cubes. HPL wrote most of his story during a visit to Charleston and Richmond in late August 1935.

HPL's segment is about three to four times as long as that of any other writer's, taking up about half the story. Robert E. Howard, who had been talked into taking the fourth installment, displays Campbell (in the body of a centipede) suddenly reviving from a fainting fit to engage in an orgy of slaughter against his slimy opponents, while Long—whom HPL had talked into coming back on board the project after he had walked away in a huff when Schwartz had dumped his initial installment—concludes the story by showing the centipede-bodied Campbell becoming a god on the distant planet while the human-bodied alien degenerates into mindless bestiality. It's all good fun of a sort, although even HPL's segment—clearly the most substantial of the lot (it has actually been published separately as a self-contained narrative)—cannot claim much aesthetic value. The science fiction version is, if possible, even worse.

Texts: Fantasy Magazine 5, no. 4 (September 1935): 221–29 (HPL portion 223–27); in *Beyond the Wall of Sleep* (1943); in *Miscellaneous Writings* (1995) (HPL portion only).

1. The Eltdown Shards had been invented by Richard F. Searight (1902–1975) for the story "The Sealed Casket" (*Weird Tales,* March 1935). It is often thought that HPL revised the story; but, although he read it in January 1934, there is no evidence that he performed any revisory work on it. In a letter of 1935 he copies out a passage from the Eltdown Shards, designed as an epigraph to the story (*SL* 5.112); but HPL elsewhere admitted that the passage was written by Searight, and that HPL altered only a single word of it (*Letters to Richard F. Searight* [West Warwick, RI: Necronomicon Press, 1992], 17). (The epigraph was not in fact published in *Weird Tales,* and the Eltdown Shards are not mentioned in the story proper.) HPL has, however, invented the details about the 1912 translation.

2. An obvious reference to the Great Race of "The Shadow out of Time" (1934–35).

The Disinterment

"The Disinterment" is the second story that HPL revised for Duane W. Rimel. This tale—very similar in atmosphere to some of HPL's early macabre stories, especially "The Outsider"—is to my mind either wholly written by HPL or a remarkably faithful imitation of HPL's style and manner. Rimel has emphatically maintained that the story is largely his, HPL acting only as a polisher; and correspondence between the two writers—especially HPL's enthusiastic initial response to the story—seems to support this claim. Consider a passage in HPL's letter to Rimel of 28 September 1935: "First of all, let me congratulate you on the story. Really, it's *splendid*—one of your best so far! The suspense & atmosphere of dread are admirable, & the scenes are very vividly managed. . . . I've gone over the MS.

472

very carefully with a view to improving the smoothness of the prose style—& I hope you'll find the slight verbal changes acceptable" (ms., JHL). The critical issue is what to make of that final sentence (the manuscript or typescript, with HPL's putative corrections, does not survive). The fact that HPL refers to "slight verbal changes" should not lead us to minimize his role in the tale, since this may simply be another instance of his customary modesty. It is, moreover, odd that Rimel subsequently wrote nothing even remotely as fine (or, at any rate, as Lovecraftian) as this tale. Rimel (or HPL) has taken the hackneyed "mad doctor" trope and shorn it of its triteness and absurdity by a very restrained portrayal, one that suggests far more than it states; and although the "surprise" ending is hardly a surprise to the alert reader, it follows the lead of many HPL stories in which the narrator cannot bring himself to state, unequivocally and definitively, the hideous truth until the very last line.

The story was initially rejected by Farnsworth Wright but then, in early 1936, accepted; it was not published in *Weird Tales,* however, until about a year later.

Texts: Weird Tales 29, no. 1 (January 1937): 95–102; in *HM* (1989 ed. only).

Further Reading: Will Murray, "Facts in the Case of 'The Disinterment,'" *Lovecraft Studies* no. 17 (Fall 1988): 30–33.

1. Possibly an echo of Soames, the butler in "Facts concerning the Late Arthur Jermyn and His Family" (1920; *D* 81); also of Sidney Sime (see n. 14 to "Medusa's Coil").

The Diary of Alonzo Typer

HPL worked on this story in mid-October 1935,

revising a handwritten draft (see Appendix) for William Lumley. Lumley (1880–1960) was an occultist and devotee of weird fiction from Buffalo, N.Y., who came in touch with HPL in 1931. HPL wrote of him: "[Lumley] says he has witnessed monstrous rites in deserted cities, has slept in pre-human ruins and awaked 20 years older, has seen strange elemental spirits in all lands (including Buffalo, N.Y.—where he frequently visits a haunted valley and sees a white, misty Presence), has written and collaborated on powerful dramas, has conversed with incredibly wise and monstrously ancient wizards in remote Asiatic fastnesses . . ., and not long ago had sent him from India for perusal a palaeogean and terrible book in an unknown tongue . . . which he could not open without certain ceremonies of purification, including the donning of a white robe!" (*SL* 4.270–71).

Lumley had produced a hopelessly illiterate draft of the tale and sent it to HPL, who, feeling sorry for the old codger, rewrote the story wholesale while still preserving as much of Lumley's conceptions and even his prose as possible. In Lumley's version we are taken to some spectral house, evidently in upstate New York, where strange forces were called up by the Dutch family that had resided there. The narrator, an occult explorer, attempts to fathom the mysteries of the place, but in Lumley's version the tale ends quite inconclusively, with the explorer awaiting some mysterious fate while thunder and lighting rage all around. Some parts of his account are unintentionally comical. HPL, while preserving as much as he could of this farrago of nonsense, has at least made some coherent sense of the plot. HPL thought that Lumley would dump the story upon some fan or semi-professional magazine like *Marvel Tales,* but Lumley enterprisingly sent it to Farnsworth Wright, who accepted it for *Weird Tales* in early December for $70.00. Wright noticed the traces of HPL's style in the piece, and one wonders whether this had anything to do with the long delay in its publication. HPL magnanimously let Lumley keep the entire $70.00.

Texts: A.Ms. (JHL); *Weird Tales* 31, no. 2 (February 1938): 152–66; in *Beyond the Wall of Sleep* (1943); in *HM* (1970/1989).

1. See n. 6 to "The Man of Stone."

2. Batavia is the county seat of Genesee County, in the far western portion of New York State, near Buffalo.

3. HPL refers to the American Society for Psychical Research, founded in 1885. This society was and is independent of the original Society for Psychical Research, founded in England in 1882.

4. Attica is a town across the southern border of Genesee County, in Wyoming County in western New York.

5. Fictitious. The name refers to a city in Israel cited occasionally in the New Testament; it is one of the cities where, according to medieval legend, the Antichrist would be born. HPL's essay "Some Causes of Self-Immolation" (1931) is said to have been written by L. Theobald, "Professor of Satanism and Applied Irreverence in Philistine University, Chorazin, Nebraska" (*CE* 5.77).

6. Cochin-China was a name that at this time designated the lower third of South Vietnam, encompassing the city of Saigon and the surrounding area. It was a French colony from 1862 to 1948.

7. The term Aklo had been invented by Arthur Machen in "The White People" (1904), where its use was deliberately mysterious: the girl whose diary is reproduced in that story merely refers to "the way to make the Aklo let-

ters." HPL appears to have assumed that the term referred to a language, citing it as such in Wilbur Whateley's diary in "The Dunwich Horror" ("'Today learned the Aklo for the Sabaoth'" [*DH* 184]) and in "The Haunter of the Dark" ("The text was . . . in the dark Aklo language used by certain cults of evil antiquity" [*DH* 106]).

8. See n. 6 to "The Horror in the Museum."

9. For the *Necronomicon,* see n. 21 to "Medusa's Coil." The *Livre d'Eibon* is a French rendering of the *Book of Eibon* (for which see n. 5 to "The Man of Stone"). It appears to be an invention of HPL's, as Clark Ashton Smith never cited the title in French. See HPL to Smith (11 February 1934): "One recalls the disquieting suggestions in Jehan d'Artois' Roman des Sorciers concerning the huge black cats captured at those very singular sabbats on the rocky hill behind Vyones—the cats which could not be burned, but which escaped unhurt from the flames, uttering cries which, though not like any known human speech, were damnably close to the unknown syllables forming part of the Tsath-ritual in the Livre d'Eibon" (ms.). Ludvig Prinn's *Mysteries of the Worm* was invented by Robert Bloch in "The Secret in the Tomb" (*Weird Tales,* May 1935). HPL read the story in August 1934 (see *Letters to Robert Bloch* [West Warwick, RI: Necronomicon Press, 1993], 52). When he read "The Shambler from the Stars" (*Weird Tales,* September 1935) in April 1935, he fashioned the Latin title of Prinn's work, *De Vermis Mysteriis* (see *Letters to Robert Bloch,* 65) and cited it first in "The Shadow out of Time" (*DH* 374).

10. For Shamballah and the *Book of Dzyan,* see n. 5 to "The Tree on the Hill." For Lemurians, see n. 11 to "Medusa's Coil."

11. Yian-Ho appears to be an adaptation of Yian, cited in "The Whisperer in Darkness" (*DH* 223); Yian itself

is taken from Robert W. Chambers's story "The Maker of Moons," in *The Maker of Moons* (1896), where it appears to be a city in China. Yian-Ho was first cited in "Through the Gates of the Silver Key" (*MM* 435). The term appears in Lumley's original draft (see p. 427).

12. See n. 6 to "The Battle That Ended the Century."

13. An adaptation of Lumley's *Book of Forbidden Things* from his original draft (see Appendix, p. 431).

14. For Yaddith, see n. 13 to "Out of the Aeons."

In the Walls of Eryx

HPL worked on this story in January 1936 in conjunction with the young Kenneth Sterling (1920–1995), a science fiction fan and writer who had moved to Providence in the spring of 1935. He was still in high school at the time. Sterling has stated that the idea of the invisible maze was his, and that this core idea was adapted from Edmond Hamilton's celebrated story (which HPL liked), "The Monster-God of Mamurth" (*Weird Tales,* August 1926), which concerns an invisible building in the Sahara Desert. Sterling wrote a draft of 6000–8000 words; HPL entirely rewrote the story ("in very short order," Sterling declares) on a small pad of lined paper (perhaps similar to the one on which he had written "The Shadow out of Time"), making it about 12,000 words in the process (see Sterling's "Caverns Measureless to Man"). Sterling's account suggests that the version as we have it is entirely HPL's prose, and indeed it reads as such; but one suspects (Sterling's original draft is not extant) that, as with the collaborated tales with Price and Lumley, Lovecraft tried to preserve as much of Sterling's own prose, and certainly his ideas, as possible.

The authors have made the tale amusing by devising

nasty in-jokes on certain mutual colleagues; I suspect these are HPL's, since they are roughly similar to the punning names he devised for "The Battle That Ended the Century." The already hackneyed use of Venus as a setting for the tale is perhaps its one significant drawback. It should be noted that the spectacle of a human being walking without much difficulty (albeit with an oxygen mask and protective suit) on the surface of Venus was not preposterous in its day. There was much speculation as to the surface conditions of the planet, some astronomers believing that the planet was steamy and swampy like our own Palaeozoic age, others believing that it was a barren desert blown by dust storms; still others thought the planet covered with huge oceans of carbonated water or even with hot oil. It was only in 1956 that radio waves showed the surface temperature to be a minimum of 570° F, while in 1968 radar and radio observations at last confirmed the temperature to be 900° F and the surface atmospheric pressure to be at least ninety times that of the earth.

HPL's handwritten version of the story was presumably typed by Sterling, since the existing typescript is in an otherwise unrecognizable typewriter face. The byline reads (surely at HPL's insistence) "By Kenneth Sterling and H. P. Lovecraft." The story was submitted to *Astounding Stories, Blue Book, Argosy, Wonder Stories,* and perhaps *Amazing Stories* (all these names, except the last, are crossed out on a sheet prefacing the typescript). Finally it was published in *Weird Tales.*

HPL, according to Sterling, had helped his young friend on this story because he wished to give him some practical advice and encouragement in story writing, although both HPL and Sterling sensed even then that the latter's career lay in science and not literature. Sterling had, however, previously published a story entitled "The Bipeds of Bjhulhu" (*Wonder Stories,* February 1936), whose title was consciously meant to evoke Cthulhu, although there are no Lovecraftian touches in the tale itself.

Texts: T.Ms. (JHL); *Weird Tales* 34, no. 4 (October 1939): 50–68; in *Beyond the Wall of Sleep* (1943); in *D.*

Further Reading: Kenneth Sterling, "Caverns Measureless to Man," *Science-Fantasy Correspondent* no. 1 (1975): 36–43; in *LR* (1998).

1. The name means "New Earth" in Latin.

2. *Akmans* is an allusion to Forrest J Ackerman (see n. 12 to "The Battle that Ended the Century"). *Skorahs* refers to William F. Sykora, a science fiction fan and member of the Science Fiction League. *Tukahs* refers to Arthur Wilson "Bob" Tucker (1914–2006), a science fiction fan and writer.

3. The name *Dionaean* derives from Dione, the mother of Aphrodite. In 1684, the astronomer Giovanni Cassini gave this name to one of the moons of Saturn.

4. *Ugrats* is an allusion to HPL's derisive nickname for Hugo Gernsback (see n. 28 to "The Battle That Ended the Century"). *Darohs* is an allusion to the science fiction fan Jack Darrow.

5. A pungent reference to Farnsworth Wright (1888–1940), editor of *Weird Tales* (1924–40).

6. An allusion to the Science Fiction League, a fan organization to which Kenneth Sterling belonged.

7. The name is a clear reference to Herman C. Koenig (see n. 21 to "The Battle That Ended the Century").

The Night Ocean

HPL and R. H. Barlow worked on this story during Bar-

low's stay in Providence in August 1936. We are now able
to gauge the precise degree of HPL's contribution to this
tale, as Barlow's typescript, with HPL's revisions, has now
surfaced. Prior to this discovery, all we had to go on were
various remarks in letters and certain other documents.
HPL told Hyman Bradofsky (who published the tale in
the Winter 1936 issue of the *Californian*) that he "ripped
the text to pieces in spots" (HPL to Hyman Bradofsky, 4
November 1936; ms.); but in a letter to Duane W. Rimel
upon appearance of the work, he waxed eloquent about its
merits: "The kid is coming along—indeed, the N.O. is one
of the most truly artistic weird tales I've ever read" (HPL
to Duane W. Rimel, 20 February 1937; ms., JHL). It would
be uncharacteristic of HPL to praise a story in which he
had had a very large hand; and sure enough, HPL's contribution probably amounts to no more than 10% of the
story. He was in any event correct that Barlow had been
"coming along," as the latter's "A Dim-Remembered Story"
(*Californian*, Summer 1936) is a superbly crafted tale but
one that does not seem to bear any revisory hand by HPL
at all. HPL repeated his praise for that story in a "Literary Review" that appeared in the very same issue of the
Californian as "The Night Ocean." Curiously, the final two
paragraphs of the tale had appeared (as "A Fragment") in
the *Californian* a full year before the story itself, suggesting
that Barlow had been working on the draft for well over a
year.

Texts: T.Ms. (on a microfilm of Barlow material at
JHL); *Californian* 3, no. 2 (Winter 1935): 73 (extract; as
"A Fragment"); *Californian* 4, no. 3 (Winter 1936): 41–
56; in *Uncollected Prose and Poetry* (1978); in *HM* (1989
ed. only); in Barlow, *Eyes of the God* (2002).

Further Reading: Brian Humphries, "'The Night

H. P. LOVECRAFT

Ocean' and the Subtleties of Cosmicism," *Lovecraft Studies* no. 30 (Spring 1994): 14–21.

Appendix

Notes to "Medusa's Coil"

These notes are found in a transcript in AHT. They exemplify HPL's recommendation to draw up two synopses for a story—one listing events in order of occurrence, the other listing events in order of narration (see the essay "Notes on Writing Weird Fiction"). The mention that Marceline is a negress, "as in original text," suggests that this was Zealia Bishop's climactic scene in a draft or synopsis she had written.

Texts: AHT; *CE* 5 (2006).

Notes to "The Challenge from Beyond"

These notes outline the plot of HPL's segment of the round-robin story, picking up the narrative after the segments by C. L. Moore and A. Merritt.

Texts: A.Ms. (JHL); *Lovecraft Studies* no. 9 (Fall 1984): 72–73; *CE* 5 (2006).

The Diary of Alonzo Typer

Lumley's original draft of the story, exhaustively revised by HPL, who nonetheless attempted to preserve some of Lumley's occult terms and citations, along with some of the prose.

Texts: A.Ms. (JHL); *Crypt of Cthulhu* no. 10 (1982): 21–25.

The Sorcery of Aphlar

This story was written by Duane W. Rimel in the summer of 1934. HPL read it in July; at that time it was titled "The Sorcery of Alfred." Finding the use of a common English given name in what purported to be a Dunsanian fantasy unconvincing, HPL changed the title to "The Sorcery of Aphlar" and also made a "few changes" (HPL to Duane W. Rimel, 23 July 1934; ms., JHL) in the text itself. The tale appeared in the *Fantasy Fan* and then in the *Tri-State Times* (a small local newspaper published in upstate New York) for Spring 1937; in one copy of the latter publication someone (R. H. Barlow?) has written next to the story: "revised by HPL." On the basis of this note I reprinted the work as a Lovecraft revision, but I now do not believe that HPL's changes (which again must be inferred only by internal evidence) are significant enough to warrant such a designation.

Texts: Fantasy Fan 2, no. 4 (December 1934): 57–59; *Tri-State Times* 1, no. 1 (Spring 1937): 3–4 (as "The Sourcery of Alphar"); in *Uncollected Prose and Poetry* (1978).

1. Cf. "The Quest of Iranon" (1921), where Iranon is "a singer of songs" (*D* 111) and has "no heart for the cobbler's trade" (*D* 113), but is told: "All in Teloth must toil . . . for that is the law" (*D* 113).

Bibliography

A. Primary

The Ancient Track: Complete Poetical Works. Edited by S. T. Joshi. San Francisco: Night Shade, 2001.

The Battle That Ended the Century/Collapsing Cosmoses (with R. H. Barlow). West Warwick, RI: Necronomicon Press, 1992.

Beyond the Wall of Sleep. Edited by August Derleth and Donald Wandrei. Sauk City, WI: Arkham House, 1943.

Collected Essays. Edited by S. T. Joshi. New York: Hippocampus Press, 2004–06. 5 vols.

Dagon and Other Macabre Tales. Selected by August Derleth; Texts Edited by S. T. Joshi. Sauk City, WI: Arkham House, 1986.

The Dunwich Horror and Others. Selected by August Derleth; Texts Edited by S. T. Joshi. Sauk City, WI: Arkham House, 1984.

Essential Solitude: The Letters of H. P. Lovecraft and August Derleth. Edited by David E. Schultz and S. T. Joshi. New York: Hippocampus Press, 2008. 2 vols.

The Hoard of the Wizard-Beast and One Other (with R. H. Barlow). Edited by S. T. Joshi. West Warwick, RI: Necronomicon Press, 1994.

The Horror in the Museum and Other Revisions. Selected by August Derleth. Sauk City, WI: Arkham House, 1970. Rev. ed. (by S. T. Joshi), 1989.

Marginalia. Compiled by August Derleth. Sauk City, WI: Arkham House, 1943.

Miscellaneous Writings. Edited by S. T. Joshi. Sauk City, WI. Arkham House, 1995.

O Fortunate Floridian: H. P. Lovecraft's Letters to R. H. Barlow. Edited by S. T. Joshi and David E. Schultz. Tampa: University of Tampa Press, 2007.

Selected Letters. Edited by August Derleth, Donald Wandrei, and James Turner. Sauk City, WI: Arkham House, 1965–76. 5 vols.

Something about Cats and Other Pieces. Compiled by August Derleth. Sauk City, WI: Arkham House, 1949.

Uncollected Prose and Poetry. Edited by S. T. Joshi and Marc A. Michaud, West Warwick, RI: Necronomicon Press, 1978–82. 3 vols.

B. Secondary

Barlow, R. H. *Eyes of the God: The Weird Fiction and Poetry of R. H. Barlow.* Edited by S. T. Joshi, Douglas A. Anderson, and David E. Schultz. New York: Hippocampus Press, 2002.

Bishop, Zealia. *The Curse of Yig.* Sauk City, WI: Arkham House, 1953.

Cannon, Peter, ed. *Lovecraft Remembered.* Sauk City, WI: Arkham House, 1998.

Joshi, S. T. *I Am Providence: The Life and Times of H. P. Lovecraft.* New York: Hippocampus Press, 2010. 2 vols.

CPSIA information can be obtained
at www.ICGtesting.com
Printed in the USA
LVOW12s1239011217
558111LV00017B/221/P